Bloodied Waters

To Venassa

I hope you're not to
shucked!

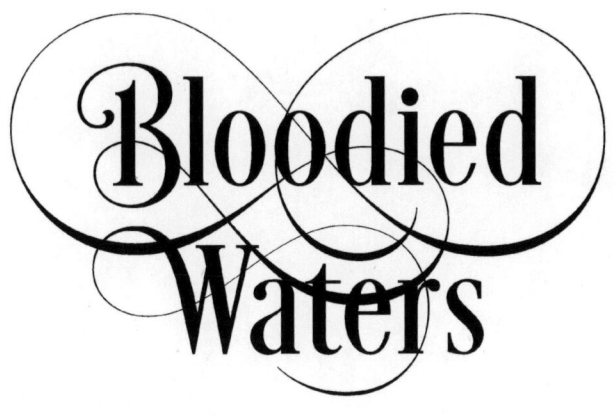

Bloodied Waters

RAYMOND HUGH

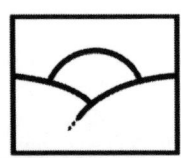

MORNING MIST

Poole

Dorset

BH16 6FH

Email - info@morningmist.co.uk

A CIP catalogue record for this book is available from the British Library

ISBN 9781838409272

Printed in Great Britain by

Biddles Books Limited, King's Lynn, Norfolk

My thanks to all who helped me in my research for this book and understandably wish to remain anonymous. You know who you are.

CHAPTER

—1—

Wissant – France

Late September

It was a glorious sunset. Throughout the day the low Autumn sun had been brightening a cloudless sky. Now, as the sun set over the sea, dark clouds were racing in from the west and as they did so the sun's rays became trapped, bloodying what up until then had been a perfect blue sky. Almost, the whole of the sky was now coloured with a dark bloody red broken here and there by a dappling of grey, a grey that was turning darker by the minute. It was obvious to anyone watching that the grey would soon take over completely and as it got angrier turn to black.

Maureen, she hated her name, she felt it exemplified a period in time which gave clue to her age and presented to men, no English men, a woman who was good at washing the dishes, leaning on the polished railings of her balcony gazed in awe as nature's spectacle unfolded. In the distance two ferries were passing each other in mid Channel. They would probably be the last two making their way between Calais and Dover that day as "the storm of the decade," century even according to some media outlets was forecast to hit that night. Clues to the impending storm were increasingly becoming apparent. What during the day had been a refreshing breeze was fast becoming a playful wind hiding unexpected gusts that increasingly had the potential to do damage. The waves in the Channel or rather La Manche as the French called

1

it, for she was gazing out from the French coast were beginning to swell and white tipped rollers were racing all the more frequently to shore, exploding in a wrath of white on Wissant's famous expanse of sand. Not far from her apartment, even though there had been warnings not to, a group of surfers were making the most of the conditions.

Maureen took in a deep breath, relishing the fine sea spray carried by the wind and landing with force on her face. She rolled her tongue and gently pushed, exploring her lips whilst sucking in droplets of salt water. Sea water, she was sensitive to, had a very different taste to salt mixed in tap water. It had life. To allow her body to take full advantage of the conditions she stretched her arms skywards. Her short flimsy nightie, all she was wearing rising with them until the hem line hovered just below her waist. Becoming aware suddenly of her nakedness she quickly dropped her arms, laughing inwardly as she did so. A few months ago she would have been horrified at such exposure. Now she found it a thrill and physically shook with excitement at the thought somebody might have seen her. Not that there was any danger of that. Apart from the surfers who were too far away to spot any detail and three men who were too busy boarding up the beach brasserie to notice her, the seafront was deserted.

It was a good hour since her young lover had left her apartment and as the wind sought to discover her body, it lifted his scent, wafting it across her face. Momentarily this brought the memory of their love making back to her. He had been a good 40 years younger than her, perhaps more. Frustratingly she'd discovered the age difference had been too great. Although his body had been tone perfect and his enthusiasm and excitement an unbelievable turn on for her, his inexperience meant that he had failed to fully satisfy the woman that she was. She loved foreplay and liked to orgasm repeatedly with the intense attention of an adoring man before it progressed to full intercourse. Penetration for her although she enjoyed it was she thought, more of tool for a man to orgasm than for a woman. Too quickly her young lover had penetrated her. Within minutes he had orgasmed and although, being young he could recover quickly. his too predictable, rhythmical thrusts and the feeling of his fiercely erect penis inside her went quickly from being exciting to merely mildly enjoyable and after a very short time to boring. As he pounded her excitedly she had let her mind drift to other lovers, lovers that in the past had left her limp, gasping for breath. Normally doing this she could make herself cum giving a disappointing lover the illusion that he had done a good job but today that hadn't happened and to bring proceedings to an end had faked her orgasm. Visibly pleased with the result of what he imagined had been his handiwork her young lover had left her apartment with his male feathers puffed up. No doubt later he would boast to his mates about his experience. She didn't mind, perhaps it would encourage one of them to try their luck and she could look forward to that.

The sun's rays were now fading to pink, soon they would disappear behind darkening clouds, and the Baie de Wissant, a 12km perfect crescent of sand nestling between two rugged capes would only be lit by the twinkling lights from farms and close knit villages that hugged the coast. Dusk over the bay was always a beautiful experience and Maureen never tired of it. Throughout the day or night, rain or shine the view from her balcony was constantly stunning, it never dissa-pointed. Maureen never grew tired of it. She was, she knew extremely lucky to live where she did. Her mind wandered back to her first day in Wissant. Having driven back, a long and tiring drive, from a holiday with her husband in the Languedoc they had arrived in Calais only to find the local "pecheur" blocking the port with their fishing boats. The queues both at the sea port and tunnel had been horrendous. Her husband demonstrating a very rare show of inspiration, not to mention spontaneity, decided rather than hang around a very crowded port to explore the old coast road between Calais and Boulogne. The road had been a revelation. The coast was spectacular and the steep twisting descent of Cap Blanc Nez, (White Nose Point, so called because of its spectacular chalk cliff face), was nothing short of breath-taking.

Within minutes of arriving they had both fallen in love with Wissant. The long sandy beach was and still is the best she'd ever seen. A long sandy shelf stretched miles out to sea and as the sun shone it warmed the waters pulled by the tide flowing over it. The result, the water in the bay, year round was comparable to the temperature of the Mediterranean. Such a phenomenon of course made Wissant an attractive beach resort and in summer the place was buzzing with holiday makers and day trippers, including savvy people from across the water. Despite the summer crowds and the rather tacky promenade built on Hitler's defences against a possible invasion, Wissant had managed to hold on to its charm. At its heart lay a small square with a 15th century church, overlooked by the rather grandiose Hotel Normandy, complete with a mock painted Norman timber façade. Nearby an old mill had been converted to a hotel. The hotel's bar and restaurant had a typically rustic wooden terrace where you could sit and enjoy a cold drink overlooking the mill pond. The surrounding streets were dotted with elaborate villas largely built at the end of the 19th century. Famously General de Gaulle had one of these villas and infamously used to rent the villa adjacent to house his mistress.

Her husband had loved the place so much, on an even rarer show of impulse he insisted on booking into the Hotel Normandy. The hotel's old world charm had intoxicated him, the ultimate escapism from his job in the city and what had been planned as a one night stay turned into a week and then a second. Maureen had never seen such a change in her husband. He had started to talk about retiring and before she knew they had bought a first floor apartment on the Digue de Mer with spectacular sea views. It had not been cheap, property prices in Wissant were comparable to the UK but despite this, within a month they had moved in and left their humdrum life in the UK behind. Retirement for her husband had meant lazing in their apartment and enjoying the many eateries in town. He was rarely on his feet and it was probably this inactivity which killed him.

Barely six months after they had moved into their apartment, Maureen on returning from one of her many excursions had found her husband dead sitting in his favourite chair. She was surprised at how peaceful he looked and this on reflection had helped her get over the initial shock.

Life without her husband, had at first been hard, very hard and very lonely. They had married when she was just 18 and throughout her life she'd known no other man and never been tempted by another man. She'd been brought up by her parents to treat marriage as sacred and for better or for worse this is what she had done. In Wissant they had lived as a couple, not making any friends and if she were honest, making no effort to make friends. The occasional nod or bonjour to a familiar face was the extent of their friendships.

After the funeral she had continued her life in the same fashion but now of course, alone. Her rather dull existence only started to improve with the arrival of Spring and with it, the sun. The temperature rose and so did Maureen's appetite for life. With the first signs of summer approaching she brought herself a couple of colourful and rather flimsy dresses. Typically French they were designed to show off, emphasise the positives of the female figure. The hem line on both fell just above the knee and buttoning up at the front both dresses also allowed the wearer to expose as much cleavage as the wearer wanted or dared. For Maureen the purchase was completely out of character, during her married life her dresses had all reached her ankles and typically sewn together using heavy dark materials. The material and colours of her recent purchase embraced life and even more her femininity. Trying them on at home had made her feel both scared as well as excited. Both dresses made her feel good, she loved the light touch of the material which was so delicate in places that when the light caught it at a certain angle an attentive admirer would see through it. Maureen stretched, twisted and turned in front of the bedroom mirror, admiring the results. Her figure though heavy set was she recognised, all woman. Apart from her rather too ample stomach her limbs, both arms and legs, though large were firm. Her breasts too were ample but even at 64 still didn't need a bra to support them and her generous, (her husband's tailor's description), behind was well rounded and stood out from the top of her thighs. Chunky was how her husband had described her figure and he had been right but now she recognised chunky in the most womanly sense. Admiring herself in the mirror perhaps for the first time in her life she felt sexy, and immediately felt guilty by thinking in such a fashion.

Wearing her new wardrobe outside, she almost immediately noticed a difference in how people reacted to her. Both men and women smiled in greeting as they passed and more than once she'd been stopped for a chat. It felt good and within days Maureen had added to her wardrobe. Her make up too she changed, out went the subtle colours to be replaced by more vibrant shades, shades that had a pulse. To complete her new look Maureen had made a visit to the local coiffeuse. The lady doing her hair she remembered had tutted disapprovingly at her old fashioned perm. "Your hair is the style of an old woman," she had told her. "You are not old"! Maureen had agreed to let her do her thing, "let me go wild," the coiffeuse had told her and she had. When she had finished, gone was the perm, replaced by a cut that was daringly short and fashioned in sleek lines. "You have a strong neck," the coiffeuse purred, "show it off." Looking in the mirror once she'd got home, she had to admit the coiffeuse had been right. The cut had taken years off of her. She still looked her age but a young 64, a vibrant 64, a sexy 64. Yes sexy and she was beginning to welcome the feeling.

Chapter 1

Two days later her new look changed her life. It was a beautiful sunny day and Maureen had been determined to embrace it. She started by enjoying a Kir Royale sat by the window in her favourite promenade bar. It was not even 10 o'clock, yet the beach was filling up and several people were already enjoying a civilised morning beer. A group of lads she guessed in their late twenties, were playing baby-foot, their enthusiasm was infectious as well as noisy. She couldn't help but notice that now and again they would glance in her direction with admiring looks. She enjoyed the attention and crossed her leg nearest to them so her dress slipped down her bare thigh, at the same time in the most nonchalant fashion she could muster, she unbuttoned her dress by two holes. Her breasts held by the briefest of bras told anyone who noticed that the lady sipping her Kir Royale by the window was definitely all woman.

"Do you mind if I sit down?" The request, in French, had startled her. Stood by her table was a smartly but casually dressed male, she guessed in his late thirties. His hair was a mass of tussled curls and he had the confident poise of a man used to money. With money came confidence and the man hadn't waited for her to answer, he quickly sat down at the same time, deftly signalling to the waiter. Minutes later the waiter had appeared with a freshly poured beer, another Kir Royale and a bottle of champagne that was half full.

"The bottle used for your Kir," the stranger gestured to the bottle. I thought we could finish it off. Maureen found herself nodding in agreement and with amusement she noticed the attention from the group of lads playing baby-foot had turned from glances of admiration to glances of envy. It made her feel good. She could hardly remember the next hour. The stranger had she remembered smelt delicious, he'd been effortlessly funny and in just minutes was holding her hands in his. They'd finished the champagne together and within an hour were naked in her bed. For the next three hours, Maureen had experienced

7

pleasure that she hadn't until then imagined existed. The stranger had worshiped her body as though it was his last day on earth. It had felt at times as though he possessed 10 hands and 5 tongues. She had lost count how many times she'd orgasmed and realised after he'd gone that before their liaison she'd never had an orgasm before. Several hours later her body was still twitching involuntarily. as more tiny orgasms escaped.

Twice more she enjoyed the stranger, the fact she didn't know his name somehow made their liaisons more exciting, he was to her, forbidden fruit and she didn't care a jot. He disappeared as suddenly as he had appeared but Maureen didn't care. She had discovered a newly found confidence and during the summer season had made the most of it. She regularly entertained men at her apartment plucking them from the many bars that opened for the summer season. Being a sea resort there was a regular turnover of fresh male meat and Maureen made the most of it. She never tired of sex and quickly came to realise, that with her newly discovered sexuality came power, power over men. This often transcended to the bedroom. Her legs and arms had a strength she hadn't realised before and she enjoyed trapping men during sex with both, holding them rigidly in a position she enjoyed until they had made her cum. Her conquests appeared to be turned on by this and Maureen was fast understanding the French expression Femme Fatale. Nearly all of her lovers she considered, would if she asked, do just about anything for her. Perhaps even lay down their lives.

Reflecting on her summer of love, Maureen found herself becoming turned on once more. The spray from the sea was now constant and still standing on the balcony Maureen had become wet through. With the combination of wind and water she started to shiver with cold but she hardly noticed. Almost oblivious she gazed out to sea, the surfers were still there despite it being almost dark and the water increasingly angry. The wind was starting to race and Maureen held her nightie tight to avoid it blowing over her head and away completely. Gusts blew up her legs playing with her still sensitive clitoris. She moaned softly enjoying the sensation, it made her think of her most exciting lovers. Juices she couldn't control started to dribble down the inside of her sturdy legs. The wind quickly turned them cold and instantly she knew she had to finish what her inexperienced young lover had failed to do. Turning swiftly she stepped into the lounge closing the balcony doors behind her. The doors battered by the wind rattled in protest. She lifted the handle and two bolts slid easily into place, securing any crack through which the increasingly angry wind could enter. Silence.

Impatient now, Maureen stepped quickly across the tiled lounge floor to the bedroom pulling off her nighty as she did so and throwing it on the table. Her bedroom was carpeted, the one luxury she had insisted on when they had bought the apartment. The warmth on the soles of her feet was welcoming. Opening the first bedside drawer she pulled out her favourite vibrator. Sliding onto the bed she lay on her back and opened her legs. Determined to build her orgasm slowly she at first let her vibrator play with her clitoris for a while before moving it gently but firmly inside her. With her free hand she caressed the inside of her thighs and base of her bottom before moving to her clitoris as her other hand expertly moved the vibrator inside her body. She moaned loudly as the sensations began to build. Suddenly she screamed and her lower body thrust violently upwards as her orgasm exploded. Her body collapsed back on the bed and then pumped the air several times more before finally settling on the now soaked sheets. Maureen lay back gasping for breath, her body gently shaking along with the odd violent twitch. It was a good ten minutes before everything was calm. Slowly she drew herself up and reached for a decanter on the bedside table. It contained her late husband's favourite brandy. She poured herself a glass and took a long hard sip. She let her head fall back enjoying the slow burn of the brandy as it slipped down her throat. She closed her eyes and within seconds the glass slipped out her hand, the remaining liquid spilling onto the quilt. A few more seconds passed before a slow rhythmic grunt escaped from her lips. Maureen was asleep, oblivious to the hell that was unfolding outside.

Maureen had been wrong about no one watching her on the balcony. On the beach below three men were trying to secure a beachfront brasserie. The brasserie was mainly constructed from wood with an awning out front. It was of course vulnerable to any strong wind and tonight the "storm of the century" had been forecast. Despite this the owner had insisted on his commerce staying open for as long as possible. To the very last minute. It had been a glorious day, perhaps the last good day of the season. The beach had been packed and the trade had been comparable to the best days of summer. Only minutes earlier had the last customer left and the three men were now fighting a losing battle against a strengthening wind to take down the front awning which beach side was supported only by scaffolding poles resting on the sand. After this there was still the terrace furniture to be stored and the windows which were of normal glass, boarded up. Alexandre had just turned 18 and was working at the Brasserie before starting an IT apprenticeship in Lille. Whilst trying to take in the covers he had immediately spotted the rather stocky woman on the balcony above. He could see that she was almost certainly naked beneath her "robe de soir". The woman stretched her arms and the rise of her night dress confirmed his suspicions. An erection began to grow beneath his trousers, the woman looked powerful and he loved that. At that moment he made his mind up that he was going to have to try and make her acquaintance. At the same moment a violent gust of wind caught the awning ripping one of the roof supports from the wooden cabin. The support, a heavy 6 metre steel pole swung in an arc, carried effortlessly by the billowing awning. There was a shout of alarm from the other two men, Alexandre turned his head in their direction only to witness the steel pole seconds before it killed him.

Chapter 1

Farm House – Escalles, France

The wind had really started to pick up and Antanois was thankful when he finally turned into the drive of his rented farmhouse. His car, an entry range Citroen was not good in this weather and there were moments when driving over Cap Blanc Nez that he feared the Citroen with him in it may be blown out to sea. The car hadn't been his choice but his organisation wanted to avoid any unwanted attention or curiosity and a small Citroen blended in perfectly. Maybe so but it was shit in this weather and he found the compactness disconcerting. He much preferred his sturdy Mercedes, one felt safe in a Mercedes and you could spread your limbs. As he stepped out of the Citroen a gust of wind almost blew him over. The car rocked violently and the wheels that were coast side actually lifted for a few seconds. Antanois shivered, he was glad he was relying on own two legs and not the 4 wheels beside him. A piece of board flew past him, he ducked instinctively. He needed to get inside, from all accounts there was to be one hell of a storm tonight. How he yearned for his homeland, he'd been away far too long. Home was Lebanon, the country may have its problems but it still had a lot going for it and one, when compared to here was the weather.

He searched his pockets for the key to the garage door. The key was so small it always took a while to find, he really needed to add it to a ring. Especially when you considered what the garage concealed. If he lost it there would be hell to pay. He might even pay with his life. The last thing the organisation wanted was a complete stranger having to fix a new lock. With a sigh of relief he found it, struggled with the wind to put the key in the lock and struggled again to lift the rusty door, which really badly needed replacing. Minutes later the Citroen was safely tucked away and the garage door locked. There was no danger of the garage being damaged in the storm as it was cut into the steep grassy slope of Mont d'Hubert a hill connecting with Cap Blanc Nez.

A succession of gusts almost blew Antanois off his feet. He looked up to the summit of Mont d'Hubert, the Eastern scarp rising behind the farmhouse was pitted with craters courtesy of RAF bombers during the 2nd World War. They had been trying to destroy a network of bunkers dug into the hill, part of Hitler's Atlantic Wall. On the surface the RAF had largely succeeded but not entirely. What the British hadn't known, was that Rommel had extended the defences deep underground. If the British had discovered and destroyed these, his presence and expertise here would not be needed, there would be nowhere to operate from. At the summit of the Mont stood a red and white painted aerial mast. Antanois wondered if it would survive the oncoming storm. No matter, it wasn't his problem. Another piece of debris flew past his head, he needed to get inside.

The farmhouse hadn't been a house to a farm for over thirty years. When the last farmer had passed away his oldest son had sold the land and converted the farmhouse into a gite. An outbuilding had been converted into two much smaller gites. The organisation had offered to rent all three gites at the high season rate for 5 continuous years, with a ten percent rental increase each year. At first the son had been reluctant but changed his mind when he was offered cash. The organisation insisted on not having a written contract, good old fashioned trust is what they offered and expected. The son incentivised almost entirely by greed accepted with a handshake and almost immediately regretted it. He liked to have paper work, a written contract but sensed if he went back on his word and asked for one it might be all the worse for him. Although the people who'd paid him had been all smiles and friendliness, there was something sinister about them. Drugs was what he suspected. He wouldn't ask any questions and that is exactly what the organisation wanted.

Antanois switched on the tv. It was tuned constantly to a local news channel. That evening every bulletin was concentrating on the predicted storm. The program flicked from one fixed camera to another recording every minute of the storm unfolding. A mobile phone lay on the coffee table, Antanois picked it up. There were no messages. He wasn't surprised, the mobile was only to be used in an emergency. The reason for the organisation's growing success was, that there was no proof of its existence, no phones and no paper trail. Everything was done by word of mouth, the reason for his drive to Lille, to meet a fellow operative who had a message or to be more precise instructions for him. He knew five operatives in total and there were, he'd been told, hundreds, perhaps even thousands of operatives worldwide. He had no idea who the man was at the top or those immediately below him. Except for those at the very top each operative knew just five other operatives. The organisation communicated through a giant web of Chinese whispers, though relaying a message wrongly would almost certainly cost you your life. Each operative was responsible for a particular project and all were working towards the same goal. No one spoke about it though and if honest most weren't even sure what it was.

Going to the fridge Antanois took out a beer. Lebanese beer, it was the one reminder of home he allowed himself and if the organisation found out, he'd probably be in serious trouble. Flipping the cap he walked to the nearest window. Outside the landscape was going mad with the wind. He shivered involuntarily, as he thought of his scary traverse of Cap Blanc Nez. He would need a second beer if he was going to get any sleep and walked back to the fridge.

CHAPTER
—2—

Marbella – Spain

John loved the Mediterranean, he'd travelled extensively over the years, visiting nearly every corner of the globe but there was something about the Med that mesmerised him. Driving along the A7 towards Malaga he was pleased to have left the glitz of Marbella behind. He found it vulgar and that, despite his life and job revolving almost exclusively around the rich, he'd always found the seedier side of life more attractive. Granted Marbella had plenty of that but it was still too showy for his liking. It was the army he reflected that had introduced him to the dark side of life. Her Majesty's government had sent him to most of the worlds cesspits, especially when he'd joined the special forces and where others often hated the experience he'd revelled in it. He admired the characters who lived in the shadows, even if many of them were out to kill him. After leaving the army he'd been invited to join the secret service, MI5 mainly but not exclusively. With the service he'd been sent to more cesspits though they'd tended to be a little more upmarket and although this world was dangerous everybody in it, including the enemy tended to play by an unwritten set of rules.

The seafront to his right now was in darkness, strict restrictions had been placed by the Spanish government on developing this part of the coast. He squinted as cars passed, coming from the opposite direction. He was looking for a dirt road on his left leading into the limestone hills that lent badly needed drama to this part of the coast. He knew it was just before a small set of whitewashed villas, the last development before virtually all construction was banned. The car had GPS but he had expertly unplugged it, he didn't want the inquisitive knowing where he had been. He could see the development ahead now, it stood all alone, rather like an oasis in the dessert. Almost at the same time he saw the road he was looking for, a large double posted sign helped him. It read 'El Jardin de los Encantos,' and underneath, restaurant and bar in English. His Spanish was good enough to translate the name into English too. 'Garden of Delights,' he wondered what that meant exactly. Almost missing the turning he swung the wheel hard, at the same time engaging the brakes, his hired car complaining loudly at the extra effort.

The road was now almost exclusively dirt with only the worst pothole badly filled. After around half a mile a chain of festooned lighting announced the restaurant and bar. Resting on the side of a valley the main restaurant was a converted finca, as the name suggested it had an extensive and surprisingly tasteful garden, the main delight being a huge barbecue which when he arrived had several whole legs of lamb roasting on it. Something he already knew the restaurant was locally well known for. The restaurant was owned by the gentleman he'd come to see. He hoped he wasn't at work, it would be much easier to meet him at his house. Needing to check he swung the car right, (more complaints), into the badly pitted car park. The car park was almost full, something he hadn't expected and something of an annoyance to him. A waiter greeted him as he crossed the threshold.

"Restaurant or garden," he enquired. The waiter was obviously English and flamboyantly very gay.

"Just a drink" John offered shortly.

The waiter looked dissapointed. "Sit anywhere you like," he waved his hand vaguely and returned his gaze to the clip board he was holding.

16

He chose a table almost at the top of the garden, from there he could, with ease, survey the scene and plan for any unexpected scenarios. The clientele he observed were mostly English with a spattering of Spanish. Litre jugs of sangria were being liberally consumed and many of the English diners were tucking into a whole leg of lamb on their own. Another waiter arrived at his table.

"The drinks menu sir?" the waiter also obviously English offered him a rather well-worn card.

"Have you a local beer?"

"Cerveza," the waiter looked surprised.

John nodded and the waiter disappeared. He was back in an under a minute. Placing a mat and a fine stemmed bulberous glass on the table he offered to pour from the bottle, dripping wet from having been in a cooler.

"I'll do it." John gestured to the waiter to simply leave the glass along with the bottle. The waiter made to leave but John touched his arm.

"Is the owner around, John pretended to look at his phone, "a Mr Michael Swinton?" The waiter, John observed looked unnecessarily nervous by his question.

"No I'm afraid he isn't sir, Mr Swinton never works in the evenings."

"Then I'll find him at home then," John phrased this as a statement not a question whilst smiling reassuringly.

"I've really no idea sir," the waiter was in a hurry to leave.

John held his hand firmly, "and his house is just up the valley? Am I right? The waiter gave the slightest of nods. "Thank you, I'm an old friend and want to surprise him." It was a lie of course.

By his manner it was very obvious the waiter wasn't convinced and hurried away just a little too quickly. John knew he or someone in the restaurant would be phoning his client and this is exactly what he wanted. He hadn't come all this way to find his client not in and time as the saying goes, is money. He swiftly finished his beer and made his way to the car. He knew he was being watched. Seconds later he was back on the dirt track heading for the hills. He knew at the end of the track there was a small wooded parking area and an old Roman aqueduct. The car park was used mainly by hikers for it was perfect walking terrain. John had once been a keen hiker himself but too much alcohol and a love of Cuban cigars had put pay to that, his body a long time ago had stopped being a temple. Stupid he knew for someone in his game but he liked to think that guile and clever talk could persuade most of his clients to do his bidding. If they didn't, well he had people who could take care of that.

His clients house, he knew was a newly built villa, on the Northern side of the valley. How he'd got permission to build was anyone's guess, money almost certainly had played a part. And it was money John was there for, for his client owed a small number of people a great deal of money, people who wanted it back and didn't really care how they got it. There was also the small matter of an Aston Martin DB4 Vantage sports. The car was worth around half a million pounds and his client had driven off having paid a deposit of just £50,000 pounds and that was over a year ago. The dealer wanted the car back and had employed him to get it back. £50,000 was the price for a successful outcome. In total if he satisfied all of his commissions he stood to make a cool quarter of a million. The trouble was he knew Mr Swinton no longer had the money. Despite this he had a proposition and Mr Swinton would be stupid not to take it. And if, as he suspected his client wasn't stupid, he was still in the frame to collect the quarter of a million.

For someone who was meant to be in hiding, the villa was madness. It was bright, had too many clean lines and had no right being in a rustic Andalucian valley. It boasted, 'look at me, I'm home to an English gangster'. And that's exactly what his client was or had been before younger more determined men had taken over what had been his turf in Manchester. A freshly laid drive formed an S up the valley side to a landscaped parking area. It didn't quite reach the villa and the rest of the climb was completed by an exaggerated series of steps twisting between a set of statues which, now it was dark were spot lit. Taking a deep breath John turned up the drive, taking care not to hurry and all the time looking for the slightest movement ahead. His client, (he always liked to think of them as that), he knew, would almost certainly have a fire arm in the house and by reputation wouldn't be afraid to use it. In fact it was pretty stupid of him to make his client's acquaintance without a partner but he preferred to work alone, always had done. For him a partner was too much of a crowd and if anything kicked off he didn't want to feel responsible for someone else's death. For he was the boss and he would be responsible. The drive curved gently into a parking area which he estimated could easily fit four large cars. He could now see that a wide garage had been dug into the valley side and sat centrally under the garishly lit villa. Other than his, there was one other car parked in the parking area, an Aton Martin DB4 Vantage Sports. John wondered why it was parked in full view on the drive, why his client had made no attempt to hide it. He'd expected there to be no sign of it. Perhaps it was a silent peace offering, "go on take it," there again it could be a dare.

John circled the hire car and parked it facing and blocking the drive way access. Still there was no sign of anyone being at home. The Aston Martin was parked beside the beginning of the steps. As he passed it, there was no need to touch the bonnet, the engine was still radiating heat. So, his client had only just got home. He scanned the villa, several cameras adorned the walls. That's why there was no sign of life, he was being monitored digitally. He smiled and waved at the cameras, he wanted his action to reduce any sense of threat he might pose and hoped it would be seen by his client that way. To further reduce any sense of threat he had removed his jacket and left his fire arm, a Glock 17 Gen 4 pistol, under the passenger seat. He knew this left him vulnerable but at the same time reduced any risk of confrontation. With every job he took on he was prepared to die and found this quietly amusing, as he'd ultimately left the military and the secret service to avoid exactly that. He'd quickly become bored though and knew too many retirees because of their inactivity had met an early and quickly forgotten end. God built humans to be both mentally and physically active. When both stimuli were gone, what was the point and in his view God obviously thought so too.

It was ex colleagues who suggested he took up debt collecting, a surprising number of ex-military he discovered had found their way into the field. He'd quickly discovered he was very good at it, exceptionally good. At first he dealt purely with legally collectable debts, then as his reputation grew he received more and more approaches from people who weren't interested in going down the legal channel. At first he'd been hesitant, after all he'd always worked for Her Majesty and was proud of his loyalty and devotion. But he'd quickly discovered that there was serious money to be made outside the legal route, and so successful was he, quickly found himself receiving commissions, (he liked to call them that), from all over the world. These days most of his work was almost entirely outside of the law and some of it decidedly dangerous. Her Majesty's government had even become one of his customers, though they'd never admit to it and were also very careful not to leave any sort of trail, paper or electronic. His success became so great, he'd had to start a legitimate business simply to introduce some of the money he was earning into the system. In Putney he now had a bakery special-ising in continental bread and pastries. His delivery drivers were all ex-military, a couple, like himself, from the special forces. They were all mentally scarred and would never find a job in civvy street. He gave them a good living, security and if he were honest and they were honest with themselves, the excitement they craved from their military days. When a client was difficult it was their job to finish the job off. They nearly always succeeded and if they didn't they would offer up a tortured and very dead body to the customer who had commissioned his services. For this service too, he was handsomely paid. He now had millions in the bank and could and probably should have retired years ago but he didn't really have anything to retire too and if he was honest with himself was a little scared that he may go the way others he knew had gone, once they retired. Also if he was honest with himself, like the ex-serviceman he employed he missed the excitement the army and MI5 had given to him. Anyway he thought, better to go out in a blaze of glory than sitting on a toilet. He laughed inwardly and started to climb the steps to the house.

He didn't have to knock the door. As he approached, the door opened, not by his client but a child! A young girl, not more than around twelve he considered. This threw him, he hadn't expected this. Morally it was abhorrent but he recognised a very clever move by his client.

"My Daddy says to come through, " the girl beamed, "oh and would you mind removing your shoes." Another clever move.

The girl showed him into a large and spacious lounge. The floor was white marble which sparkled under the galaxy of ceiling lights. A large, dark and highly polished grand piano hugged one corner, the only other furniture was a series of sumptuous armchairs and sofa gathered around the largest glass coffee table he'd ever seen. They all faced a ginormous picture window which doubled as a wall. The view it afforded would be hard to beat anywhere in the world. Apart from the girl there were two other people in the room. An over tanned man sat on the sofa, once muscular his muscles had run to fat and his chin had tripled. His head was bald, his nose flat, (from a fight in his early days John knew), and his eyes were almost perfectly round, almost like marbles. Behind him with her hands on what was almost certainly her husband's shoulder stood a woman. Not the glamorous blonde with false boobs, normally associated with gangsters but a dark haired badly ageing woman, her skin wrinkled from a lifetime of smoking and eyes which lacked any lust for life. She had, John could see at once, had enough and he knew instantly that this was going to be easy.

"The keys are there, take them." The man nodded to the coffee table.

On the table lay a small set of keys with a stylish Aston Martin key fob. Instead of picking them up, John settled into one of the armchairs. Clasping his hands together he rested his forearms on his knees and leaned forward. Both the man and the woman eyed him warily.

"Can we talk?" John smiled kindly, "but." He gestured with the slightest nod of his head to the young girl who had sat herself on the arm of another of the armchairs.

"Lucy do you mind making us some drinks, sorry we haven't offered you anything." The man smiled weakly at John.

"Coffee please, black, no sugar." The girl leapt up and ran out of the room.

The man spoke again. "I knew who you were when you asked for me by my real name."

"Then you know it isn't just about the car?" The man nodded.

"I haven't got it, the money, I could sell this but it wouldn't cover a fraction of what you're looking for."

The woman started to cry softly, her knuckles white from clutching her husband's shoulders too tightly. John almost felt sorry for them, how they'd got themselves into this mess he'd no idea. They both knew only too well what the people they owed money to could do to them if they didn't pay up and it wouldn't be pleasant. Indeed it would be hell, days and days of hell. At the back of John's mind was the knowledge that the broken man before him had once had a fearsome reputation. The torture he was hiding from now he'd handed out many, many times to others in the past. But there was the sweet little girl, she didn't deserve this and John recognised they had used her in a last desperate attempt for mercy. They needn't have stooped that low. He was going to offer it to them anyway.

The girl came back with a large mug of coffee and placed it on the table before him. Nothing for her parents. She was visibly shocked to see her mother with moistened eyes.

"Lucy, give us a little while will you." Her father tried hard to raise a smile. John beamed one at her, hoping his effort would help relax her. Lucy smiled bravely back and trotted off.

"You have a beautiful daughter," John paused, "you shouldn't have used her." At this the man looked deeply ashamed and his wife's tears turned into uncontrollable sobbing.

"I don't need to tell you what the people who have employed me would do to you if I revealed your new identity and address." No reply, they knew, their eyes said it all. "And I know you don't have the money." Their expressions changed, their eyes spoke to him, simultaneously, "then why are you here?"

John took a sip of coffee, it was good. "look," they stared, "I can give you a way out of this."

"How?" it was the woman.

"I can make you disappear."

"What a new identity? I've already tried that and look you managed to find me."

"A new identity is up to you to sort out, no I can make you disappear, and I can guarantee your creditors will stop looking for you."

"I don't see how." The man looked doubtful.

John cut in, "I promise you they will, anyway what other choice have you got than to trust me?" They hadn't any other choice and they both knew it.

"You pay me £250,000, and I'll make your problem go away, I'll make you disappear." He knew they had that in several secreted accounts and enough after he'd been paid to live a modest life in Spain until the end of their years. There was of course also the villa. He saw from their expressions that they knew he knew. "Shall we talk details?"

Several hours later John was driving away in a classic Aston Martin, the only legal part of his evenings work. Sod the plane ticket, he would enjoy himself driving back through France. The hire company would charge him quite a bit to collect the car from the villa but he didn't care. He was £250,000 richer.

Chapter

—3—

Marseille - France

There was nothing exceptional about Chez Monique and that's why it had been chosen. The café- hotel was almost anonymous in an anonymous narrow street, part of the labyrinth of narrow streets which made up the old Le Pannier quarter close to the original port. The rather glamorous name was after an owner from the 19th century when the café was popular with sailors needing to rinse the sea salt from their mouths and taste something much more to their liking in the rooms upstairs. Today the café was mainly popular with locals down on their luck and tourists wanting to experience the "real Marseille." The hotel was cheap and the clientele didn't expect anything fancy. What the hotel undersold was its character. The crooked, creaking wooden staircase led up to a maze of narrow wooden landings lit by lamps that were the colour of walls stained with cigarette smoke. Those of a certain age will know the colour. Each room was unique and uniquely French in character. They were frozen in time from when the owner had been Monique. The only exception was a room over the kitchen at the back. EU laws had forced the building of a modern ventilated kitchen and above this a new bedroom had been built. It was not for general let but for a special customer and her name was Fatima.

As we join, the café had the usual evening trade. A couple of men well into their 'troisieme age' sat on tall rounded wooden stalls in front of the bar as they had done, every evening for as long as they could both remember. In all that time none of the staff in the café had changed, they'd just all become older. The café itself was softly lit with dark walls and two windows, one at the back and one at the front. The windows were so heavily draped with nets that it was sometimes, once inside hard to distinguish night from day. Their deep sills were home to an array of heavy set plants that took full advantage of the little light that somehow managed to filter through. Anybody coming in from the bright Marseille sun outside would take several minutes for their eyes to adjust. The walls were adorned with a number of cheaply framed touristy prints of the city and adverts for Pastis, the traditional drink of Marseille. Above the door leading to a corridor that led to the hotel staircase out the back were two black and white photographs. Taken in the nineteen twenties they were of the café's clientele back then. Several were proudly wearing sailor's uniforms and nearly all looked very stern. In between the photographs, the symbolic hand of Fatima.

The tables and chairs were from Monique's time. As was the mode back then, the tables were made of wood, round and in testament to their age, scarred with circles and cigarette burns. The matching chairs had curled frames with punched hole patterned seats, they too were made of wood. The café had done well to fend off the shiny plastic furniture that had found their way into so many French cafes. The one modern feature was the bar. It looked tacky which it was, and very out of place. Behind the bar were two posters, one of the Marseille football team that won the Champions League in 1993, still the only French team to do so and the other, of the modern day team. A number of Olympique Marseille pendants hung from the bar.

Apart from the two men at the bar, the café was in the main hosting couples. It was hard to tell exactly but the majority were probably in their late forties or early fifties, the one exception being a couple by the window who were almost certainly in their late teens. Finally there was a group of three men and two women sat around a table too small for all of them. They had ordered food and were struggling to eat comfortably. Apart from the two men at the bar all of the men, even the young lad sat opposite his very beautiful girlfriend were throwing sly, guilty glances to a table positioned in a corner close to the bar. All were doing their best and all were failing the longer they looked to be discreet. It was the only table to have a single occupant.

Sipping a strong black coffee, sat a woman. All the men who were secretly admiring her assumed she was Arab for she wore a pale hijab which crossed neatly under her chin before effortlessly clinging to her shoulders. They all assumed wrongly for the woman came from Iran, she was Persian. Like all Persian women her face was blessed with model like features, a luxuriant skin tone and eyes that shone dark, almost water like drawing you beneath the surface if you looked too long. Apart from her hijab the rest of her clothes were dark. A dark dotted blouse she wore unbuttoned just enough to hint at a magnificent cleavage. Her blouse was tight enough to also hint at why the cleavage would be so impressive. Over the blouse hung a modest but rather expensive looking black jacket. Her legs were crossed and a strong thigh faced the rest of the café. She wore no stockings, her legs were bare and because of the length of the skirt she was wearing there was more than a hint of what lay beneath. Luxurious, smooth olive toned skin adorned pronounced calves and finishing just above the knee the skirt had risen to reveal the beginning of a perfectly shaped thigh. On her feet were a pair of very western fashioned shoes, black with a strong stiletto heel. Apart from a stud in her nose, a pair of discreet silver earrings and a silver chain around her neck, the woman wore no visible jewellery. She knew she held the attention of nearly all the men in the café and enjoyed the sense of power it gave her. Deciding to play a game she lifted her crossed leg an inch higher. In response her skirt dropped down her upper leg revealing just a fraction more of a strong muscular thigh. She felt rather than saw the tension in the men observing her, she could feel their desire. Everyone one of them she knew wanted to test her in bed and were desperately trying to imagine what it would be like if they succeeded. Wearing a hijab they all assumed she was forbidden fruit, untouchable. And she was acutely aware that every single one of them secretly thought the experience would be unforgettable, much more exciting than the women they were sat with. And they'd be right, any man who had the privilege to sleep with her became hooked, they wanted that experience repeated over and over and would do anything to have the privilege again. She'd learnt from a very young age that despite her large frame she held a certain power over men. Now approaching 50, she felt her power had gotten even stronger and more importantly, she had learnt how to use it. This was why she was so good at her job and so sought after, she had found as the country she was in called it, her "raison d'etre." She loved what she did and revelled in the expression the French language used to describe a woman like her. Only the French language could pigeon hole her, other languages were far too clumsy. Femme Fatale described her perfectly, and she made a very good living from it.

"Fatima."

The woman working the bar call whispered loudly. The Femme Fatale, turned her head. Fatima was her working name, she wasn't even sure anymore if there was anybody left living who knew her real name. Her family in Iran had all been killed by the brain-washed servants of a brutal regime. Alone, she had experienced rape by those in authority, more times than she cared to remember before escaping to Iraq and all the challenges that, that country brought. She'd escaped having no money and with no means of support. Too quickly and too young she'd discovered that men's desire for her could open far more doors than money and thus her apprenticeship had begun.

The woman behind the bar gestured to the back door. Fatima nodded, she was waiting for this. In no hurry she continued to sip her coffee, he could wait, it would increase his desire, he'd be bursting with expectation when she got to him.

Cap Blanc Nez – France

The storm had certainly taken hold and earlier than expected. It was just 10pm and if you were stupid enough to be outside you were at risk from serious injury from flying debris. Mathieu was one of those people. Young, in his twenties, he lacked the fear and caution that old age brought. An ambitious semi-professional photographer he was at the base of the Western slope of Cap Blanc Nez. He'd managed to capture some great shots of the storm at both the Eastern and Western base of the Cape. Now he wanted to take some from the summit but the local police had closed the road, siting it to be too dangerous in such strong winds. For a moment Mathieu paused, just for a moment, in just a few seconds he'd decided the police closure was an over precaution. He easily steered his ageing Renault 19 round the police sign and started up the famous zig zag climb to the summit. When at the summit even he had had to admit that he was surprised at just how strong the wind was. His car rocked dangerously and it was a struggle to open the door even. Towering above him the obelisk which stood as a monument to the "Dover Patrol", from the First World War looked completely unaffected by the wind. Looking around him Mathieu gasped, not from the wind but at the storm. It was better, far better than he'd expected, it was spectacular. Perhaps not in another 500 years would there be such a spectacle. These pictures if he captured them correctly would make him famous, he could see himself being credited in journals all over the world. Driven by ambition and partly by adrenaline he fought the wind to a position right on the edge of the cliff. He was acutely aware of the danger he was in but this was an opportunity of a lifetime. He raised his camera, he had an almost perfect line East towards Calais. But not quite, he shuffled on his knees to a point where he could almost see the furious sea directly below. Perfect. He again lifted the camera and started to screw his camera to a small tripod. He almost had it when there came a thunderous noise. Mathieu glanced up to see his car tumbling across the car park. For a second he lost all concentration. It was to be a second that cost him his life. Another gust and he was falling backwards over the cliff edge. The violent water at the base of the cliff approached almost as if he was falling in slow motion. Another gust, thud, his skull split open as his head smashed against rain drenched chalk. Seconds later he hit the water. Semi-conscious, as the waves pulled him under he found himself walking through the most beautiful garden with the trees full of bird song. Briefly he remembered seeing a documentary where people had died and been brought back to life. Every one of them interviewed claimed they'd entered a beautiful garden with birds in full voice. So this was it then, he must be dying.

Chez Monique – A Café In Marseille, France

At the time a young man was falling to his death in the North of France, Fatima knocked on the door to the bedroom that was never let to anybody else but her. The number on the door read 19. Cautiously the door opened.

"C'est moi."

The door opened quickly and Fatima with a lightness that defied her frame stepped inside. The door hastily closed behind her. In front of the door his right hand still on the handle stood a man, very obviously in his late sixties. He was smartly dressed in navy blue slacks, an open neck crisp white shirt and a "Husbands" light blue jacket. Try as he might,

Louis could never blend in, he was dressed far too smartly for the area and they both knew, that was extremely dangerous for him.

"It's there," Louis gestured to a crisp brown sealed envelope sitting on a 'build at home' dresser.

Fatima picked it up and slowly tore it open with her long finger nails. She was aware that her smallest of moves was turning her man on. Without even touching him she was bringing him to a state of ecstasy. In a deliberate move Fatima sat on the low cushioned dressing stool, crossing her legs to let the hem of her skirt slide almost down to the bottom of her waist. If she moved ever so slightly she could expose just the tip of her knickers and she did this, at the same time removing the contents of the envelope. At a glance she knew Louis had excelled himself. The papers detailed all of the proposed actions of the local police, the gendarme and most of the specialist units in the coming days, weeks and months. Her client would be one step ahead of the Marseille law enforcement for the approaching future.

Now for his reward for Louis was stood like a dog, sitting with a paw out waiting to be fed a treat. Fatima went over to him and feeling his crutch with one hand started to undress him with the other. Laying him on the bed she slowly disrobed herself above him. At all times she was in total control and the man beneath her respected that. Whilst Louis was naked, Fatima was not, she never completely disrobed. She always kept her hijab on and one other item of clothing. The item of clothing changed each time but the hijab always stayed. The hijab was to remind her man, (sometimes woman), that she was, in their eyes, forbidden fruit and the other item of clothing to frustrate and at the same time excite. Her victims, not how she pictured them, would never see her completely naked, though each time they hoped they would. This added to her control and controlling their hope was a very powerful tool.

Two hours later Fatima closed the door behind her. Louis was still lying naked on the bed, exhausted, his body almost broken. She handed the envelope to the woman behind the bar, in turn the woman handed Fatima a smaller envelope but one that bulged. Inside Fatima knew there would be 50,000 Euros, not bad for around three hours work. At the same time the information she'd obtained from her "victim," was probably worth millions to her client. Who her client was, she had no idea. She was always contacted when she wasn't expecting it and never by the same person. She'd been given a codeword, "Pitgam. " Often she would be passed in the street and a stranger would pass her by whispering the word, "Pitgam." If this happened she knew to follow the whisperer, usually to a café where she would be given instructions. The contact would also inform her how much their client was willing to pay. It was always more than enough.

Louis remained on the bed for a good half an hour after Fatima had left. Always after their reunion he felt a deep sense of guilt. As Le Capitaine de Gendarmerie de Marseille, he was entrusted with and responsible for just about every criminal investigation in the city. What he was doing went against his every natural instinct. By his liaisons with Fatima he was betraying everybody he worked with and followed his command, some were good, very good friends. His greatest fear was, by handing over the city's law enforcement's deepest operational secrets he was putting the lives of those who trusted him, in danger. He had no idea who Fatima was working for and wasn't sure he wanted to know. Despite his deep sense of guilt he couldn't help himself. Fatima was like a drug. Her love making brought him to levels of ecstasy he'd never, until now thought possible. She was firm, always in control and seemed to always know his deepest desires. He knew there was never going to be a good ending to their liaison and he dreaded the day it arrived. He'd thought long and hard about what he would do if his betrayal was ever exposed and suicide was increasingly looking like the only option. Without realising It, he'd mentally been preparing for such an outcome from the first day he'd done Fatima's bidding. A modern day Femme

Chapter 3

Fatale, that's what she was. Only now did he understand the power behind the expression. Before he'd thought the expression had just been some sort of fantasy.

CHAPTER
—4—

Calais - France

It was eleven thirty in the morning and the good people of Calais were busy clearing up after the storm which the weather people had sweetly named Monica. A similar clear up was taking place all along the coast. On the summit of Cap Blanc Nez the local police were examining an upturned old Renault. It was registered to a local photographer but there was no sign of him to be had.

The storm had blown itself out surprisingly quickly. By eight in the morning it was virtually nothing more than a stiff breeze and by nine, apart from the odd mischievous flurry, everything was calm.

The sea in contrast was taking a lot longer to find any sort of calm. Although no longer angry there was a definite swell, and anyone who is prone to sea sickness, will know only too well that these are the worst conditions to sail in.

The school party, consisting of twelve and thirteen year olds were on the first sailing to leave Dover that morning. Booked to sail the evening before they'd spent the night in their coach at the port of Dover. Ecstatic to leave their cramped conditions now they were on the ferry, most of the children though having had little or no sleep, were exploring the ship with gusto. The teachers after a lecture about ship safety and respect for other passengers, retired to a comfy lounge to try and get some shut eye before the drive to the Somme battlefields. They'd been told the roads were in a dreadful state, with trees down almost everywhere. It was going to be a long eventful drive. Their charges were delighted with their new found freedom. Most, despite the conditions, managed a full English breakfast after which the majority went to discover the delights in the games room. Only when the French coast approached and the ferry started turning to port to run parallel with the beach at Sangatte did a number go on deck to have a look at what the French coast looked like.

Excited voices split the air and arms stretched pointing at anything and nothing. Play fighting took place as a number of the boys pretended to throw some of the girls overboard. Shrill but good humoured screams were thrown. Other passengers smiled at the scene remembering wistfully what it had been like to be young. The screams became more exaggerated as the game progressed but always playful, then a scream rang out that stood out from the rest. It was louder, shriller and definitely not playful. As one, all turned to the girl who had uttered it. Almost hysterical she was screaming without taking in breath, her eyes fixed on the sea below. Seconds later she collapsed on deck, having fainted. Hurriedly the others leant over the side to see what all the fuss was about, as did one or two of the passengers. Another helped the fallen girl inside. There passed a rather surreal few seconds then came the sound of someone being sick and quickly after, another. An elderly lady started sobbing and more girls started screaming. "Oh my God," uttered one of the boys.

To their credit most of the boys started ushering their female school mates into a lounge. A woman could be seen having a hurried conversation with one of the bar staff, calling to a colleague he followed her to the outside deck. There was still a gathering of passengers all leaning over the side. Bobbing in the water below were what at first appeared to be a number of footballs. The barman looked harder and it quickly became apparent what all the commotion was about. They weren't footballs at all, but severed heads, swallowing his desire to vomit he counted. One, two, three, he paused, he didn't want to count the same one twice and the waves were playing tricks. Three, he'd been right, four, five. Beside the ship there were five heads floating in the water, there was something else too. It looked rather like a large rag doll and it's movements were strangely grotesque but he couldn't be sure what it was. He turned to raise the alarm but other members of the ship's crew were already there. Quickly they ushered the ghoulishly curious gathering of passengers from the deck and closed all access.

The bridge was quickly informed.

"Five heads! Fucking Hell." It was uncharacteristic for the captain to swear and the other officers manning the bridge looked across at their boss in surprise. The captain had only just become used to discovering the bodies of 'illegal' immigrants floating in the water. Their desperation to get to the UK, resulting in the ultimate sacrifice. He despised the people traffickers for whom life didn't matter, for whom money was far more important. Yes he was used to finding floating corpses but this was different, heads and five of them. "Fuck."

Turning he barked to his First Officer, "alert Le Cross." Le Cross or, Cross Envoy Secours Maritime, their official title, were responsible for safety and security for the French side of the Northern reaches of La Manche or English Channel. They operated from a base on the summit of Cap Gris Nez, (Grey Nose Cape or Point) at the Western tip of the 12km long Plage de Wissant, 'Wissant Beach.' It's twin, Cap Blanc Nez sat at the Eastern tip.

"What shall I tell them?"

"That we've found five fucking heads in the water and they need to come and fish them out, NOW. Don't forget to give them our position."

The First Officer didn't need to be told, he'd already noted it.

Le Cross answered their call almost immediately, luckily most who took the calls there spoke good English or at least operational English.

The captain listened as his first officer relayed their situation and their macabre discovery. He could hear the operator at Le Cross tapping the details into a computer. When he had finished there came from the operator a very slowly pronounced, 'Fuuuck.' His French accent made the word sound like the name of a perfume.

Within minutes the operator had made a call to the SNSM station at Boulogne Sur Mer, the SNSM are the French equivalent of our RNLI. The operator there asked the man at Le Cross to repeat the message several times. "It was definitely only heads?"

"Oui, oui, oui. Only heads."

"Merde. Ok." Both the operators at Le Cross and the crew in Boulogne were shocked. They were very used to picking up bodies in the water, nearly all going unreported by both the French and English media. They were only really interested when an entire boat capsized and most of the passengers ended up drowning. But this was different, just the heads. This looked sinister.

A lifeboat was quickly launched from Boulogne and operators from both Le Cross and SNSM contacted the Procureur in Boulogne, to warn him of what had happened and that there was almost certainly going to be the need for a criminal investigation.

The Procureur's office quickly made a call to the Gendarmerie at Calais and when the ferry docked the Gendarmerie were waiting. Nobody would be going anywhere soon, they needed statements.

The lifeboat had no trouble in finding the five bobbing heads. Three fishing boats were circling. Not from ghoulish curiosity but to protect the scene and to help guide the lifeboat to the correct position. The crew were used to witnessing some distressing scenes, especially when it involved a child. But none of them had ever experienced anything like this and as the third head was hauled aboard and placed carefully into a bag, one and almost immediately after, a second crew member threw up over the side. Floating close to the heads there was also a naked torso, the loose skin was a sickening ash white. It looked to be badly mutilated or maybe even badly chewed. It was hard to tell, it wouldn't be the first time the inhabitants of the sea had been grateful for an easy meal. Placing what were the remains of a once living person, none of the crew ever forgot that, into a body bag they turned the boat and started heading back to Boulogne. There an ambulance would be waiting to transport the remains to the morgue at the main hospital, grandly named Centre Hospitalier Boulogne Sur Mer. As they rounded Cap Blanc Nez one of the crew gave a shout and pointed. The rest of the crew searched in the direction of their colleagues out stretched arm. There floating almost lazily in the swell, bobbed another body. This one, unlike the torso looked fresh. It was very unlikely but there was always a remote possibility that whoever it was could still be alive.

The pilot opened the throttle and the boat raced forward leaping and then crashing between the waves. Hauling the body over the side, from experience they all recognised in an instant that the man, whoever he was, was never going to take a single breath again. Half his face was missing and if that hadn't killed him then the sea had finished him off. He was fully clothed and well wrapped up, almost certainly to protect himself from inclement weather. Round his neck hung two cameras, they both looked expensive and one was exposed, not in its case. It didn't take a rocket scientist to work out what had happened. They were directly below the towering chalk cliffs of Cap Blanc Nez.

"Bloody idiot!" whispered one of the crew.

Their discovery was radioed back to base, where notice of their latest find was immediately passed on to the Procureur.

CHAPTER
—5—

Wissant - France

It was early afternoon when Maureen slid out of bed. Only now was she ready to brave the world. She had brought herself to one of the hardest orgasms she could remember and her body was still revelling in the experience. She hadn't wanted to lose the feeling by getting up. In the end needing to wee forced the issue and she padded to the en-suite bathroom. After relieving her bladder she washed her hands with fine smelling French soap and liberally splashed water over her face. When she had finished she dared examine herself in the mirror. Her skin was glowing and there was a glint in her eye. Yesterday had been good, very good. Then she remembered the brewing storm from the evening before, funny, she hadn't heard anything in the night. Perhaps after all the hype it had been no more than a storm in a teacup, the weather people always loved to put the fear of God into their public. They must lead very boring lives, she considered. Being a little more self-aware now it was daylight, Maureen tied on a slightly too large dressing gown and after making herself a large mug of black coffee opened the glass lounge doors to the balcony.

What she saw shocked her. The beach bar directly below was nothing more than splintered wood and twisted metal and the normally immaculate beach was strewn with all kinds of debris. Everything from a snapped tree to garden furniture, a satellite dish and most impressive of all, an upturned van which must have been blown off the promenade. Directly below her, what was left of the beach bar had been cordoned off and two local police officers were standing guard. Presumably, to protect the place from looters.

How on earth, Maureen wondered had she slept through all of that. She felt a little guilty. Suddenly she felt the urge to see the rest of Wissant, her paradise found. Showering quickly, she picked out one of her more modest dresses, the occasion needed modesty she felt. Strong showy heels she couldn't resist, to finish she chose a long belted coat by Max Mara, purchased with money left to her by her husband.

Wissant she decided, almost resembled Beirut during its most turbulent years. An exaggeration yes but that's how it felt to her. The streets were littered with loose masonry and all sorts from her neighbours gardens. More than one window had been shattered and a number of street signs had disappeared as had a number of display signs attached to local businesses. Her route to the boulangerie, (fresh baguette and patisserie were an essential, nobody should do without), took Maureen along the Rue Du Professor Lelour. It was the main thoroughfare from the town centre to the beach and as she walked, travelling in the opposite direction to her, heading for the seafront, passed a line of vehicles, blue lights rolling and sirens blaring. Their dark blue livery instantly recognisable as the gendarme. She stood still and watched as no less than six vehicles passed, one a van and just as she started to walk again an ambulance also passed.

When she arrived, Maureen found a number of customers waiting to be served. She couldn't remember a time when there wasn't.

"Bonjour Maureen," several of the customers sang as she entered.

She never tired of the French accent, those who went through life never experiencing it were missing out. Everybody waiting knew her love for the male species and nobody ever judged her. Quite the opposite she was respected. The attitude was so different here in France. If you kissed in the street, passers-by tended to clap and cheer where as in England you'd hear a leering, "get a room."

Maureen expected the conversation that morning to be all about the storm and the wreckage it had caused all over town and how long it would take to clear up. But it wasn't, it centred on the dead. Apparently a man had died trying to secure the beach bar directly below her balcony. Worse still a severed head had been found, washed up on the beach near to Escalles and almost directly below the chalk cliff of Cap Blanc Nez. As a consequence the authorities had decided to close the whole of the beach. All twelve kilometres of it. And news had just reached them that more heads had been found floating in La Manche, perhaps as many as ten along with a number of bodies. These revelations shocked Maureen, they shook her to the bone. As she walked back all she could think about was the young man who had died almost directly below her apartment. He must have been one of the three men she'd seen trying to secure the awning whilst standing on her balcony. The thought sickened her. The feeling almost certainly would have been a lot worse if she had discovered just seconds before his death, the dead man had been watching, even more, desiring her.

Farmhouse - Escalles

Antanois had almost finished. He stood up, rested his hands on his lower back and leant backwards. After three hours of bending low his back was complaining loudly. He looked around needing to admire his handiwork. The garden was almost back to normal, another ten minutes and he'd be finished. Three hours, three hours it had taken him to clear up the mess from the storm, But it had been worth it, he'd grown to love the simply planned verdure that surrounded his temporary home. One of his favourite ways of passing time since moving into the farmhouse was to take tea or enjoy a cold beer on the rough stone patio whilst revelling in his surroundings. The scenery about him was wild, verging on the spectacular but at the same time intimate. Very, very different from his home back in the Lebanon. And he loved the fact that it was.

The sound of police sirens broke all serenity. The interruption annoyed Antanois. In the distance he could see several gendarme vehicles followed by an ambulance rapidly coming down the road which led into Escalles. He wondered idly whether in Escalles the small convoy would turn left to pass his farmhouse or continue along the coast road. He waited, the sound of the sirens faded, confirming they were continuing along the coast. Antanois let out a small sigh of relief and quickly realised before the passing gendarme, something else had been bothering him. As he'd been stretching his back, he'd heard another sound. It was alien, he didn't recognise it and he couldn't make out what it was or where it was coming from. With a jolt he realised the sound was still with him and that it was coming from the mobile phone he'd been given by the organisation, the phone that never rang was ringing. And it had been ringing for an inordinate amount of time. He'd been given strict instructions not to use it. He wasn't even allowed to have his own mobile phone. In a panic he sprinted across the bush dispersed lawn and through the back entrance, almost tearing the old wooden door from its hinges as he barged it open. On the equally old kitchen table, the simple Nokia phone was doing a frenzied dance. Antanois dived for it and just as he'd grasped it in his hand the ringing stopped.

"MERDE, MERDE, MERDEMERDE."

The phone rang again and Antanois, this time almost dropped it in his surprise. Nervously he hit the accept call button and even more nervously, waited for a voice.

"Jul.man."

Antanois almost dropped the phone a second time, he hadn't known what to expect but not that. The voice, male, steady, slow and calm continued not allowing him time to reply. He spoke in Akkadian, ancient Akkadian from ancient Babylonia. The language was long thought to be extinct but this man spoke it and so did Antanois. He had been taught it whilst taking holidays with his parents in the Shuf Mountains. He had always been encouraged to keep his knowledge a secret. Out of respect to his parents he had always done that, never really questioning or understanding why. He'd never needed it in everyday life and his knowledge had long been forgotten or so he thought. For now his knowledge came flooding back to him, he could understand every word the man was saying.

In just a few seconds the man had cut off. The message had been short and to the point.

"There has been a break, evidence in the sea. What are you doing about it? Peace be with you."

The man was gone.

"MERDE."

"Antanois instinctively looked at the TV, permanently tuned to the local news channel. He was meant to monitor it constantly.

"MERDE, MERDE, MERDE."

He could be in serious trouble. On the screen a female reporter, her loose hair waving in the wind was almost shouting into her microphone. Antanois recognised where she was immediately, she was reporting from the summit of Cap Blanc Nez. His eyes widened and his ears pricked up. The narrative was all about the storm and the number of dead confirmed so far, thought to have been as a direct result of "Tempete Monica." The media always delighted in reporting on the number of dead, never on the positives. There were five officially reported dead so far. If the media were honest, the number was smaller than had been expected, but reporting that wouldn't make good headlines. Unexplained though, the reporter continued, were the as yet unconfirmed reports of several severed heads, perhaps as many as ten, picked by the SNSM in the waters just below where she was standing, Cap Blanc Nez.

Antanois's blood froze. Seconds later he was sprinting out of the back door and without bothering to close it running towards the garage. On the television the female reporter continued to report. Her training forgotten, in almost panicked tones, she related that what had been confirmed was a severed head washed up on the popular tourist beach at Escalles.

Antanois didn't hear her. He pushed up the rusting door of the garage and after switching on the light quickly closed the door behind him. Resting against and in front of the far wall were typical garage storage, old crates, boxes, a wine rack, bicycles, garden tools, a mower. You can picture the scene. Antanois quickly moved a number of old boxes to expose a large section of the wall. The boxes looked as though they'd been carelessly placed but a trained eye would recognise that in fact the opposite was true. A small, dry powder fire extinguisher hung on the back wall. It was covered in dust and had probably hung there for decades. Antanois went to it, pulled out the safety pin and squeezed. No powder was expelled, instead if you listened carefully you would hear the sound of an electric motor starting and the seemingly fixed wall began to rise. Antanois replaced the pin and picking up an innocent spray can pointed to and sprayed the fire extinguisher. It, once more was covered in dust, showing no evidence of recent use.

In haste, for Antanois knew he had just thirty seconds, he started the Citroen and waited. The back wall came to a halt, revealing, behind it a brightly lit tunnel, wide and high enough for a large vehicle to travel along. He put the car into gear and shot forward. Seconds later the wall dropped behind him. Someone would be along shortly to replace the boxes, the raising of the wall will have sent an alarm to a cottage in Haute Escalles. His mouth bitter with adrenaline, Antanois drove at speed. There was plenty of room. Built by the Nazis on Rommel's orders

Chapter 5

Mount d' Hubert and Cap Blanc Nez were a mass of undiscovered tunnels. There was almost a small town beneath Cap Blanc Nez and Montd'Hubert, completely hidden from the outside world. An incredible example of German Engineering. It was almost a miracle that they'd never been discovered but then nobody knew they were there, except that is for the organisation. How they had known, he had no idea. The thought of the organisation worried him and Antanois put his foot down on the accelerator, perhaps a little too hard.

CHAPTER
—6—

Gendarmerie Nationale – Calais, France

Theirry Maubert, Capitaine Maubert to the officers under his command, drove purposefully into the Gendarmerie car park and pulled up sharply in his designated space. Capitaine Maubert did everything purposefully as well as decisively and couldn't understand people who didn't live their lives in the same fashion. There were no grey areas in his world. His daughter regularly complained at his attitude to life.

"Pappa runs this house as though it's his Gendarmerie," she would, almost on a daily basis moan to her mother. And she no longer lived there. Capitaine Maubert took this as a compliment, that's just how he liked it and how it should be. His one guilty pleasure was what the French call hard rock, to the English heavy metal. Whenever he had the opportunity he would go to concerts where almost the entire audience were crazed teenagers. He didn't care, it was his release. In his office at home, he would often don some expensive headphones and play Motorhead, or something similar at full blast.

Exiting his car he gazed at the plastic looking, red brick box that was his life, the gendarmerie on Rue Mollien. In its design there had been no attempt at beauty. The tricolore hanging out front, offered the only colour. The building looked and was, boring, somewhat forbidding and purposeful. The building was perfect, Capitaine Maurbert had always considered. With purpose in his stride he made his way to his office on the first floor, acknowledging curtly but with respect everybody he passed on his way.

Once at his desk, he phoned for a coffee and settled down to study the latest reports on the findings after the storm. He had just driven back from the port where his officers were attempting to take statements from a largely, tired and disgruntled set of passengers. To make it worse the majority taking the statements spoke very little English and he'd only managed to secure three interpreters. There were also a mix of other nationalities on board and finding interpreters for them would take time. They would not be happy and he pitied any officer who eventually had to sit down with them.

Six severed heads and what looked like a mutilated body. Fuck! What the hell was going on? He had no idea where this investigation would lead. It was going to be big and the media had already somehow gotten hold of it, so his gendarmerie was going to be under siege and under enormous pressure to come up with answers and quickly. Worse still everything they did would now be under scrutiny and open to, what he already knew would be unjust criticism. Then there were resources. Almost a third of his officers were on bloody beach patrol at the request of the British. Bloody British. He'd seen news reports of British politicians promising money to help pay for the extra patrols. The way they spoke, they made it look as though France were taking it, pocketing it and in return not doing a great deal. And yet he knew from the Mayor's office, that to date they hadn't received a penny and as a result his balance sheet was looking crap.

Leaning back in his chair, the capitaine reflected on what he knew so far. After the so called, 'storm of the century,' he knew today was always going to be a difficult one, but he hadn't expected anything like this. Shortly after the SNSM had confirmed their recovery, a call had been received from the local police, confirming another head had been found, this one on the beach close to Escalles and not far from Wissant. After a conversation with his equivalent in Boulogne they had agreed it was wise as well as urgent to close the whole of the 12km sandy beach between Cap Blanc and Cap Gris Nez. There was a possibility of more bodies or body parts being washed ashore, God forbid, and the whole bay, (Baie de Wissant), might hold vital clues as to what had happened. The decision wouldn't be popular with the local Mayors, the summer weather hadn't been great and local businesses had as a consequence suffered badly and were still suffering. The weather over the next few days looked very promising and even now, only hours after the storm the clouds had cleared to a bright blue sky. Local businesses would have been looking forward to a last gasp summer and his gendarme will have snatched it from their outstretched palms. Still, if he'd wanted to be popular, he wouldn't have joined the force.

Another group who wouldn't be happy, were the people traffickers. There was no way they'd be able to float a dinghy over the next week or so. The coast would be swarming with his officers and the local police. The thought caused his lips to form a wry smile. The British too would be happy. His smile turned into a grin.

The initial and still the most popular theory was that the heads, the deceased had been tossed from a passing ship during the storm. As a consequence he had asked Le Cross, who monitored all the shipping using La Manche, for a detailed list of all of the vessels that had passed through the channel in the past week. He'd also got his officers to contact the Gendarmerie Maritime. They would have detailed knowledge of the currents and wind force/direction over the past few days. He wanted to know if using their expertise they could track back to where the body parts may have originated from. Impatient, he buzzed through to his secretaire.

"Colette, have the SNSM or Le Gendarmerie Maritime come back yet?"

"No Monsieur Maubert," she was the only person in the station who didn't refer to her boss as Capitaine. She completely ignored his dissatisfied grunt, she was used to them and she knew they meant nothing, they were just his way. "Monsieur Maubert the Voix du Nord has been chasing me for an update and France 24 are being very insistent, there are others of course but these two are being the most annoying." La Voix du Nord, (Voice of the North), was arguably the most important and influential local rag and France 24 a national channel which offered a detailed local news service. Capitaine Maubert felt inclined to tell them to go fuck themselves but he knew he might at some point need their services, he had to remain civil, even if it was through gritted teeth. He knew, without Colette telling him, that there were many more media harassing her. The noisy radio stations, Radio 6 and Sky Rock were always in their face, plus undoubtedly the one truly local rag, Nord Littoral. Colette was doing a sterling job protecting him. But he had to stop thinking local, this was fast becoming national news, perhaps even International. He considered his next move.

"Colette, get the media team, (team was an exaggeration, the "team," was just one person who covered an area much bigger than his gendarmerie), on the phone, tell him to let the wolves know, that we'll hold a press conference tomorrow. I'll give them an exact time in the morning. We will hold the press conference at the Hotel de Ville, they have the space, I suppose we'd better let them know." At the other end of the phone Colette smiled, the Mayor will love that. "Oh, and Colette."

"Oui Monsieur,"

"From now on refer all media enquiries to our media team."

"Oui Monsieur Maubert. You mean Monsieur Hivin?"

"Oui." The Capitaine allowed himself a loud chuckle. That will give that lazy bastard something to do.

A soft click told him Colette had rung off. Next, he needed to know how far they were with an autopsy. He knew the Procureur will have put considerable pressure on the morgue at Boulogne to carry out the necessary immediately. Scrolling through his mobile phone he quickly found the number for the chief pathologist. The phone rang just twice before it was answered. The voice on the other end sounded young. He recognised it immediately as being that of a trainee, why anyone would want to become a pathologist, he couldn't imagine.

"Monsieur Hubert, is he there?"

The trainee was used to Capitaine Maubert, he knew not to try and make small talk, instead he signalled silently to his boss.

"Hubert." The pathologist could have been born the capitaine's twin.

"Jean-Paul, it's Thierry, Calais."

"Yes I know. I was just about to call you. Listen I think you'd better come over. Come and have a look, it would be easier."

The capitaine sighed, he'd arranged to visit his, belle-mere, (mother in law), that evening and she had promised to make him Baba au Rhum, no one else could make a Baba au Rhum like his belle-mere could. A trip to the morgue and back would mean he would have to put off enjoying his promised dessert to another day. Plus he'd have to face her on another day and that would be hard for she never understood or accepted his official duties as an excuse for a no show. She was family and families are more important than work, even if his was with the gendarmerie. With his belle-mere at the forefront of his mind he decided to try and put off his visit to the morgue till early tomorrow morning. Jean-Paul was always there by six am, the guy practically lived in the place.

"Jea....." On the other end of the phone sounded an electronic monotone. The pathologist had rung off, he was expecting him. "Merde."

In under an hour Capitaine Maubert was pulling into the morgue's car park, in the grounds of Boulogne's main hospital, the Centre Hospitalier Boulogne Sur Mer. The journey from Calais along the A16 had been quick and trouble free, he'd pondered on taking the coast road. Doing so, would have given him a chance to see how his teams were doing but had quickly dismissed the idea. He recognised, modestly that at times his presence, could be a hinderance.

After scrubbing up and donning a disposable set of coveralls and gloves , the capitaine was shown into the main operating theatre. On popular television programmes you often only see one pathologist engaging a detective and his or her assistant. In reality or at least at this morgue, the place was a hive of activity, there were several pathologists, all beavering away over a body. Capitaine Maubert hated the place, in particular he hated the smell. Although highly sanitised you could never completely get rid of, even if the body was fresh and many were not, the smell of dead human flesh.

Jean-Paul on seeing the capitaine greeted him with a firm hand shake.

"You wanted to show me something?" Capitaine Maubert offered. He wondered if it was really all necessary, he never understood why the pathologist couldn't just email him his report. Although practical to a tee, there was still a sense of drama about him. Jean-Paul liked the theatrical and his theatre was his own personal stage.

"Yes, I needed you to see so you'd better understand." The pathologist smiled, a kind of personal apology for dragging the capitaine away. Jean-Paul was short, a little over 5ft in height and wore round rimmed spectacles. The capitaine in contrast, was nearly 6ft 4 and for close reading or examination owned a pair of thickly black framed glasses. The two of them together resembled a little, Mick Fleetwood and Sam Fox at the Brit Awards.

The pathologist led them over to a trolley table , surrounded by a pale blue curtain. On a paper cover, though barely recognisable lay a human male, torso. Missing were the arms and legs and also the head, the skin was a ghoulish greying yellow and apart from the aforementioned the torso looked incomplete. It looked almost as if the outer flesh were caving in on itself. The pathologist picked up a long metal scalpel that glistened in the harsh, bright light.

"Observe," he gestured and carefully prised apart the skin and flesh, where it appeared to have been cut. "No they're not stab wounds." The pathologist saved the capitaine from asking the obvious question. And he was right, for the capitaine had just been about to. "No they've been made by a professional, a surgeon. And from what I can see, a skilled one."

The capitaine's mind whirled. "Why?" I mean, "what for?"

"To remove the organs." Jean-Paul announced triumphantly, pure theatre, "the kidneys, the liver, the heart. All of the vital organs have been removed. And as I've just told you by a professional, and I repeat, a skilled one."

Capitaine Maubert, stood silent, staring down at the pathetic looking pile of flesh. Once a breathing, living human, their life had ended and now displayed in such sad indignity.

"But why?"

"That's your job Thierry, I'm just the pathologist."

"How long has he been dead, any idea when this," the capitaine waved his right arm at the crumpled torso, "the surgery could have been done?"

"That will take time, to be sure. You know I don't like to guess but from its condition I would guess he's been dead around a week, as for the surgery," he paused. " Well common sense would guess the same time. As for age, at this stage I can't really tell but at a rough guess, over thirty, under fifty."

That's three guesses the capitaine pondered and you don't like to guess.

"And of course then there's your heads, they've caught the media's attention."

Capitaine Maubert couldn't disagree. Whilst driving, a rather flustered, Monsieur Hivin had radioed him to let him know that the severed heads had made the main television news, not just in France but throughout Europe, oh and "thank you very much!" The next few days would be hell.

The pathologist led the capitaine through to another, this time, rather grey room flanked on either side by differing size drawers. Walking to the far end, he proceeded to pull out a series of smaller drawers. Originally designed to hold the body of a deceased infant, each now held a rather macabre looking severed head, all were male. Every head lay slightly to one side looking up to the ceiling. At least they would have been looking up if they'd had eyes, for four of the heads didn't. Where their eyes should have been was now simply a black space, an empty socket.

"Did the fish to that?" The capitaine, was trying to avoid their empty gaze, it unnerved him. He had heard somewhere that the first thing fish ate of a dead human were the eyes.

"No," the pathologist paused building the dramatic. Get on with it the Capitaine urged silently. "No, like the torso they were surgically removed and again by an expert."

"What about him?" Capitaine Maubert gestured to the only head which still had eyes.

"I can't tell you that, but I'm guessing, (a fourth guess), if you look at the age, the severed head still with eyes, is a lot older than the others. I'm guessing when I examine him properly that I'll find that his eyes were defective." The capitaine went to speak but the pathologist held up his hand. There's something else, all of these, (he meant the heads), have also been surgically removed from their bodies. The cuts are clean and professional. None of the heads were hacked off."

"Do any of the heads belong to our torso over there?"

The pathologist shook his head, "No Thierry, they do not, it's one of the first things I checked. There are six dead people here, not five." The capitaine took a deep breath, bloody hell!

"There's one more thing you should see." The pathologist pulled out another small drawer. With this drawer, the capitaine observed, he was much more careful. He, for some reason was treating this, whatever it was with much more respect. He soon saw why. Positioned in the same fashion as the others, lay another head. This one also like the others had, had their eye sockets removed. What was very different to the others, this head belonged to a young girl. At a guess no older than twelve and despite the horror inflicted on her, she still somehow managed to retain her beauty.

The pathologist slowly closed the drawer. "This is the head found on the beach at Escalles." He shook his head in disbelief that someone could do such a thing to a mere child.

The next hour was spent in the pathologist's office. Thierry listened carefully as the pathologist went into greater detail about his findings so far. He was also furnished with a preliminary report and several sets of detailed photos of both the torso and all of the heads. On one set of photos the pathologist had marked the findings of his investigation to date.

Driving back along the A16, the capitaine felt exhausted. He had never in all of his career had to deal with anything like this. And the young girl's expression still haunted him, her face kept appearing on the road in front as he drove. When he was leaving the morgue, the pathologist with an emotion he had never seen before, had touched his arm and in a low, steady term whispered loudly. "Thierry, I hope you get the bastard who did this." Bastards he had thought, for he doubted this was the work of one person. All the signs pointed to organised crime.

It was with a sense of great relief when the capitaine reached home. Home was a restored rather eccentric villa just outside the medieval town of Ardres. His only neighbours were cows and a small stream meandered through the garden. It was his own miniature version of paradise. His beautiful and long suffering wife had dinner waiting on the table. Eating it faster than was respectful for all of his wife's efforts, he retired to his office. Selecting a CD, he pressed play. Lounging in a deep leather chair he covered his ears with a ridiculously expensive set of headphones. His fingers soon started tapping to a fairly new English artist called Yungblud. Apparently he was all the rage with the 'underground' adolescents. Thierry soon started to relax. He was liking Yung Blud.

Chapter
—7—

The GMC Building, Euston Road – London, England

Habib stood, waiting nervously, as were most of the other candidates to the right of the main reception area on the ground floor of a large glass building on Euston Road. Home to the GMC, the General Medical Council. He'd only arrived in the UK late last night. The 'organisation,' that's all he knew them by, had booked him into a small private hotel in Bayswater. On the corner of Porchester Gardens and Inverness Terrace, The New Dawn as it was called, had been simple, his room compact, very compact but it had been clean and an unexpected bonus, the receptionist had spoken Arabic.

This was his first time in the UK and yet Habib spoke almost perfect English. Again he had to thank the 'organisation' for that. He had needed English to apply for the exam. The proof he needed for this this was an IELTS certificate, again the 'organisation' had helped him achieve this. Soon after starting his training to become a doctor at the FMT, (Faculty Of Medicine Of Tunis), he had been approached by a woman, who casually , perhaps a little too casually told him she belonged to some international organisation which required doctors with certain skills to work abroad. The money they were offering was eye watering. Ten times what he could earn in his own country, Tunisia. After signing a contract which bizarrely he was not allowed to keep a copy of, he was driven to a medical centre, somewhere in the Tataouine mountains, in the south of the country. The whole complex he remembered was below the surface, hidden under a mountain. There he'd received specialist training. His teachers, he'd found easier to follow than those at the FMT, their way of teaching could be described as being almost hypnotic. He never forgot or misinterpreted an instruction. It was a surprise for no-one, including himself that he successfully qualified as a doctor. Shortly after, at the request of the 'organisation,' he applied to practice in the UK. The Tunisian medical system is justly reputed to be the best in Africa and respected worldwide and the GMC on receiving his application and doctors certificate, quickly, eagerly almost asked him to sit a written exam known as the PLAB 1. The sitting for this had taken place at a GMC examination centre in Cairo, Egypt. Habib had found the examination paper surprisingly easy, he'd passed, of course and now here he was in London, the city of opportunity, waiting to take PLAB 2, the practical part of the exam. If he passed this he would be allowed to practice as a doctor in the UK.

Habib rubbed his palms, they were sweating. It was the organisation. If he passed they'd told him, he would be picked up and driven to his new home. If he failed he'd be taken straight back to Tunisia for, 'retraining.' It was the word 'retraining,' he didn't like. The way the organisation had used the word had, Habib thought had a sense of menace about it. They'd been told by the GMC to arrive at eight. One quality of being an Arab was getting up early, it was in their blood. As a consequence he'd arrived an hour early and more to pass the time than anything else he'd enjoyed three cups of surprisingly good coffee in the Black Sheep Café which conveniently was only a few paces from the main entrance. Now it was nearly time, he needed the loo but worried if he went he'd be in danger of missing the group rendezvous. Looking around he could see by their faces several others were almost certainly suffering the same predicament. There were, he counted ten candidates in all, mostly judging by their appearance from the Middle East and

Asia. One candidate he recognised was Tunisian like himself and he'd even seen him from a distance, in the medical centre where he'd trained. The 'organisation,' whatever the circumstances had pre warned him to never show any signs of recognition. He couldn't understand why but respected their wishes. It was silly perhaps, but for some reason he thought it could be dangerous to do any different. He gave his fellow countryman a split second glance and that was it, no more. In return the man showed zero signs of recognition. Maybe but Habib knew deep down the guy had recognised him too, he just knew.

Bang on eight am two women turned up to greet the nervous group of applicants. For most, their hopes, ambitions, and for a few, family, depended on the next few hours. In small groups they were led by lift to the 2nd floor and into a pre-prepared waiting room . Once there, the exam process was explained in some detail. Security was extremely tight, all candidates from here on in, were chaperoned, even if or when they went to the toilet. All personal belongings were to be left in a personal locker, especially mobile phones and there was to be no conversing with other applicants. Any deviation from these rules would result in instant disqualification. Before anyone could take the exam, documents were checked and photographs taken for a security lanyard. Without it you could not get into the examination quarter. The whole process was very intimidating but once into the examination process nearly all tended to relax, this is what they'd been trained for and for most, practised on a daily basis.

Habib found the practical examination, like the written, surprisingly easy. He had expected a lot worse. He was very confident he had passed. Very, very confident. He almost skipped out of the main doors and jokingly nodded to the manikin gazing through the window. Outside he started to walk, a new found assuredness in his step, towards the pedestrian crossing that would take him across Euston Road and to Warren Street Station.

"Pitgam"

Someone had whispered the word firmly in his ear. A man was walking away, heading for one of the two cafes in Regent's Place. Habib followed him. Not far away, another applicant, also a Tunisian could be seen walking closely behind another man. They too were heading for one of the two cafes.

Wissant – France

Maureen stood on her balcony, just as she had done the evening before. This time however she stood fully clothed. The weather unlike the evening yesterday was in complete contrast. The air was still, not even a whiff of a breeze and as a result the sea was a virtual millpond. The air was also clear and across the water lights twinkled in the darkness, sketching the line of the English coast. It was almost impossible to imagine the hell that had passed yesterday. Standing, looking out at the serenity before her, it felt to Maureen as though the storm had happened years ago, not yesterday.

Her gaze turned to the shore and promenade directly below. The tide was in and the water lapped somewhat apologetically against Wissant's famous white sand, almost as though it were asking for forgiveness. Maureen never tired of the sound and unless she had company she always slept with the balcony doors open. Forget sleeping pills, there was no better soporific than the sound of the sea. The storm was almost forgettable until eyes were exposed to the heap of rubble that had once been a popular beach bar. Maureen remembered the poor man who had died there, only hours before. Remembering him, her first emotion like every normal person was one of sadness, then other feelings started to make their presence felt. Feelings that had no right being there. The thought of the poor man's death brought a thrill that snaked through her veins, she started to feel tense with excitement, sexual excitement. She shouldn't she knew, be feeling like this but the fact that it was shocking made the excitement somehow greater. Standing below, not far from her balcony stood two gendarmes. They were on night watch, guarding the beach, others Maureen knew were posted at the East and West extremities of town. A small reddish glow highlighted that one was smoking and her tongue could taste the rising cigarette smoke. It's taste excited her even more. The two were in deep conversation, oblivious to her voyeurism. As she watched one broke off and entered the café across the way. Through the steamed glass windows she could see him taking a place at one of the back tables. He hadn't just ordered a coffee, he'd asked the serveuse to bring him a menu, he would be there a while. Driven with anticipation Maureen knew what she needed to do, if she didn't try she wouldn't sleep that night. She felt a little disgusted with herself but quickly contained her guilt. Working with haste, she shone her legs, made her face with bold daring colours and pulled over a dress blessed with a material that magically clung to places that mattered most to the average male. Standing, instinctively she dropped her knickers and already braless, decided to leave it that way. Killer heels and a dark blue faux-fur and she was ready. Less than five minutes after she had made up her mind to do this she was ready for the kill.

The two gendarmes were already struggling with boredom. It was eight in the evening and tomorrows shift designated to replace them weren't booked to arrive until six the following morning. Another ten hours to kill and after just only two had passed they were both bored senseless. Although it was forbidden, they'd been ordered to always stay as two, they decided between them that they would each do two hour lone shifts. Their squad car was parked in full view of whoever remained on guard and they would take turns sleeping in it. After tossing a coin it was Andre who won the first break. As the Promenade café was still open he decided rather than get cramp in the car, he'd take advantage and enjoy a coffee and a hot meal. He promised his colleague he'd bring him a coffee too.

Not long after he'd ordered his food, a Welch, a woman entered the café. He along with several other men he noticed, even the youngsters, for she was obviously in a nice way over sixty, appreciated her. The woman looked around, and he could have sworn, deliberately caught his eye and then taking bold strides chose a table adjacent to his. Removing her coat the woman sat down. As she did so she crossed her leg nearest to him. The lower half of her high split dress fell away revealing a strong, womanly thigh that glistened in the shine of the ceiling lights. For her finale the woman looked directly at him and holding his eyes with hers she gave him her best, most engaging smile.

The gendarme couldn't remember feeling this way since he'd been a teenager. His trousers were becoming uncomfortably tight as an erection started to strain the material, all he could think about was making love to that woman. Nothing else mattered. He couldn't help himself from throwing her guilty glances and on each occasion the woman caught them and flashed him a smile. As his glances became bolder he realised that the woman wasn't wearing a bra. And as time passed she slowly, and Andre half thought, purposely brought her leg up so that if he dared look long enough he could see she wasn't wearing knickers either. She was completely naked under that dress. His erection was now so hard that it was no longer uncomfortable, it was beginning to hurt him. He risked another glance and again the woman caught it and smiled his way, this time he smiled back. The next thing he knew the woman was sat opposite him, leaning towards him, her breasts threatening to fall out of her low cut dress.

"I hope you don't mind but being in here alone I feel uncomfortable with all those men staring at me. You're a gendarme, I feel safe with you." The woman looked directly into Andre's eyes, at the same time, with the back of her fingers, she gently rubbed the back of both his hands.

From her accent the gendarme realised instantly that the woman sat opposite him was English.

"I speak English, a little," he stammered. What a stupid thing to say he thought and immediately regretted it. His English was practically non-existent.

"No don't," the woman purred, I find your language so soothing, so reassuring, soooo sexxxy."

The woman gently pulled her hands away and taking a sip of her coffee pulled a face. "This coffee is so rubbish," she held his eyes. "I make much better coffee, do you want to try some of mine?"

"I'm meant to be working, I could lose my job."

The woman stood up "That's all part of the excitement isn't it, my apartment is number six, opposite here. I've been watching you from my balcony. Finish your meal and then come up. Here's the key to the apartment entrance." The woman discreetly slid a copper colour key under the edge of his saucer. With that she stood up and strode out of the café not giving Andre the opprtunity to refuse.

Around fifteen minutes later, after finishing his Welch the gendarme crossed the road and after explaining to his colleague, he needed to stretch his legs went in search of the woman's apartment. He soon found it and after opening the door bounded up the stairs, three steps at a time. He couldn't believe his luck, He just prayed it wasn't some sort of cruel joke.

Sitting in a car, parked deliberately so not to be easily visible, in viewing distance of both the café and the English woman's apartment sat a smartly dressed man. Slim, almost certainly in his late thirties his head boasted a mass of tussled curls. The man glanced at his watch, a Patek Philippe, held on by a leather strap. He breathed in contentedly. He had been watching the English woman on and off throughout the summer. After their initial liaison the woman had become expert in seducing and controlling men, but a gendarme was a step up. They were warned to resist such approaches and if he were caught, it would almost certainly result in instant dismissal. No the woman had done well, very well. His intuition had been right, she may be just what they're looking for. After pressing the ignition, he engaged the gears and the car sped silently away.

Maureen waited, pacing the lounge. It was almost fifteen minutes since she'd left the gendarme in the café. Wasn't he going to come? Her vagina was throbbing with anticipation. Perhaps she had been too bold, too intimidating. Perhaps she should have been more subtle. As she pondered there came a knock at the door. Her gendarme, in a little under 10 minutes she had seduced a complete stranger, someone probably half her age and a gendarme at that. She was very, very pleased.

Opening the door, Maureen grabbed and dragged the man inside. He just had enough about him to kick the door shut, no one must see him. In seconds Maureen was holding him tight in her strong arms kissing him passionately on the lips, her tongue, prising open his mouth, exploring deep inside. As he responded in kind she drew her tongue back sliding along, teasing the tip of his tongue. He responded well, playing the same game, happy to follow her lead. Maureen felt his hands starting to explore her body and moaned deeply as his fingers brushed against an erect nipple. Acknowledging her enjoyment he went back and squeezed her nipple through her dress. Maureen shuddered, her head falling back. The gendarme's head was now buried in her neck. That was enough. Maureen pushed him off. Turning, and still wearing her heels she marched, taking deliberately long strides, to the open doorway of her bedroom removing her coat and immediately after her dress, as she did so, letting both slide to the floor.

Andre watched, fascinated. Never had he met, seen a woman like her. In truth he'd never really looked at an older woman, a larger woman. His wife was a size 10 and only just turned thirty. Whoever she was, he suddenly realised he didn't even know her name, she was two hundred percent woman and never in his life had he felt so turned on. When he reached the bedroom door he found her, already lying on the bed, her back raised, resting on what looked like silk pillows. Her right leg was drawn up, the other one flat revealing just a hint of semi shaved vagina.

"Hurry up." Maureen commanded, her vagina felt as though it were about to explode. The gendarme needed no encouragement, he started to undress. Maureen saw that he was carrying a gun, this only added to her excitement. She drew her other leg up and started to gently finger her clitoris. Living close by death, the gun, the uniform, a gendarme and a married gendarme she observed, was forbidden fruit twice over. With everything rolled into one Maureen's sexual nervous system was on fire and this young man would soon know it.

For the next two hours, the gendarme experienced love making like never before. He became lost in the woman's body, her hands, arms, legs and mouth were everywhere, she completely controlled where he went and what he did. And the more the woman orgasmed the more she wanted, more she demanded of him.

After two hours of intense love making Maureen was close to having a massive climax, every nerve in her body was telling her this. She knew exactly how she wanted to cum. With ease she pushed her gendarme down so his head was between her legs, his mouth inches from her vagina. She swung each leg over, clamping his back with her ankles and still using every muscle in her legs pulled him towards her. Even if he'd wanted to he wouldn't have been able to escape the clamp her legs had him in. She was too strong. His tongue started to explore her vagina, moving slowly around her clitoris. Maureen started to moan, arching her back as she did so. She reached down and grabbing his hair pulled gently. She had to manoeuvre him into just the right spot. She quickly found it for him and shouted out loud as his tongue started to explore some more. She pulled hard on his hair not wanting him to lose the spot. She heard him gurgle in her juices as he experienced pain. Maureen didn't care, this was all about her. She pulled his hair harder pushing her vagina hard into his face. He knew he was struggling to breathe but didn't care, he'd have to learn to breath though his ears. Then it came, the orgasm that had been building for the past two hours. Maureen screamed her lower body arching upwards. The gendarme yelled as his body contorted before his head came to rest on the woman's stomach. His whole head was soaked in sweet tasting cum. Maureen let her legs relax and in response they slid off the gendarmes back. She continued though to hold his head, enjoying the feeling as her body experienced follow up orgasms causing her body to twitch, on occasion violently.

Ten minutes later Andre was showered and back in his gendarme's uniform. He said goodbye with an almost innocent kiss, the sort you'd greet an old friend with. Walking down the steps outside he could hardly believe what had just happened. He'd never experienced sex like it. Only now he was outside did he realise that he hadn't cum once and yet he'd never felt so excited in his life. The woman, he still didn't know her name, had shown him completely different possibilities. The trouble was he wanted more. He wanted to experience it again. The woman was the worst kind of drug and he was totally addicted.

Returning to his post, his colleague was visibly displeased. "Where the fuck have you been? You've been gone nearly three fucking hours, we agreed two."

"Then take four, Andre cantered, I don't mind," and he didn't.

"Well where the fuck did you go?"

Andre paused and after a second's reflection decided to tell him.

"Bollocks, in your dreams," and his colleague walked off to take his break. After a few steps he stopped. "Oi and where's my fucking coffee you promised?" The café was no longer open.

Andre shrugged his shoulders, grinning as he did so.

"Fucking hell," and with that his colleague opened and after climbing in, closed the car door.

Andre looked up to what he assumed to be the woman's balcony. He thought he saw a movement, no, there was nothing, it must be his imagination. Hands in pockets, he stared out to sea, preparing himself mentally for what he knew would be hours of boredom.

Farmhouse – Escalles, France

It was dark outside and the only light in the lounge came from a television. Antanois watched intently, he was lounged in his favourite chair and the brandy resting in his right hand was his fourth. The other three hadn't touched the sides. He wanted their normally mellowing effect to act quickly but his brain was stubbornly resisting the assault. He took another long sip, his throat burned, it was a waste of his bottle of Janneau VSOP he knew. Brandy should be enjoyed when your body was relaxed, when the smooth burning liquid could stimulate a calm that was already there. It wasn't designed to bring about a sense of calm, if you used it for that it would simply bring on a headache and Antanois could already feel one approaching.

There was nothing new on the news about the findings in La Manche or the English Channel and that was a something of a relief. His biggest problem now, was that a great number of the world's media not to mention gendarme were camped above his hidden town. He couldn't afford anymore slip ups and more importantly the organisation couldn't. Even more important they wouldn't accept anymore. He wasn't sure if they'd accept this one, he'd find out in a few days. The thought made Antanois take another long sip of his Janneau.

His mind wandered back to the events that afternoon, events that he'd rather forget. In his haste to get to what the organisation called the 'centre of operations,' he'd almost crashed his car against one of the many piles of chalk that littered the tunnel. Rubble left over from the tunnel's construction, rubble because of the circumstances the builders hadn't had time to remove. Two parked refrigerated vans signalled the end of his short but eventful drive. Waiting for him was a huddle of both men and women, all wearing an expression of concern. They were a mix of races which reflected the organisation's international make up.

An elegant, rather lanky woman stepped forward as Antanois pulled up. She opened his door before he had fully come to a halt, giving him a single shake of the hand before stepping back to let him exit.

"We've had a break." Her voice was matter of fact, steady but her tone failed to hide her concern.

"I know, I've been contacted." The woman's facial expression turned from one of concern, to surprise. She wanted to know by whom but knew better than to ask.

"The whole bloody world knows." Antanois added.

"Maybe, but not where the break is." The woman countered cautiously.

"Not yet," came Antanois's curt reply, "and let's hope for all our sakes they don't discover from where."

There was an uncomfortable silence. All those gathered had been listening to the short, what maybe should have been tete-a-tete. All knew the consequences if the organisation even suspected their secret underground operation. The organisation, would almost certainly want every single one of them dead for risk of any of them breaking under interrogation. And all knew that the organisation would be quick and efficient in their task. They'd all known the risks when they'd joined. Antanois scanned their worried faces. These were the professionals, they were all very well paid along with a promise to be looked after for life if they served the organisation well. However he was only too aware that they knew, though none standing before him had been threatened, what would happen if things went wrong or much worse, if you made a mistake that could jeopardise the operation here. The threat was always a silent one and thus all the more powerful. The fact that one day a colleague you'd been working alongside for months, possibly years, the next day simply vanished without any explanation was evidence enough that the threat was real.

Antanois bore no real sense of guilt when it came to those who were earning a good salary and to their eventual destiny, but he was also responsible for the unpaid, people who had no hope, no future. These people the organisation had picked up from the streets of despair. Offering them hope, a bed and a hot meal if they were loyal and worked hard. For these workers a hot meal and a bed were welcome but the offer of hope was always paramount. The outside world would call these people slaves and Antanois hated that description. Although not a saint by a long chalk he did possess a conscience, a weak one maybe but a conscience all the same and perversely perhaps, he cared for them more than the professionals employed and earning a good salary.

"Where's the break?" Antanois aimed the question to the woman who'd greeted him.

"In the room we never mention."

"Show me."

The woman nodded to the gathering who took it as a signal to disperse and with a nervous silence they did just that.

With an outstretched arm the woman began walking Antanois through a series of tunnels. All of the tunnels were spacious and in places heavy steel doors were set into the walls. German stencilled writing painted on the wall adjacent to some of the doors, indicated the original use of the room behind the steel. The swastika was everywhere and if you ran your fingers along the walls you would find messages etched into the chalk. Almost invisible to the naked eye in the brackish yellow light they were nearly all left by the soldiers who had once lived, worked, perhaps even died in the tunnels.

Antanois didn't need to be led, he knew exactly where they were going and if you weren't sure, as you got closer to 'the room that's never mentioned,' you simply had to follow your nose. The stench was gut wrenching and dark stains on the tunnel floor as they approached was evidence of many stomachs that had passed before and given up the contents of their host. Finally they came to the end of a very broad and dimly lit tunnel. In front of them barring their way a huge armoured steel door. Above the door hung a large sign. Like all the rest it was in German. Achtung. The word was underlined, "Danger."

The woman pressed what was quite obviously a recently installed button and the heavy steel door, with very little effort started to slide open. As the first gap appeared a rush of foul smelling air escaped into the tunnel. The two of them though experienced, instinctively covered their face. No matter how many times you experienced the 'room that was never mentioned,' your senses never quite got used to it. The door movement was excruciatingly slow and it was several painful seconds before it shuddered to a halt revealing what at first appeared to be a giant cave. The floor was concreted and covered with a thin layer of foul smelling water. The walls and ceiling in contrast were mainly exposed, roughly hewn chalk. In places the water was almost an inch deep, what at first appeared to be folds of bathroom tissue were everywhere. Their movement boarded at times on the grotesque. Possibly because they weren't paper at all but remnants of rotting human tissue. Both the woman and Antanois knew this. In the centre, built into the floor, lay a huge circular pit lined with steel. At the far side, the circle was broken and extended into a wide arc. Both the arc and the circle were completely flooded. Against the far wall, the chalk wall that held back the sea, another titanic armoured door was fixed, though this one had two halves and opened vertically. You could tell this because the doors were locked open. On the other side of the door, more bare chalk had been exposed, in through which flowed a current of fresh sea tasting air. The air was proof that somewhere there was a fissure, though it was not immediately obvious where. The woman reached to a hook in the wall from which hung what looked like simple plastic carrier bags. Tearing a couple off she handed them to Antanois.

"If you're intending going in there, you'd better put these on" They were shoe covers taken from the medical department.

Antanois needed no further encouragement and suitably booted he stepped into the chamber, followed by the woman who was also suitably booted. A movement in the shadows, distracted them both and a man shuffled into their vision. A thin gaunt looking man with haunted eyes, a beard that badly needed trimming and a whisper of hair that stuck to his scalp with grease. He was bare foot and wore black trousers that were covered with stains, they were also soaked up to his knees. On his upper body a grey shirt was almost entirely hidden by a fully zipped parka. The man's name was Armani not that anyone here cared or even knew and so never reflected on such an irony. His home was Eritrea where he had, many years ago, been a proud farmer but fighting and a very real threat to his life had forced him to flee. He'd heard stories about the streets of London being paved with gold and he wanted to find out for himself if the rumours were true. Travelling almost entirely by foot he had journeyed to Calais. On arrival he'd discovered on the very first day, that to complete the final stage of his voyage he would need money. Unlike many of the others residing in the so called 'Jungle' he had no money to buy his way to Britain. So near and yet so far. He had all but given up when one day, a couple, he thought they were French, took pity on him. They had been part of a team serving food at one of the many charitable food stations dotted around town and so he trusted them. A clandestine rendezvous one night saw him climb into the back of a van.

Ever since he had been in this 'hole' that never saw daylight. He had no idea how long he had been there. Certainly months, perhaps even years. There were no days, just electric light that never turned off. And it was a 'hole' yes but not hell, not quite. He had a bed, it was in a dormitory shared with nineteen others but it was still a bed and whoever it was who had taken him provided him with three meals a day. His job was disgusting he freely admitted that, but he had slowly got used to it and like the rats that were everywhere he now viewed the rotting flesh that he had to transport and clean up after, as just another waste. The only thing that got to him occasionally, was the stench. It was worse, when he fell behind with his work, at times it became almost overpowering and when this happened he could be sick several times in one day. To balance his hunger he had shamelessly started to eat some of the scraps about him. At first he'd been horrified at what he had become but time heals and better still, accustoms one's mind to the most disgusting. And anyway he found eating the root of the smell, helped to quell his nausea.

Armani observed his visitors nervously. Normally nobody came to this room, only to let him in and out, that was all. Yet that afternoon there'd almost been a crowd. For several minutes nobody talked, the man he knew to be Antanois slowly walked around the huge circular pit occasionally glancing into it with a look of disgust. He reached the armoured steel doors that were gaping open.

"Who opened these?"

Armani shaking, raised his right arm as though he were competing with a crowded room.

"Why?"

"The smell, to relieve the smell. " The man shook as he answered the question put to him.

Antanois felt sorry for him but his action had put the whole operation at risk and he knew the organisation would not forgive. Armani had very little time left in this world and he knew Armani knew it too.

"Why are they still open?"

"I can't close them." Armani had pointed to a rusting wheel bolted to an arm of concrete rising from the floor. Nearly everywhere the organisation had replaced the world war two mechanics with modern electrical switches but this door had never intended to be opened. The cavern had been built to hold a gun, it was in fact a casemate, a huge one, designed to defend against a British attack from the sea. The thick armoured door had been built to protect the cavern from incoming fire. The builders had yet to break through the thin layer of chalk that hid the structure from the outside world. The end of the war meant that breaking through had no longer been necessary. And so the status quo remained until the night before when the 'storm of the century,' finished what the Germans hadn't.

Another man had appeared at the door. He looked flushed and his cheeks matched almost the redness of his head of hair and beard. He wore sturdy black boots and ignored completely the shoe coverings hanging from a hook in the wall.

"Charles." Antanois acknowledged the man.

Charles was a very English name for a fiercely proud Scot. Back home he had been an engineer in Aberdeen's booming oil industry. Whilst ashore he'd shared a house with two other engineers. All were divorced and one to supplement his already exaggerated salary was dealing drugs. One day their house was raided and Charles although he wasn't involved was arrested, charged with dealing and found guilty, receiving a two year prison sentence. To make matters worse, whilst there his mother had liver failure, probably from years of drinking scotch. Without a donor she was destined to die and Charles was prepared for the worst. That is until a Serbian, also in for dealing offered to help. I know people, an organisation, he had called it, who can help and he had added, "they could use a man like you". Promise to work for them when you come out and I'm sure they will help. It sounded like one big fantasy to Charles but what had he to lose. He promised and in under a week his mother had been whisked away. Two months later she had mysteriously reappeared. She was weak through her operation and still going through recovery but she had successfully been given a new liver. By the time Charles got out his mother was like a born again teenager.

He couldn't thank the people who had helped him enough and wondered how he could join what the Serbian had referred to simply as the organisation. A few days later he found out. Whilst walking to the betting shop a van had pulled up alongside. Two men jumped out and bundled him into the back. Apologising profusely for the way they had handled him, the two men hurriedly explained they were with the organisation that had saved his mother and that their unusual method of recruitment were entirely necessary to protect the sanctity of the movement. The two men looked as though they could handle themselves and Charles felt he'd had little choice than to accept his fate. They had offered him a scotch to welcome him to the 'cause,' and the downing of it was his last memory before ending up here, wherever here was. He still wasn't sure, though after the fissure, or the break, as everyone here kept calling it, he knew he was near the coast. His job he'd discovered immediately was to be in charge of all aspects of engineering, in wherever they were. He knew the construction was originally German and almost certainly from the second world war as swastikas and signs in German were everywhere. Although life here was more than weird , he actually enjoyed it. He had no contact with the outside world, except for a weekly supervised phone call to his mother. She had access to his bank account and confirmed that a great deal of money was paid in from a foreign bank on the first of each month. He was being regularly paid as promised and paid well, very well. The food was good, there was a bar, a gym and he had his own, very comfortable room, with cable tv, though strangely he couldn't access a single news channel. Through his work, on the lowest level, he'd glimpsed, what looked like an underground hospital. He hadn't been able to confirm it as the area was restricted. Everyone referred to his employer as the organisation. Who they really were he had no idea. He guessed they were based in the middle east as those in charge all appeared to be from that region and were Muslim. He knew that as calls to prayer were regularly relayed through the speaker system and close to the leisure area there was a prayer room. No one had attempted to convert him however, and that was a great relief. His contract, (unwritten), though he trusted them, was for five years, after which they'd promised him, if he wanted to, he'd be free to leave. With the money he'd earned he'd probably be able to retire. The only condition, he'd have to sign a strict confidentiality document and that was fine with him.

"Report." Antanois directed his order to the engineer.

"There's a small opening just below the lower door. The weight and force of the waves must have found a weak point. It's only small…"

"Large enough for some of our waste to escape through."

"Yes, yes, large enough for that," the engineer had to agree with Antanois. "But on the plus side the opening is at the very back of a chalk shelf. It isn't visible from the ground, and from the air or out at sea, if visible at all, would probably appear as a shadow."

Antanois was quietly relieved to hear this but had no intention showing it. "I don't like the word probably, especially with all the attention outside."

What attention? Charles knew their operation was clandestine but this was the first time he heard of any unwanted attention.

Antanois ignored the question. "So what are you going to do about it? "

Charles had been prepared for this and answered without hesitating. " There's plenty of loose chalk, rubble in the old tunnels, we'll fill it, the opening with that and cement it in. Then we'll close the doors." The engineer gestured to the aperture. No one will ever know."

"I hope you're right, ok, get on with it."

The engineer, turned and jogged back up the tunnel.

"Ok, clear this mess up Armani."

It was the first time anyone in charge had ever called him by his first name and Armani almost wept. "Yes sir," he just about managed.

There came no reply. The door was already locked shut. He was alone once more, alone in his own disgusting little world, which no one ever mentioned.

Antanois and his female colleague, returned following the same tunnels but in reverse. As they walked, the two conversed intensely. Home for the woman was Egypt, though she hadn't lived there for years. She was medically trained and oversaw all things related to her training. Nobody knew her real name, she simply liked to be called Seth. Their discussion, was purely commercial. The break, meant they would have to stop operations for a while. Orders were already piling up and Seth complained she had very little stock with which to work. Soon her supplies would be exhausted and she couldn't see any fresh stock being delivered any time soon. Their customers would not be happy and more worryingly, the organisation, would not be pleased. Antanois, didn't need to be told, he already knew and this was his deepest concern.

Before returning to his farmhouse, Antanois wanted to see for himself the orders that were being received. He didn't trust Seth, she tended to exaggerate. Just off the main parking area behind another armoured door, there was a modern looking office. Only the German stencilled writing on the back wall, gave away that this was no ordinary office. There were files, computers, wall charts, even a coffee machine. Four young women, all wearing the hijab were hard at work.

"Busy?" Antanois' question was almost nonchalant in its tone.

"Very," the woman nearest to him answered. "Especially London, they're being very demanding."

"Can I see?" The woman clicked her keyboard and a list of orders appeared on the screen. All these are just from today and we're being chased for earlier orders already. The trouble is London wants mainly Caucasian."

Antanois studied the screen intently. A weekend in Paris, several week long holidays in Thailand. Three VIP around the world cruises.

"Three VIP," Antoinas whistled.

"Yes," the woman confirmed and London have warned us there's more in the pipeline.

"Ok," Antanois let out a long sigh, "ok, thank you."

"You see," Seth's tone was almost accusing.

"We're going to have to sort it."

"Yes you are." Seth retorted and closed his car door harder and louder than was necessary.

Hardly paying attention anymore to the television, Antanois reached once more for the bottle next to him. This would be his fifth glass but the brandy wasn't having the desired effect. Maybe one more glass would do it.

His two main concerns were re-starting the operation and avoiding being discovered by the gendarme or come to it, by anybody. The main entrance to the underground complex was at the summit. His tunnel had been built by the Germans as an emergency exit. Nearly all the bunkers that were part of the Atlantic wall had been given one. The main entrance was in plain sight of anybody on the summit but like the entrance to the escape tunnel, it was cleverly disguised. He doubted if the gendarme would even look for it but if they ever found reason to, he worried what electronic sensors were capable of and might uncover. It was paramount that the gendarme never found reason to search in the first place.

Once his concerns were satisfied they'd be able to start operations again. He'd been surprised at the number of orders coming in, especially from London and the type of order. Three VIP cruises around the world, code of course, wow. There was little more he could do than have the break closed as quickly as was feasibly possible and he trusted Charles to do that. Charles was excellent. After that there was little more that could be done, except pray that the gendarme would decide sooner rather than later that there was nothing to be found on the Mont and as a consequence the world's media would soon get bored and leave too, to go and be annoying somewhere else. The organisation had taken years to renovate and fit Rommel's bunker and spent millions in the process. They would be very unhappy if it all went tits up. The thought made him take another swig of the warm liquid in the glass and immediately regretted it

It took just under two hours to close the opening with cemented chalk. It had taken a little longer to close the armoured doors. The doors had put up stiff resistance but oodles of grease along with the muscle power of several men, and the heavy doors though protesting every step of the way, were once more forced tightly shut. Job done, satisfied or partially satisfied for Charles wasn't too confident about the chalk filling holding, he retired to the bar where he ordered a double shot of Johnny Walker Blue Label. He felt he deserved it whatever the outcome.

Chapter
—8—

Bayswater – London, England

The water was piping hot. Habib hadn't expected it to be, it was a pleasant surprise. Stepping out of the shower, he dried himself with gusto. He'd been advised by the man who'd met him outside the GMC building that it may take up to 10 days for his results to come through, though first signs were positive. How did he know?

What was also strange, he could remember everything the man had told him and instructed but he couldn't picture the stranger at all. He couldn't remember in the slightest what the man had looked like and yet it had been only a couple of hours ago. How bizarre and quickly Habib forgot all about it. He had been told to stay at The New Dawn until otherwise notified. The hotel would be booked automatically. There was no need for him to do anything.

Habib had every intention of making the most of his new found freedom, and in one of the world's greatest and most vibrant cities. After checking himself in the mirror he sprayed himself perhaps a little too liberally with scent he'd brought from home. Satisfied he looked his best Habib stepped out to experience, first-hand the delights of London. As he strode up Queensway he had not a care in the world.

He held no fear, after all what danger was there for a young Muslim in such a civilised city.

Langstone- Hampshire

Langstone was beautiful, few could argue with that and if you did, you'd be on the losing side. Made up of little more than a few cottages and a modern close, the hamlet hugged the coast at the start of the sea bridge, crossing to Hayling Island. The hamlet though tiny boasts two waterside pubs, The Ship Inn, formerly an old mill, beside the main Havant to Hayling Road and the much painted and photographed, Royal Oak which when the tide's in, you can only reach on foot or by boat.

The only real road, grandly named, The High Street leads from the main Havant to Hayling road down to the water's edge and Langstone Harbour. The road frequently floods and a row of chocolate box cottages, some thatched, all have slots in front of their door to house their own wooden flood barrier.

The hamlet was almost perfection personified. Shame then that such a horrific discovery had been made in one of the cottages. An anonymous caller to 999 had asked for an ambulance to attend as their 'friend,' had stopped breathing. When the paramedics arrived they had found the front door to be slightly ajar. The door entered directly onto the lounge. The caller had been right. Their friend had stopped breathing alright for his head had been decapitated and was sitting on the coffee table.

Within minutes the Hampshire constabulary were on the scene. Detective Inspector Philip Johnson and his sidekick, Sergeant Wesson, weren't unused to coming across a corpse but this was entirely different, this was horrific in the strongest terms. Resting upright on the seat of a winged back arm chair, sat a naked torso of a man. His arms and legs had been removed, his arms were stuffed in a large glass vase meant for flowers. The flowers were strewn all over the floor, and his legs in the log basket. The victim's torso was heavily scarred from what looked like possibly hours of torture. His torso was also missing his genitals. They were to be found on the low coffee table, hanging from the mouth of the decapitated head.

The police photographer was next to arrive. "Jesus," he breathed surveying the scene. "I could sell these for a fortune on eBay."

He quickly realised his remark had been a mistake and proceeded to record the evidence through a lens.

"I want nobody else apart from forensics coming in here." The sergeant nodded. "And none of this is to get out. I don't want the media getting hold of it." From the inquisitive group of bystanders already starting to gather outside the cottage, the sergeant, considered this order may prove to be a little more difficult. As if reading his thoughts Detective Inspector Johnson added, "and get uniform down here, I want those ghouls outside held right back." The D.I. hated the curious, often morbid Joe Public. They always made his job that little bit more difficult.

"Right."

The only room to the rear of the cottage was the kitchen. An open staircase led up to a double bedroom and bathroom. Nothing at first glance looked out of place. Forensics may uncover more. Returning to the lounge, the two observed the grizzly scene, trying their hardest to remain professional. On occasions such as this it was easy, too easy for your emotions to get the better of you.

"I hope the bastard who did this has left some DNA. Once forensics have finished, tell the lab I want the results tomorrow. Don't let them give you any bullshit. The Met I know can get DNA results within hours."

The sergeant hoped his boss was right, personally he was doubtful.

"I wonder if his name's Simon?"

"Pardon?" Detective Johnson failed to understand his sergeant's interjection.

"Simon de Montfort, he was killed at the Battle of Evesham. He was decapitated and his genitalia displayed around his mouth."

"Are you being seriou…."

There was a shout from the photographer. "If you want to know the guy's name, look." He was photographing the upstretched arms in the vase. Squeezed between the two hands, carefully placed, was a driving licence. The photograph confirmed it belonged to the corpse, the name on the card though was not Simon but Martin. The surname however, clearly printed was, de Montfort.

Gendarmerie Nationale – Calais, France

It was almost five am and Capitaine Maubert was already at work. Well almost, in his parking slot sat a dark coloured, almost new Peugeot 308. Even though there was only moonlight to see by the car's metallic finish shone through in the darkness. Very subtle the capitaine muttered to himself. He knew exactly who the car belonged to. Late last night he had been woken by a call from a man who introduced himself simply as Baptiste. Further explanation, revealed that he was attached to the BRB in Paris. BRB standing for Brigade de Repression du Banditisme. A similar outfit in the UK, would be the National Crime Agency. He'd wanted to know if the capitaine would be kind enough to grant him an early morning meeting. Capitaine Maubert had already booked a meeting at six with a representatives from the Le Cross and the Gendarme Maritime and had been about to suggest that he could see him after, when the man from the BRB had cut in.

"Fine, I'll see you at five then. At your office?" The line had clicked dead. The way Baptiste had raised his tone towards the end, made it sound like he'd been asking a question, but Capitaine Maubert knew better. He was expected to be at his office at five in the morning and as the man from the BRB was coming from Paris, he could hardly complain.

He parked in a space designated for visitors, tough, he wasn't in a particularly good mood and the fact that it was still dark depressed him. Soon it would be winter and he hated that time of the year.

Capitaine Maubert found the man from the BRB already sitting in his office. He was sitting crossed legged, thankfully not in his chair, drinking a cup of freshly made coffee from his Nespresso machine. The machine had been a present from his wife. It would help him be "less grumpy," she had told him, especially when he had an early start. Well he felt grumpy now and simply acknowledging Baptiste with a nod started brewing his own. Baptiste in return didn't rise out of the chair to greet him. It wasn't a good start.

"Bonjour, I assume you know why I'm here?"

No he didn't, he had an idea but no one had bothered informing him and that frustrated the capitaine greatly. He liked formality, good communication, order. This man had just swanned in as though he owned the place and now expected him to be a mind reader. He sat behind his desk, leaning back as though he were settling down to watch a drama on the telly. He wasn't going to let this man intimidate him.

"No one has told me, but I assume, it's to do what was found after the storm."

Baptiste nodded, "you assume right." He reached into a smart black leather briefcase on the floor beside him. The capitaine observed his every move, you could tell a lot about a person by the way they handled themselves, and by the way they dressed. Baptiste's attire was what we call, smart casual. On top, hanging smartly an almost tweed blazer which he wore over a soft blue shirt and a dark blue crew necked jumper, his trousers were chinos and a dark tan. Everything Baptiste was wearing shouted, 'quality.' His body could best be described as sinewy and the capitaine recognised, if trapped in a corner, Baptiste could handle himself and almost certainly get out successfully. Perhaps what surprised the capitaine the most were the man's facial features, they were distinctly dull. Nothing stood out. Not at all what he'd expected for someone working in the BRB. Baptiste would definitely never find a career in the movies.

From his briefcase Baptiste retrieved a well stuffed brown, envelope. Placing it carefully on the desk between them he rested both his hands on his crossed knee and gazed intently at the capitaine.

"Have you a theory as to what you have found." Baptiste's voice was soft but full of confidence. This man was very self-assured.

"Not really, we've only just started our investigations," Capitaine Maubert, shook his head, more in frustration, than from giving a negative response. He hated the fact that he had to admit as much to this man. He reached for the envelope.

"Don't open it now, let me explain first and why this is of interest to us."

The capitaine nodded and casually patted the envelope. "Ok."

"You'll find facts and figures of what I'm about to tell you in there." Baptiste nodded to the envelope. He took a long sip of his coffee after which he gazed thoughtfully around the room. The capitaine, wished he'd hurry up and get on with it.

"Capitaine." Baptiste gazed intently at the capitaine's face. Capitaine Maubert didn't flinch, he held the man's gaze. "Have you ever heard of the Red Market?". Baptiste used English for 'Red Market.'

Capitaine Maubert nodded. "I've heard of the expression, and I assume you're not referring to the street market in Paris but that is all. I've never come across it here" The capitaine spread his hands. Baptiste knew by the word 'here,' the capitaine meant Calais. The BRB wouldn't normally involve the gendarme but resources he knew were stretched and the man sat opposite him had an excellent reputation. Almost as soon as the capitaine entered his office, Baptiste took a liking to him. He'd never show it of course, most important of all, he knew he could trust the man opposite.

"The Red Market is a worldwide expression for the illegal harvesting and sale of human body parts. It is if you like a typical black market except it involves the illegal commercialisation of the human body, hence the expression red." If the capitaine was shocked he didn't show it and Baptiste, speaking calmly, continued. "The whole of the human body can be harvested and you might be surprised to know that you or I, if we died, being white, Caucasian and from Europe, could be worth as much as 600,000 Euros on the red market, a lot more if the heart was included. My body would probably fetch a little more than yours." Baptiste smiled for the first time that morning. It was his attempt at a joke and the capitaine in recognition of the fact respectively smiled back. Baptiste continued.

"The red market is a worldwide multibillion dollar industry. Only in Iran is the market legal. There is an increasing shortage of human organs for transplant. In North America alone there are well over one hundred thousand Americans at any one time waiting for a transplant. Worldwide it's estimated over three hundred thousand people, including children are waiting for a life-saving transplant. A good percentage of these are very willing to pay a small fortune if it meant staying in this world and not departing to the next. Facing death or the death of a loved one, especially a child, people will go to incredible lengths to preserve life and the illegal market is responding to those demands. In the past human organs harvested and sold illegally mainly came from the Indian sub-continent or China. In China it was to some extent state sponsored, organs from executed prisoners were openly sold to the highest bidder. Under pressure the Chinese government has mainly stopped this practice but not entirely. Thus the shortage has become even greater. I said just now that in the past the bulk of the red market stemmed from the Indian sub-continent or China."

Capitaine Maubert nodded.

"Well that is until now, increasingly we believe that Europe is also becoming a source. So far, there's no firm evidence, it's what us, and other law enforcement agencies in Europe are hearing on the ground . Especially the UK.

"And you think our findings could be related to this red market?" It was obvious that's what the man from the BRB was leading to.

"Almost certainly, I understand that the torso you recovered had had it's vital organs removed ."

"And drained of blood." The pathologist had told Capitaine Maubert this just as he was leaving.

"Blood is another commodity." Baptiste confirmed. "Tell me about the heads, the media love them,"

The capitaine sighed his agreement. "Well the pathologist told me, that all the heads had been surgically removed and by someone skilled in the technique.

"And their eyes?"

"Yes all the heads had had their eyes removed, all except one," the capitaine remembered.

"Reason? Have you any idea?

"Yes, Jean-Paule, sorry I mean the pathologist believes it's because the eyes were in poor condition."

"Anything else?"

"About the heads?

"Yes"

"I don't think so, oh yes," the capitaine remembered, "one head was that of a child, a young girl, ten to twelve years, Jean-Paul estimates."

"And her eyes?"

"Missing," the capitaine confirmed.

"Bastards, " Baptiste whistled through gritted teeth.

"I agree." At that moment the two were in silent agreement. Both wore the expression that read they were determined to find whoever had done this and bring them to justice.

"A dead child's body is worth far more to the traffickers, than an adult one. A child's body parts can be worth up to a third more than a healthy adult's, sometimes more" Baptiste's voice dropped a tone.

"Traffickers?"

"Yes that's what we call them, after all that's what they are, dead people instead of living, traffickers." Baptiste paused before continuing. "Here in France as you know, we have a system unlike the rest of Europe, where, when you die, unless you opt out when alive, the state assumes you're happy to donate your body for the purpose of saving other people's lives. Consequently we assumed wrongly that in France the red market didn't exist. Just under a year ago, an Algerian national, collapsed on the street in Paris. He was taken to hospital where it was found that he'd received a kidney transplant, a very badly executed one. Whilst conscious he told the doctors that he had bought the kidney and had the operation somewhere in Paris. This was a shock. The gendarme were booked to interview the man the next morning but in the night the patient disappeared. No way was he in any state to walk out so we can only assume he was kidnapped. This would indicate an underground organisation was involved and no small one at that. To kidnap someone from a Parisian hospital would have required a great deal of expertise. This is when the BRB became involved and we're, you might say surprisingly, also working with the BRI on this." Capitaine Maubert was surprised to hear this, the rivalry between the two serious crime divisions was almost legendary, partly because the lines between them, operationally were often blurred and frequently crossed over.

"Law enforcement in other countries," Baptiste continued, "are helping and sharing intelligence. But it's not much. The red market isn't taken seriously by many European governments, you could argue that many see the red market as doing them a favour. Providing a service which otherwise their creaking and under resourced health services would have to provide. Of course all of them will deny this if asked. Have you any theories as to where the remains may have originated from?"

The sudden question, took Capitaine Maubert by surprise.

"At the moment the assumption is that they were most probably swept overboard from a seafaring vessel during the storm. But it's only a theory."

"And a very probable one." Baptiste agreed.

"My meeting at six is with the Gendarme Maritime and the SNSM, they might be able to throw some light on the theory."

"Do you mind if I sit in?"

The capitaine knew he couldn't refuse and smiled. "No. Not at all." And if he was honest with himself, he really didn't mind.

For the rest of their time together, before the hour arrived at six, Baptiste went into more depth about the perceived red market in Europe and the capitaine went into a little more detail on what they had discovered so far, which wasn't much.

Later that morning, there was an operations meeting planned, where all the officers on the case were to be briefed and at the same time an opportunity for feedback including alternative views. Baptiste asked if he could sit on this too and the capitaine readily agreed. He gave him a pre-prepared information pack which included photos taken at the morgue. Capitaine Maubert, then invited Baptiste to the press conference which was planned for four that afternoon at the impressive Hotel de Ville. This invitation the man from the BRB declined. Capitaine Maubert thought he might.

Just before six, there came a knock at the door. The capitaine was just about to shout, 'come in,' when Baptiste held up his hand.

"I don't want the media getting hold of this, everybody involved must be made aware of that. There must be no leaks."

Capitaine Maubert looked puzzled. "The media are already aware. They're all over bloody Calais, even outside here. You even commented on them yourself."

"No, I mean the body trafficking side, we, I don't want them to know the route our investigation may take. This has been made clear to me at the highest level."

The capitaine knew by, 'highest level,' Baptiste meant government.

"But why, we may need the assistance of the public in this and the best way to get to them is via the media."

Baptiste looked vaguely anywhere except at the man sat opposite him.

"I'm afraid I'm not at liberty to say but it's imperative, for now that we keep this in house. They're not my orders you understand."

The capitaine didn't respond, instead he shouted loudly, "come in." and the two men booked for the six am meeting entered the room. They both looked surprised to see a stranger sitting in the office and even more surprised when he was introduced. Capitaine Maubert explained why he was here and repeated Baptiste's instruction that it was imperative that any investigation that led down the body traffickers route remained in house. Their expressions quickly changed from one of surprise to one of shock. Neither had really heard of the Red Market, and neither had remotely considered this a possibility.

Baptiste asked, before the capitaine led the meeting if he could just expand on what they'd already discussed. "It would be for the benefit of everybody."

"Go ahead," the capitaine smiled though he was a little irritated by the request.

"Sorry, we ran out of time earlier," the man from the BRB smiled apologetically, he sensed the capitaine's frustration.

"That's fine." Except of course it wasn't and everyone in the room knew it wasn't.

Baptiste back rolled his chair to one side so he could front everyone equally.

"Capitaine Maubert has explained that the most likely theory is that the, let's call them body parts, were washed overboard, during the storm from a passing seafaring vessel."

Both men acknowledged this, "I think that's why we're here," confirmed the representative from Le Cross, he looked at the officer from the Gendarmerie Maritime, sat beside him who nodded, confirming that was his understanding too.

The man from the BRB looked satisfied. "Let me tell you our stance on this. And why your theory matters greatly to us." He was deliberately throwing them a compliment, Baptiste needed them on his side. Desperately so." I've explained a little about the red market, it's a billion Euro market, probably several billion so it's up there with the drug trade. It's a huge problem but never really spoken about. As I explained to the capitaine just now, possibly even, in some countries, it's deliberately ignored."

Both men were listening intently, this was all new to them and shocking. Baptiste continued, relieved he had their absolute attention.

"The demand in Europe has been growing steadily and until recently, to some extent, we could track the source of supply back to Asia and in particular China. This however appears to no longer be the case. The supply it looks, and we don't know how, is somehow being met locally. More worrying the European market is becoming more and more demanding, clients are insisting that the body parts they buy are from Caucasian Europeans, more troublingly still, the American market is leaning towards this too. American's it seems don't want body parts from their own countrymen."

"Have the BRB any idea where these body parts are being harvested and who is doing the transplanting? Surely you're going to need something like a hospital to do this."

Chapter 8

"You're bang on," Baptiste acknowledged the capitaine's question. "The short answer is, no we haven't a clue. London it's thought is the centre for body trafficking and private transplanting in Europe. And their NCA, National Crime Agency have noticed a considerable number of wealthy individuals, known to have serious health problem flying into Britain. Though they're monitoring it, like us they are under-resourced and the red market is seen as low priority, as it is here. Until now that is." He added after a short pause.

"Why now?" it was the man from the Le Cross, though all were mentally asking the same question.

"Because it's taken a step further, read into that what you will. I'm afraid I'm not at liberty to say any more than that." The room fell silent as all considered this. Baptiste keen to prevent any more questions moved on swiftly.

"Capitaine," he threw a glance at the man behind the desk. "You asked if we knew where, and no we have no idea. And the obvious question is how can such a huge operation remain hidden from the authorities. The growing theory is, somewhere operating in international waters is a hospital ship. Harvesting organs and body parts from a dead body and possibly even doing the transplant on board. Now both of you," Baptiste nodded towards the two newcomers to the meeting, will be aware how many ships go missing ever year, and how it is almost impossible to find them. Some are insurance scams and when this happens it's not unknown for the ship to then be re-registered under a different name. There are many rogue states that will turn a blind eye to this. Other ships are simply stolen, altered a little and then re-registered. Am I right?

The representative from the SNSM and the Gendarme Maritime both nodded.

"You mean somebody can simply steal a ship and sail it all over the world without anyone noticing?" Capitaine Maubert was incredulous.

"In a word, yes. Am I right?" Baptiste turned to the representative from the SNMS.

In response the man from the SNMS laid a large manual on the capitaine's desk. He turned open and flicked through the pages. What stood out were the many black silhouettes of ships.

"This is a manual of ships that have gone missing over the last ten years. For some insurance has been claimed but the insurers believe they might be operating, registering under a different name in a country that either turns a blind eye or encourages it for political reasons. They are of course the usual suspects. Now at least two, often many more large, and I mean large, disappear without a trace every year. Some perhaps are stolen, the truth is we just don't know. There are many more smaller ships that go missing." The officer from Gendarme Maritime was nodding his agreement.

"The question is," the man from the BRB cut in. Has one of these missing ships been turned into a floating hospital and was it operating the night of the storm, near our shores?"

"Capitaine Maubert was flicking through the manual, some of the ships were huge. How could a ship simply disappear? And looking at the summary there were literally hundreds of them.

Cargo ships – 360

Passenger ships -75

Bulk carriers -70

Container ships – 35

Chemical tankers – 46

Oil tankers – 11

And many, many more.

"How can you lose a bloody oil tanker?" The capitaine's question was aimed at anyone in the room who had an answer. Nobody did.

"There were two suspicious ships, the night of the storm, both registered in Africa that resembled very closely, cargo ships that had disappeared recently from the Indian Ocean. We've checked with our British counterparts and they've concurred that they suspected these two vessels as well." The man from the Le Cross took back his manual from the capitaine and slapped the two pages where the missing vessels were listed. "Both," he added, "were owned by Indian companies and we have no reason they had any involvement their disappearance."

"If these ships were both suspicious, why didn't we board them? Bring them into port?" The capitaine still couldn't believe what he was hearing.

"There are laws and regulations that exist for the sea. We as a country have signed up to them. We can't go boarding or commandeering a ship simply on suspicion alone. We are not Iran." This time it was the officer from the Gendarme Maritime speaking. He turned his attention to the capitaine. "As you requested sir, we've studied the currents and the effect of wind direction on the night of the storm and the conclusion is, that for the hea.., I mean body parts to be washed up or found so close to our shore." He paused for breath. " To be found on, or close to our shore they would have had to originated from a source on our side of La Manche. It's not a perfect science of course, because there are other factors to be taken into consideration but we estimate, if the parts were from a vessel it couldn't have been sailing more than eight or nine km offshore. If it had been, the chances are, the parts would still be somewhere mid channel or washed up on the British shore. As I said though, it's not a perfect science."

Very helpful, was Capitaine Maubert's silent, sarcastic reaction. He liked hard facts, not wishy- washy maybes. "And how far out were these two suspicious ships.?" They were using the North Eastern entryway, so our side of La Manche," the gendarme explained helpfully.

"They were both approximately twelve kilometres from shore," the man from Le Cross added.

"Don't they have to register their presence to you lot?" Capitaine Maubert aimed his question at the man from Le Cross.

"Yes they do, but only if their tonnage is three hundred or over."

"And let me guess, both these ships were under that and so we've no right to know what they're doing in our waters and where they were going?" Capitaine Maubert wondered what idiot in government signed up to these regulations.

"They were both just under three hundred tons, so no. The man from Le Cross looked uncomfortable. "I didn't write the rules capitaine, anyway the rules are there for the purposes of safety not to monitor criminal activity."

"There is another theory we need to consider. "All turned to look at the man from the BRB. "The body parts may have been thrown overboard deliberately, knowing that we'd find them."

"Why on earth would anyone do that?" it was Capitaine Maubert who asked the question all three men wanted to ask.

"To laugh in our face, to threaten us, to dare us, to throw us off the scent. Who knows but it's something we have to consider."

The meeting ended with handshakes all round and the capitaine offering everyone a cup of coffee before they left. No one accepted. The briefing was scheduled at ten am and Baptiste having time to kill decided he wanted to visit Cap Blanc Nez , to get an 'overall' view of the scene. Capitaine Maubert agreed that it was a good idea and it would allow him time to prepare.

Soon after the man from the BRB had left, Colette arrived with a steaming fresh cup of coffee and two, still warm, butter croissants from a nearby boulangerie. Thanking the smiling Colette, (Colette was always smiling, he couldn't imagine her doing anything else), the capitaine settled down to read the papers contained in the envelope given to him by Baptiste, the man from the BRB.

There was a report on the investigation that Baptiste had already touched on. It went into much more detail without really solving anything. Some of the papers were condensed summing ups on already well documented cases, mainly taken from investigations by broadsheet journalists. Some of the sentences had been highlighted by marker pen. Around ten pages concentrated on Europe and the hospital ship theory. From what Capitaine Maubert could see, most contained within these pages was just that, theory. One phrase stuck out, "possible involvement of terrorism." Where did that come from? There was no mention of terrorism in any of the other documents. Three pages listed people who were suspected of purchasing and receiving an illegal transplant. Nearly all had travelled to London, some thirty odd, three in Germany, Berlin, one in Holland and two in Belgium. France wasn't mentioned. He recognised some of the names, they were pretty unsavoury characters and rich through criminal activity. Nearly all had travelled to London, and whilst there had simply vanished only to reappear, weeks, sometimes months later in their own countries, fit as a fiddle. There was even a mafia boss who had been widely reported as having a serious heart problem, he too had travelled to London and not so long ago had been filmed jogging on the streets of Palermo. That would mean he would have had to have had a heart transplant. The capitaine whistled. Where on earth would you get a heart transplant on the black, or even red market. He wasn't a medical professional but he knew a heart surgeon and one capable of doing a heart transplant was extremely rare. And he would need a team of highly skilled professionals assisting him. There would also be the need for a very well equipped operating theatre. It was beginning to dawn on him how big an operation this was. There was serious money involved backed by professionals in their field and some very deep resources. This wasn't up there with drug running, this surpassed it, the level of sophistication to run such an operation was way beyond that needed by the drug barons. And the biggest question of all, for him was, where was all the money going to? What was happening to the profits? This was not a few thousand Euros but possibly billions. The money question brought him neatly to the last few pages. It was a list of the going price for body parts in different parts of the world. He wasn't interested in body parts around the rest of the world, he was only interested in Europe.

On finding the right page the capitaine settled down to read. At the same time he took a bite out of his second croissant. It was a mistake because what he read, made him choke and he needed the rest of his coffee to recover.

Havant Police Station – Havant, Hampshire, England

D.I. Johnson stood at the window with hands in his pockets, staring across to the town hall. He wasn't concentrating on the view but on the matters surrounding the brutal and horrific murder they'd discovered yesterday.

A number of things puzzled him. The driving licence deliberately placed between the hands. It was as if the murderer or murderers. (The pathologist had told him in a phone call earlier that morning, that from the intelligence he'd gathered so far, in his view the murder must have been committed by at least two people, possibly, no, almost certainly more). It was as if whoever had murdered Mr de Montfort were trying to send a signal to the police. Why? For what purpose? Records confirmed that the man who lived there was one Mr Martin de Montfort, it had taken under a minute to confirm. Why the very public display of the driving licence.

Then there was the almost copycat mutilation of the corpse to one that happened in the 13th century and to someone with the same surname. This couldn't simply be a coincidence. As it turned out his sergeant wasn't a history buff but had seen a documentary on the telly a few nights before. He had done some research online. Simon de Montfort had been killed at the battle of Evesham on the 4th of August 1265 by a "death squad" commanded by Prince Edward, later to become King Edward 1. His body had been badly mutilated, his limbs cut off along with his head and genitalia. The man's testicles had then been hung either side of his nose and like this his head had been delivered as a gift from the prince to his wife. Bloody hell, he was glad he hadn't been a D.I. back then, where would you start?

Thirdly the initial findings from the pathologist. In his view, backed up by the amount of blood found at the scene, the victims limbs and genitalia had probably been severed whilst he was still alive. It was almost certainly the decapitation of the head that killed him. Up until then the victim would have most certainly still been breathing, and if he hadn't passed out, aware of what was happening to him. "Jesus Christ," had been the D.I.'s response. Therefore the pathologist deduced, there must have been at least a second person involved, to enable to hold the victim still, almost certainly more.

What sick person or persons could do such a thing. Were drugs involved? Initial checks had found Mr de Montfort to be a model citizen. He'd worked at the local supermarket, and for a while as a barman at the Royal Oak and in his spare time liked to sail. He had quite a nice little yacht moored in Langstone Harbour. There was no mortgage on the cottage, he had paid for it outright. The only question that had arisen was how could he afford such a property and a yacht on a supermarket salary. There could be a number of reasons, inheritance, redundancy, a higher salaried previous job. All the possibilities were currently being looked into.

"Detective."

D.I. Johnson spun round. A young female P.C. was holding up a phone. "Yes?"

"It's the lab, they want to speak to you."

"Ok, thanks."

"I can put it through to your office."

"No I'll take it over there," D.I. Johnson moved towards the P.C.'s desk.

"D.I Johnson." As he answered his sergeant entered the office. More than one person mouthed silently, "the lab," waving at the D.I. In response Sergeant Wesson hastily drew up beside his boss.

"Mr Johnson," the lab never used his police title, "it's Johnathan from the lab."

"You've tested the DNA?" The D.I.'s impatience sounded in his voice.

"Yes, look you're sure the DNA was collected correctly, you're quite sure?"

The D.I. was a little ruffled, "yes of course, as sure as I can be, why do you ask?" The D.I. put the call on speakerphone so his sergeant could hear the answer."

"Well there is only one set of DNA and if collected and labelled correctly, that's from the victim."

Everyone listening, had the same reaction. All were deflated. With such a messy murder there had been high hopes that the perpetrators would have left traces of their DNA. DNA samples were always taken from the victim to distinguish their DNA from any others left at the scene.

"So what's the problem?" The sergeant shouted at the mouthpiece.

"Well," all could hear the man at the lab gathering his notes. "Well you say the deceased is a Mr Martin de Montfort?"

"Yes."

"You're quite certain?"

"Yes, of course we are." Not just the D.I. but everyone listening was trying to figure out why the doubt. Why all the questions.

"Well, not according to the DNA database he isn't"

"WHAT? "That's not possible." The D.I. glanced at his sergeant.

"We do not make mistakes Mr Johnson and the database doesn't lie. The man you have there is one Roger Preston, not a Martin de Montfort, and according to the records, Mr Preston died five years ago," there was a pause, "oh, yes, from heart failure."

"Are you sure?"

"Good day Mr Johnson," and the phone went dead.

"Jesus bloody Christ." It was the D.I.'s second blasphemy that morning.

Gendarmerie Nationale – Calais, France

At around the time D.I. Johnson was taking a call from the lab, officers were gathering at the gendarmerie in Calais for a briefing on the various recorded deaths, after what the media were still describing as the 'Storm of the Century with some now sensationalising it as 'La Tempete de la Mort', 'the Storm of Death' or 'Death Storm.'

Earlier that morning Capitaine Maubert had made a call to the morgue at Boulogne, asking for an update. There really wasn't anything new. DNA samples had been taken but there was little hope, it was thought, that any of the victims were to be found on a modern database. All were, in the pathologist's considered opinion, guess thought the capitaine, from North Africa, the Middle East or the Indian Subcontinent. In other words migrants, the capitaine had asked. "You're the detective," had been the predicable response.

Less than quarter of an hour before they were due to start, the man from the BRB reappeared from his reconnaissance mission.

"Capitaine Maubert," Baptiste gently held the capitaine's elbow. "Before we go in can I have a quick word?" The capitaine raised his eyebrows as a sign to the affirmative. "In your office," Baptiste gestured.

"It'll have to be quick," Capitaine Maubert was a stickler for punctuality, he didn't want the man from the BRB causing him to be late.

"No, no, of course, of course." Baptiste held up his hands in understanding. "I just want to make it clear that I and the bosses at the BRB see this as your operation. I have put you in the picture as we see it, and a possible avenue that perhaps needs exploring but, we will leave the groundwork to you. We, I promise, will not be getting involved in your day to day running of the investigation, we will not be stepping on your toes. You have full control. I am sure that you're very relieved to hear this." Baptiste almost grinned.

"Yes," Capitaine Maubert was, very, "but why? It's not like the BRB to let somebody else run an operation if they feel they're involved."

"I know," Baptiste agreed, "but in this case we feel that it may be better investigated at a local level. By officers who know the locality, the people. We will of cause be demanding, asking," Baptiste realised his mistake immediately, "asking for regular reports and in return I promise any intelligence, we feel relevant, we'll share with you."

"Relevant? Who decides whether it's relevant?"

"Capitaine, please trust me, we really do want to help you in this. Trust me." Baptiste said again.

What choice have I got Capitaine Maubert thought to himself. None was the answer. "Ok," and opening the door gestured Baptiste through. "Shall we go."

Havant Police Station – Havant, Hampshire, England

Both D.I. Johnson and Sergeant Wesson were staring at a computer screen, searching to see if the victim, now known to be one Roger Preston had a police record.

The D.I. whistled.

"Fucking hell, you've got to be joking." Sergeant Wesson was less discreet.

The D.I. knew he had recognised the name from somewhere. Mr Preston had a rap as long as his arm. Serious stuff, gangster stuff along with suspected stuff that had never been proven. Drug smuggling, gun running, even murder, more than once. The investigation of the mutilated corpse they'd found, was inevitably about to take a very different turn.

Gendarmerie Nationale – Calais, France

All were waiting when Capitaine Maubert and the man from the BRB entered the room. There were twelve officers in all, all of varying rank and specialist interest.

The capitaine started by introducing the man from the BRB, Baptiste. All looked surprised at his introduction, a minority were quite obviously shocked. Why were the BRB involved? Capitaine Maubert, next went on to briefly explain why, and left Baptiste to explain to his officers one possible theory for the body parts that had been found along the coast. The result was a largely stunned silence. There were the inevitable questions and the capitaine allowed one or two before interrupting, asking that they for now take notes and keep questions for the end.

Next Capitaine Maubert went through a list of everyone who had been killed by or on the night of the storm. One by one he covered each. All could easily be explained except the local photographer, whose car was found overturned in the carpark on Cap Blanc Nez. " It looks like he literally got blown off the cliff, but at this stage we can't rule anything out. For the moment his death must remain open." He appointed an officer to concentrate purely on this one death. To check the car, which was now in the police pound, to follow up on the pathologist's report and to see if there was anything in the man's background or private life that might have given rise to foul play.

They now came to the body parts recovered from La Manche and the beach close to Escalles. Capitaine Maubert went through, one by one the heads and the torso they'd recovered the day after the storm. As he described each find he displayed slides, photographs taken at the morgue. All were horrific but when the girl's head flashed up on the screen, there was an audible outburst of disgust. Somehow despite the girl's mutilation all officers present were astonished at how the dead girl's face still retained an innocent beauty. The capitaine, deliberately perhaps left the image on screen for longer than was necessary. He was very aware that most of the officers before him had children around the same age and he wanted to galvanise their determination to find and punish those responsible. The image of the mutilated girl's head was a blunt tool in achieving that desire.

The Capitaine then went over the varying possibilities of where the body parts originated. Following on from this, he revisited the increasingly likely theory that the gruesome finds may be victims of body traffickers, their bodies mutilated in harvesting body parts for a profit.

"Where do they get the bodies in the first place?" A young officer couldn't wait till the end.

"Can I take this?" Capitaine Maubert granted the man from the BRB the floor.

Baptiste didn't wait. "In Asia, the bodies have been sold by hospitals or relatives of the dead. A common practice in China is for the government to sell organs harvested from executed prisoners, though this is becoming less common. Here in Europe? Or France, it's hard to say, though we cannot rule out that people may be being murdered for their bodies. Baptiste went on to detail other sources available to traffickers, but most weren't listening. Taking organs from a person already dead was one thing, taking them from someone who was still alive was quite another. The girl's face was still on the screen. Is this what had happened to her?

Baptiste stepped back and Capitaine Maubert once more had the floor.

He removed the slide of the dead girl. "You have seen that with the exception of one head all the eyes have been cut from their sockets." There was a nodding of heads and murmurings of 'oui.' In the body parts market the corneas is one of the most saleable parts of the human body. In layman's terms the cornea is the front of your eye. If it becomes damaged, it can cause pain, sensitivity to light and blurred vision. A skilled surgeon can, in some cases affect a cornea transplant in under an hour and often under local anaesthetic. The cornea is also very easy to harvest and transport. So you can see why the eyes will appeal to a trafficker. The price for a cornea transplant can be as much as 25,000 Euros. A large percentage of that will be for the purchase of the corneas. I'll let you do the maths." Most, already were.

The capitaine proceeded to detail some of the other body parts. Those in the room were shocked to learn, virtually every part of the body was marketable, even the skin. And the prices various body parts fetched left nearly everyone with their mouths gaping open.

After the corneas, kidneys were the most marketable and if they were from a reliable source could fetch close to 200,000 Euros. And that price did not include the transplanting. Waiting lists for kidneys throughout Europe were huge, adding to demand and the price.

The most expensive organ, provided you could find someone to do a transplant is the heart. Purchasing a heart with a transplant could cost over 2,000.000 Euros. The capitaine cited the example of the Mafioso, travelling to London, maybe being an example of this. Baptiste didn't disagree, which indicated to the capitaine that the BRB might know more than they were letting on. So much for trust.

The capitaine finished by confirming that a body part from a verified Caucasian European could fetch five times that from elsewhere in the world and a body part from a child, a third, possibly double that again. There were more murmurs from the listening officers, murmurs of disgust.

So, Capitaine Maubert finished dramatically, you or I, our bodies on the red market today, are probably worth upwards of 600,000 Euros, perhaps even as much as a million, more than if the heart can be successfully transplanted. It was an exaggeration, the capitaine knew but seeing Baptiste, nodding, agreeing, he wondered if it really were.

"Blimey, I might sell my wife," one officer joked and was about to add to his attempt at humour but seeing the expressions on the faces of his colleagues, stopped. "Sorry," he finished meekly.

Another officer spoke up. "I know earlier you said that the BRB believes that much of the operation has moved here." His question was aimed at Baptiste. " But why? And surely if mass murder was being committed to obtain body parts, we'd very quickly know about it."

Baptiste stretched. "Why," he started," is very simple. Although, new processes have enabled body parts, particularly organs to be preserved for a much longer period of time, in general that time is still very short. The sooner a harvested organ can be transplanted, the greater percentage, the probability of success. Not many rich Europeans or Americans are willing to take their chances in a third world hospital or one in the developing world. And transporting an organ from Asia, which is where most illegally harvested organs are still sourced, to here is a long and not an easy process. The chances are, by the time the organ has arrived it's deteriorated so badly to render it useless". Baptiste paused, giving those in the room time to digest this.

Baptiste continued by asking a question. "How many people go missing in France every year?" The response was a sea of blank faces along with a few shrugs. "Exactly, we in France have really no idea. Enshrined in our law is the individual's right to disappear. A similar law exists in many other European countries including Germany. As a result no records are kept and a further consequence, many people simply do not bother reporting a missing person. They feel it would simply be a waste of their time. The answer, therefore, to my question and reflected in your expressions, we really have no fucking idea." Swearing, Baptiste felt, brought home the message he was trying to get across. "Across the water in Britain, they run a missing persons database. On average every year over there, 180 to 200,000 people are reported missing. Now yes, a high percentage are found but over 5% are never found. That's more than ten thousand people who disappear off the face of the Earth. Ten thousand! Think about it, where are they? Answer, nobody knows, and that's from just one country." There came a rustle of astonishment from the room. "And, and that's just the adults, how many children? Anyone want to take a guess?"

"Five thousand?" The only female officer present answered, hesitantly.

"Noooooo," Baptiste had them just where he wanted. "No you're wrong, the answer is over 112,000., here it's over 60,000, in Germany over 100,000. You extend that to Europe including Russia you're talking every year, every year. ONE MILLION CHILDREN, disappearing in Europe alone. One million! Like the adults over 5% are never found. That's over 50,000 children never found. How do you know body traffickers haven't taken a percentage of these?"

A bubble of conversation broke out amongst the officers, they were all shocked. Not one of them had considered what the man from the BRB was putting to them.

"Let's return to the adults," Baptiste waived a hand for silence. "Many countries in Europe, like ours, because the way the law is phrased, simply don't record missing adults. The APRD, the "Assistance et Recherche de Personnes Disparues", recorded nearly 70,000 reports of missing persons here in France but I think we can safely say the true figure is closer to the UK's. So we're talking well over a million adults disappearing in Europe every year. I think that's quite a large pool for the body traffickers don't you?"

Everyone agreed and there was a period of general discussion, before another observation was put forward.

" All the heads that you've just shown us, I don't want to appear rude but they don't look French do they?"

"They may well be French, " Capitaine Maubert cautioned, "I think what you're trying to say is they're not white Caucasian."

The officer, looking rather uncomfortable, nodded.

"You're right, we're still waiting for DNA confirmation but the pathologist believes they're almost certainly from the usual suspects, countries where the majority of the migrant population here in Calais originate from. So to rephrase your question for you, and the point I think you're trying to make is. Are they, or do we think, the victims are from the migrant population. And if you want my response, I think it's one of the first avenues we need to follow up."

"Are we going to make the photos of the heads, the deceased available to the media? Maybe if they were published, someone may recognise one of them?" It was another question.

Baptiste, quickly cut in. "No," his answer was firm. "No they're too horrific, the reaction could be one of hysteria and that would be very unhelpful."

"Why not create un portraite robot, (artist's impression), for each head, as the artist sees each victim. With their eyes of course. The question was from the female officer.

"I think that's a good idea," it was Baptiste. "But I think we should discreetly show them to the migrant population first before we let the general media have access. What do you think Capitaine?"

Capitaine Maubert agreed and there and then designated the female officer along with the youngest officer in the room with the task of seeing if any of the migrants would admit to knowing the deceased. Both the chosen officers had kind faces and were popular because of their relaxed and happy disposition. The migrants in general didn't trust the police, even less the gendarmerie. If anyone was going to get a result it would be these two officers.

"I suggest you tie up with some of the charities helping these people, the migrants trust them. They may be very useful with introductions."

The chosen two, didn't appear convinced, neither did they appear too enamoured with their order. And perhaps for good reason. After the 'Jungle' was destroyed by the authorities in 2016, the migrants didn't leave they just dispersed. They were now living in small groups all over Calais and her environs. It was going to be one hell of a task.

The reunion ended with everyone being given a specific role, or task. Before leaving for Paris, Baptiste gave capitaine Maubert his card. "My mobile's on there should you need it."

The capitaine thanked him.

"Oh and if you want me to book you a medical expert to give a briefing, let me know."

"I will," promised the capitaine and after a shaking of hands the man from the BRB sped away in his gleaming 308.

Capitaine Maubert looked at his watch. The press conference was booked at five that afternoon, to be held in 'le Grand Salon, de l'hôtel de Ville," (The large hall, at Calais's Town Hall). The Mayor as it turned out was almost pleased to welcome the world's media. "Our magnificent building will be on view to the world," he was overheard telling someone.

Capitaine Maubert once again looked at his watch. He had more than enough time to follow in the footsteps of the man from the BRB. He wanted to get a better feel for the case by visiting Cap Blanc Nez and the beach at Escalles, where the girl's head had been found. After giving details of his intentions to Colette, he sped off through Calais Nord, heading for the D940 coast road, the original road connecting Calais with Boulogne. Colette watched from her window as her boss drove off, just a little too quickly. His Peugeot 308 was clean but badly needed a polish. She'd mention it to him when he returned.

Leigh Park – Near Havant, Hampshire

Maria Collins, lived in Billy Lawn Avenue, Leigh Park. It was half an hours walk from the police station at Havant where she worked part time as a typist. Life hadn't been kind to her. After two failed marriages, she was living in a council house with her three young children. Neither father despite going to court were paying her child maintenance. And truth be told neither father gave two jots about their offspring. Money was tight, very tight. She was forty five years old, well past the looks that would attract a decent man and looking around at her meagre belongings, ashamed of where she was. This was all she had to show after forty five years of not life, but existing. She was embarrassed, thoroughly embarrassed and desperate to give her children more.

Social services had pointed her towards her job at the police station. It was only a few hours a week but she loved it. The work was really interesting and her colleagues, although often stressed were great to work with. Now though she was in a quandary. She'd overheard something that morning, which she knew would be of great interest to the press and almost certainly be worth a great deal of money to the right paper. But she would be betraying her job and more importantly her colleagues, the thought disgusted her. For half an hour she pondered and pondered. It was the tv going off which swung her decision. She'd run out of electricity on her pre-paid meter. Her electricity company had forcibly installed it after repeatedly failing to pay her bill. She now had a choice, live in the dark and give her children a half decent meal, or have light and the children go hungry. Or there was a third choice. And she took it, she deserved better. After making several calls, she'd been promised more money than she'd ever dreamed of.

A couple of hours later. D.I. Johnson slammed the phone down and shouting at everyone and no one. "Who leaked this to the fucking press. Fucking hell," and after kicking two desk legs stormed into his office.

Cap Blanc Nez – Calais, France

Capitaine Maubert stared out to sea. It was a beautiful day and the air crystal clear. Across the other side of La Manche the white cliffs of Dover were glistening in the midday sun. The port of Dover was clearly visible, ferries cut across the trails of ships ploughing the channel and smaller craft were both playing and working in between. Dover and the white cliffs, Eldorado for many, an Eldorado that people were prepared to risk their lives for. He just didn't get it. He edged nearer the cliff edge, close to where it's thought the photographer had stood before he fell. Or was he pushed? Would they ever really know? Probably not if he was being realistic. He looked down, over the cliff edge and immediately stepped back. Seeing the drop had instantly caused him to feel dizzy. He pondered about the dead photographer and his upturned car. Had he stumbled across someone disposing of the heads over the cliff and to prevent him from talking thrown him over the edge with them. It was a possibility, the police had closed the road but only using signs, there had been no police presence. It would have been the ideal opportunity to do the dirty deed.

He turned to look West, across the Baie de Wissant to Cap Gris Nez and its lighthouse. The view was quite spectacular and one hard to beat anywhere else in the world. The various Mayors were still bellyaching that the beach remained closed, If nothing else was found that night he'd have to open the access in the morning. Someone who was bellyaching and within earshot was the owner of the only restaurant on Mont d'Hubert on the other side of the D940. The restaurant was actually built into the old German bunkers left over from the war and afforded quite incredible views across the surrounding countryside. Rightly so it was described in the local holiday brochures as a 'restaurant panoramique.' Capitaine Maubert had eaten there more than once and although the food wasn't French, had to admit he'd enjoyed every meal. Once a seafood restaurant, three or four years back it was taken over by a Tunisian chef. The food was now distinctly of that country. The restaurant sold, to takeaway, a mean cass-croute and these were particularly popular with passing hikers. The police since the storm had closed along with the public car parks his restaurant too. He hadn't wanted the public anywhere near during the investigation and there was also the large gathering of media to consider.

The restaurant owner recognising the capitaine came running over. "Mr Maubert, Mr Maubert, the police are ruining my business, can't you do something?"

The capitaine not unsympathetic, looked around at the gathered media. Can you feed this lot? This he thought would get the media on his side.

The Tunisian owner, nodded. "Of course."

"Ok, cass-croute and hot drink, that's it for each person, no more. Send your bill to the gendarmerie for my attention. And don't think you can cheat the gendarme."

"Non, non, trust me capitaine." The Tunisian owner started running back to his restaurant.

Capitaine Maubert had a quiet word with his officers guarding the closure. One who spoke reasonable English informed the gathered media, nearly all suffering from thirst and hunger, that the restaurant opposite will provide them each, with a meal and a hot drink. Compliments of the Gendarmerie Nationale, Calais. At least half immediately rushed to cross the road to the restaurant. Capitaine Maubert smiled to himself. There was no way the restaurant would be ready, he imagined the chaos that was unfolding. I'm such a bastard, he smiled climbing into his car.

The D940 ran an 'S' through the village of Escalles. On the last bend, before the road led out of the village a narrow lane continued ahead past a popular campsite, ending at a public car park servicing 'Plage du Cran d'Escalles,' the local beach. Capitaine Maubert parked, and after acknowledging the lone and obviously very bored policeman on guard, took the narrow fenced path to the beach. The beach is renowned all over France and justly so. A wide expanse of sand at low tide, the views are to die for and Cap Blanc Nez towering above, adds bucketfuls of drama. The French describe it as a 'wild beach,' and as a consequence perhaps it is in the main popular with the younger generation. Appropriate then that it was the head of a child that was found here.

Two gendarmes stood guarding an area that had been taped off, an area almost directly beneath the cliff face of Cap Blanc Nez. Both his officers looked as though they'd had enough. On seeing the capitaine they both brought themselves up, disguising their boredom well.

"Sir," they both acknowledged.

"Had enough?" Capitaine Maubert smiled.

Both nodded. "I can't see the point in guarding this any longer sir," the older of the two spoke for both of them. "The tide's been in and out several times since the child was found." The capitaine liked the fact his officer referred to the head as a child, it demonstrated respect. "Any evidence there may have been has long gone, washed out to sea."

"Ok." The capitaine agreed, "pack up and get yourselves back to base." The chief forensic investigating officer, had told him he had finished with the scene anyway. There was no point in them guarding something that was never going to be examined in the future.

"Yes sir." The two officers hurriedly took down the taped barrier and were away.

Capitaine Maubert, remained, alone staring up to the summit of Cap Blanc Nez, where did you come from little girl, he questioned in his mind. Did someone throw you from up there or were you blown in by the storm. Enjoying one last moment of solitude, he turned and slowly walked back to his car. Now to deal with the wolves. The thought made him sigh, a, long drawn out sigh from one who is resigned to their fate.

Hotel De Ville – Calais, France.

ID's were being carefully checked before any of the world's media were allowed into the town hall for the eagerly awaited press conference. The queue as a consequence was long and tempers frayed.

The atmosphere inside fared little better. Monsieur Hivin had done a sterling job in organising everything and the mayor had even got a local restaurateur to lay on a buffet, based on the traditional cuisine of the region. This was an opportunity not to be missed.

However, the main content, what everybody had come for was, in the eyes of the world media, sadly lacking. The awkward looking Capitaine Maubert, told them little of what they didn't already know or surmised and was more adept at avoiding answering questions than a seasoned politician. "I promise as soon as we have more information, you'll be the first to know." And with that the man from the gendarmerie left the room. No one believed him of course, they would be the last to know.

It was gone eight when the capitaine arrived at his house, his personal heaven just outside Ardres. His home, his bolt hole, his own little paradise. Only when he was here did he truly relax. On opening the door he was delighted to see his daughter with his grandson of just six months.

His wife appeared from the kitchen and with her the smell of something delicious. He was so lucky, he considered for the millionth time.

"We've just watched you on the telly, papa," his daughter laughed, "you were like a robot."

His wife joined in the laughter. "You were really funny Thierry."

An hour later, the capitaine was in his office, earphones on. He could still hear his wife and daughter clearing up after dinner. He selected a CD, turned on his hifi and lay back. The sound of, the French hard rock group, Trust, blasted his brain. Bliss.

CHAPTER
—9—

Havant Police Station – Havant, Hampshire, England

It had only just gone eight in the morning and his station had already received a telephone call from just about every bloody media outlet in the UK.

D.I. Johnson was furious, more than furious, someone will have to stop him from killing whoever leaked this to the press. That's if they ever found out he accepted ruefully. They rarely did. On his own paper, a popular red top, the headline screamed out.

GANGSTER HACKED TO DEATH IN BRUTAL KILLING

And then a subtitle.

Picture book village, shocked by mutilated body found in fisherman's cottage.

Where they'd got 'fisherman's' from, God only knows and to be honest no one really gave a damn. The headline did the job, it created the picture, it set the scene. The rest of the story was mainly conjecture but there were enough facts to confirm a serious leak had taken place.

"This won't make our investigation easy, the bloody press will be everywhere." Sergeant Wesson was reading. "It's bloody good though."

The D.I. threw him a look. "It's not just the press, after seeing this, the NCA and our ROCU will almost certainly want to get involved. Bloody hell!" He stood up sliding his arm across his desk as he did so, knocking nearly everything on it, onto the floor. There was a brief tap and the door opened, the chief super, stared quizzically at the scene. His stare turned to the two men then directly at the D.I.

"Harry, I've had the Chief Constable on the phone."

At the same time, the phone, the only item still on the desk, started to ring.

"YES."

"Is that Detective Inspector Johnson, Detective Inspector Harry Johnson?"

"YES."

"Do you mind if I call you Harry?"

"No, I mean who is this?"

"Harry this is Roger Denton, I'm from the NCA, the National Crime Agency. I need to come and see you. I'm sure you have an idea what about. I'll be leaving in an hour, so I should be with you in...,! There was a pause, "I should be with you in say three hours. Will you be at your station?"

"Yes." The D.I. couldn't disguise the resignation in his voice. Another bloody Roger, that's all he needed.

"Good, see you shortly then. I look forward to it."

"Me too." The D.I. was a poor liar.

"The NCA?" it was the Chief Super. D.I. Johnson nodded

"That's what I had come to tell you, buzz me when he gets here."

The D.I. nodded, "Yes of course."

The Chief Super made to leave, when he hesitated. "Oh and Harry." The D.I. looked up.

"Try and be nice," and with that the chief super closed the door.

Chapter 9

A28 Service Station – Rouen, France

John examined his GPS. His ferry wasn't booked till late that afternoon. He was at La Dentelle d'Alencon services. According to the GPS Calais was a little over two hours away. It was now, he looked at his watch, 9.45am. He had plenty of time. Good time for one last, take your time, lunch, before he reached the UK. He knew exactly where that would be. A seafood restaurant just below a rocky point called Cap Gris Nez. Called La Sirene, (mermaid), the restaurant occupied an Art Decco style building sited almost on the beach itself. Most of the fish the restaurant served, were caught by a local fisherman who lived almost opposite. His boat when not in the water, parked on the approach road. The same family had run the establishment since the nineteen sixties and no matter how long it was between visits, they always recognised him as well as welcome him as though he were an old friend. They did the best 'plateau de fruit de mer,' he'd experienced anywhere in France. If you were prepared to pay there was no limit as to what a plateau could contain and he was in the mood for a bit of self-indulgence. John started to salivate at the thought. Ever since leaving Marbella John had eaten very well, very well indeed but this lunchtime was the meal he'd been most looking forward to.

On returning to his, well for another day at least, Aston Martin DB4 Vantage, he found it surrounded by admirers. Many were busy taking selfies with the car in the background. Selfies were a modern curse John considered, as was the camera phone. In his line of work it was always better to be anonymous. He'd quickly discovered, driving such a beautiful car that anonymity was virtually an impossibility. People wanted to ask questions. Although he'd loved the experience he'd be glad when he'd handed the car back.

The small crowd of admirers, parted to let John through. Before he drove off, there were a couple of requests for him to take photos of themselves grouped around the car and even sitting in the driver's seat. Summing up as much grace as he could John obliged forcing his best smile. There were several cries of "au revoir," as he drove off. Many also waved and most had their phones pointing at him with video turned on. Yes the sooner he returned this car the better. He felt far more comfortable being Mr Nobody.

Gendarmerie Nationale – Calais, France

Seven am, another early start but not quite as early as yesterday. Capitaine Maubert had always been a morning person but the public scrutiny of this investigation was already taking its toll. He hadn't found getting out of bed that morning as effortless as normal.

On his desk sat a large A3 envelope. Scribbled neatly on top, the words, "A l'attention de Capitaine Maubert." The capitaine recognised the writing immediately, it belonged to the police, portraitiste, (sketch artist). Opening the envelope he carefully removed the contents. There were six sketches, he recognised them immediately from the severed heads he'd seen at the morgue. The portraitiste, from what he could see had done an excellent job and with the inclusion of eyes had given each head back their dignity, not to mention personality. The portraitiste had also sympathetically given every portrait a neck which tapered out at the bottom of each page, giving the impression to anyone viewing the sketch that the head was attached to a body.

The capitaine made a mental note to thank the portraitiste personally. He'd put him under tremendous pressure, even asking him to work through the night. The migrant population were by nature transient. It was important that his officers started making enquiries before anyone who may recognise one of the faces portrayed was long gone. He'd learnt from the pathologist also that the portraitiste had been violently sick when presented with a severed head to draw and been forced to sketch the portraits from the original photo instead. Even more incredible then that they were so accurate.

The two officers tasked with presenting the sketches to the migrants were to work with someone from one of the local charities that cared and worked with them. It had been agreed, and a condition for their help, that his officers would wear civilian clothes. Many of the migrants regarded gendarmes as 'the enemy,' thus, simply would not cooperate, possibly even disappear, worse still, hostile towards. They were to start at eight that morning in just under an hour.

That morning the capitaine had also decided to send a couple of officers to the Tunisian restaurant on the summit of Mount d'Hubert. He realised yesterday that no one working there had been questioned, a major oversight. If the heads had been thrown from Cap Blanc Nez, whoever it was may well have been scouting the area days before, planning for the night of the storm. Someone may have seen something. It was worth a try.

Wissant – France

Although he was good under pressure, he didn't enjoy pressure. He liked always to be in total control, unhurried organised control. Recent events had meant that although still in control, it had changed to a hurried control. Urgency by nature forced a faster response and in turn risked losing control. He hated that risk and the uncertainty it brought with it.

Recent events had not only dumped on him the dreaded uncertainty but also a need for urgency, resulting in him being where he was now. A popular café on the promenade at Wissant. He was waiting for the English lady who had a first floor apartment opposite. She was, they'd learnt a woman of habit and every morning, around ten thirty enjoyed a coffee and two butter croissants in the café where he was sitting and where he'd first met her. He looked impatiently at his watch, a Patek Philippe held by a leather strap. Ten forty five, she was late. He hated lateness.

The 'Jungle' - Calais, France

What had once been a bustling shanty town was now nothing more than an eyesore. Flat with scattered sand loving scrub, the whole place was littered with rubbish discarded by people who called this home, temporarily anyway. Sheltering amongst the cover of scrub tended to be whole families including children. Nearly everywhere else tended to be inhabited by single men. Some were there simply looking for a better future. For the remainder, the majority they had little or no choice. It was either live like this but always with hope for something better, or stay at home and suffer an unimaginable existence, perhaps even a long and torturous death. For everyone there, their one crime was being born in the wrong place at the wrong time.

Few though, amongst the residents of Calais, held that view and many lived in fear of the migrants. Sometimes for good reason as several serious crimes had been perpetuated by those passing through. Though it was a tiny percentage the coverage in the media sometimes made it appear as though every migrant were a serious threat, when with the majority the opposite was true.

"Try to stop looking like gendarmes."

"We're not," the two officers protested in unison.

"You are," hissed Stephanie the one chosen to assist the gendarmerie with their enquiries. She had no reason to love the gendarmerie but recognised on this occasion that they were trying to help those whom every charity worker regarded as their extended family. Hence on this occasion only, she'd agreed to assist with introductions. They'd get nowhere though if they continued to look so stiff and official. Worse still she could lose the migrants' trust.

It took a good hour for the two officers to fall into their role and when they did migrants actually started coming forward, asking how they could help. None though admitted to recognising anyone in the sketches and by two in the afternoon, both the officers had had enough. By this time they'd reached a more wooded area called Les Dunes. All were glad of the shade the trees offered, for the late September sun was defying the season and busy baking the earth. Both officers had brought a packed lunch and two in the afternoon was way past France's traditional lunch hour. It was time to eat and telling their guide so, squatted down to do just that.

Stephanie wasn't hungry. "I'll keep trying, I might have better luck without you." Both officers shrugged, why not. She just well might.

No more than five minutes later, Stephanie reappeared. With her, accompanied by a number of youngish men hobbled a much older man. It was hard to tell how old exactly as life had taken an awful toll, but he looked well into his sixties, possibly even early seventies. He wore, what the officers recognised as traditional Afghani dress, and on his feet, open sandals. He sported a full untrimmed beard and despite the face being weathered by tragedy, his eyes somehow retained a gentleness, testament to the man's character. Floods of tears poured from those eyes and the man stood trembling from head to toe. Both officers saw that he was close to collapse and both officers instinctively rose to assist him. Their action brought smiles of gratitude from the youngers.

Stephanie held up the portrait of the young girl. "This man, is convinced that this is his granddaughter."

Wissant – France

The beach was open once more. Maureen had watched the gendarme from her balcony earlier that morning, remove the tape that stretched across the steps, preventing people access. The news spread quickly and within an hour the beach was teeming with people, walking, running or exercising their dogs. After days of only morbid interest, spurred by headlines such as "Plage de la Mort," the Baie de Wissant was doing what it does best, making people happy. Maureen was quick to join in with the others, bare foot, with her shoes in her hands, she strolled further than she intended, loving the feel of the sand between her toes and the still warm sea as it washed the grains away. It was almost eleven when she returned to Wissant, she hoped her café had saved her some croissants.

Maureen recognised the man immediately. How could she forget him. She blushed hot with the memory. As before he was expensively dressed and his hair a mass of tussled curls. Although obviously wealthy, he also had an air of nobility about him which Maureen hadn't spotted before. He was looking at his watch. She prayed he wasn't in a hurry. The man obviously sensed somebody was watching for he looked up a little faster than was natural. On recognising her the man smiled, a smile broadened by relief. For Maureen it was purely a smile of delight. The delight at seeing her. She wasn't wrong. To her pleasure the man gestured for Maureen to join him and she wasted no time in doing so.

"I thought you were simply a ship passing in the day," it was an attempt at humour coupled with a very thinly veiled hint that she'd never expected to see him again.

"I'm on my return voyage," the man smiled, joining in with her joke.

"I don't even know your name?" It had been bothering Maureen ever since their few hours of intense pleasure.

The man looked directly into her eyes and his smile turned into a grin, "let's keep it like that for now, it makes our acquaintance more exciting. Anyway, I don't know yours." It was a lie of course, he knew everything about her.

"I suppose," Maureen doubted that and hadn't liked the way he'd used the word acquaintance. She, having met the man again realised she wanted more, much more. Needing a distraction she raised her arm trying to attract the attention of the one and only serveur,(waiter). Seeing her the smartly dressed young man approached but the man with no name waved him away.

"Come on, I'm taking you to lunch. " The man stood up, and in the same motion held her hand gently raising her from her chair whilst drawing it out. Maureen loved it, gallantry meant so much to a woman and that was lost on so, so many men. After paying cash for his coffee the man escorted Maureen outside. His car was parked in a nearby street. His car was a Mercedes, of course, and to Maureen it looked like a palace on wheels. It was actually a Mercedes-Maybach S 680 4MATIC, an indulgence the man knew, but it was befitting of a major diamond dealer, and to the outside world that was exactly what he was.

"Ooooh," Maureen exclaimed as the car seat almost pulled her in.

"Nice isn't it," her new found partner smiled. "Mercedes call this the cockpit."

And that's exactly how it feels, thought Maureen, at the same time wondering if it was really sensible of her, getting into an almost complete stranger's car and with no idea where he was taking her.

As though reading her thoughts the stranger, as they pulled away reassured her. "Don't worry, it's not far."

He was right, it was no more than ten minutes. After passing through Audinghen, on the way to Boulogne, they took a right towards Cap Gris Nez and just before reaching the lighthouse forked right, descending to reach a petite, sea facing hamlet. A fishing boat was parked in the street and almost opposite, before you ended up in the sea, a freshly white painted art deco style building, which to Maureen looked as if it didn't belong. Painted above the porch, on a black background in white lettering were the words, La Sirene.

"It means, The Mermaid," the stranger translated. Maureen already knew. After reversing neatly to a halt the man maintained his gallantry by opening her car door and expertly helping her out. Not that Maureen wanted to get out, she loved the feeling of the 'cockpit,' and was wishing that his chosen restaurant had been at least an hour further. There were only two other cars parked in the parking area servicing the restaurant. One, an instantly forgettable family saloon, the other a classic that shouted, 'look at me.

Maureen's recently acquired appreciation of four wheels, walked straight over to it. "What a lovely car." And reached out to touch it.

"That's an Aston Martin," He was relieved to see the car there. The organisation knew the driver had left Rouen a couple of hours earlier and that he was booked on an afternoon ferry but it was almost finger in the wind stuff where he'd stop to eat. La Sirene was known to be a favourite of his, so he'd had to make a calculated guess and his guess had been proved right. Someone up above was smiling down at him.

"I know," Maureen replied. "Prince Charles has one."

The man wasn't listening. Gently touching her back he eased Maureen towards the entrance. "Come on," he encouraged. "Let's go eat."

He saw the man he was looking for immediately. They both did, though Maureen was ignorant to the fact that he was so important to the man treating her. He was sat with his back to them, at a table beside one of the many windows offering unforgettable views out to sea. On the table in front of him stood a pyramid of plates with all manner of seafood piling each level. Cascading over the sides, hung two halves of lobster and an array of crevettes rose. It was a sight to behold. Maureen clapped her hands with excitement.

"Look at that." He knew she was referring to the driver of the Aston Martin's, Plateau de Fruits de Mer.

"Do you want me to order you one?"

"I could never eat all that," Maureen confessed, in fact she was horrified at the thought of trying even.

"Come, we'll share one," the man steered Maureen skilfully to a table not quite opposite but all the same facing the driver of the Aston Martin. He made sure that it was Maureen who was directly facing the driver, he chose to sit to one side offering him a more discreet view. As he predicted Maureen crossed her right leg exposing a large but strong and shapely thigh. The man smiled with satisfaction as the driver was noticeably distracted by her presence. It had been a long shot but his plan up until now was working out perfectly. Maureen was oblivious to all. She was disappointed that they weren't sat beside a window and complained so. "This is my lucky table," he explained, "besides watching the sea makes me terribly sea sick."

Why come here then questioned Maureen but kept her thought to herself.

Gendarmerie Nationale – Calais, France

It had been an awkward conversation. Capitaine Maubert was extremely unhappy that the apparent grandfather of the girl whose head was resting in the morgue had been told she's dead. He hadn't wanted that to get out and he'd expressly wished this to be the case to all the officers concerned. Now in all probability the majority of the migrant population had good reason to believe that the severed heads found in the sea were one of their own. There was now also a distinct possibility that the press would find out.

The officers had protested that they hadn't told him. That the charity worker had, and not deliberately. The man had instinctively asked if his granddaughter was dead, and completely unprepared for such a question, Stephanie's face had said it all. "You should never have left her to question migrants without you being there," Capitaine Maubert had expressed his dissatisfaction in no uncertain terms.

Aside from the negative, the two officers had gleaned some new information which may prove valuable to the investigation. Fortunately one of the younger men, an Iranian, spoke French as well as Pashto and so was able to translate. The old man had explained that cross channel traffickers had offered to take his son and granddaughter but not him. His younger two hadn't wanted to leave him behind but the traffickers were adamant and they'd departed in the main, to offer the little girl, his granddaughter a chance of a better life. He didn't know where the traffickers had picked them up, they'd told him it was better for him not to know. Around a week ago the two, during the night, simply disappeared. They'd proceeded to show him the other sketches but the old man was absolutely positive that none of the sketches depicted his son. The two officers had tried to escort the distressed old man back to the gendarmerie but he had refused and in danger of the situation escalating into a riot, they had left him there.

The news that one of the heads had been identified, suggested to the capitaine that the heads and torso had originated from land and not from a passing boat. If this was the case, the decision to re-open the beaches might have been an erroneous one. He was annoyed with himself for bowing to pressure. The officers interviewing the staff at the Tunisian restaurant on Mont d'Hubert had returned empty handed. As the police had closed the road over Cap Blanc Nez, they had closed the restaurant. Nobody had been there and nobody had seen anyone behaving suspiciously in the week leading up to the storm. The English always behaved strangely, they'd told his officers and from his experience, the capitaine had to agree.

He'd received a phone call from Baptiste of the BRB earlier. It was mainly to see how the investigation was going, though right at the end he'd told him that the BRB had received information that a criminal organisation was killing to order, specifically to harvest body parts. That was all he could tell him. So really you're telling me nothing, Capitaine Maubert considered. Useless, bloody useless.

He'd also received a communication from the annoying Brits. They wanted his officers to look out for a man driving a classic and expensive car. He was booked onto a ferry at four forty five that afternoon. If they knew that why did they need his officers to look out for him? As if they hadn't enough to do. He alerted control, to the communication. Job done. He was just about to unpack his lunch when Colette buzzed through.

"Capitaine?" She knew it was, why did she always ask?

"Capitaine, I have a call for you. It's about the migrants."

"Is it urgent?" The capitaine rarely, took calls direct from the public, his officers were there to do that.

"Capitaine I think you should speak to her, it's Marie."

Capitaine Maubert knew immediately who Colette meant. Marie ran an organisation, supporting the migrants. Not only feeding and clothing them but politicly campaigning for their human rights. She was constantly holding his gendarmerie to account and could be at times, a real thorn in his side. Looking wistfully at his neatly packed lunch, he asked Colette to put her through. Lunch would just have to wait.

Havant Police Station – Havant, England

If anybody else wanted to join him in his office, he would have to bring in builders to create an extension. D.I. Johnson looked at those gathered before him. Never in his career had he witnessed such a powerful gathering of law enforcement officers. His chief super was there. It was in his office their meeting had originally been planned but somewhat obligingly the toilet directly above had sprung a leak and at that moment you wouldn't have wanted to be within a hundred metres of his office.

Standing to one side was his Chief Super, immediately before him, sitting, two men from the NCA, also sitting, a man he knew, Richard from SEROCU,(South East Regional Organised Crime Unit) and lastly standing in front of the door, the only woman in the room. The Chief Constable.

He couldn't begin to wonder what had prompted such a gathering. He knew it must have something to do with his murder. But he'd investigated brutal murders before and gangster related murders, and some of these had involved SEROCU but never the NCA. And the Chief Constable normally only asked for an update, he'd never known her to get involved in an investigation. Whatever the reason was it must be big.

It was the Chief Constable who spoke first. "Harry," she'd called him by his first name, that was a good sign. If he'd stepped over the line it would have been, D.I. "Harry I expect you're wondering why we're all here."

The D.I. spread his hands. "I'm assuming it has something to do with the murder we're investigating."

"The one the whole world knows about." The sarcasm was voiced by one of the men from the NCA, Roger Denton, the guy who'd called him earlier that day. The D.I. had already taken a dislike to the man and this unneeded comment made his dislike even worse.

"We're dealing with that aren't we Harry."

"Yes Ma'am, I'm as annoyed and as frustrated as everyone here that this has been leaked. We shall find out who's responsible."

"I'm sure you will," more sarcasm, "and it's imperative from here on in that you only involve trusted officers. Use an enclosed room for reporting and operations and don't allow any civilian staff to become involved unless you absolutely know them to be trustworthy. Remind everybody working on this case of the Official Secrets Act and the penalties for breaking it, emphasise that if found guilty, they could be locked up for 14 years. What we are about to discuss must not, under any circumstances get into the media."

Everyone in the room nodded their understanding and confirmation.

"I'll let you continue then Roger." The Chief Constable gave the man from the NCA, the floor.

"Thank you." Roger dragged his chair to one side so he was facing all in the room. He didn't though, stand up. "Yesterday I received a call from Interpol. They had been contacted by our friends in Spain, (what a surprise thought the D.I. it's where most of this country's most successful criminals are camped), about a particularly vicious murder, or I should say murders. For it involves three murders."

"All Brits?" the D.I. asked.

"Yes Harry, all Brits. A father, mother and their twelve year old daughter." There was a hushed silence. Whenever a minor was involved the atmosphere changed completely. "It was a particularly unforgiving and brutal murder. And we think the mother and daughter were forced to watch the torture, slaying, mutilation and decapitation of their husband/father. Their end mercifully by comparison was swift, for they were both shot using a CZ-99." The silence was now one of shock. "These are photographs taken by the Spanish authorities of the crime scene, I warn you, they are not pretty." The second man from the NCA started to hand around envelopes.

"How did the Spanish authorities discover the killings?" the question came from the Chief Constable. The D.I. realised she almost certainly knew the answer. Her question was probably for his benefit.

Roger obliged. "I was just coming to that. The police received a call, requesting an ambulance, giving the victims address."

Just like his murder. The D.I. began to realise why the ensemble. The photographs confirmed it. Apart from the furnishings being different the photos could have been of his victim. Uceremoniously placed on the coffee table sat the man's head. His mouth had been forced open and his genitalia stuffed inside. There wasn't a vase, instead his arms lay across the same table. Carefully squeezed between the hands, was a Spanish driving licence.

"We now know the driving licence is a forgery. It was made only yesterday by a forger in Malaga who also happens, when he wants to be, a police informer. Apparently the victim was a onetime associate."

"Associate?"

"Yes Harry, associate. DNA results came back late last night. That's why Interpol were in such a hurry to get hold of us. The man, or rather the pieces of man, you see in the photograph, DNA tells us is one Michael Swinton. "

The D.I. couldn't contain his shock. He knew the NCA had been looking for this man for decades. At one time he had been one of this country's most feared gangsters and was suspected of committing or ordering multiple murders. He had been for years Britain's main drug importer but the authorities had never been able to find enough evidence to convict him. Whoever had done this didn't give a shit about evidence.

"Well whoever's done this has done us all a favour." The D.I. couldn't agree more with his Chief Super.

"Possibly," agreed Roger, but whoever has committed these crimes obviously has clout as well as resources and evidently they aren't afraid to stretch their muscles and aren't afraid of us either. Which in our book makes them a threat to national security. Who knows what partner's bed they're happy to crawl into."

The D.I. had to admit the man from the NCA was right. Terrorists and organised crime were often very happy to scratch each other's backs, resulting, collectively in a formidable and dangerous foe.

"How did he get a Spanish driving licence if he's British, don't you need a Spanish I.D. card to obtain one? The question came from Richard, he'd worked closely with the Spanish in past cases.

"Yes you do," the man from the NCA confirmed, our Mr Swinton was in the process of changing his identity. His new identity was to be Jorge Gonzalez Smith." There was a spontaneous outbreak of laughter. Roger ignored it. "Born to a Spanish father and an English mother."

There was still laughter.

Roger continued to ignore it but had to raise his voice to regain everyone's attention. "There's one more thing. According to the GRO's, (General Records Office), records Mr Swinton has been dead for over five years, before you ask, cause of death , sudden arrhythmic death syndrome. To you and me, heart failure. We know this not to be case for quite clearly, up until yesterday Mr Swinton was alive and kicking. The record somehow has been falsified."

"Just the same as my murder, JESUS."

"Yes Harry, Jesus indeed. Somehow, whoever is doing this has access to our GRO records and is manipulating them. You don't need me to tell you how serious this is. It's the perfect disguise for us to stop chasing someone and by the looks of it, other people less tolerant than us too."

"Have you checked with the doctors, named on the death certificate?"

"We'd love to Harry but both doctors named, passed away a few years ago."

"How convenient," Harry came back, there were several mutterings of agreement. Roger pulled a face which acknowledged he concurred with the room.

"So how did whoever did these murders find out?"

"That's the million dollar question, Ma'am, how? We have no idea at the moment."

"And why were they murdered, and why use such brutality?"

"Again Harry, at the moment we have no idea. They were of course both gangsters, ducking and diving in the gangster world, they were bound to have accumulated many enemies along the way."

"Yes, but this is different, both had long been in retirement. They were no longer a threat to anybody. A roughing up or perhaps a knee capping, but not this." The chief super, tapped the photos to make his point.

"We're only guessing they went into retirement, just because they're no longer on our radar, doesn't mean to say they're not still active. They might have simply got cleverer at hiding their activities." It was the Chief Constable offering these pearls of wisdom.

Roger nodded, "You're right, we cannot make any assumptions, and going by the evidence they're almost certainly connected in some way."

"Is there nobody the NCA has in their sights?" It was Richard from SEROCU, who asked this question.

"There is one man." His assistant once again handed everybody an envelope. Inside each found three photos. One resembled a passport photo and at a time when the man was obviously younger, the second rather bizarrely had him smiling and holding up a baguette and the third, almost certainly the most recent looked as though it had been taken from a security camera. "This Roger proclaimed is John Mitchell, some of you may have heard of him." Everyone's faces remained blank. "Well he used to be one of us. From special forces he move to MI5, retired in 2011 and now runs a continental bakery out of Putney, hence the baguette." There came a ripple of laughter. "This photo," the man from the NCA held up the most recent, "was taken by the security camera installed at Michael Swinton's villa."

"On the night of the murder?" More than one person asked this.

"No a few days before and our man here made no attempt to cancel out the cameras, so I think we can assume, he can't have been too concerned about them. It would appear that he was on a debt collecting mission to collect a classic car. To be precise an Aston Martin DB4 Vantage Sports." Photos were handed around. A few whistles sounded and cries of 'nice car.' "Yes a beauty isn't she and worth a cool, half a million. Apparently our Mr Swinton hadn't been keeping up with his payments and Mr Mitchell was on a contract to get it back." Roger held up his right hand. "Before you ask, apart from not informing HMRC, it looks as if the operation was completely legit. We've been in touch with the seller concerned and they confirmed they'd employed one John Mitchell to get the car back for them on a no collection no fee basis."

The D.I. "Wait a minute, if there was CCTV, didn't the cameras, pick up the bastards that did this?"

"Good point, all security was controlled by a central office in Marbella, apparently Mr Swinton hadn't paid his bill so the cameras were switched off that morning."

The D.I. whistled, "What bad fucking luck."

Roger. "Possibly Harry but I'm not so sure. The thesis is that whoever did this knew. Apart from cutting the main wire, no attempt was made to take out the CCTV. This by all accounts was a very professional job, executed by people who knew exactly what they were doing."

"Just like my murder," The D.I. repeated his comment made earlier. "If he succeeded how much was this John fella in for?"

Roger. "What for collecting the car?" The D.I. nodded.

"The dealer refused to tell us Harry but I think we can safely assume it will be at least a five figure sum plus expenses. And I think we can also assume that the payment will be in cash."

"Do you think this is a one off, or are there more?" It was the Chief Super.

Roger. "What do you mean?"

"Well is there evidence that John here," the Chief Super tapped the photos, "has done this sort of thing before?"

"Not that we can find, there's no evidence but the car dealer who employed him, did tell us he came recommended. So I think we can safely assume by that, that he has. But as I've just said, we haven't found any evidence, to date."

"It's bloody obvious he has." The D.I. threw up his hands.

"I agree. But to date, we haven't found a trace of evidence." Roger repeated.

"Do we know where this John is now?" It was the Chief Constable.

Roger drew in a deep breath. "As a matter of fact we do, well roughly. It's hard to hide driving a car like that." Roger held up the photo of the Aston Martin.

All agreed.

Gendarmerie Nationale – Calais France

"Marie?" Capitaine Maubert couldn't hide the caution in his voice and the woman on the other end of the line, realised it.

"Don't be like that Thierry," The capitaine hated the fact that the woman always insisted when addressing him, in using his first name. She made it sound as though she were a friend, and she definitely was not, far from it.

"Like what?"

"Having your guard up, I'm not the enemy." Aren't you the capitaine pondered. "Anyway I'm here to help." The capitaine raised his eyebrows but of course the motion went unseen.

"Help me?"

There was a pause as Marie considered the question. "Well yes, yes, you and the migrants" Ah thought the Capitaine. "Well with your investigation, the one all over the press and on television, fucking everywhere. Merde, you know what I'm talking about Thierry. I have someone I think you need to speak to."

Now the capitaine was listening, this could be the breakthrough they needed. "Ok Marie, I'm listening, you've got my attention."

"Not on the phone Thierry, this guy's, really, really scared. You need to hear it from him. He will only talk to you. For some bizarre reason, he trusts you." Thanks for the vote of confidence, thought the Capitaine. "When can you come?

"Well I don't know when .."

Marie cut in. "How about now? I'm worried this guy will run, disappear and you need to talk to him."

The capitaine thought the always over dramatic woman was being just that again but agreed. "Where Marie?"

"Café du Centre, Marck, do you know it?"

The capitaine did, "Yes I know it."

"Good I'll be sat on the terrace out back, I'm waiting, hurry Thierry. OH AND THIERRY, not in uniform and not in your car, the 308. You might as well paint on the bloody side, look at me I'm a gendarme" The phone clicked dead. Bloody drama queen the capitaine swore under his breath. This better be worth it. After changing into civilian clothes and picking up his packed lunch the capitaine after checking with the control room about progress, (there was none), walked through to reception.

"Colette do you mind if I borrow your car?"

"Of course not," the ever obliging Colette would never refuse him anything. "May I ask why?" The capitaine smiled sweetly, meaning no, you may not. "Ok," Colette smiled and after rustling in her handbag handed over a single key, hanging from a Betty Boop key ring. The Capitaine smiled again, this time in thanks, a smile that Colette returned but one that was meant as an apology for the key ring.

Colette's car was a respectable Citroen C3. Burgundy in colour, the car was discretion itself and belonging to Colette, immaculate, inside and out. The Café Du Centre was in Marck Est, a small town east of Calais. It was positioned on the Avenue de Calais, the main thoroughfare through the town, not far from the Zone de Fret Transmarck. A stop for lorries traversing the Channel, and as a consequence targeted by migrants hoping to catch a lift.

To the Capitaines delight he found free roadside parking almost directly outside the café. On entering he found the café to be empty but they were obviously expecting him for a serveuse, (waitress), quickly ushered him to the terrace out back. Marie was sitting, reposed enjoying the suntrap that was the terrace. The serveuse continued to hover as the Capitaine sat.

" A Grimbergen, pression, (draught), cvp, Marie?"

"A 1664 cvp, pression aussi. Merci Thierry"

"De rien"

The serveuse, quickly returned with their beers, after which they were alone.

The Capitaine took a long sip, after which he continued holding the glass. "So Marie, what is this all about?"

Marie, holding her glass with both hands, too took a gulp. "There is something going on capitaine, something not right."

"With the migrants?"

"Yes, I know you don't like them ."

"It's not a question of liking them, it's my job Marie."

Marie put down her glass and held up both hands. "Yes, I know, I know it's your job. You're just doing your job."

"Anyway Marie, you were saying."

"Yes, yes, there is something wrong Thierry." Capitaine Maubert took another long sip, he was enjoying his beer more than was comfortable. Marie leant forward and in hushed, (over dramatic, considered the Capitaine), tones continued. "You see, normally when a migrant reaches the UK, especially those with family there, friends or other family members still remaining here tend to get a message confirming their success and that everything's ok. Not always of course but mostly. In recent months more and more migrants are leaving but are never heard of again. It's as though, puffff," Marie splayed her arms. "They've disappeared in a puff of smoke."

"That's it, that's why you dragged me out here? To tell me that migrants are bad communicators?"

"No, no Thierry, I know these people. Something's wrong. Then the heads all the media are talking about and now Abdul-Jalil's granddaughter, the poor, poor man." Abdul-Jalil must be the grandfather who had just hours earlier identified his granddaughter. News travelled fast. "And now Ismail."

"Ismail?" the capitaine finished his beer.

"Yes, yes, the man I want you to see. He has relatives in the UK, so speaks fairly good English, I can translate." If the Capitaine was honest he understood a lot of English but rarely let on.

"Ok, where can we find this Ismail?"

"He is waiting not far from here, but Thierry." In a surprising move Marie held both the capitaine's hands. "Thierry he is very, very, scared. Please try to be less like a gendarme and more like a human being. If not you will scare him, he will not talk."

La Sirene, Rue de la Plage, Audinghen, France

CHAPTER
—10—

La Sirene – Cap Gris Nez, France

John, was at first a little annoyed at other customers joining him in the restaurant. When he'd arrived there were just two other diners, an elderly couple sitting at a table beside a curved window. He virtually had the place to himself and he loved that. With the warm welcome he'd received, it felt almost as though where he was sat, was his own private room. The new couple shattered that illusion. Now though he was much happier with their intrusion. They had chosen a table a little way ahead of him, with the woman facing. And thought John, she really is all woman. To his salacious delight, the woman crossed her legs displaying an ample but shapely thigh. As he ate, John found himself slowly getting lost in the woman. He fantasised having sex with her, how he would be her greatest ever lover. The woman must have noticed his stare as on more than one occasion she caught his eye. But rather than turn away, the usual reaction when women caught him lusting after them, this woman smiled back and made no attempt to hide her exposed leg.

John had ordered the Plateau Royal, a seafood platter with the addition of lobster. He'd also ordered extra prawns. The price for his indulgence was over 100 Euros but he didn't care, until now. With the woman sat opposite he now regretted ordering quite so much, he was what the French call 'gourmand', and his ample waistline was proof of that. His one grace was he'd ordered water not wine. He couldn't risk alcohol driving such a car.

Maureen's companion, in the end decided rather than share a seafood platter, they should each order a 'plat.' The platter he explained might take ages to eat and his time was limited. Maureen at once picked up on the hint. She assumed he wanted dessert, and ample time to enjoy it.

Taking her companion's advice they both ordered Medallion de Maigre aux Noisettes served with a wild mushroom butter and a selection of what her partner called 'forgotten vegetables.' Maureen had wanted lobster but her companion had waved her off this, explaining that nearly all the homard,(lobster), served along the coast was not local at all, but caught off the coast of Cornwall.

"Really?" Maureen exclaimed. "How funny," and laughed loudly.

As their time was tight, they decided together, to order a main course only. Maureen couldn't help showing her delight when their order arrived. Never had she seen food so beautifully presented and every fork of food she put in her mouth she wanted to remain there for eternity. As she ate she couldn't help but notice the driver of the Aston Matin's interest in her. From time to time she smiled obligingly enjoying his obvious obsession with her thigh. She must have been too obvious for her companion noticed their interaction.

"You're putting the poor man off his food," he joked, "and that mountain of seafood must have cost him a small fortune."

Maureen returned her attention to the man, the stranger sat opposite. If elegant was possible, he ate his food elegantly, almost as though he were being respectful to the plate before him. Later he was to explain to her that's how good food should be treated. With the utmost respect, not just to the food on your plate but to the person who had put so much effort into preparing it.

"If he can drive a car like that, he can afford it." Maureen replied waving her knife in John's direction. Anyway, by the look of him, I think he appreciates his food."

"I think you're probably right," agreed her partner, "though as well as respecting food you have to respect your body and I fear he may be failing with the latter."

"Ooooh, I don't know, more to work with." Maureen giggled suggestively. The combination of white wine and seafood was working quickly on his English companion observed her partner. In most European countries, men plied their women with vodka as a way of helping their women to lose their inhibitions. In France they were much more sophisticated, at least he hoped so. If you want to treat your female and help her lose her inhibitions, white wine and shellfish were the way to do it. The fact was well known in France. On this occasion he, had had to go with fish, not shellfish but this combination too appeared to be working, for his companion appeared to be rather too brazenly, losing hers already.

"Do you fancy him?" it was a fun question.

"I fancy his car," Maureen laughed.

"Think you could get him to take you for a ride in it? I bet you can't"

The bait was cast and Maureen jumped at it. "Bet you I can," and brought her right ankle up to rest on her knee, knowing that as a result the man trying to concentrate on his seafood would have a good glimpse of her knickers. Her companion poured her another glass of white. She was becoming raucously drunk and he, although professional was beginning to look forward to their time together later.

"What do I win, if I get him to give me a ride?"

"A car like his." Her companion joked. Maureen laughed.

"Deal," she offered, holding out her hand. Her companion took it. The dare was cemented. Couldn't have gone better, her companion smiled with contentment.

Half an hour later, Maureen was sat in the passenger seat, enjoying the roar that was the Aston Martin. "This car is meant to be driven," John explained. "It reacts to your personality, it's rather like a woman," he added, hoping the woman sat beside him would understand his meaning. Perhaps even take him up on his hint. Not at that moment of course. She had a male companion, though she had, unless he was mistaken, encouraged his attention in the restaurant and outside her companion had encouraged her to take a ride. He wondered about their relationship.

"What's your name," he asked.

In response Maureen put an index finger to her lips and giggled. "Secret, I'm a woman of mystery," and squeezed John's thigh.

"How exciting." John put his foot down.

In truth the one condition her stranger had insisted on if Maureen took a ride to win the dare, was not to reveal her name. Maureen had lapped that up, it added to her excitement.

John knew the area well and gave the mystery woman beside him an experience he hoped she wouldn't forget in a hurry. A circular tour that included the fishing village of Audresseles, Ambleteuse, the seaside resort that was Wimereux, a speed fest back along the A16, to Wissant, eventually returning along the coast road to La Sirene. Maureen knew everywhere they travelled but gracefully allowed the man, she now knew as John, to indulge her. Just before they reached the restaurant John pulled out a business card and passed it to his 'mystery woman.'

"Here take this, if you're ever in London look me up."

"I will," pouted Maureen, suggestively sliding the card beneath her bra.

When they returned, her stranger was stood in the car park hands in pockets, staring out to sea. John had been half preparing for a confrontation but the man was all smiles. Ten minutes later he was speeding back along the coast road heading for Cap Blanc Nez and on the other side, Calais and his ferry. What the fuck just happened, he wondered to himself, what the fuck and wished the erection that was beginning to prove uncomfortable would take a bow.

"Well?" beamed Maureen's stranger.

"He gave me his card," Maureen removed the card slowly from her ample breast and waved it in the air.

"Let's have a look," Maureen after taking a glance, handed it to him.

"Ooooh he's a baker," Maureen laughed and then, after giving the matter some thought. "He must be a bloody good baker if he can afford a car like that."

Her stranger was quietly asking himself the same question. Taking the card from Maureen's outstretched hand he glanced at it with a little more concentration than was necessary. Maureen didn't notice. Taking the card back she returned it to the safety of her bra.

"How do you fancy a trip to London," her stranger joked. Except he wasn't, he wasn't joking. He was deadly serious.

Havant Police Station – Havant, England

As Roger, the man from the NCA held up a photo of the Aston Martin, there came a knock at the door.

"Sorry sir, just wondered if you guys wanted coffee? We're just making some." The young male P.C. smiled apologetically. The coffee from the station machine was considered by many to be undrinkable, and a long time ago a kettle had appeared. Along with china mugs and without argument everyone in the office, on a weekly basis, topped up the kitty.

"Anyone?" the D.I. asked. Like schoolchildren nearly everybody put their hand up and those that didn't confirmed with an assured, "yes."

The P.C. closed the door and Roger continued. "We know, this morning he was at the Dentelle d'Alencon services at Rouen. We also know he's booked on a four forty five ferry this afternoon at Calais. So right now he's somewhere between the two. You can see from his photos that the man probably likes his food." There came a river of spontaneous laughter. "So my guess is, he's enjoying French hospitality somewhere. Border Force have been informed as have the relevant authorities in Calais."

"And two members of ERSOU, (Eastern Regional Special Operations Unit), are waiting at Calais to watch his movements on the ferry." Richard cut in.

"Thanks Richard," Roger acknowledged. "We've asked Border Force to give him a bit of a hard time, see what sort of answers he gives them. But unless they find him smuggling in drugs, or other illegal goods, to let him continue. What we don't want them to do is lead our man here to believe he's part of a wider investigation. If he does he'll probably go to ground, and that's the last thing we want."

There came a rustle of general agreement.

"Now Harry, I don't want to tell you how to conduct your investigation, but it's important you use, only your most trustworthy officers. Security must be watertight and when unattended, lock your operation or incident room. Don't even let the cleaners in, hoover the bloody carpet yourselves."

There came a ripple of laughter but everyone knew the man from the NCA was being deadly serious.

"We need to know everything there is to know about our victim here, who we now know is really Roger Preston, a retired, or assumed to be, retired gangster. Maybe not. Harry we need you to find out everything you can about this guy, how he moved here, why he moved here and what's he been up to since he's been down here. Who he's friends with, who he's fucked, even where he shits. And most importantly has he ever had contact with our man with the Aston Martin, a John Mitchell, X special forces, X MI5. John Mitchell may be a vital connection. We shall investigate him at the NCA Harry and let you know everything we find out. In return you let us know immediately if you come across anything that may be useful.

"Of course," promised the D.I. There came another knock at the door.

"WAIT." Shouted the man from the NCA. He looked around the room. "I think we're just about done here. I can't stress enough that we believe at the NCA, whoever committed these murders is a major player and a major threat and as yet we know nothing about them or who they are." He turned to the D.I. "Harry we need to discuss tactics and how we best communicate. SEROCO will be assisting you and at least one of their specialist officers will be stationed here until no longer deemed necessary."

"Sorry Harry," Richard smiled. Roger had the grace to smile too.

" My colleague here, Miles, (the man who'd handed round the envelopes), will be your immediate point of contact at the NCA. If you need his help here, with anything, just ask. "A smile and a nod passed between Miles and the D.I. "Now before we start, I'm really thirsty and it's really stuffy in here, shall we take our coffees outside? Is that ok with you Chief Constable?"

"It is," she replied smiling, and opened the door.

Wissant – France

In little over a minute from entering her apartment, Maureen and the stranger were naked and in bed. Compared to last time she was much more experienced and knowing now what she enjoyed and hungry for it. Encouraged by the wine, Maureen went about her love making with a passion that surprised even her experienced stranger. Her determination physically to reach an intense state of gratification, almost overwhelmed him but also turned him on and for two hours their bodies twisted and turned with an energy and escapism that neither had experienced before. A bomb could have gone off next door and neither would have noticed. The only thing that mattered for both of them, during those two hours was achieving an intoxication built on pleasure and pulsating excitement, climaxing in a combined state of ecstasy. The outside world could go to hell.

After they had finished Maureen lay in bed whilst her stranger showered. When he reappeared, he was fully dressed and with not a hair out of place.

"I'm serious about you going to London you know."

Maureen grinned, "you're not."

The stranger grinned back. To the English woman this was a game, and it was good to start proceedings off that way. "I am, you know." The stranger continued to grin. "How would you like to do a little job for me? Become a bit of a secret agent?" His grin widened

"What like James Bond?" Maureen's eyes glistened.

The stranger sighed inwardly, why did the English believe any secret agent must be a James Bond. However he played along. "If you like."

Maureen giggled. "You're joking."

"Well, we will have to change your name, no offence but Maureen isn't very Bond like, is it?" Maureen couldn't recall telling the stranger her name. She must have done.

"What shall I be called?"

The stranger looked pensive. "Bree," he announced.

"Brie? But that's a cheese!" Maureen was indignant. "Maureen," she knew wasn't good but it was better than being called a cheese.

The stranger's grin returned. "No Bree, spelt B r e e. It's Celtic and translates to noble and powerful. Perfect for a spy."

Chapter 10

Maureen's expression changed, "I love it."

"Ok then, I'll be in touch Miss Bree." He kissed his hand and wiped his fingers across her lips. Before Maureen or now Bree could respond, he was gone. No longer a ship in the day, thought Maureen, though frustratingly she still didn't know his name. Why the big secret?

The stranger glided out of Wissant, turning left, onto the D940 coast road. Although his official residence was in Antwerp, he owned a penthouse, fitting for a diamond dealer, overlooking Calais Plage. He regularly donated a great deal of money to charitable causes in the town and hoped if he ever needed a favour returned, the town would see him right. After his two hours with the English lady he felt exhausted. He would have to teach her to curb her enthusiasm or she might end up killing their target. He would have to teach her, if she were to work for him, to learn that the greatest enjoyment was not achieving orgasm but exercising power over her man. Having experienced first-hand her insatiable search for satisfaction, it wasn't going to be easy and they had very little time but he, they, had no choice. They could threaten their target but from bitter experience he knew how that could so easily go wrong, no this was the best way. The target had once helped one of their own. They needed to know how he had done it and perhaps employ his services again, possibly even, on a regular basis. It was essential to get the target on your side, without them knowing. This he was convinced was the best way. Bree, he smiled inwardly at her chosen name. He hadn't lied, nobility and power, were associated with the name but Bree was also his home town in Belgium. His own little bit of mischief. He hoped it wouldn't end up biting him in the bum.

It wasn't long before his car was effortlessly climbing the steep grassy slope of Mont d'Hubert and Cap Blanc Nez. The root of all his current problems. That storm and the idiot underground had created a small crisis, not just for him but the organisation. The organisation had over 100 people living, incognito, under the Cap. He prayed it would remain that way. He knew the gendarme had interviewed the restaurant owner, he was passing the restaurant now, and some of the staff there that morning, but from what he understood it had been a very soft interview. Just routine as far as he could make out. Nothing, he hoped, to worry about. The trouble was the organisation had no-one on the inside at Calais, and under the current circumstances it would be far too risky to try and recruit somebody now. He needed to know what the gendarme were investigating, what avenues they were exploring. There was somebody, he trusted, who could find out, and he had sent for her a couple of days before. His request had been relayed resembling a series of Chinese whispers. Phones or any form of technology, unless absolutely necessary, weren't ever used for communication, even encrypted ones. Interpol were becoming very adept at breaking codes. You could buy a box that could search for secure networks but even they were fallible. Not so a person, a loyal agent delivering a harmless baguette. His message should be reaching her anytime now. Hopefully by tomorrow evening, Fatima will arrive in Calais.

John enjoyed revving the Aston Martin over Mont d'Hubert. At the beginning of the 20th century, English aristocrats, used to test their cars on the slope. At the summit of Cap Blanc Nez, he decided to take a 5 minute break. He never tired of the view. Across the water, on a clear day the white cliffs of Dover. To the east Calais and beyond the Belgium coast and looking west, the magnificent Bai De Wissant. For him it was one of the greatest views in Europe. Unfortunately on this occasion there were a couple of straggling tv crews. Seeing his car, one instinctively started filming. This was the last thing he wanted, forfeiting the view he circled the Aston and sped downhill, heading for Calais.

On arriving at Calais Port he found check in teeming with gendarme and British police officers. He remembered half hearing something on the news about severed heads being found in the sea, close to Calais. Both the gendarme and border force were paying great attention to anyone travelling. It must be that. John felt his blood run cold. He was kicking himself for being so careless. He'd ignored all of his training. He'd got rid of his gun in Spain but he hadn't checked the Aston Martin. He hoped his client hadn't still been running drugs and using the Aston for transport. If he had been and they were discovered he was done for. You fucking idiot, Mitchell, he scolded himself. There was no way he could leave the queue now, it would look too suspicious. And the car, it wasn't his. They were bound to ask about the car. He had the appropriate paperwork for it, but if they did a search on the man that his paperwork evidenced he'd collected it from, the records would show he'd been dead 5 years. How had he collected a car from a man recorded as dead and for several years? Shit what a mess.

To John's relief the French douane waved him through as did the gendarme. On reaching the British border force, whilst examining his passport another officer approached. "Excuse me sir, would you mind pulling into our bay over there," the officer signalled with his arm to where several other officers were waiting. "We won't keep you a minute."

"Of course not." John slowly swung the car over, the engine sounded as though it was no longer purring but growling. He brought the Aston Martin to a stop. The officer who had told him to pull over, came across. John wound down the window. The officer leant down, leaving one hand resting on the car roof.

"Nice car sir, is it yours?"

"No," John replied, wishing he didn't sound so guilty.

"Would you mind stepping out then sir. We need to ask you a few questions."

Shit, John scolded himself. Shit, shit, shit, SHIT.

CHAPTER
—11—

Marck – East Of Calais, France

Marie didn't drive, Capitaine Maubert knew that. She'd passed her test and possessed a full licence but liked to live life as her extended family did, the migrants. None possessed a car and Marie lived life on foot so she could better understand their challenges.

The Capitaine opened the door for her and Marie slid in. "Where are we going?"

"I'll guide you," Marie pointed forward, "straight ahead. It's not far." Capitaine Maubert did as directed. Marie, as it turned out, was right, it wasn't far. After crossing over a canal, he was immediately told to turn right, and not long after, after crossing a railway line, left. Ahead of them now squatting under a bridge was a lone male. Capitaine Maubert knew the bridge, many years ago it was known as a place popular for small time drug dealing.

"That's him Thierry," the capitaine had guessed it was. "Stop, let me get out and walk, I don't want him scared. " The capitaine obliged, he watched as the two briefly hugged, then Marie turned and waved him forward. The Capitaine did as he was told, hoping all this drama would be worth it. Pulling gently to a halt, he, behaving as best he could to present himself as a normal human being, got slowly out of the car. No sudden movements. "Ismail, this is Thierry, he's my friend, he can help you." The capitaine hoped he didn't look surprised, friend? Really?

Ismail held out his hand. The capitaine took it. There was no shake, Ismail simply held it tightly.

"Thank you, thank you monsieur, thank you," and in a surprising move kissed the capitaine's hand.

"Merc…." Marie started translating.

"It's ok Marie, I understood."

"Of course."

The capitaine looked at the man before him, over. He was dressed in European clothes, though all badly needed to see the inside of a washing machine. On his right wrist, he wore what looked like a reasonably expensive watch and on his left hand, a wedding ring. He was short, just over one and a half metres, he guessed, with a plumped cheek face, balding head and haunted eyes. The capitaine recognised the look, he had seen it many times before. As a gendarme you were constantly dealing with victims. This man, those eyes told him, had been through hell.

"Shall we get in the car?" The capitaine gestured. "It's probably not sensible to be standing, so exposed here."

Marie panicked, "yes, yes of course. Ismail in the car." Marie shooed the poor man, almost as though he were a pet dog. Ismail didn't appear offended, he quickly got in.

"Marie, listen carefully. If what you say is true, there is something funny going on, it is not safe for us to park somewhere for a little chat. It could attract unwanted attention." Marie nodded her understanding. "We are going drive and I want Ismail to tell me his story as we are moving, it will be safer this way, understand?"

Marie nodded and spoke in English to Ismail. "Ok," Ismail nodded to the drivers mirror, "Ok, yes, good."

"Take this, it's a Dictaphone," Capitaine Maubert reached into his pocket and passed over a small voice recorder to Marie, sitting in the back seat." He immediately saw the disquiet etched on her face. "Don't

154

worry Marie, you have my word I won't use the voice recording as evidence. I have translators back at the gendarmerie and I want them to give me an accurate translation, no offence." Marie's English he'd very quickly understood, to be wanting a little.

"Ok, as long as you promise as Thierry, not a gendarme."

Capitaine Maubert held back a sigh. "As Thierry, you have my word."

"Ok then." Marie appeared to be satisfied by this. In her broken English, she explained to Ismail who lifted both thumbs up, signalling his ok. Capitaine Maubert had been worried if his passenger would be happy having his story recorded. He didn't want to have to rely on his memory for Ismail's story. This way he could play the recording over and over, if necessary, enabling him and his team to pick over the evidence at their leisure.

Swinging the car around he started driving back towards Calais. There may be the slightest chance that they'd pass something that would jog his passenger's memory. It was worth a try. He looked in the driver's mirror catching Marie's attention.

"I want you to tell Ismail to tell his story as though he's talking to a friend. Tell him not to hurry, to takes his time and include the slightest detail even if it doesn't seem important. It may be important to us and for us to be able to help him." Marie nodded at the mirror and turning to Ismail passed on the Capitaine's instructions. Once again Ismail held up his thumbs. "Good, ok Ismail, start when you're ready," the Capitaine smiled in the mirror and he saw Ismail smiling back. Marie held the Dictaphone and Ismail started recounting his story.

Calais Ferry Terminal - Calais, France

"Did you pack the car yourself?"

"Yes." John knew he looked nervous. Damn he'd been trained to appear calm, non-committal in the most stressful of situations and here he was sweating like a pig before a jumped up, and compared to himself, amateur working for her majesty's government. He'd put his life on the line, more than once for his country. What had this guy ever done, except give thousands of innocent people a hard time.

"To your knowledge you're not carrying anything that you should have declared."

"No," John replied, rubbing the palms of his hands with his fingers.

The border force officer knew the signs, this guy was more than nervous, he was petrified. They'd been asked to look out for him, to 'play with him a little, but unless they found anything serious to let him through. A hidden microphone was recording the whole conversation, it was being listened to by two officers from ERSOU, sitting in a car not 50 metres away. They were to join the ferry and keep an eye on Mr Mitchell during the crossing.

"Do you mind telling me how long you have been away?" John reached into his jacket pocket and pulled out his British Airways ticket for London to Malaga. The border force officer examined the ticket, deliberately taking his time. "So you flew out and are returning in this?" The border force officer stepped back examining the half a million pound car. "And your flight tickets are for a return, can you explain? I have to be sure the car isn't stolen, you understand."

John nodded. "Yes, yes of course," and launched into how he was a debt collector and there had been no guarantee that he'd even find the car, let alone able to drive it back. He produced the paperwork provided by his client and their written permission along with insurance documents. The border force officer didn't look at them, instead he asked.

"Do you mind if my colleagues take a look over the car?" John shook his head, of course he minded but he hadn't a choice in the matter. The jumped up officer might have asked a question but what he really meant was, we're going to go over your car with a fine tooth comb. "Good," the officer framed a smile but it wore no warmth, "whilst they're doing that, I'm going to examine these." The officer held up the papers John had given him. "Please take a seat Mr Mitchell, this shouldn't take long."

John did as he was told, sitting on a cheap plastic bench as directed. He watched as highly trained border force officers crawled over and under his car. In the boot they went through his suit and brief case. He saw their excitement on finding a wad of cash. There was £8,000 in notes, that was allowed, They could waste their time counting that, and a twinge of a smile appeared on his face as he saw the look of disappointment on theirs. The sound of the officer who appeared to be in control, returning, quickly wiped it.

"Mr Mitchell," The man was on the phone, and had his hand clasped over the mouth piece. "Can you confirm the name of the person you collected the car from?" This was the question John had been dreading.

"Michael Swinton." It was little more than a whisper.

"Sorry?"

Louder. "Michael Swinton."

"Ok, thank you." The officer returned to his phone conversation. John wondered who in the hell he was talking to. If he was checking records and his contact at the GRO had been his normal efficient self, then he'd have some serious explaining to do. A few minutes later the officer came over. He was all smiles. Handing John his paperwork he apologised for any inconvenience and hoped he understood why they had to check things out. He'd even joked, "Had to check that there weren't any severed heads in the boot." John, of course had flattered

157

him that he understood and with cries of, "nice car, "was waved on his way. Five minutes later, he was on board the ferry. On his tail, two plain clothed officers from ERSOU.

Once fully on board he took himself to up to the Club Lounge. He always booked the Club Lounge, it was generally free of overexcited kids and there was also a touch of 'times gone by' about it. A time when the world was a more civilised place, and John loved that. If he was being followed it was also a good place to spot the usual suspects. There were never many people in the Club Lounge and as a consequence allowed him the opportunity to suss anybody questionable out. He spotted them immediately, two men, both overly casual, and both carrying newspapers, the same newspaper, an instant giveaway. He wondered who they worked for and why they were tailing him. There could be a multitude of reasons, some good, some bad. He'd been followed before and it was not unknown for clients to have him followed to ensure he didn't run off with goods he was being paid to return. It was quite possibly that. After all he was when driving, sitting in, half a million pounds.

The waitress came with his complimentary glass of champagne and newspaper, the Daily Mail. John settled down to enjoy his champagne. He was not so worried about having the one drink now. His client had phoned him on his arrival at La Sirene. They now wanted to collect the car at Dover. It was agreed they would wait for him in the bar at the Premier Inn, close to the port. After the call he had taken out the sim of his pre-paid phone and thrown it in the sea. He no longer needed it. He'd buy a new one for his next job. The phone itself he'd crushed under his foot, and casually slid what was left under a rear wheel, when he drove off there would no longer be a phone to speak of. Looking back he wondered now if the woman who he'd taken for a ride had been a plant. His one weakness, being a man, he easily convinced himself she was not. Calmness personified, John settled back to read his paper. He stared at the headline, stared at it again and choked on his champagne.

"Man Found Brutally Murdered Is A Gangster."

'Police confirmed today that the man found murdered in an idyllic seaside cottage is wanted gangster, Roger Preston.'

John read on, not wanting to believe his eyes. The brutality of the murder was not left to the imagination, it was all there. And there too, in black and white was the victim's name. Roger Preston, vicious gangster, and where he was murdered, Langstone. Could this, John wondered, be the reason he was being tailed.

You bloody idiot, Preston, you bloody idiot. You must have broken cover. He didn't give a shit the man was dead. He had always been an A1 bastard anyway. What really pissed him off, was the man had put himself and possibly others in danger. Possibly even mortal danger. This changed everything thought John. Everything. Bloody everything. You useless piece of shit Preston. He suddenly felt, not saw the two men he suspected of tailing him, watching. Turning the pages by five he picked up on another headline. "MP Caught With Pants Down." John smiled, once more he was calmness personified.

Havant Police Station – Havant, Hampshire, England

As it always did, going through the details, reviewing the case so far and planning which route the investigation should take, took longer than everybody had anticipated. One thing the D.I. gave Roger, the man from the NCA credit for, was his attention to detail. By the time they had finished they would know every breath the dead man had taken, before his sudden demise. Whilst they were meeting Roger had received a call, everyone assumed from either Border Force at Calais or ERSOU. All he said was, our man's at Calais and from all accounts he's close to shitting his pants. Everyone in the room laughed but there was no further explanation forthcoming.

It was close to eight and dark outside by the time the last cup of coffee had been drunk and everyone felt they should call it a day. Roger to his credit, felt rather than returning to London that night he and his colleague should book into the Premier Inn on the road to Hayling Island and the D.I. could join them for a drink. It would, he proclaimed give them all a chance to get to know each other outside the stresses of work. The D.I. was slowly warming to the man. He had a human side and that was often kept hidden by senior officers.

Opposite the hotel there was a purpose built pub and carvery but instead of going there, the D.I. persuaded his new colleagues to take a ten minute stroll down to Langstone and grab something in the Royal Oak.

It was a good choice, a log fire, when they arrived was burning, warming the ancient stone slabs that for centuries had covered the floor. And being surprisingly quiet, the three settled beside a window, through which they could admire Langstone harbour in all her natural beauty. The D.I. never tired of this pub. You could if it wasn't busy imagine yourself being in another time, when candles were the only source of light. Outside the harbour could have been a scene straight out of "Moonstone," by Wilkie Collins, the D.I.'s current read. He could see his colleagues from the NCA were captivated by it too and all too easily the narrative changed from an unsolved murder to family, football and anything but. A taxi took them all home. On the way they stopped briefly to chat to the officers guarding the crime scene. 'Who would want to buy this now,' was the main topic of conversation and it was true. Who on earth would want to buy the cottage after such a horrific murder. It was gone 1am when the D.I.'s head finally hit the pillow. Never, was his last thought before he fell into a heavy slumber. Never have I been involved in an investigation such as this, and somehow he had the feeling this was only the beginning, the beginning of something much, much bigger.

Wissant – France

Maureen or Bree as she now liked to think of herself stood on her balcony listening to rather than watching the sea. The surf was slightly up confirming the forecast of wind and rain the next day. She felt deeply satisfied, both sexually and mentally. Her life so far had always been comfortable thanks to a devoted husband but it had on reflection been extremely boring. Now she felt she was on the verge of a new excitement, not sexual but an adventure. It might of course all be fantasy but deep down she had a strange feeling it wasn't. Now completely, she understood the expression, 'live for the moment as tomorrow may never come.' That is exactly how she felt now and couldn't wait for tomorrow to dawn.

Gendarmerie Nationale – Calais, France.

Capitaine Maubert sat at his desk reading the transcript, provided by the interpreter of Ismail's story. If it was true it was deeply disturbing. They had driven for over an hour whilst Ismail recounted what had happened just over a week before. So disturbed had he been, that more than once he had collapsed into tears, his experience here in Calais too similar to those he'd experienced in Syria. Calais, Syria, a similar experience and on his patch. This really disturbed the capitaine. On his patch, under his nose, if this was really happening, then he and his gendarmerie had failed not just the migrants but his country too. He was determined to put things right, Ismail's story would not be swept under the carpet as the mad ramblings of a 'Kosovo,' as Calaisiens tended to refer to all migrants.

It was dark outside and he made a call to his wife to let her know he wouldn't be too long now. His wife as usual had been the epitome of understanding along with the promise of a hot meal. He was so lucky. One day he was going to spoil her rotten. He then made a call to Marie. Marie answered with a tease.

"Thierry, to what do I owe a late night call, are you feeling lonely?"

"Very funny, how's Ismail?" Marie's humour left her.

"He's fine, I called my friend and she said after a good meal he had a shower and went straight to bed. Last time she checked he was sleeping like a baby. It's probably the first time he'd slept in a proper bed in months maybe years even."

They had earlier, dropped Ismail off at a friend of Marie's living in Les Attaques, a commune almost attached to Calais, hugging the St Omer – Calais canal. Her friend lived with her boyfriend in a rather non-descript terraced house, typical of the area. The house was instantly forgettable and thus ideal as a hide away. Her friend and her boyfriend both volunteered at the many food stations feeding migrants all over town and so were ideal to offer shelter.

There was a long pause as Marie waited for the capitaine to reply. She sensed he was struggling with how to word his next sentence. Eventually, "Marie."

"Yes Thierry?"

"We're having an operations meeting tomorrow, here at the gendarmerie, it's at 10am, sharp. How do you feel about attending?"

"Whyyy?" Marie answered cautiously, for this was like being thrown to the lions, whilst in the lion's den.

"To tell my officers what you told me, so they can hear it from the horse's mouth so to speak. I think it would help convince my men that we need to take this seriously. Will you do it? I'll send a car for you."

"No you won't," Marie was quick to answer. "Yes ok Thierry I'll do it but I'll make my own way there, ok."

"You're sure?"

"Yes, quite sure."

"Don't be late." The Capitaine couldn't refrain himself.

There sounded a sigh. "I won't Thierry, bonne nuit." The line clicked dead.

A few minutes later the Capitaine was driving home. He had the transcript with him, he wanted to read it again. Coq au Vin, from a slow cooker was waiting for him when he arrived home. His wife massaged his scalp as he ate, she worried about the stress this new case was bringing. After chatting for half an hour his wife retired to bed. He promised her faithfully he wouldn't be long and as he did every night retired to his office. Selecting AC/DC from his collection he put his earphones on and settled down to have another read of the transcript. As guitar screams sounded, his eyes started to close and the transcript fell to the floor. He was remembering when they'd seen the band live in Paris. It had been a really great night. Eyes closed tight the Capitaine started to dream. For the Capitaine AC/DC were the perfect soporific.

Dover – England

John watched the two men he thought were possibly tailing him, get in their car four rows back. As he drove off the ferry and out through the port he kept them in his sights. The Premier Inn was virtually at the port and in a couple of minutes he was pulling into the car park. He knew the two, if they were tailing him, wouldn't risk following him in, they'd instead find a space somewhere along the seafront with a view of the hotel. Hastily he parked round the back so his half a million pounds car was not in clear view from the access road that ran along the seafront. With a haste that defied his figure, he flicked the boot and picking up his bags walked round the front to reception. There he spied the two reversing into a roadside parking space. He was tempted to wave but that was for the movies. He took great pleasure knowing that they were watching him enter the hotel. They will assume that he had booked in for the night, at the same time cursing the fact, that they'd have to spend a night in their car.

Two men approached him as he entered the bar, smiling they offered their hands. John shook and somewhat despairingly handed over the keys. He'd miss that car but not the attention it brought. One of the men gave him a paper along with a bulky envelope.

"Confirmation we've collected the car from you," John read the document and nodded, "And the other half of your fee is in there," the envelope. "Jeremy has estimated your expenses and doubled them, he hope's that's ok."

"It will be." John knew there'd be more than enough, clients always treated debt collectors well.

"Ok then, we'll be off then, the car's?"

"Round the back."

The two men shook hands again and were gone. John remained in reception hands in his pockets, surveying the seafront road. The two men were both reading their newspapers, already bored and resigned to their fate. He couldn't help laughing out loud as the Aston Martin drove past them followed by a family saloon, driven by the second man. He continued to laugh as they struggled to pull out and do a quick U-turn. They failed miserably in achieving both. Very discreet John mused.

Still laughing he walked up to reception and booked in. His client had, he knew reserved and paid for a room. Once in the room he made it look as if he'd stayed the night. Leaving the television on, he left, closing the door and leaving a, 'Do Not Disturb,' hanger. In a few minutes he was back in the bar where he ordered a whisky and a taxi in that order. Twenty minutes later, he was at Dover Priory Railway Station booking a train to London, London Bridge. Two hours later he was at bustling London Bridge waving down a black cab and in just over half an hour later he was sliding a key into to front door of his bijou flat at the northern stretch of Drury Lane. WC2B.

His flat was small but comfortably furnished and he loved the fact that stepping out the door he was at the centre of everything that mattered in London. His country estate, as he called it, was a large house with a garden running down to the river at Goring on Thames. He only really stayed there when London wore him out, which these days was with increasing frequency. Tomorrow he would visit his bakery but now he felt like partying. He would start with his favourite pub, The Cross Keys, just five minutes' walk away in Endell Street. He had spent his youth in Covent Garden and lots had changed since then but this place hadn't, it was exactly the same as the day he'd first discovered it in 1981. Inside it was comparable to an antique shop, every available space was taken up either with a picture, mirrors or a decorative ornament. It was both eccentric and stately at the same time. As he stood at the bar enjoying his first pint he wondered where his tail was now and started laughing out loud, again.

A216 Aprroach Road – Calais Ferry Port, France.

The wind was picking up, bringing with it the first touches of an Autumn chill. It wasn't pleasant but he didn't care. This world had taken everything from him. He'd always been honourable, throughout his life he had striven always to do the right thing. And how had he been repaid? Life was so unfair. He was ashamed to want to go out this way, it was a sin in Islam to take your own life, life was seen as a gift from God. He prayed his action would be looked upon mercifully and he'd be allowed into paradise. He'd love to be honoured as a martyr but knew that his exit wouldn't be seen as such. It would be seen as shameful.

A passing car, its wheels only inches from his head, focused his attention. It had to be a lorry and one was coming now. This was his moment.

Cobham – England

The two men from ERSOU, watched as the Aston Martin pulled into a forecourt with a number of 'out of reach' cars parked. Even more, further 'out of reach' cars starred in a brightly lit showroom. The two officers parked across the road waiting for their target to step out. It had taken all their skill to catch up with the Aston, thankfully for them, Mr Mitchell hadn't been in a hurry. A few minutes later a second car pulled in, a characterless family saloon. The officers watched with intensity, this was more like it. The driver's door to the Aston opened and out stepped a slim lanky man sporting a moustache. In disbelief coupled with horror they watched as the man locked the car door, walked across to the saloon and got in. With no other option they followed the saloon, radioing back to control what had occurred. The language that followed is, I'm afraid, not possible to print. The man who'd been driving the half a million pounds Aston was dropped off at a respectable semidetached and the saloon driver ended his journey at something similar. Checks found they were both employees of the garage.

At Dover two more officers were stationed at the Premier Inn. Showing their ID, they explained to the two girls on reception that they were interested in the man in room 17. They didn't want to disturb him, just watch his movements. With cups of coffee they settled down for the night in the office behind the reception desk. Both wished their colleagues, now somewhere in Cobham, every bloody harm.

CHAPTER
—12—

Gendarmerie Nationale – Calais, France

There was no sunrise that morning, just a lighter shade of grey. The colour captured Capitaine Maubert's mood perfectly. He was already in his office starting the morning, exactly as he had ended the day yesterday, reading the transcript from Ismail's recording.

According to his testimony, he along with several other migrants had been offered free passage to the UK by a couple, male and female who he thought were French. They had told him they worked for an organisation who wanted to help people who were genuinely fleeing for their lives, to get to the UK. People because of their misfortune, hadn't the funds to pay traffickers. These people were like angels, sent by God, he had recorded.

It had been agreed, the following evening to wait at a food station, in a suburban district of Calais. By Ismail's description it sounded to the Capitaine to be in a district called, Les Quatre Ponts. It was a new food station he recounted. He thought he knew all the food stations, but not this one. When they arrived all were given a welcome hot cup of coffee to stave off the cold. Ismail didn't drink coffee, however accepted anyway as he didn't want to offend. He'd taken one or two sips then discreetly poured the rest away, not liking it. A little while later a white van had turned up and they'd been ushered inside. There had been nine of them including himself, Ismail was adamant about this. Not long after the van had driven off, everybody had started to fall asleep. Not a natural sleep but an enforced sleep is how Ismail had described it. He tried to wake his fellow passengers up but it had been impossible. At first he worried they'd all died but on checking he found them all to be breathing, he just couldn't wake them up. As for himself, he felt a little drowsy but not enough to fall asleep.

The van he remembered after twisting and turning started to speed up and continue at a pace, maybe for about ten minutes when it suddenly slowed and came to a halt. He'd at first thought they'd be let out, but no. The van remained still but no doors were opened. He could hear voices. He couldn't work out any words but the tones in which they spoke sounded as though they were frustrated and as the wait went on, the tones became more excitable. After maybe an hour, possibly two his fellow passengers began to stir. He was at first relieved, before slowly they all began to fall asleep again. This time though it was different. He had seen this sort of sleep before, in Syria, where he once worked. It was when the army used a certain sort of gas, people just fell. It was like this. The van had also started to chill. He could smell nothing but knew the signs for gas. As he had been trained in Syria, he lay flat with his nose to the floor and up against the door. Once again all around him were motionless. He remained the only one conscious.

Without warning the van started to move, at this point he was experiencing a pain in his chest and close to blacking out. He may have done even, he wasn't sure. The next thing he can remember were people opening the rear doors. He deliberately lay motionless, pretending to be either dead or unconscious, he wasn't sure which. He just lay still. With occasional glimpses through barely open eye lids he could just make out they were parked in some sort of garage. The doors had been left wide open as he can remember seeing the stars in the sky. For a moment there was silence and he took his chance. He'd rolled out of the back and run for the outdoors. All the time he'd expected someone to chase him but no one did. He remembered there was quite a lot of verdant cover and he scrambled under a bush. From his vantage point he'd seen men, in some sort of uniform or overalls, he wasn't sure, start to lift the bodies out of the back. Then somebody closed the garage doors and that was it. He waited maybe half an hour, an hour, maybe two even and then he'd made his escape. There was a nearby road for he heard and saw the lights of the odd car passing. He was too scared to take the road so he walked down hill through open countryside, heading towards lights he could see in the distance. The rest is a blur, maybe because of shock or maybe because of being drugged, he was sure he had been drugged. He'd walked blindly until he started to recognise the odd building, and realised he was back in Calais. Returning to the camp wasn't an option. He'd slept rough, alone, and never in the same place until he'd found Marie. The rest is history.

"What sort of van was it, can you describe it?" The Capitaine, reading, heard his own voice.

"Not really, inside it was a bit like a fridge."

The Capitaine, lay the transcript on his desk and hands in pockets, walked across to the only window and looked out. What was going on out there, and right under their noses. What Ismail had described was, almost certainly a mass kidnapping and even worse, quite possibly murder. Were they, he wondered connected to the findings of the severed heads and torso. Very possibly, it was too much of a coincidence, which would mean quite a large and organised team were operating. He had shown Ismail the portrait robots, (artist sketches), of the severed heads, in the hope they may have been his fellow passengers. But Ismail hadn't recognised anybody or possibly didn't want to admit or was simply too scared even to confirm that they had been. Capitaine Maubert thought it was the former, he simply hadn't recognised them. Which meant there were eight more, possible disappeared.

There came a knock at the door.

"Oui."

"The door opened and there stood a fresh faced officer. The capitaine recognised him as just coming off the night shift."

"Sir I thought you should know, we picked up a body during the night on the A216, a migrant. He'd been killed by a lorry. Most likely, trying to board it."

"So," the capitaine was now sadly used to migrants being killed trying to board a lorry, truck or train whilst in motion. Although wrong, they were to him now, simply a statistic to a problem politicians failed to resolve.

"Well, it's not been confirmed yet, but we have good reason to believe it's the old man who identified the girl, who's head we found. The one who'd claimed to be her grandfather."

The Capitaine turned, "are you sure?"

"Almost certain, yes."

"Ok, thanks for letting me know." The officer gave a single nod in reply and closed the door softly behind him. Merde breathed the Capitaine, merde, merde, merde. He needed a coffee and buzzed through to Colette. She wasn't in yet. Merde.

Marseille – France

Fatima loved Marseille, she compared it to a cooking pot full of different cultures. She could be almost anything and she would fit in. Yes the cultures sometimes clashed and the city, it was often claimed was run by corruption or gangsters but that made the city an exciting place to be, for her anyway.

It was a beautiful morning, the sun was warm, there was a strong sea breeze, but the glass terrace walls protected her from that, at the same time magnifying the heat from the sun. Not working she was dressed in colourful western clothes, not designer but close to it. Everything she was wearing came from good cloth. She took a sip of her coffee, it was good strong coffee, like Persian coffee, reminding her of home. One of the few good memories of home.

Fatima was sat on the terrace of La Suite. A popular café/brasserie facing the old port. The terrace afforded views over the port and being North African run, shisha was on the menu and the service although friendly, could at times be a little chaotic. Fatima loved it. You had to be patient but your patience was always awarded. She sometimes spent hours here, she felt safe here, exposed but safe. Her mind wandered, contemplating everything and nothing. As she often did, she wondered where she'd be in ten maybe twenty years' time. By then she may have lost her looks and her current job. What would she do then? The job suited her, it was a lonely existence but she didn't mind that. To have friends would mean having to have trust and she trusted nobody. No she was happy, very happy with her own company. She often wondered at her job. She loved it, not the sex, she didn't not enjoy the sex but it was more something she simply had to do. What really gave her a kick was the power it gave her over men. She could control a man, spitting him out whenever she wanted. She knew how to hold the attention of a whole room of men, they were a pathetic sex and yet she still took her commands from mainly men.

"Pitgam," the word shook her and she made to stand up. The smart but casually dressed man, who had uttered the code stopped her. "We can talk here, another coffee?" Fatima nodded, a waiter was already hovering. "Two coffees."

Fatima could tell by the way the man was dressed, and by his accent, that he was almost certainly Algerian. She often wondered how big the organisation was as she never met the same contact twice. They weren't all Muslim either, one had admitted that he was a member of the Armenian Apostolic Church. No one really told her what they stood for, or who was in control. Almost certainly a turban wearing, bearded man, hiding in the desert. And what they stood for? All she'd been told was that the organisation was anti-corruption and were active in supporting women's rights, particularly in the Middle East. Their methods may be questionable, but considered Fatima, what little she'd been told as well as learnt, was good enough for her.

She felt the man examining her. "I love it here, it's one of my favourite places in Marseille." Fatima knew he was lying, she'd never seen him here and she had a photographic memory for faces. She doubted even, if he'd visited Marseille before.

"Hmmm I love it too."

"I'm afraid your service is required in colder climes." The waiter arrived and placed their coffees. Her fellow coffee drinker pulled out a packet of Montana cigarettes, lit one and after pulling on it took a long sip of his coffee. Fatima took a sip of her fresh coffee, remaining silent, waiting for him to expand. "Yes there won't be many days left where you are going to enjoy the warmth of the sun." The man smiled still with the cigarette in his mouth.

"I look forward to it," Fatima wasn't lying, Autumn in Marseille brought with it a curtain of melancholy. There was no explanation, it was just there.

"Good," the man took another long sip of coffee. He had almost finished it. "You are to travel to Calais, I've placed your ticket under the menu." Fatima looked at the menu, lying flat on the table. He was good, she hadn't seen him place it. This man, she realised suddenly was a professional and yet he looked harmless, a nobody. That was his greatest skill.

"Merci, when do I leave?"

The man finished his coffee. "This afternoon, you will have to change at Lille. Your hotel reservation is there too. Two weeks."

"What about my work here?"

"Not needed at the moment." The man stood up. "I must be off, good luck." Fatima watched him pay the waiter and then he was gone, milling with the idlers roaming the port.

Fatima reached under the menu and slid out an envelope placing it in her hand bag. She had to pack and finishing her coffee, parted in the opposite direction. No coincidence she knew. Calais, she'd never been there, she hoped she'd like it.

Gendarmeie Nationale – Calais, France

Marie arrived at 9.45am. Capitaine Maubert had never seen her looking nervous before and now she looked almost scared out of her wits.

"My men don't bite, Marie," a poor attempt at lightening the mood. He was dreading what he was going to have to tell her. Marie threw him a look, which simply made things worse.

"Really?"

The Capitaine smiled unconvincingly. "Look Marie, there's something, before we go in I have to tell you."

"How to my protect myself?" The remark was unfair and Marie knew it. "I'm sorry."

The Capitaine waved her apology aside. "It's fine Marie. Look last night another migrant died trying to board a moving lorry." He wished he could avoid Marie's stare. "It's someone we both know, or at least have both heard of." Maries stare strengthened, it wasn't hostile just concentrated. "You already know him or of him. It's Abdul-Jalil, the man who claims to be the grandfather of the little girl's head we found on the beach at Escalles. I gather my men gave you the sketches." Marie nodded her confirmation. Her next reaction was completely unexpected, she simply crumpled before him, bursting into loud floods of tears. After interviewing the lorry driver and reading the report from his officers it was pretty obvious that this had been no attempt at mounting a lorry. The old man had simply had enough of life. Looking at Marie, it was pretty obvious she knew this too.

Dover – England

It was approaching noon and their target still hadn't checked out. The two officers from ERSOU had already, unfairly faced the wrath of their boss and they were beginning to have a bad feeling about room 17. Chances are, and they both were beginning to feel this way, that Mr Mitchell could well be lying dead, on the other side of that door. Dead on noon they asked the manager to unlock the door to the room. Treading carefully at first, their caution catapulted into a sense of urgency and both men almost flew into the room.

Nothing and no one, a great big zero. To trained eyes it was obvious the room had been rigged to make it look as though it had been slept in. Where the fuck was Mitchell? The two officers looked at each other. Who's going to call this in? Neither of them fancied the job.

Ten minutes later, the head of ERSOU was expecting a difficult conversation with his counterpart at the NCA. Roger listened intently, before replying.

"I know he's not there, he's in his flat. I'm stood outside, I can see him through the window." With that Roger cancelled the call. He smiled to himself, wondering how many testicles in ERSOU would be skewered over the next few hours.

After crossing the road, he knocked on the newly painted burgundy door. A rather stout man who's body had seen better days answered. He was still in his dressing gown and revealing enough to let anyone who cared see that he was naked underneath.

John looked at the man from the NCA. "Hello Roger, I've been expecting you."

"Morning John, do you mind putting some clothes on before I come up."

John laughed, "as you wish," and started mounting the stairs. "Close the door behind you." Roger did as he was told.

Wissant – France

Maureen, fully dressed watched through her window at the grey sea and a reflective grey sky. A new dawn had brought with it miserable weather. She didn't care, her personal dawn brought a thrill that exercised her blood. Once more she thought back to yesterday. She was now Bree and starting a new and exciting life. She wondered when Mahon would next contact her. Could it even be today. Mahon was his code name, he had told her. It was to be their own little secret, Bree and Mahon. She still didn't know his real name but she didn't care. Mahon was good enough for her and anyway a code name was far more exciting than using a name given at birth.

How would Mahon next contact her, she was sure he wouldn't risk coming to her flat. She would wait in her usual café. Take longer over her coffee and croissants, give him ample opportunity should he need it.

Five minutes later Bree was sat beside a steamed up window, in her promenade café, wind and rain lashing the outside. Four other tables were taken, one with a young woman, possibly in her early twenties and three couples, all, almost certainly married. The three men all had one thing in common. They all secretly desired the shapely woman sat by the window, enjoying her coffee and two croissants.

Gendarmerie Nationale - Calais, France

The hum of conversation slowed as their Capitaine entered the operations room, and abruptly halted when they recognised the woman with him.

Marie stared around the room. She didn't need to interpret the expression on the sea of faces facing her. The atmosphere as she'd entered had immediately turned hostile. She could feel it polluting the air. Rather than cowing her, it made her all the more determined to get her message across.

"Morning all," the greeting was cheery, Capitaine Maubert either wasn't picking up on the hostility Marie thought or he was doing a bloody good job at ignoring it. "You all know Marie," the Capitaine turned and smiled, Marie beamed back. Rumblings of discontent sounded from those already in the room. The Capitaine held up his hand. "Yes, yes I know we haven't always seen eye to eye but with this investigation, we're all on the same side and Marie has come forward with some valuable information." The Capitaine handed around copies of the transcript from Ismail's testimony. "Before we start, I want you all to read this. It's the transcript of a conversation I had yesterday with a migrant introduced to me by Marie." Marie smiled confidently at the room. When you've finished reading I'm going to ask Marie to tell you all what she has recently experienced amongst the migrants and her concerns."

There was silence as all read the transcript. During the reading, the atmosphere visibly changed from hostility to one of shock. One by one, papers were lowered and faces brought up. When the last to finish lowered his paper and looked back at the capitaine, Capitaine Maubert spoke again.

"I think you'll all agree that from the interview. If he's telling the truth, and having met the man, I believe he is. There is little doubt that a mass kidnapping was attempted. Possibly and probably, in light of recent events, leading to mass murder." There came a round of agreement from the room. "Now I'm going to let Marie tell you what she told me yesterday. Please put any resentment to one side and listen to what she has to say with an open mind."

Marie stepped forward, facing her enemy with a smile. "Morning." She was greeted by a collective morning from the room. It was a good start.

After taking a deep breath, Marie recounted what she had told Capitaine Maubert just before they had met Ismail. That a greater than normal percentage of migrants were simply disappearing after they had left with people traffickers. She sensed the scepticism building in the room as she followed up with her suspicions, that this was simply not the norm. Like the capitaine, when she'd first voiced her suspicions, it was obvious most in the room were doubtful. They were basing their doubt on their own experiences, wayward teenagers and with several, their own characteristics. Bad communicators. Marie took the bull by the horns, "Yes, yes I know, many could simply get lost in their new found lives, but you must believe me there has been a noticeable difference recently, so noticeable that I and several others have picked up on it. And in light of Ismail's experience, I simply feel we can't ignore it."

The capitaine stepped in before the officers had a chance to voice any of their doubts. "I think Marie has a point, especially in the light of the find after the storm and now Ismail's experience. Marie's is a voice on the ground, she knows life amongst the migrants far better than we do. In light of everything I personally feel her views have to be taken seriously, at the very least investigated." There was a collective hum of agreement from the room. Marie looked visibly relieved and smiled a silent, 'merci' to the capitaine. If he saw it, the capitaine didn't acknowledge it. He had the room and wanted to capitalise.

"Now you've all read the transcript, can I have your initial thoughts." As though they were back at school, several hands shot up. The capitaine proceeded left to right. The first was a very experienced officer who had turned down promotion several times. He loved being at street level and feared promotion might take that away from him.

"If what the Ismail bloke says is right and Marie's suspicions," a silent acknowledgement passed between the two, "are correct. That's potentially a hell of a lot of people going missing. And if this is down to a possible red market, these people are being kidnapped for their body parts. Well," the officer spread his arms. "You're going to need a hell of a large building for that and one that is well equipped. You couldn't do this in your garden shed using a scout's knife. Sorry, excuse my bluntness." The officer smiled at Marie. Marie smiled back but her smile failed to conceal her shock. The Capitaine wondered if he'd told her about their investigating possible 'Red Market,' activity here in Calais. He couldn't remember. Possibly, even probably not. Merde! That was inexcusable. He should have told her and have her swear her silence. He needed to do that before she left. The officer hadn't finished. "And surely that sort of operation must be almost impossible to hide, someone will have seen something suspicious and reported it, someone would have talked, surely we will have noticed. How could we not?"

All of the officers concurred with their colleague's assessment, more than one confirming that they had been of the same opinion and had wanted to voice it too.

"I agree," the capitaine started.

"Who notices a missing migrant?" Maria cut in. Several faces in the room looked embarrassed. No one was the silent answer.

" I agree," the capitaine repeated, "which means that if this is happening, here in Calais, right now and right under our noses, it's a highly professional and organised operation. Excuse the pun." Nobody laughed. "We need to start asking our contacts on the ground questions, could this be a terrorist run operation? BRB, reading between the lines, I suspect believe it could be. And there must be large amounts of money involved, both coming in and leaving. Where is it coming from and where is it going to? And going back to the original point. Where do you hide an operation such as this?"

"There'd be a hell of a stink, I mean where, how do you dispose of the rotting corpses. You couldn't just put them in a bin." The comment came from a different officer.

"Good point," the Capitaine agreed. "Which brings me back to my original point, this must be a very well organised and professional operation."

"Are we still looking at the possibility of a so called, 'hospital ship' being involved?" A third officer asked this.

"I don't think we can rule anything out," answered the capitaine.

"Perhaps that's how they're disposing of the bodies, they're weighing them down and dropping them out at sea. That would explain our find, the storm released the heads and corpse that hadn't been properly weighted and bagged. Sorry," another apologetic smile was directed at Marie.

"Another good point," the capitaine acknowledged and one we need to investigate." Capitaine Maubert made a note. "Now any views on the van? Ismail said the interior resembled a fridge."

"Can he not remember what the van looked like from the outside?" Another question where several other officers audibly concurred. The consensus of opinion was that the man must be able to remember something more about the van, more than simply it was like the interior of a fridge inside. "It must be a refrigerated van." This was also a general opinion.

"Maybe not," a lone voice. "It could simply be soundproofed."

Marie stepped in. "I'm afraid he doesn't remember anything about the outside of the van, I've pushed him on it."

"That'll be the drugs, they'll have wiped his memory." Another lone voice followed by mutterings of general agreement.

Capitaine Maubert stepped in. The discussion was running out of control. "Ok, ok. First things first. Yes the van at first sounds like it could be refrigerated but again, and good point, it could just be soundproofed. What do you think about Ismail's comments on his fellow passengers falling asleep? He compares it to a gas attack he experienced in Syria. Any comment?" This time there was a ten second silence before a lone voice piped up.

"If it was made to look like a refrigerated van, couldn't the cooling engine housing be for gas storage instead? No one would even notice." There followed a mix of excited chatter as the room considered this.

"Good point again, I'll put the question to those more technical than us. "And are we all as one, in thinking the coffee contained some sort of tranquillizer or date rape style drug?" There followed a resounding, "oui".

"Have forensics checked the site yet? The site where they were picked up. They may have left traces of whatever nasty it was." Another lone voice.

"Not yet," the capitaine was quick to answer, "and I think we have to take a view as to how we investigate this. Both the BRI and BRB want us to be," the capitaine paused, "how can I phrase this, softly-softly in our approach, almost as though we're not investigating at all. Their combined opinion," there were jeers at this. The infamous rivalry between the two elite forces, meant they were notorious for never agreeing. The Capitaine smiled, "yes I know a minor miracle but they both feel, if we go in heavy handed the big chiefs will just shut up shop. We have to try and catch them in the act. That's their view. Forensics examining an old food station will immediately send out the wrong signals, anyway, we're not sure where it was set up. We only have a rough idea."

"Well how the hell are we going to investigate this, if we can't ask questions, and what about searching premises? How are we going to do that?" It was another lone voice but it could have been the whole room. "Marie do you know where this food station was?"

Marie shook her head. "No," but before she could expand another voice cut across her.

"Yes and if we're looking for a false refrigerated van, how are we going to find it if we can't stop and search?" Once again it was a lone voice but it may as well have been the whole room.

The capitaine held up his right hand for silence. "We'll come to that, Marie you were about to answer."

"No," Marie confirmed, "What, wherever it was, it was not an official station." There was a snigger from one or two of the officers. They didn't really recognise any of the stations as being official.

The capitaine gave them a look but stopped short of rebuking them. He persevered, "Marie can you let me know if you hear anything on the ground about a new food station."

Marie nodded.

"And that goes for all of you," the capitaine returned his attention to the room. "Just because we're going softly with this, doesn't mean to say we can't use our contacts. Just don't give too much away. As for the general investigation, we're going to pretend we're looking for drugs. Assisting us from tomorrow, will be members of the specialist drug unit. They will be familiar faces to some of the criminal fraternity so will bring credence to what we want to portray. Anybody have a problem with that?" Nobody did and nearly all voiced their opinion as it being an excellent idea.

"Now," the Capitaine returned to Ismail's story. "What do we make of Ismail's revelation that after a few minutes the van came to a stop and remained stationary, in his opinion for around one or two hours, possibly more?"

"Do you think it was a planned stop?" One of the officers asked.

Several officers chimed in, with a definite. "No."

"I agree," the capitaine was just about to expand when an officer normally seconded to traffic, raised an arm.

"I think I may have an explanation."

"Go on." The room, following their capitaine's example was listening intently.

"I'll have to check the date, but around a week or so ago there was an accident on the west bound A16. It blocked the autoroute for just over two hours. May I?" The officer moved to a large scale map of Calais and the surrounding area, firmly screwed to the wall. Placing his right index finger at a place on the map he slowly moved it demonstrating, in his view the possible movement of the suspected van. "This is Les Quatre Ponts, where we suspect the food kitchen may have been. Our man describes the van taking several twists and turns before accelerating and keeping a steady pace. Les Quatre Ponts is something of a labyrinth, which would explain the twists and turns. We can then safely assume, they joined the A216, the road leading from the port and if my theory is correct, continued onto the A16 heading for Boulogne. The accident happened just before the sortie, (exit), for the D304 and the D940." The officer tapped the map, "from Les Quatre Ponts to here, depending on your speed would be roughly seven to ten minutes. And it took roughly two hours before the accident was cleared." The room remained silent as the officers took this in.

"It fits," came the first audible comment.

"Makes sense," quickly came another.

Capitaine Maubert stroked his chin. Both his officers were right, the theory fitted and made sense. "Can you, after we've finished, confirm the date and times this took place. It fits but we have to be sure."

"Of course sir, I'll have the information minutes after we've finished. I'll come to your office."

"Excellent, now assuming this to be correct, where do you think the van could have ended its journey. How long was it, Ismail estimated that the van finally stopped after recommencing its route?" The Capitaine scanned the transcript.

"He doesn't say," an officer in the room piped up.

Marie spoke up, "He told me originally that it wasn't long, maybe ten minutes, but im not sure how much credence you can give to that, he may have been blacking out."

The traffic officer was still standing in front of the map, he waved his hand in an arc. "If we take ten minutes as a rule, that would mean they could have finished anywhere here roughly, inland from Wissant." The area the officer indicated was mostly hilly terrain almost entirely rural.

"Bloody hell, that's going to take ages to cover," another officer quickly agreed.

"Yes but we're looking for a large building, there's not many of those."

"Rubbish, the area is dotted with farms, they all have large outbuildings."

The capitaine once again held up his right arm and the room quickly fell silent. "Remember Ismail described walking downhill and seeing lights in the distance which we know to have been Calais, that narrows the options down quite a lot."

The officer, still standing by the map, moved his hand across a much smaller area. "That roughly takes in this area. Still not much to go on."

Capitaine Maubert studied the map intently. He was remembering the heads found off Cap Blanc Nez. He turned to Marie, "Marie did Ismail say anything about hearing the sea?"

Marie shook her head, "no, I'm positive."

"Can you try and find out before you leave the gendarmerie, you can phone from my office, it's completely private, I promise."

Marie nodded, "yes no problem." She was then asked to leave the meeting, as much of the remaining time would be taken up discussing operations. With a broad smile to the room Marie got up to leave to her relief nearly all of the room smiled back and just about audible, there was even the odd 'merci.' Outside she found Colette waiting, who escorted her to a waiting area in reception and a very welcome café noir.

Another forty five minutes was spent mainly going over everything in more detail before planning for the next stage of the investigation. Those gendarmes with contacts on the ground were tasked with gathering as much information as they could. The port and harbour, considering that the investigation had started at sea, it was decided that should be the first stage of the investigation. They couldn't start searching boats without the permission of the Procureur and there was no guarantee they'd get that. Plus it was well known les pecheurs could be, at times, a little sensitive and the last thing they wanted was a confrontation. It was agreed, as requested to tread, 'softly- softly,' and start by using a casual form of questioning and if anyone appeared suspicious they could put in a specific request to the Procureur.

On returning to his office, Capitaine Maubert immediately buzzed Colette to show Marie in. After politely thanking her for her contribution to the meeting and enquiring sensitively as to whether she'd found her experience all that traumatic, he without waiting for an answer asked her to call her friends housing Ismail.

For both in the room, it felt as though the phone was going to ring forever, when to their combined relief a female voice answered. Marie turned her back on the capitaine. Shooing him away with a hand gesture, she exchanged pleasantries with her friend before asking if she could speak to Ismail. There followed a short silence before she started talking in such a hushed voice it was almost a whisper. The capitaine watched with frustration, wanting to hear every word that was being spoken. After what to Capitaine Maubert felt like an eternity, Marie turned to face him, replacing the handset as she did so.

"Well? Did he hear the sea?" The Capitaine was almost physically straining, wanting to know the answer.

"No, Ismail can't remember hearing the sea." The capitaine's facial expression dropped, it was obvious he'd been hoping for a different answer. "But" Marie continued, "he does recall in the distance an inky blackness with the odd light. Different to the cluster of lights nearer to him. On reflection he considers, what he may have seen was the sea and the odd lights, passing ships."

The capitaine couldn't hide his satisfaction at hearing this. He thanked her profusely and offered another coffee which Marie declined. If she stayed any longer she was in danger of starting to think like a gendarme. It was a joke she reassured him. After the capitaine had convinced her that nothing she had heard today must be spoken about outside, Marie left. As she walked down the street, her main thought was on Capitaine Maubert. If he wasn't a gendarme she considered the man could almost be a good friend. Feeling ashamed she quickly pushed the thought from her mind.

Alone in his office Capitaine Maubert sat at his desk. Laid across the top an unfolded IGN map 2103ET, Calais, Site des Caps. As the officer in the room had done, he ran his finger along the suspected route the van may have taken. As he did so there came a knock at the door. As promised the officer had the information on the A16 accident. The date and time fitted. It was their first big break. After the officer had left the Capitaine continued to trace a possible route with his finger. He sketched a route along the D243 through Peuplignes to Escalles and then Cap Blanc Nez where he rested his finger. Cap Blanc Nez. It fitted perfectly, roughly a ten minute drive, perhaps a little more, Calais was spread out below the Mont and so was the sea. The one thing that was missing, was a large building. On Mont d'Hubert, there was the 'restaurant panoramique,' the Tunisian restaurant that offered the best casse-croute the capitaine had ever tasted. It could hardly be described as large. Even so, maybe they should take another look. A much closer look.

Covent Garden – London, England

Roger eyed his former colleague and loosely in the loosest sense of the word, friend. They'd hardly seen each other since he'd left Her Majesty's service. In fact on the rare occasion they had spoken it was usually because the man sat opposite him had needed a favour. He had never refused and he wished now that he had done as the pit in his stomach belied a horrible suspicion that those favours were about to come back and haunt him. After a troubled nights sleep at the Premier Inn, he had left Havant at four in the morning. Once in his office he had spent the next few hours examining what records there were, on Mr John Mitchell. He hadn't found much. There was his service record, much of which was classified and since his departure he had set up and run a continental bakery in Putney. Anyone leaving the service is tracked for a few years after and his choice of direction had raised a few eyebrows. There were suspicions that he was debt collecting for a few dubious clients but this hadn't been followed up and if the truth were told a blind eye had probably been turned. He had known about the debt collecting almost as soon as his ex-colleague had started, for John had asked him to trace the debtors for him using the NCA's database. In return he had been paid thousands of pounds in cash. Something now he deeply regretted. How had he been so bloody weak, so bloody, bloody stupid.

John, now fully dressed looked quizzically at the man sat opposite him. He, if he wanted to could bring his ex-colleague tumbling down and the man sat opposite him knew it. At the same time it would be stupid to try, Roger was more useful to him alive than dead and he knew that if he did, it would probably be his last day walking this earth as well. In their business you became acquainted with characters who walked on the dark side of life. Characters who at the blink of an eye would kill out of loyalty, just as much as they would for money. In the secret services you sometimes had to hold hands with such characters. In return it would, to them be dishonourable not to help out in a crisis. Killing someone wouldn't be given a second thought. Going to the fridge he cracked open a couple of beers, he hadn't asked, he knew Roger would accept and he did. Sitting back down he raised his glass.

"To laying past ghosts."

"To laying past ghosts," Roger toasted. It had been their personal toast when in the services and applied even more today. "So John I hope you're keeping your nose clean." John in reply, pulled out a colourful handkerchief and rubbed his nose. Finishing he spread his arms wide, making a point. Roger ignored the gesture. "You know the NCA, SEROCOU, ERSOU and the Hampshire Constabulary are all very interested in you, and I in my role at the NCA have had to encourage it. Even direct it."

"Is that why those two goons were following me?" John guffawed, taking a swig of beer. His actions were all bravado, underneath he was a bag of nerves.

Roger smiled, "They made sure the Aston Martin was delivered safely." Both men couldn't help chuckling at this, resulting in the atmosphere lightening slightly.

"I suppose you've come to see me about this." John held up yesterday's paper with the headline announcing the brutal murder of a known gangster in Langstone.

"Actually no, I want to know what you were doing in Spain. But." Roger paused, "if you want to tell me about that," Roger nodded at the headline, "too, I'd be very interested to hear."

John silently kicked himself. He'd assumed it was about Langstone and the murder of Roger Preston. Now he'd given away that he knew something. SHIT. "Spain? But you know what I was doing in Spain, collecting a car."

"From whom?"

John knew his former colleague had him, the man he was about to name, if the NCA had checked the records, and they will have done had been registered as dead for over 5 years. How can he explain that.

"From a Michael Swinton."

"The gangster and all round bastard?"

"Yes."

"And you didn't think to let me know, even though you knew all of the UK law enforcement were looking for him."

"Come on, he retired years ago Roger."

Roger ignored this. "I won't ask how you found him, a favour no doubt," a slight discoloration touched John's cheeks. "If I show you a recent photo do you think you could do me the honour of identifying him?"

John shrugged his shoulders, "of course, why not?" Roger pulled out a large photograph from an A4 envelope and placed it face down on the low table between them.

He leant back, "can I have another?" John gave a single nod and pulled out two more beers from the fridge. This time he didn't crack them open. He passed one to Roger who cracked it himself and poured the amber liquid into the empty highball.

"Well, aren't you going to take a look?" John knew the tactic, placing a photo face down was to make the other person nervous. And John had to admit he was, why play this tactic on him? Slowly he turned the photo over and had to breathe in deeply to stop himself from gagging. The photo depicted the severed head of the man he'd only days before, collected the Aston Martin from. His widened eyes suggested he'd almost definitely died whilst being tortured and his genitalia may or may not have been stuffed in his mouth before or after he died.

John tried to make light of the photo before him. "Well he wasn't like that when I left him." Roger ignored him and placed two more photos face down on the table. John raised an eyebrow.

"Take a look," Roger gestured. John turned each one over. In one photo he recognised, obviously dead, the wife and in the other, the man's sweet daughter who had made him coffee. She was also very obviously dead.

"The bastards," John whispered. He was more shocked by the photo of the girl than his client's severed head. Yes the head was disgusting but it took a certain sort of person to kill a child. Roger wasn't stupid, he had read John's expression as he turned each photo over. The shock was obvious, he knew nothing about the murders. At least not the daughter's.

"Agreed, Roger nodded, can you tell me anything? Even if you don't want to. I promise no one will know where I got it from."

"It was a debt collecting job. I had to get the Aston back, you know that."

"Nothing else? Rumours on the dark side are that Michael was into someone for a lot of money. You weren't sent to collect that?"

Michael shook his head, "no nothing more."

"Look at the girl John, we need to get the bastard responsible for this."

John picked up the photo of the dead girl, a tear rolled down one cheek, there came a painful silence after which John shook his head. "No nothing more, just the Aston."

Roger sighed, "Ok John, if you say so, then can you explain why Mr Swinton is registered as dying from a heart attack five years earlier?" Again, John shook his head.

"Sorry, no, I've no idea."

"And how did you find him John, we've been looking for this bastard for years, how come you found him when we couldn't?"

John looked at his old colleague, straight in the face. "You know I can't tell you that Roger."

"I know," Roger suspected it had been John's only straight answer and the only one he could expect. If it had been the other way around he wouldn't have given up his source either.

Roger pulled out another photograph and laid it on the table, this time face up. The face of Roger Preston, the man murdered at Langstone stared back at them. His eyes contained the same terror and his, slightly smaller genitalia were protruding from his mouth. Roger caught the flicker of recognition in John's eyes. It was impossible to hide. "Want to tell me about him? You can see the resemblance." Roger held up both photos of the severed heads.

"He was a client."

"Client?"

"It's what I call people I'm contracted to collect money from."

"Really? That's nice. Was it the same people who contracted you for Mr Swinton?"

John wasn't going to be caught out. "No, Mr Swinton was purely the Aston." John knew that Roger knew he was lying, it was a game that had to be played though, by both of them.

"Ok and can you tell me, if Mr Preston paid up?"

"Yes he did."

"How much?"

"I can't tell you that Roger but it was a lot of money."

Roger examined his former colleague's face. "John you know we can examine anyone's accounts." John shrugged. "We've examined Mr Preston's accounts, all of them and we can find no significant movement of money. Thousands yes but not tens or hundreds of thousands. How did he pay you?"

"Cash."

"And have you told the Inland Revenue?"

John smiled, "what do you think?"

Roger actually smiled. "And can you explain that according to records held at GRO, Mr Preston also died of heart failure around five years ago, can you shed any light on that?"

"I'm sorry Roger, I'd like to help, I really would."

"Ok John." Roger finished his second beer. "Look John you've seen the photos, whoever did this doesn't take prisoners. If you really don't know anything about who did, I think that somewhere you may have a leak which you might want to close. And take great care not to piss anyone off or it might be your head I'm picking up and your prick is so small, no one will notice it's even stuffed in your mouth."

"Very funny." John stood up to see his ex-colleague out.

"Don't worry I can let myself out and John," Roger turned, "if you do hear anything, please give me a call, I'm asking as a friend."

John nodded, "actually there is something, something that happened yesterday and still bothering me, it may be connected."

"Go on."

John described what happened at La Sirene restaurant in France. The oversexed woman hitching a ride in his car.

"Sounds like a plant, John, let's face it, you're not exactly God's gift are you. Roger patted John's stomach.

"I had the Aston."

"Ah," Roger admitted, "that changes everything, did you get her name or number?"

"No but I gave her my card."

"Well if she gets in touch, which if she's a plant, she will. Get her name and number and I'll check her out for you."

"Thanks Roger."

"It's nothing, but one good turn deserves another."

"I know."

"Ok, take care John," and with that Roger let himself out.

From his window John watched his ex-colleague make his way north towards the A40 and Museum Street. Roger never took the tube, somewhere he either had a car or a police driver waiting. Almost certainly the latter, with instructions if a certain amount of time passed to knock on his door. Finishing his beer he put on his coat. He was going to make a rare appearance at the bakery. That was the only place there could be a leak. What Roger had told him had shaken him to the bone. His operation was beginning to unravel and that would mean only one end. Somewhere he must have been careless, fuck, fuck, FUCK! Going to his microwave he pulled off the back cover. Neatly clipped he pulled out a Glock 17 pistol and silencer. Tucking them into his coat, he descended the stairs. Out on the street he started walking to the tube at Covent Garden. There were, as usual, hundreds of strangers thronging the street. Any one of them could be his enemy. It was not a nice feeling.

Wissant – France

Maureen or Bree as she now liked to think of herself had been sitting in the café for over two hours. She couldn't drink anymore coffee. She had shopping to do, she'd do that and perhaps come back to the café later that afternoon. Maybe she'd treat herself to a Kir. Pulling her coat close, she started running up the street to the local shop.

She didn't see the young man sheltering in a nearby doorway. Last time she had seen him he'd been wearing a uniform. He watched her as she ran past. He couldn't forget their few hours together. It now seemed like it had all been a dream but his stiffness told him otherwise. He was infatuated with that woman. He simply had to have her again. Even if it cost him his job.

Chapter 12

Gendarmerie Nationale – Calais, France

Capitaine Maubert spent the rest of the afternoon in his office. Regular reports came in from his officers on the ground but with each report, there was always nothing to report. Not even a hint of anything untoward. Les pecheurs had to his surprise, in general been more than cooperative, but there also his officers had found nothing to report. Nothing remotely suspicious. How could, if their suspicions were correct, such a large operation simply go unnoticed. It just wasn't possible. Only Marie, up until now, had spotted anything worth reporting and he had almost dismissed her. He smiled inwardly recalling her courageous stand with his officers. Having got to know her a little, he was finding he actually liked the woman. A woman who previously had been such a pain in their backside.

Once again he went back to questioning how such an operation could go unnoticed by his officers. Between them they knew just about every face in Calais. Perhaps not directly but through a friend of a friend or an extended family member. Somebody somewhere would have seen and said something, but nothing. It was as though a ghost was running whatever it was. Or a stranger, perhaps a group of strangers, someone new to the area. A light started to shine, where before there had been none. He buzzed through to Colette. "Colette, can you contact the Hotel de Ville. Tell them I need a list of every house purchased or rented in the last five years, for the latter I'm particularly interested in long term rentals and purchases from people outside the Calais area."

"They're going to love you."

"I know." The Capitaine smiled to himself, he could almost hear the protests already. Once again he found himself looking at the map. Perhaps he was biased but everything they'd learnt so far seemed to point to Mont d'Hubert and Cap Blanc Nez. It had taken some persuading but the Procureur had agreed to a raid or rather a search of the

Tunisian restaurant on the summit of Mont d'Hubert. It was scheduled for seven tomorrow morning when they'd be busy taking in deliveries. The Capitaine having some sort of relationship with the owner was to lead it himself. The raid was to be carried out in a friendly fashion with the pretence that they had received a tip off regarding drugs.

Baptiste from the BRB had phoned earlier asking for an update and to his surprise when learning of the planned raid, had asked if he could tag along. With his specialist experience, he suggested, he might spot something an ordinary gendarme might miss. The capitaine felt he couldn't really object and readily agreed. Like last time, Baptiste had told him he would be staying at the Hotel and Restaurant de la Plage, facing Calais beach. Perhaps this time, especially if the raid turned out to be successful the Capitaine might care to join him for dinner. This too had been a surprise and he'd accepted. He might even learn more about how the BRB operated.

Baptiste had also asked, no it had been more like an order, to feed the media with the idea that it was generally thought by the authorities, that the find off Cap Blanc Nez and the plage, (beach), at Escalles were drug related. Monsieur Hivin had been tasked with this and at least three newspapers had reported back that this information would feature on their front page tomorrow. Nowhere was the basis of the real investigation, the red market, mentioned.

With darkness closing in, the Capitaine decided to call it a day. It was to be an early start tomorrow and his wife deserved to spend an evening with some company for once. Instead of her cooking, he promised her he would bring back something filling from a friterie. It was far from fine dining but it was a tradition loved in his household. They spent the evening, eating heart stopping food, snuggled up on the sofa watching Peaky Blinders, an import from Britain. After each finishing a bottle of 3 Monts beer, they retired to bed. For five minutes they made love, not especially exciting but sensual and full of feeling. It was confirmation that both cared deeply for the other. When they'd finished his wife fell into a deep satisfied slumber. Thierry, with tomorrow's raid on his mind twisted and turned, struggling to do the same. In the end, worried his restlessness might wake his beloved, he left his bed for his office. Searching on his computer he downloaded an album recommended by a friend. It was by a group from Pays de Galles, (Wales), called Neck Deep. Placing his earphones over his head he settled back into his chair to listen. Before the end of the second track, the Gendarme had joined his wife in a deep slumber.

Covent Garden – London, England

John returned to his flat feeling very frustrated. He had found nothing at his bakery that hinted at a leak, yet it was too much of a coincidence that two of his previous clients had been murdered. He had arranged their disappearance. They'd no longer existed. How had they been found and so quickly, one after the other. The leak must have come from his operation, one of his ex-servicemen must have squealed, probably for a great deal of money. If this was the case, it put his whole operation at risk and more worryingly his life. Roger was simply being honest when he had told him he couldn't protect him. He'd scanned the Spanish media. There was not a hint of what had occurred. He was impressed how Roger and the Spanish authorities had kept it under wraps. Unlike here.

John went to a decanter sitting on a duck egg blue painted cupboard. Pouring himself a brandy he moved over to a window overlooking Drury Lane. It was early evening and the street was busy. Any one of the strangers passing below may be hired to kill me, he thought. How would I even know. For the first time in his life it felt as though someone was a step ahead of him and he hated such a feeling. Just yesterday life had felt so good and now he felt as though he was being dragged into an abyss, an abyss he would never escape from.

Thinking of yesterday, he wondered about the oversexed woman who had asked for a ride in the Aston. Had she genuinely had her head turned by the car or was she a plant? At that moment the phone rang. Picking up the receiver he heard a woman's voice.

"Hello, is that John? John Mitchell?

Wissant – France

It was late afternoon when Maureen returned to the café, in the continuing hope of being contacted by Mahon. There was a storm brewing out at sea, not a fierce one but strong enough to make one want to run for cover. Maureen watched as wind and rain battered the steamed café window. Every time the door opened she hoped it would be her stranger but each time she was to be disappointed, it was mainly people seeking shelter from the weather. A rather annoying young man had entered the café. He kept smiling and trying to catch her eye. He looked vaguely familiar but his behaviour was a real pain. She was forced to spend most of her time trying to avoid his stare. In no way did she want to make eye contact. After a while it became too much, she simply wasn't in the mood that evening. She paid the waiter and strode purposely out of the café, all the time she held her head high, avoiding any unwanted attention.

The young gendarme watched Maureen leave. He'd tried his best but she hadn't noticed him. It was apparent she'd had something on her mind. He wondered about ringing her apartment bell. Surely she'd let him in when she remembered their hours of passion. No, he thought better of it. He was off again tomorrow and he'd come back then and try to initiate, to her, a surprise meeting. As he left the café, he thought through the rain he glimpsed his woman getting into a smart Mercedes. His training clicked in and he automatically noted the licence plate. He could always check it out. He looked at his watch, he had to get home. He'd told his wife he was going fishing. Only mad fisherman and Englishmen go out in this weather but as the rain and wind intensified, he knew it was becoming less and less believable.

Maureen was just about to put her key into the lock of the door of the lobby when, "Bree."

She spun round. She recognised the Mercedes and her heart jumped.

"Bree," the passenger window was wound down. She saw a smartly dressed arm beckoning. "Bree, get in."

Maureen didn't hesitate. Within seconds she was sat in the 'cockpit' and they were gliding out of Wissant. Mahon smiled at her but said nothing. Where was he taking her? Maureen didn't care, she simply didn't care.

Gare De Calais Ville – Calais, France

Why do people choose to live here was Fatima's first thought as she stepped off the train. That morning she had been enjoying a coffee, in the warmth, under a blue sky, wearing summer clothes. Now she was buttoning up to her neck to keep out the cold and wet and battling the wind to stay on her feet. As she left the station ticket hall a small saloon pulled up. The car stopped and the driver got out. Apparently oblivious to the conditions, he enquired, "Fatima?" Fatima nodded. "Please get in." The man walked around opening the rear door. He was about to take her suitcase but Fatima held him off, the case was staying with her.

With the doors closed, Fatima casually uttered, "Pitgam."

The driver, nodded. "Of course Madame, your hotel is on the seafront. I hope you like sand."

It was the right response, word perfect. "Take me there." Fatima commanded.

Fatima watched through rain slashed windows as they voyaged down the brightly lit Rue Royale, past the Place d'Armes, past the harbour and then along the rain battered seafront. Her hotel was halfway along. Modernish it was comfortable without showing off. The rooms were out the back with the bar and restaurant affording sea views. The hotel was equally popular with both French and international clientele. Her staying there wouldn't arouse the slightest attention. It was the perfect and Fatima knew, deliberate choice. Her booking had already been paid. Within minutes she was in her room, clean with clean lines, it was perfect. After half unpacking, she ventured to the bar. She'd already eaten on the train and was happy to settle down with a Ricard. A side table held several newspapers, mostly local. She picked one up. It was two days old she noticed, everywhere there was the story of the severed heads and torso found in La Manche, after the 'storm of the century.' There's a 'storm of the century' out there now Fatima thought to herself. Turning the cover page, on the inside there was more about the same story. Inset was a smallish photo of a man in uniform. He was, so the paper claimed, the man leading the investigation. A Capitaine Thierry Maubert. Fatima recognised the photo, he was also to be her next target. Hello Thierry, she whispered to the photo. I look forward to meeting you.

Wissant – France

For several minutes Mahon drove without talking, his facial expression wore a seriousness she had never seen before but his persona remained friendly. She didn't feel uncomfortable, just curious.

"You're sure you're ready for this Bree?" His first words surprised her.

"For what?"

"To become a spy." For the first time since she'd got in the car Mahon smiled, in fact he grinned.

"Definitely." Maureen had never been so certain of anyything.

"Good," Mahon nodded. "Good." Maureen saw that they were approaching Audresselles, an attractive seaside village with a large square, famous for its crab fishing and mussel collecting. The square was often used by English motor clubs as a meeting point. Mahon guided the Mercedes into the square and circled. He didn't stop but proceeded to return along the coast road towards Wissant.

"You've still got the card, the card of the man with the Aston Martin?"

Maureen nodded proudly, "Of course."

"Good, I want you to ring him, tell him you're coming to London. Joke with him, hint at wanting another ride in his car. You know what I mean."

"I do," Maureen grinned, she knew exactly what Mahon meant and she knew her newly acquired skills meant she was bloody good at it. "Do I do this as Maureen or Bree?"

"I've thought about this, I think it's best you travel under your own name but with your target," Maureen felt a thrill run through her veins at the mention of the word target, "play our game. Tell him you're called Bree. If he begins to suspect there's no need to keep up the pretence, tell him your real name. The fact that you used an alias, will intensify his excitement."

"What exactly am I meant to do?" Maureen still wasn't sure. She suspected Mahon wanted her to seduce her target, in that she was very confident. It would be easy, but then what?

"I'll fill you in tomorrow." They were approaching Wissant now and Mahon silently guided the car into town, coming to a rest in the old square dominated by its 15th century church. Leaning to the back seat he gave Maureen an envelope. "Here are your ferry tickets, and train to

London. We've booked you into the Fielding Hotel in Covent Garden, it's right in the centre, you'll love it." Maureen couldn't believe what she was hearing, surely this must all be a fantasy. "I've booked you a taxi, meet me for lunch tomorrow at the Hotel de la Plage on Calais seafront, the taxi has instructions to take you there first. It will pick you up sometime after eleven tomorrow morning."

Maureen nodded, she looked disappointed.

"I'm sorry I can't come up," Mahon leaned across kissing her gently on the lips." Before Maureen could respond he pulled away. "I'm sorry I can't come up," he repeated, "I'm working tonight and sorry I can't drop you back to your door, I'm already late." Maureen nodded her understanding and quickly exited the car. Slowly she started to walk back to her apartment, she was so turned on that she almost felt like grabbing any man who passed her in the street. As fate would have it, no man did and minutes later she was in bed, in her apartment pleasuring herself to orgasm. Mahon had in fact wanted to come back but as he had picked Maureen up he had spotted a man in his mirror paying a little too much attention to his car. He was old and wise enough not to invite trouble. Anyway he had an appointment to keep and she was almost certainly already waiting for him.

Chapter
—13—

Cap Blanc Nez – France

The rain from last night had reduced to a drizzle. The wind had subsided to a stiff breeze, uncomfortable still if you weren't well wrapped up. Neither really bothered the capitaine but what was a worry, was the sea mist that enshrouded Cap Blanc Nez. You could hardly see your hand in front of your face and the lack of visibility could hamper their operation. There was a point where the general thought process was to delay it by a day but being the coast there was no guarantee what the weather would hold tomorrow, and a decision, prompted by Baptiste of the BRB, was made to go ahead.

Four vehicles would approach from both the East and West of Cap Blanc Nez. Along the D940 coast road. On arrival at their target, twelve officers were to surround the restaurant, to ensure nobody attempted to get away. This may sound easy but the restaurant was cleverly housed in a WW2 bunker with the surrounding terrain being distinctly rough, pitted with craters, courtesy of the RAF and interspersed with scrub. The mist would make this task all the more difficult.

Baptiste joined the Capitaine in his 308. He came dressed in almost military fatigues and wearing a stab vest, something the Capitaine hadn't been expecting. As they mounted Cap Blanc Nez the wipers had to be on full, wiping the windscreen free of water droplets from the mist, only to be replaced in seconds by thousands more. It meant the climb up Cap Blanc Nez was something of a crawl. Blue lights and sirens were turned off to aid the element of surprise.

The vehicles carrying those tasked with surrounding the restaurant, parked alongside the D940 and blocking the vehicle entrance and exit to the restaurant's car park. The twelve officers quickly and silently, aided by the lights from the restaurant, surrounded the designated area. A signal was passed to the Capitaine that all was ready and the raid began. The remaining vehicles raced up to the restaurant's entrance. To one side of the restaurant two large doors were open, receiving a delivery from a refrigerated van. Parked to one side was the restaurant's own refrigerated van, used mainly for their "service traiteur.," (catering). Several officers targeted the delivery and storage area whilst the Capitaine, Baptiste and four other officers banged on the customer entrance door.

A familiar and rather frightened looking face answered the door.

"Capitaine what on earth's going on?"

"I'm sorry Karim," the Capitaine was all smiles. "We've had a tip off for drug running here, it may be one of your staff. We have no option but to take these allegations seriously you understand. You're not alone, we will be checking other places too."

The owner opened the door, stepping back to allow access. "Please, please, come in." The officers accompanying the capitaine silently and efficiently rushed through. The capitaine turned to Baptiste, what is it exactly we're looking for?"

"Medical knives as opposed to kitchen, PPE, tables that could be used to lay bodies on. To be honest I don't really know. Anything that doesn't belong in a restaurant."

Very helpful, went through the capitaine's mind but said nothing.

"I'm going to look at the storage area, perhaps best if you keep an eye here." Baptiste didn't wait for an answer, he was gone.

"Do you want a coffee capitaine? Whilst your men are working."

I'm working too thought the capitaine but accepted the owner's offer. When the owner returned, the capitaine gestured for him to sit down.

"Karim, you're sure you've seen nothing untoward up here, we've had a tip off that drug traffickers are using refrigerated vans to conceal their operation."

"I promise you nothing, nothing." The owner shook his head.

"How many vans do you have?"

"One refrigerated and one ordinary."

"Can my men take a look?"

"Yes of course," the owner stood to get the keys but the capitaine stopped him.

"We'll wait till my men have finished here." The owner sat down again and the two engaged in almost friendly conversation whilst the search continued around them. A little more than twenty five minutes later the four officers searching the restaurant's public area and kitchen, arrived to report.

"Clean Capitaine, nothing out of the ordinary as far as we can see. We've even removed a couple of panels and nothing. Though I'm not really sure what we're looking for. "

"Good, so far so good," the capitaine smiled at the owner. "Now let's check your vans."

Outside the search of the delivery and storage area was in full swing. Baptiste was very thorough, the capitaine had to give him that. Every box had been opened and officers were expertly tapping walls checking there was nothing concealed behind. A dog trained to find traces of human blood was hard at work. Outside in the carpark all the workers were lined up, looking very bewildered.

"Anything?" Baptiste called seeing the capitaine. Capitaine Maubert shook his head.

"No, nothing. You?"

"Not yet," Baptiste was remaining positive but the capitaine had a sinking feeling, they weren't going to find anything. He had been wrong and yet he'd been so sure. The refrigerated van proved to be clean, the fridge motor was a fridge motor, not altered to hold gas. The second van was kept in a garage, once a bunker, and like all the other buildings , secreted into the hill. This van also proved clean and the garage too. At the back there was a walk in freezer, it was the biggest the Capitaine had ever seen. It had come from a warehouse the owner had explained. Inside hung joints of meat and on shelves all manner of frozen produce. Everything inside was checked too but nothing that shouldn't be there was found. Last but not least, the walk in fridge was searched and the delivery van. Again nothing. The dog showed an interest in both the fridge and the freezer, but crucially it didn't bark, something it was trained to do if it sensed traces of human blood or tissue. The dog was just being a dog, interested in its next opportune meal. The men surrounding the restaurant were called in from the mist, resulting in quite a crowd gathered out front. The enterprising owner offered all coffee. Why not, considered the Capitaine but out here in the carpark not in the restaurant. Fifteen minutes later the last gendarme vehicle had left the premises. Before leaving there had been much shaking of hands, thanks for the coffee and several apologies for the intrusion. The Capitaine was also handed a bill.

It was a short drive back to the gendarmerie but to the capitaine it seemed to take forever. He couldn't help but let his despondency show. Baptiste was less so.

"That's police work Capitaine, we have to pick ourselves up and start again. At least we've ruled out one theory. It will no longer distract us from looking elsewhere."

The capitaine had to agree, but where the hell did they look next?

Chapter 13

Covent Garden – London

It was gone ten when John stepped out of the shower. Although the warm water had helped, his head still felt heavy from emptying the decanter of brandy the night before. Wearing only a towel for protection he walked to the lounge window that overlooked Drury Lane. London town unlike the City of London wasn't an early riser and very few people trod the pavements below.

Putting on a gown he made his way to the kitchen. A God almighty fry up was what he needed. Going to the fridge he took out four rashers of bacon, three sausages, two slices of black pudding and two eggs, From a store cupboard a tin of baked beans, and from a wicker basket, two field mushrooms. He was going to enjoy this. He patted his stomach. He knew this part of his body along with his south hugging bottom put the opposite sex off but he was past caring. He'd have to accept if he wanted a sex life he'd have to pay for it, or buy a really flash car. The thought brought him back to the woman in France. How could a woman like that, remotely find him attractive. She'd been so glamorous, so full of life. He was an idiot if he felt she was interested in him. If it wasn't the car she must be a plant. But why? Perhaps he was over estimating his importance in that respect too. The phone call last night had been an insurance agent. He should have been expecting it. He'd forgotten. Age had nothing going for it his grandmother had once told him, God rest her soul. She had been bloody right.

Pouring oil into the frying pan, he turned on the gas. He didn't hear it at first, it took several rings before he realised his phone was ringing. Picking up the receiver, sounding a little breathless from rushing to pick up he answered simply, "Hello." A woman's voice answered.

"Hello, is that John, John Mitchell, are you alright?" the voice sounded concerned.

"Yes, yes, sorry I was in the shower when the phone rang."

"Oh sorry," the woman on the other end giggled. "John I don't know if you remember me, we met in France, outside the fish restaurant. You gave me a ride in your lovely car. You gave me your card. Remember?"

"Yes, yes I do, how are you? Sorry I don't believe you ever gave me your name." He was shaking, she must be a plant but an erection was already growing with the thought of seeing her again. Why were men born so weak?

"Bree, Bree Fowlis, B-r-e-e, not the cheese" the woman answered. "I hope you don't mind me calling you, but you gave me your card." Maureen was kicking herself for revealing her surname. That hadn't been her plan.

"No not at all."

"Well you said if I were coming to London to look you up, and I am, this afternoon. Will you oblige me by giving me a ride in your beautiful car again?"

"Of course," John lied, how long are you staying for?"

"Not sure yet," the woman he now knew as Bree answered excitedly. "A few days, maybe a week. Depends how much fun I have," she laughed. John felt his erection growing. "Anyway must go, my taxi's outside. I'm staying at The Fielding in Covent Garden."

"Ring me when you get here," John almost begged.

"I will, I promise." The line went dead. John looked at the display on his phone. It recorded a French mobile. He wrote the number down before entering it in his phone. Did he care if she was a plant. He wasn't sure if he did. If he could experience a body like hers, it, the consequences, no matter how bad, would be worth it. He picked up the receiver again. It would be prudent to check her out anyway, to be prepared…

WHOOSH!

The sound came from his kitchen. Pulling open the door he was greeted by the sight of flames leaping from the frying pan.

Chapter 13

"SHIT. – SHIT,SHIT,SHIT."

A Private Hospital – South Kensington, London

A consultant was trying to placate a large American patient. He had flown in for a liver transplant. Something he'd have to wait a long time for in the states and time wasn't something he had.

He'd arrived in London with the promise of an immediate turn around and five days later he was still waiting for his operation and this dick head was telling him he still couldn't guarantee when it would be. He'd paid over a million bucks for this shit, typical crap British service.

"We have a liver ready for you sir but you won't accept it."

"I don't want a liver from a someone who's a funny colour, I want one from someone the same colour as me, white, jeeze is that too difficult to understand?"

"Yes sir, but caucasian livers are much rarer."

The American's skin colour went from white to almost red. He pointed his finger, "you fucking told me you had one, you were happy to take my fucking money, now I want my fucking liver, even if you have to kill somebody for it!"

Little did the American know, that's exactly what had to happen.

Wissant – France

The gendarme had waited all morning in the café, hoping to spot his so far, 'one off,' lover. From where he sat he had a view of her apartment's lobby door. Still not a sign. He was just about to give it up as a bad job when a taxi pulled up outside. And there was his woman, HIS woman exiting the apartment block. She was dressed to kill and carrying a medium size, designer suitcase. The driver opened the door and in she slid, immediately the taxi started to pull away. Leaving more money than was necessary on the table the gendarme left to find his car. Two minutes later he was speeding out of Wissant. If his woman was carrying a suitcase she was almost certainly making for the ferry port. Or possibly the airport at Marck. Working on this supposition, he swung his car recklessly onto the D940, racing, breaking every speed limit, heading for Calais. At the summit of Cap Blanc Nez he had the taxi in his sights, he'd been right. Immediately he braked and thereafter he was careful to keep a discreet distance behind. After passing through Sangatte and Bleriot Plage the taxi turned left to run along the beach front road of Calais Plage. Instead of continuing to the ferry port, halfway along the taxi turned into the hotel guest parking for the Hotel de la Plage. The gendarme did the same. Like the taxi he didn't bother to park in a bay, simply resting across two. He watched as his woman got out, he saw her wave to three men sat at a table in the restaurant window. One of the men waved for her to wait, probably in reception. His woman then disappeared through the reception doors. He decided to park and follow her in, always at a safe distance, he didn't want to alarm her. Any meeting had to look accidental. Choosing a parking bay facing reception, he reversed, turned off the engine and cracked open the door. He hadn't opened the door more than an inch when he heard his passenger door being pulled open and something wrapped around his neck. Helpless he slumped back into his seat. Within a split second someone outside had slammed his door shut and could be seen casually, hands in pockets, walking towards reception. He heard his passenger door slam shut and with relief, felt the tie around his neck loosen. Something hard was pressing against his stomach, he turned to see a man of Mediterranean appearance sitting in the passenger seat. He wore a smile, not a friendly smile but a smile that gloated satisfaction. In his hand he held a pistol with a silencer attached. That's what was pressing against his stomach.

"Drive."

"Where to?" The gendarme's voice was hoarse with fear.

"Left out of the car park. I'll direct you from there." The gendarme did as he was told, trying to keep the motion of the car as smooth as possible. As he turned onto the seafront he felt his stomach give and a damp feeling in his underwear. Swallowing, he glanced at his captor. The man made no acknowledgement of what had just passed. Only his smile was broader, displaying even greater satisfaction.

Gendarmerie Nationale – Calais, France

There were a pile of newspapers waiting at reception when the Capitaine and the man from the BRB arrived back at the gendarmerie. Most had picked up the line fed to them by Mathieu and printed a story connecting the severed heads to the drug trade. None though ran it as a headline. How quickly the media forget. There were no International media left in Calais and no media presence when they raided the restaurant. The office was still getting daily calls but nothing like the harassment experienced a few days ago.

For the next few hours, Capitaine Maubert spent his time with Baptiste, going over what action they had taken so far, and what they had discovered, which wasn't a great deal. Together they once again looked at the theory of the accident and delay on the A16 and together they looked at other alternatives. There didn't appear Baptiste admitted to be many. Perhaps there was another explanation. Perhaps the van had been waiting for something, possibly a boat. Yes but the capitaine had countered, how do you explain the hill and the lights of Calais below. Perhaps the boat had been delayed or for whatever reason, unable to dock. Perhaps where the van finished was an emergency operation, an alternative if something went wrong.

Both men agreed it was a possibility and that the search of boats and port areas should be extended to the East to Dunkirk and to the west as far as Etaples.

The Capitaine went on to explain his theory that if the operation existed at all, then it must be being run by strangers, otherwise his officers would have heard or seen something. He explained his positive action of having the Hotel de Ville furnish him with all the new house purchases in the region over the last five years and all the new rentals, especially long term. He'd been told that he could expect the results by the end of today.

"I bet they love you," Baptiste remarked. The Capitaine smiled.

"Funny you should say that."

The conversation then turned to Ismail and the food kitchen. "We need to explore this further Baptiste suggested. We need to keep an eye on all the food kitchens, who's running them and who's working at them." The Capitaine commented that this may be a very delicate matter as many of the people who ran these kitchens saw his officers as their arch enemy. And see any questions they may ask as confrontational, not asked in the migrant's best interests. Then we need to convince them that they are, Baptiste countered. A comment from someone who knew nothing about the local environment. Capitaine Maubert was beginning to realise why the BRB wanted localised officers running the operation. I have someone who could probably help, the capitaine was thinking of Marie, perhaps even Stephanie though with the latter he was still blaming her, even if only a little, for the recent suicide. The Capitaine painted a positive picture of Marie.

"Do you trust her?" was Baptiste's immediate question.

"In this, yes." Capitaine Maubert was definite.

"Then give her a call."

After Baptiste had left, with a promise to meet him later for dinner at the Hotel de la Plage, the capitaine gave Marie a call. She was quick to pick up. Gone was the reservedness, the suspicion that had always dogged their previous dealings. Marie was all enthusiasm, keen to help if she could. Yes she would come to the gendarmerie tomorrow morning. Eight thirty sharp. Deal. She would bring breakfast.

After the call, Marie found herself smiling. She was actually looking forward to going to the Devil's Den, the gendarmerie. And in particular she was looking forward to seeing Capitaine Maubert. He was forbidden fruit and she found herself giggling.

Covent Garden – London, England

It took a good couple of minutes and the burning of two tea towels before John managed to put the fire out. The whole flat stank of burnt smoke after and despite the inclement weather, he opened every window. The cleansing fresh air was welcome but only for as long as it took to clear the smell of burning. The resulting cold definitely wasn't welcome and the towel robe was quickly replaced by warm clothing. After ten minutes all the windows were once more closed. John went back to the kitchen, throwing the burnt pan in the bin he pulled out another. He was determined to enjoy his breakfast. Once more he added oil to the pan and turned on the gas. As he did so the phone rang again. Swearing, this time John turned off the gas.

"Yes." He immediately recognised the voice on the other end of the phone, it was Roger. "I was just about to ring you. Why are you ringing me?"

"I thought I'd warn you John, the Met are going to investigate your bakery. They've received a tip off, they're not going to find anything are they John." It was a statement not a question.

"Of course not," John knew that Roger was asking not for his benefit but his own. Roger was worried. "What sort of tip off?"

"I don't know John, I can't be seen to be poking my nose in, questions might be asked. From what I understand at first they're going to put your premises under surveillance so keep those goons posing as delivery drivers under control."

"They'll be as good as gold," John promised

"Anyway why were you going to ring me?"

"Maybe it has something to do with it," John said slowly, could the Met be running a honey trap?"

Roger laughed. "No not after Colin Stagg, they've learnt their lesson and before you ask, no it's not us, I'd be the first to know. Why do you ask?"

"That woman I told you about, the one I met in France, the one I gave a ride to."

"Yes."

"She's been in touch, she rang me this morning. She's coming to London, wants me to give her another ride in my car."

"Well she'll be disappointed," Roger joked. "Did you get her name?"

"Yes, hang on." John searched and found the notes he'd made. "Yes Bree, spelt B-r-e-e, not the cheese, Fowlis."

"I don't suppose you have a date of birth?"

"No." He heard Roger whistle the other end.

"Ok, I'll see what I can do. I have to say she does sound like a plant, who have you pissed off John?"

"Half the world."

"Only half?" Another joke. "Oh and John."

"Yes."

"You know I can't protect you."

"I know."

"Not even from the Met."

"I know."

"Ok, just so long as you realise that. Alright I'll see what I can find out about this woman. In the meantime keep your nose clean and take care, be aware of who's walking behind you. Do you have a gun?"

"Yes."

"I didn't hear that, but I suggest you carry it always."

"I am, don't worry."

"I'm not," and the line clicked dead.

John returned to the kitchen. He grabbed the frying pan handle and held it, not moving. Who had he pissed off? There was always someone but no one enough to want to bring him down. And why the honey trap, for he was now sure that's what it was. He trusted Roger to find out. Even if it was, he'd play the game and damn sure he'd see her naked. Once more he felt an erection building in his trousers. Cursing he put everything away. He didn't feel like cooking anymore. He'd eat out. His favourite local café, Diana's Diner had recently closed. Back in the eighties it had been something of a secret celebrity. The original Diana used to create, good honest English food. Once a week her windows were heavily steamed as she made her legendary steamed steak and kidney puddings. People, famous people from the pop and film world, could be seen eating there on a regular basis, enjoying Diana's food without the fear of being disturbed by intrusive fans. Diana had retired, a succession of owners had followed, all still offering a reasonable breakfast and now, not long ago it had closed its doors completely. For John, Covent Garden was moving in the wrong direction. In an even worse mood he slipped his gun into his jacket and stepped into Drury Lane. If anyone pissed him off anymore he'd surely kill them.

Hotel De La Plage - Calais, France

Mahon as Maureen now knew him, saw her taxi pull in. She was early, he hadn't quite finished with his guests. Quite obviously tailing the taxi another car pulled into the car park. Mahon watched intently without giving away his interest to his two guests. He recognised the driver immediately, he'd been trained to notice such things, he was the one taking such an interest in his car the day before. Smiling he waved to Bree as she was to be called from now on, to wait in reception. She acknowledged her understanding with a smile. A single finger movement sent a message to two men, outside sitting in a saloon car. He watched without anyone noticing as the two men dealt with the man tailing her.

Standing up he shook hands with the two men opposite him, thanking them for coming. Moving to the centre of the restaurant, he beckoned for Bree to come and join him. He had to admit she looked a million dollars. A little over the top perhaps but that didn't matter. Her job to some extent was to brighten up a sad man's life, and that she would do effortlessly.

Maureen smiled at the two men who had been sitting with Mahon as they left, neither gave her a second look. Dressed in suits they were almost certainly business associates. Far too busy to notice her. Maureen excused them.

"You're early." Maureen thought her contact looked a little irked in the way he greeted her.

"The taxi was early," Maureen replied, feeling she had to defend herself.

"No matter," Mahon smiled broadly. "You look dressed to kill Bree."

"Do I," Maureen, alias Bree did a twirl, swinging her Faure Le Page handbag, as she did so.

In a corner, deliberately hidden from view, sat a more modestly dressed woman. Wearing a pale mauve hijab that wrapped around her neck before trailing gracefully over her bosom, she watched with interest.

"Come sit down," Mahon gestured to one of the chairs not long vacated by a suit. Maureen did as she was asked.

"Is this a business meeting or social?" she grinned.

"More business than pleasure I'm afraid," Mahon apologised

"That's ok, I thought it might be." Maureen smiled sweetly.

Before they got down to business, Mahon asked if she was hungry. He wasn't he told her but feel free to order. Maureen was starving, she hadn't had breakfast but not wanting to be seen taking advantage of his generosity, ordered a Welch Complet. It was one of the least inexpensive choices on the menu, accompanied by a glass of house white. Mahon simply took bottled water.

"So how are you feeling?"

"Excited," Maureen admitted.

"Have you any idea, what your first mission as a spy is going to be?" Mahon smiled, holding her eyes with his.

Maureen didn't hesitate, she wasn't stupid. "I guess you want me to seduce the fat man with the nice car."

"The large gentleman with the classic Aston Martin," Mahon corrected, always respect your targets Bree. That's probably the most important role as a spy. Never take your target for granted. And yes, we need you to seduce him, but more than that we need you to control him."

"Like a dominatrix?" Maureen was quickly warming to the idea.

"No, no. Not at all, when I say control him I mean you need to make him yours. To create a scenario where you are in total control of your relationship. You must make him want you, need you, desire you. To a point where when you're not with him he's counting the seconds until you are. When you know he will lay down his life for you, that's when you have total dominance. Not physical, but mental. Mental dominance, you have in your hand his heart and his mind. They are both yours to destroy if you wish.

Wow, Mahon was impassioned, Maureen loved the thought. "How do I do that?" She had an idea but needed to be sure.

"Through sex." Mahon was blunt. "But not through normal sex. Your task is not to seek orgasm but power, power over your target. Orgasm if you want but never let him feel he has the power to achieve this for you, it must be your own doing. And never let him inside you, never allow full intercourse. Instead tease him with it, hint that one day you will allow it. With full intercourse it is the man who takes control, who has the power. You must make intercourse his dream, his fantasy. Nothing more."

Maureen felt her tongue sliding between her teeth, this was turning her on and there was nowhere and no way she could satisfy it. She mustn't let her mind wander, she had to concentrate. At that moment her Welch arrived. Mahon gestured for her to eat. Great timing.

"Go ahead, I'll carry on if that's ok." Maureen nodded, wanting to rub his leg with hers but with some effort, restraining herself.

Mahon continued. "You're a strong woman Bree, use your strength as you did with me." Maureen almost choked. "Use your arms, your legs to control him, you are the master in the bedroom. Make him know you're powerful. Dictate the proceedings. Men like your target are in total control of their lives, being controlled sexually by a powerful woman is a great release for them. It's their ultimate fantasy, to abandon their power to a woman, to be controlled, dominated by a woman. Use your strength, your weight to control his submission. Use your body to make it difficult for him to breathe, use your imagination Bree, I know you have one." Maureen made to speak but Mahon hadn't finished. "It's not just the bedroom Bree. When you're out with him make other men desire you, make him jealous. Make your target desire you again even if you've only just finished sex minutes before. Achieve this Bree and you'll have your target eating, drinking, sleeping, breathing you."

Maureen found herself tingling at the thought of achieving her mission, and she was going to be paid for it, or so she thought. Money hadn't been discussed. She had a question. "What am I meant to do, when I have my target under control?"

"We need information Bree, information only your target can give us. I can't tell you what that information is yet. As an organisation we have a password, Pitgam. P-i-t-g-a-m. Whenever anyone, a stranger mentions this word you must trust them. If someone passes you in the street and mouths this word you must follow them, do their bidding. It's how we make contact. We don't use normal methods of communication like phones. We will watch you in London Bree, if we need to pass information to you it will be by this method. Nothing must be written down. Do you understand?"

Maureen nodded, this was becoming more and more exciting. "What's the name of the organisation, who am I working for?"

"You're working for me," Mahon said quickly, "that's all you need to know." In truth Mahon didn't know, it was simply the organisation to him as well. Maureen accepted that, for some strange reason she trusted Mahon even though she knew nothing about him, this was crazy, but she didn't care. She was, she thought like a drug mule, except the drug was sex.

"How do I contact you Mahon?"

"You can't, Mahon replied quickly and you must never speak of me." He still had her eyes and now he forced this through with a stare. "When you have your target where you want him you must go to this half price ticket booth in Leicester Square." Mahon handed her a brochure. Ask them if you know of a show called Pitgam. They will take you from there."

Maureen was dissapointed, very, that she couldn't contact her best ever lover. She however bowed meekly to his request, or rather command.

"Also Maureen, when in London, you must concentrate one hundred percent on your target. There must be no other contact with any other man. If there is the organisation will not be pleased. Is that understood?" Maureen nodded, she understood. She was disappointed but she understood.

"What if I have an emergency? Who do I contact?" Maureen though it a sensible question and Mahon agreed.

"The ticket booth Bree, always the ticket booth but only if you have an emergency." For the next hour Mahon went into more detail and answered any questions she may have. Mahon also enquired how her telephone call with their target had gone and appeared pleased when Maureen relayed their conversation, earlier that morning. At the end of the hour, Mahon kissed her cheek and bid her both good luck and farewell. The same taxi was waiting for her outside. As they rode to the ferry port Maureen opened her handbag to check her passport. Her passport was there but so was something else. A thickly stuffed envelope she'd never set eyes on before. Leaving it in her handbag Maureen prised it open. The envelope was stuffed with ten and twenty pound notes, a quick thumb through, Maureen estimated there to be around five thousand pounds. Not bad for a weeks work.

In the restaurant Mahon ordered a beer, he thought he deserved it. He hoped he was doing the right thing. Normally it took months to train an operative and here he was sending one out after just a few days. He wanted Bree to succeed. He genuinely liked the woman. As he pondered another woman seated herself opposite him. As she did so she swung the trail of her hijab over her shoulder.

"Hello Pierre."

"Hello Fatima, it's good to set eyes on you."

"Axsti," they both said in unison.

Chapter 13

Putney – London, England

John sat in his office. The office that presented his legitimate life. Baking. In front of him sat six men. His delivery drivers. All had seen the worst side of life. All had been involved in special ops and all were prepared to defend the other with their lives. All were mentally scarred and all had been prepared to make the ultimate sacrifice for the society who had now abandoned them. John had helped them regain their respectability, a regular income and at times, satisfy their lust for violence. Violence that had become an unwanted addiction.

John had recounted what he had been forced to suspect but not one of them had flinched. The leak hadn't come from any of these men, of that he was sure. He was also greatly relieved. Apologising he furnished each with a beer and a handshake.

After all had left he sat back in his chair fondling his gun. Rarely had he been lost in life but he was at a crossroads now and he had no idea which direction to take. Who, who, who was messing with him, the bloody bastards. He kicked his waste bin across the floor. At the same moment his mobile rang. The screen told him it was Roger, maybe he had something. Quickly he thumbed the screen to accept the call.

"Hi Roger."

"Hi, it's about that woman, her name is definitely Bree Fowlis?"

"That's what she told me."

"Well John she's lying. There is no one registered in the UK as Bree Fowlis."

"You're sure?"

"Quite sure."

"Anything else?" There came a spluttering at the other end.

"The NCA is not here for your personal bloody use."

" Sorry, I didn't realise"

"You take care, I don't want to see your ugly mug and your thimble sized genitalia on the front page of a red top."

"Fuck off Roger."

"Thanks would be nice," and the line went dead.

John attached the silencer to his Glock 17. Holding the gun in two hands he pointed it at the wall in front of him. "Hello Miss Bree," he mouthed slowly, "and how are you today?" He pulled the trigger, there was a click but nothing else. Pulling open a drawer, he took out a ready loaded magazine and attached it to the gun. Now fully loaded, he once again pointed the gun at the wall.

Hotel De La Plage – Calais Plage, France

Pierre, alias Mahon, ordered Fatima a drink, a Ricard. After exchanging pleasantries, Pierre asked Fatima what her first impressions of Calais were.

"Have you seen the film, Bienvenue chez les Ch'tis?"

Pierre admitted he hadn't. "Well it's like the film, you need to watch it, first impressions aren't great but it's already growing on me."

"I hope so for you may be here a while, it depends how quickly you can win over your target."

"The capitaine? I saw his picture in the paper. He looks like a capitaine, even without his uniform I'm sure he still looks like a capitaine." Fatima smiled. She had worked authoritative men before. They were all the same, they needed release even if they didn't realise it. And she would be his release. The fantasy he wasn't aware he had.

"What do you think of our new recruit?" Fatima knew he was referring to the woman who had just left, dressed as though she were about to appear on stage.

"She's flashy, perhaps too flashy, she could bring unwanted attention. And she's like an adolescent in a woman's body. You're sure you can control her Pierre?"

"She'll be carefully monitored in London." Fatima took this as an admission, he wasn't sure he could. "I needed more time to mould her but events have left me with no choice. What has happened here has demonstrated we need a second source, maybe a third, fourth, fifth even. We have clients in London who are growing very impatient. This man, if what I suspect is true, could hold a golden key. I do have every confidence that she will achieve finding out and then it's up to us."

Fatima pulled a face that read, 'I'm hope you're right for I'm not so sure.' After taking a sip of her drink, she played with her glass, rolling the stem with her fingers. Looking out at the sea, she looked miles away but Pierre knew she was deep in thought. The lady sat opposite him he knew was never absent minded. She'd be plotting, scheming, her life had forcibly taught her that skill.

"What do you mean by source Pierre?" Pierre, alias Mahon simply smiled. "Ok, so when am I going to meet my target?"

This question he answered. "He's dining here tonight, with his wife and a man from the BRB." Fatima smiled, a deep satisfying smile.

"This should be interesting," and she finished her glass.

A Farmhouse – Escalles, France

Antanois couldn't refrain from helping himself to one more glass of Janneau. He knew he'd regret it tomorrow morning but at that moment he couldn't care less. The pressure on him since the storm and the break in the wall, had been growing by the hour. He hadn't heard anything from the organisation. Just a big fat silence. A big fat heavy silence. A silence that was worse than death. What were they thinking, were they blaming him? He needed answers. And today he'd got half of one. He'd been approached whilst shopping in Boulogne. After the usual password, Pitgam, he'd been told to meet the Egyptian, tomorrow morning eight o'clock sharp, in the bunker. The Egyptian, nobody knew his name, it was always simply, the Egyptian, was loosely in charge of the organisation's security. His reputation was fearsome, if you crossed or let down the organisation in anyway you'd be in danger of having to face the Egyptian. And nobody in their right mind would want that experience. And now here he was, summoned to do just that.

Running, he knew wasn't an option. The organisation would track him down and the consequences terrible. The thought made him fill his glass again. He took a swig and immediately felt his head starting to throb.

Covent Garden – London, England

Maureen couldn't believe her luck. Covent Garden was heaven on earth, it was vibrant and incredibly beautiful. If she could reincarnate, she would come back as Covent Garden. Her hotel too, the Fielding, was just as magical. It was she thought, both discreetly glamorous and the epitome of simple luxury. It was also right in the heart of Covent Garden.

She couldn't believe her luck. She was actually getting paid for doing this. For seducing a flabby man with a nice car. Pinch of salt.

Not a million miles away, John was ready for bed. The shower had helped him to some extent wash the stress out of his thinning hair but not entirely. The pressure of not knowing, still nagged away at him. The phone rang, it was gone ten, John took the call in his bedroom. He recognised the voice immediately, bright, laughing full of the joie de vivre. It was Bree. Immediately his mood softened, either she was just simply delightful or she was bloody good at her job. On hearing her voice, an erection immediately started to form. Honey trap or no honey trap he was going to have her body.

"I'm in Covent Garden," Bree laughed. "I love it."

John couldn't help smiling, in so many ways Bree was like an overexcited child, a breath of fresh air. "At your hotel?"

"Yes it's lovvvvvely, I'm lying on the bed, I've just had a bath."

John felt his erection growing.

"Shall we meet tomorrow?" Bree didn't wait for an answer, "I'll call you after I've had breakfast."

"Ok."

"Can't wait."

"No me neither," but Bree had already put down the phone. After a second's thought John dialled Roger's number. Within two rings he answered, though didn't speak. "Roger I'm meeting that woman tomorrow, she may be of use to you, perhaps."

"I'd already thought of that, get her picture, full face and frontal and I'll run a face recognition scan. See what comes up."

"Ok, will do."

"And John, be careful."

"I will," but Roger had gone, he was obviously busy. John slid into bed. His erection was now annoying him, he'd have to deal with it.

Hotel De La Plage – Calais Plage, France

Darkness enveloped Calais. Fatima had showered and just finished dressing for the evening. She'd chosen an Arab style shift dress with western influences. It was bright enough to get noticed but subtle enough not to be showy. When standing the material though hanging loose was tight enough to give any admirer a hint of her Rubenesque figure beneath. And when sitting, if she positioned herself in a certain way, could show quite an expanse of leg to anyone who was watching. The exposure though deliberate, would appear unintentional to the voyeur and once she knew she had the voyeur's attention she could tease her prey by revealing as much or as little as she wished. Fatima had had the dress made for her in Marseille. Her demands had sometimes driven the seamstress mad but the end result was perfect. The dress was a cleverly disguised uniform of her trade, designed to her specifications, to help her lure an unsuspecting prey. Her finishing touch was a perfume, like the dress, created for her, acting on her specific demands. For this she had employed the services of a young Egyptian perfumer in Rosetta. He specialised in recreating the scents popular when the Pharaohs reigned and recognised the mystical qualities behind each fragrance. The main ingredient for her, a pure extract from the blue lotus flower. The flower not only had mystical qualities but also narcotic, intoxicating anyone who came close enough. To finish she'd chosen a long flowing hijab which trailed both down her back as well as her front and strong high heels which when on her feet, helped to accentuate her figure.

Physically prepared, Fatima now had to concentrate her mood. Placing a Bluetooth speaker on a bedside table she started to play Ya Sidi by Orange Blossom. As the music started Fatima began to sway, her arms rising slowly as the song intensified. By the time the Algerian singer's emotional tones entered the fray, Fatima was lost in the moment. She danced with a passion, swirling with abandonment. Her hands sometimes smoothing her body, at other times reaching for the unknown. The song was about a woman who believed she would never find true love except the love of God. That was her, Fatima, she truly believed this. SHE WAS READY.

At eight o'clock the gendarmerie received a call. It was the wife of one their officers. She wanted to know if her husband was there. He was off duty and they were meant to be at a dinner with friends half an hour ago but he hadn't come home. With everything that was going on she thought he may have gone into work to help with something. She'd tried phoning him but his phone was off which was most unusual. She was starting to worry. The operator buzzed a number of his colleagues but no one had seen him. The one peculiarity, earlier that day he had called requesting the name of an owner of a car, giving a Belgium registration number. Because it wasn't French it had taken a little longer. The number had come back as Pierre De Fauw, a wealthy diamond dealer from Belgium who had a residence on Calais Plage. Why he had requested the information when he wasn't working and why he wanted it he'd never said. Feeling it better to keep this information from his wife the operator, said, sorry, no, no one's seen him. Sensing something might be wrong she passed details of the call to an on duty officer. The officer, extremely busy, looked at it and immediately dismissed it. He'll turn up, he's probably either enjoying a beer or fucking some random woman. He'll turn up and the officer dismissed it from his mind.

Light's flashed twice through Fatima's hotel bedroom window. They were close by. Calmly she picked up her clasp bag and taking long strong strides down the corridor, headed towards reception. She passed a young couple on their way to their room. As she passed the man looked back over his shoulder receiving a playful punch for his trouble. Fatima smiled, the man was at least half her age, she was feeling the power. The trio were entering as she arrived, timing was everything, expertly she headed for the restaurant a pace ahead of her prey. Just as she was about to find a table she made an abrupt turn almost colliding with the capitaine who was guiding his wife with one hand.

"Sorry, gasped Fatima," making sure the capitaine had her gaze. "I've left something in my room."

Capitaine Maubert stepped aside to let Fatima pass. "No, no," he stumbled, "it was my fault." A tug on his sleeve told him he was following the woman with his eyes longer than was necessary.

"Thierry," his wife encouraged. "Let's find a table."

"Yes," Baptiste agreed. "Come on capitaine."

Fatima, was delighted, it couldn't have gone better. She felt her target draw in her perfume, she saw the effect it had had on him. She had already managed to control him for a few seconds with her eyes and as she strode across reception she'd sensed him watching her. This was going to be easier than she had first thought.

In a few minutes she was back in the restaurant. At a glance, she saw the trio had chosen a table by the Eastern window. The capitaine and his wife were facing her, with their male friend displaying his back. Perfect. Fatima took slow bold strides into the restaurant, strides that read underneath all this, her clothes, I'm one hundred percent woman. She was confident she'd catch the capitaine's attention and she did, the capitaine looked up from his menu, Fatima displayed no facial emotion but devoured him with her eyes. The capitaine had the decency to blush and felt his wife gently squeeze his hand. He immediately felt guilty and too quickly lowered his eyes to the menu. Fatima sat down choosing a table, not too close but close enough and facing her target. As she settled in her chair she loosened her hijab, hinting at an elegantly shaped and strong neck, covered by skin that shone youth like in the restaurant's subtle light. She watched as the capitaine lowered his menu, laying it to rest on the table in front of him. Fatima knew the signs, he wanted a better view of her, he could now glimpse her without making it obvious to his fellow guests. Fatima smiled inwardly, so far it had been easy, she had him dangling. The next and much bigger challenge was to take her control in the restaurant to the bedroom. She had to make him want her so badly that he would abandon his cloak, sewn with family values and respectability for a risk factor that could destroy his life and everything he'd ever worked for.

The rest of the evening gave her the confidence that it shouldn't prove that difficult. She had played it very carefully. Not once did she look directly at the capitaine but she made sure her body language did. Only once did she reveal her leg and even then only for a few seconds, but in just those few seconds, she knew she had him. For the rest of the evening the capitaine kept glancing over hoping for another view, he was to be dissapointed, she wasn't going to give him the satisfaction, not yet anyway. Only when they left did she look him in the face.

"Bonne soiree," Fatima smiled at all three but her expressive eyes were for the capitaine alone.

After they'd gone, she ordered a Grand Marnier to finish. Sitting back in her chair she became aware of the rest of the restaurant. Every single man, most accompanied by their wife or girlfriend, she knew were admiring her. All, she also knew, wished she was their guilty secret. Men were pathetic, who said men were the stronger sex. They were so, so wrong.

Thierry lay next to his wife, her head on his shoulder. As soon as they'd got home his wife had demanded him to undress and to get into bed with her. In the restaurant he had been fascinated by the Arab woman, or she may have been Persian. Never had he felt so turned on. His wife had felt his erection and mistaking it for him wanting her had encouraged it with her hand under the table. Something she hadn't done for years. Not once during the meal had his erection subsided. And when for a few seconds the woman had had an unfortunate robe malfunction which had exposed one leg, his erection had grown to such an extent, he'd been worried he might bust his zip. His erection didn't subside on their drive home and his wife, now they were alone continued to encourage it, unzipping him and sliding her hand inside. Their love making that night had been much more passionate, for his wife because she hadn't seen her husband show such an interest for so many, so many many years and for Thierry because he spent the whole time picturing and imagining his wife was the woman in the restaurant. Not able to sleep, he gently lifted his wife's head onto the pillow and went, still completely naked to his office. That evening he selected a French band, Gojira. Headphones on he sat back in the leather to enjoy the music. As the thumping increased rather than relaxing he thought of the woman, he'd been secretly admiring earlier, in the restaurant. He kept playing the few seconds, leg exposure over and over in his head. He could smell her perfume, he'd never smelt something so intoxicating, so sensual. After just a few minutes of playing Gojira he felt another erection forming. Throwing off the headphones, he returned to the bedroom to wake up his wife.

At eleven pm, the gendarmerie received another phone call from the wife of one of their own. Her husband still hadn't turned up and this time she was convinced something had happened to him. Secretly, so did the operator though she didn't say. A call went out to search for him and his car.

CHAPTER
—14—

A Farmhouse – Escalles, France

The alarm had rung on three occasions and on three occasions Antanois had hit the snooze button. Now light was streaming through his East facing window, he had no choice but to get up. His head felt heavy and a dull pain told him he'd had too much Janneau the night before, when would he learn. There was a sick feeling at the bottom of his stomach one that reached up to his lower throat. This was not from the brandy but the thought of his appointment in just under an hour's time. Going to the bathroom he ran the shower with cold water only. Stepping in he inhaled deeply as the icy droplets bounced off his skin. The natural reaction was to step out but he forced himself to stay, a form of mild self-flagellation using water. After drying himself his head though much improved, still throbbed. Antanois didn't believe in taking tablets. Half filling the wash basin with cold water he went to the freezer in the kitchen and broke open a bag of ice. Minutes later the ice cubes were added to the water. Satisfied Antanois plunged his head underwater, gasping as the cold hit home. Ten minutes later he was dried and dressed, ready for anything, anything but the Egyptian. Forcing back rising vomit he made for the garage. He knew he'd be sick if he took the car, so after closing the false wall, he started to walk the Nazi built passage that would take him deep under Mont d'Hubert and to where the Egyptian, he knew would be waiting.

Ardres – France

Capitaine Maubert woke in the morning, wearing a deep feeling of guilt. Last night now felt surreal, what had got into him. It must be the pressure of this investigation. It was going nowhere fast. It was not even going somewhere slowly. Seven, maybe more, many more dead and he had to admit, his gendarmerie didn't have a clue. After kissing his wife gently through her hair he showered in warm soapy water. Dried and dressed he felt a new man, ready for anything the world could throw at him. At that moment his mobile rang, it was the gendarmerie. Closing the door so as not to wake his wife, he answered.

"Maubert."

"Sir," he recognised the voice as one of his more experienced officers, soon to retire. "Sorry to ring you so early but I thought you should know, one of our officers is missing."

"Missing?"

The officer explained what had occurred last night and another call they'd received just over an hour ago. The missing officer's wife had rung this morning around six, a broken woman. Her husband still hadn't returned home, she'd just managed to say this between floods of tears.

"Is anybody with her?"

"Two officers are on their way to her now."

"I'm on my way."

"Sir." The line clicked dead. Six o'clock, she was a strong woman. If his wife had disappeared he'd be on the phone every ten minutes, all through the night. The thought made him re think the night before. He adored his wife, the feeling of guilt made him feel sick. Grabbing his coat he left for his office, not now really wanting to face today.

Chapter 14

Covent Garden - London, England

It had just gone ten, when John's phone rang for the first time that morning . If the truth be known he'd been waiting for it to ring ever since he'd woken around five. No calls meant, hopefully there were no problems at his bakery but also that Bree or whatever her real name was hadn't yet thought about him. He knew he was being stupid, behaving like a teenage virgin anticipating his first bite of the apple but he simply couldn't help it. He knew she was probably dangerous, a plant but like a true professional, she had got under his skin. He really didn't care, he'd always wanted to go out with a bang and if Bree was to be his executioner then so be it. Better than a bearded, tattooed Russian or a brainwashed Jihadi, worse still a bullet in the back fired by Mr or Mrs anonymous. No, Bree, if he had to have an executioner would do nicely. The thought actually started to turn him on and an erection soon became proof of this.

It was past eight when Maureen alias Bree first woke. She had, she decided never slept in such a comfortable bed. The first thing she did was check her phone. The only message was from an old girlfriend who'd she'd promised to visit whilst staying in London. So her target was playing hard to get, well she could play at that game, she'd message him after bath and breakfast though in the end she reversed this to breakfast and bath. The bath was placed conveniently at the bottom of the bed, an excellent idea to Maureen's mind. Bathroom's could be such lonely places. Also from the comfort of her bath she could watch tv and as she lay back to soak, she turned on Sky News. It was nine thirty and the last half hour of Kay Burley. Five minutes in there was an article on the opening of a private hospital in Dudley. The health minister was there alongside a representative of the company, New Dawn Health Services. This is the third hospital the company has opened in the UK, the reporter announced, the other two both being in London, South

Kensington and Kings Cross. The minister went on to enthuse how this was a perfect example of how the private sector could work with government and the NHS. The government helped with a grant for start up costs and in return the company gave the NHS preferential rates for all kinds of operations, taking some much needed pressure off. The new hospital the representative boasted had state of the art facilities and could operate the most complicated transplants, something of a speciality. The hospital could become something of a life saver to so many stuck on a waiting list. Maureen wasn't really listening, she was too busy studying the representative of New Dawn Health Services. She had seen him before and now she remembered where. He'd been one of the two men with Mahon when she'd arrived at the seafront hotel yesterday. She had a good head for faces, yes it was definitely him. Singing, she stepped out of her bath. What high circles she was moving in, who'd have thought, her Maureen and she laughed out loud.

If Maureen hadn't have been caught up in her own little world she would have seen Mahon's other associate on screen. Also appearing with a minister. He, it was announced, was the main player responsible for opening a high tech factory in the North East of England. The factory would specialise in manufacturing advanced surveillance equipment and could eventually replace the state's and especially the police's reliance on Chinese technology and all the risks that came with that reliance. Like the hospital earlier the start-up costs would be made easier with a grant and on top, favourable tax breaks. By the time Maureen returned to the TV, Kay Burley had finished and so had Maureen's interest. The TV went off. It was time to contact her target. Maureen felt a shiver, not from cold but from the thrill of her mission. He would soon be eating out of the palm of her hands, she was very confident in that.

Chapter 14

Mont D'hubert – France

Why couldn't he shrug off the feeling that he was a dead man walking. Antanois wanted to feel positive but the dead man feeling seemed to grow heavier with every step he took along the tunnel. And the tunnel didn't help, it was soulless, the only distinguishing marks being piles of rubble and the odd stencilled sign in German. Every step echoed, accenting every heartbeat that allowed the next stride. It felt like hours but in fact it was no more than ten minutes when he arrived at the central parking area and the busy sales office. A small group were standing, waiting for him. He recognised Seth and gave her a fleeting smile. Her expression in return read, what the fucks going on? coupled with, I'm scared. There were five others, at the front a stout balding man with his shirt and most of what it covered trying desperately to get out. This man, Antanois knew was the Egyptian, he'd never met him, he just knew. The three accompanying were dressed in medical fatigues, he assumed they were doctors and the remaining two, wearing suits, were undoubtedly security. They blended like water in a desert. The Egyptian held out his hand.

"Assalamu alaikum."

"Wa alaikum salaam," Antanois replied appropriately.

"We have a little problem to sort out," the Egyptian attempted a smile but Antanois read it more as a salacious leer. The Egyptian was all smiles, charm even but what lay beneath?

"Problem?"

"Yes, well two actually, I'm afraid I've commandeered a couple of your operating rooms to engineer a solution. I feel I've trod on the toes of your very capable lady," the Egyptian gestured towards Seth. I'm sorry for that, I promise it won't be for more than a couple of days, three at the most. It's important though you see what we are doing." The Egyptian motioned to an adjacent tunnel. Like in a James Bond film there were electric passenger buggies, available to ride in but it appeared the Egyptian preferred to walk and at a pace belying his cumbersome figure. The medical staff followed and then Antanois walking alongside Seth with the two security taking up the rear. The last two making it very obvious that no one had a choice, other than to follow.

For nearly half an hour the group marched, descending to the lowest levels of the world war two bunker. A security door announced the end, as well as the purpose of their descent. On the other side Antanois knew were medical facilities, his authority had never reached beyond those doors and thus he had never visited. All that was about to change. The Egyptian stepped back motioning for Seth to open the door. This was no easy matter. It required a card, a palm print and facial recognition. Seth, eventually satisfied all three and the door slid open.

The other side could have been another world. Bright lights, ultra-smooth, shiny floors, walls and ceilings and a strong smell of disinfectant. Seth motioned to a soap dispenser and all dutifully obliged, she then presented everyone with coveralls and a mask. Again everyone obliged.

"Operating theatre three please Seth, " the Egyptian couldn't have been more charming. Antanois had never had an idea what exactly the medical facilities were down here but at least three operating theatres was astonishing. It was evidence of just what the organisation was planning and to what extent.

"Whatever you think of Hitler and the Nazi regime you have to admire their ingenuity." The Egyptian waved his arms, indicating , Antanois assumed, all of this. "It was they who built the original medical facilities down here. All we've had to do is bring them up to date. They designed them so nobody would know and we're simply carrying that on. It's perfect, they're perfect. The brainchild of our master."

It was at least a ten minute walk until they arrived at operating theatre three, and the Egyptian talked all of the way. It was something of a relief for all of them when they arrived at their requested destination.

Their destination was immediately recognisable for it was denoted by an electricity fed figure '3', a figure that glowed blood red. The redness Seth explained warned anyone in the corridor that the operating theatre was in use and not to enter. Operating theatre three was different to one and two that they'd passed, in that one of the walls was made of glass, allowing special guests to observe the operation inside. Six airport lounge style chairs made for comfortable viewing.

The Egyptian motioned for all to sit down. All, Antanois realised, meant the Egyptian, Seth and himself. The two security remained standing and the three others, accompanying had quietly vanished.

"Sit back and enjoy the show." The Egyptian was rubbing his hands. "I shall."

Antanois waited for whatever horror was about to unfold. He didn't have to wait long. Double doors on the opposite wall of the theatre opened and three men, undoubtedly the vanished men, dressed head to toe in coveralls wheeled in a patient, completely naked, on a gurney. At first everything appeared to be normal, that it is until they tried to transport their patient to the operating table. It very quickly became apparent the patient didn't want to be there and two more staff quickly entered the theatre to help. Antanois immediately realised this was no routine operation and the patient wasn't laying on a standard operating table. He was literally strapped down, unable to move. Even his head was forced motionless and his mouth stretched open for a ball gag. The doctors now with their patient compliant, albeit unwilling angled the table so it sloped facing the viewers the other side of the glass wall. It was then Antanois recognised the 'patient.' It was Armani from the room that nobody talked about. And he looked terrified.

Gendarmerie Nationale – Calais

Capitaine Maubert sipped on his coffee. It was only just gone eight and he was already on his fourth cup. On top of everything he now had the worrying news of a missing officer, and the unauthorised request of a licence number, when the missing officer was off duty. Why? And why Pierre De Fauw, a wealthy diamond dealer. He personally knew Pierre and liked the guy. He was always personable and despite his wealth, never aloof. He had often attended charity events with the man and had always found him to be good company. Again, why had his missing officer been interested in him and why when he was off duty, not when he was on duty. It just didn't make sense.

There came a knock at the door.

"Entrér."

The door cracked open and a smiling Marie poked her head round. "Am I welcome? Oh your lady in reception let me up, she knew you were expecting me."

The Capitaine nodded, "Yes, yes, of course, come in, come in." Marie entered with false caution. The Capitaine recognised the joke and apologised. "Sorry Marie, I've already had a crap morning."

"And it's only just gone eight," Marie finished for him. "And I'm early, that's probably made things worse." She gave him her best smile.

"No, no of course not, if anything you're a welcome distraction." Well that's a good start, Marie thought quietly to herself. Marie sat down, crossing her legs. She was wearing a much shorter skirt than last time, much shorter. The Capitaine forced himself not to look. For the moment he had enough of the female form. Especially legs.

Sitting himself, the Capitaine pulled out a file. "Marie as part of the investigation we need to take a look at the migrant food stations around town. Not to check on them you understand but to see if anyone who means harm has infiltrated them. Infiltrate to build up trust, to present a friendly face, ready to help, when their true intention is quite the opposite. It's to take advantage.

Marie nodded. "Yes of course, I understand but I don't see how I can be of help?"

"Marie, the migrants, the people you work with, they trust you. You're almost their public face, their PR. We the gendarmerie, and I admit it's because of the insensitive way, sometimes, we have handled things, are their sworn enemy. The enemy to both migrants and helpers. You could be our eyes and ears Marie. Now you know our, my, agenda I think at least you can trust us." The capitaine stopped. He looked almost desperately at the woman, attractive woman he now admitted, sat opposite him on the other side of his desk. She was more important to them, the gendarmerie, than she realised. She was their one road into the daily life of the migrants and the people who supported them. Without her trust, her willingness to help, they'd have an ocean to cross without a paddle.

Marie leant her elbows on the desk and placed her chin in her cupped hands.' Only sometimes' she thought, thinking the capitaine's word through. 'Only sometimes'. The gendarmerie had never shown any sensitivity towards the migrant's plight, quite the reverse. Why should she help them. Firstly she supposed, because of the man sat opposite her. He'd shown her a side she hadn't considered possible, even in a gendarme. She now realised he could be sensitive, genuine and even humble. On top of that, although it wasn't a defining reason she found him quite attractive. Moving quickly on from the thought she remembered also, the faces of his officers in the incident or operations room. At the end of the meeting, they were all, well nearly all, behind her. She owed them for putting their trust in her.

"Ok capitaine I will help you." Marie leant back, she recognised the visible relief in the capitaine's face. "But not for the gendarmerie, you understand. To get the bastards who are taking advantage of people's misery."

Capitaine Maubert nodded. "I expected nothing else Marie, but please accept my thanks, at least allow me that."

"Of course Capitaine, and I accept your thanks, thank you. I hope I live up to my billing." Marie gave him her best smile. What was it with men. One minute they could be so authoritarian, so dominant, so masterful and the next second, so very vulnerable. No wonder the world was in such a bloody mess.

"To work, Marie," the Capitaine's expression had changed to one of concentration and he was back to his authoritative self. "The first thing I need is a list of all the distribution des repas, (food stations), official or unofficial, permanent or temporary."

Marie pulled a paper from her bag. "I thought you might, I prepared this, everything you've just asked for is on there. I've kept a copy by the way."

There were several sheets, the Capitaine unfolded them and flattened them with his hands. He started to read. Just as Marie said, she had made a detailed list of all the food stations known to her, where they set up, what time they set up and for how long they stayed open. Details also included who tended to run them though that info was, he thought, a little suspect. He recognised some of the food stations, the two main ones being, Quai de la Moselle, in the sports centre car park and Zone Marcel Dore, near the Metro trade market. Some, embarrassingly, he hadn't known existed and there was no mention Les Quatre Ponts. Perhaps he had assumed wrongly where Ismail had been picked up. Perhaps there never had been a food station there, in which case their theory as to the route the van that had allegedly picked up the migrants took, was shot to pieces. He sighed, a sigh Marie recognised as one of exasperation.

"Can I help then?"

Chapter 14

"Yeees," another sigh, "yes, yes Marie." The Capitaine looked thoughtful. "Marie you were at the last meeting, you know Ismail's story perhaps better than all of us. Do you think it's possible that someone, an organisation, is going around setting up false food stations, to entrap migrants. For whatever reason?"

Marie thought this over for a few seconds before she spoke. "It's not impossible," she admitted. "Some migrants don't even trust me and thus keep things from me but I think it's unlikely. People talk, something, I'm sure would have got back to me, leaked out. If they are doing it, they're extremely clever for no one's talking."

"Clever, or they're putting the fear of God into the people who know."

"Possibly," Marie admitted, "though remember, many of these migrants have already been through hell, many have been tortured. It would take a lot to scare them."

"I don't mean scare in that way, I mean dash any hopes of crossing La Manche. 'Talk and you will never get across,' that's the threat demanding silence."

Marie uncrossed her legs and crossed them in the other direction. Her action didn't go unnoticed. "Quite possibly," she admitted, they could weaponize their promises. But I still think I would have heard something."

"You hadn't heard of the food station Ismail attended," the Capitaine pointed out.

"True." Marie sucked her bottom lip. A silence fell between them as each considered the possible consequences of their conversation.

It was the capitaine who spoke next. "Marie," Marie waited, the Capitaine looked pensive. "Marie would it cause you a problem, I mean put you at risk if you eavesdropped for us. Some people if they suspected might see it as you spying for the gendarmerie."

Marie almost grinned. "Thank you for your concern Capitaine, but you needn't worry, I'm a big girl and can look after myself. When you say eavesdrop, what do you want to know?"

"I'm not sure," the capitaine admitted. "Anything not run of the mill, strangers offering to help out, migrants you know are still in Calais not turning up to be fed. That sort of thing. I can provide protection if you wish."

"No way," Marie was adamant. "Your guys may mean well but you need to train them to look normal before they get within a mile of me."

The Capitaine was gracious enough to laugh. "Ok Marie, if you're sure."

"Bloody sure. How do I report back?"

"This is my personal mobile, contact me on that." The Capitaine scribbled a number on a notelet and slid it across the desk. Marie took it, looked at it and slipped it in her handbag.

"Ok, I'll start straight away." Marie stood up and blew the Capitaine a kiss before leaving. The capitaine to his surprise found himself blushing. What the hell was happening to him. There came a knock at the door.

"Entrér." One of his more senior officers entered.

"Sir we've found his car." The missing officer's, the Capitaine knew without asking.

"Really? Where?

"La Foret de Guines," (Guines Forest), in a parking area."

"And ..."

"No, no sign sir, just the car. Forensics are on their way now. Do you want me to get a team together to search the forest?"

"No not yet, organise a dog handler first, see if they can pick up a scent. And let me know if forensics find anything."

"Yes sir." The door closed.

Another bloody mystery, was this foul play or did his officer want to go missing. Perhaps he had another life nobody knew about. It wouldn't be the first time. People had a right to go missing in France. It was enshrined in law. Then again it could be foul play. Bloody hell, what a mess. And if it was a disappearing act, what bloody bad timing, how bloody inconsiderate. The capitaine immediately felt guilty. Perhaps his officer was in serious trouble. He made a note to visit his wife. If nothing turned up. It was the least he could do. The phone rang.

"Maubert."

"Thierry, it's Baptiste."

"Bonjour, are you on your way in, I've had an officer go missing."

"Really." Baptiste sounded shocked. "If I can help in any way. And er no, I'm not coming in. I've been called back to Paris. Is there anyway you can pop by and see me before I leave. Just for a face to face, an update. I intend on leaving around two."

What a bloody pain, this was the last thing he needed. Then the capitaine thought of the Muslim woman from the night before, the woman who had had such a strange effect on him. It was completely illogical but he felt a strong desire to see her again. "Of course Baptiste, no trouble at all. Around midday ok?"

"Perfect, see you then." The phone clicked dead. The capitaine sat back in his chair, what had he just done and why. Was he going mad? Yes he knew it was madness but a sense of excitement he simply couldn't suppress was already gripping him. Knowing there was the remotest possibility that he would set eyes on the woman again was forcing him mad. Mad! Yes madness, an illogical madness, an insane madness, a madness that he simply couldn't control. It should scare him but it didn't, he wanted this madness, worse still he desired this madness.

Covent Garden – London, England

"John? It's Bree, I'm fed, watered, bathed and ready for anything," she laughed. John knew who it was the second Bree opened her mouth. Bree had a wonderful sense of happiness about her which shone through in her voice, with every word she spoke. And like the French, she didn't speak, she sang her sentences. He loved everything about Bree, everything.

"Morning Bree, you sound happy."

"I am," Bree sang, "I'm in a wonderful city and about to meet a wonderful man, with a wonderful car." She laughed again. I'm going to disappoint her on two fronts he thought sadly. "When are you free John?"

"Now if you like." John surprised himself, it wasn't the answer he'd wanted to give but he couldn't help himself. Some sort of madness had gripped him.

"Can you wait for an hour John? I just need to prepare myself." John felt a surge of excitement, he was picturing Bree getting ready for him.

"I think I'll survive." It was corny, but a joke all the same.

"Great, I'll meet you outside the tube station, Covent Garden, say midday-ish?"

"Perfect."

"Can't wait." Bree rang off.

Bree couldn't help experiencing a strong sense of excitement. Not sexually, her target wasn't exactly God's gift but for her mission. It was an assignment she was determined to excel at. De robing she started to rub oil into her strong legs, there would be no abrasion. Choosing one of her more delicate perfumes she sprayed inside the top of her thighs, her lower abdomen and carefully the skin surrounding her vulva. Gently rubbing the scent in she then sprayed under her breasts finishing with her neck. Her target was in for a treat. Now to dress.

Chapter 14

John stood motionless, for a minute at least after Bree had terminated her call. What was he doing, why was he taking such a risk. It went against everything he'd ever trained for. Naked he examined himself in the mirror. He had to admit his body was a mess. The result of enjoying his food too much, alcohol too much and the odd cigar. If you looked carefully you'd appreciate that once his body had been better than most, but you needed to look hard, very hard. He had to come to terms that Bree wasn't entertaining him for his looks. It was either because of the Aston, or perceived wealth because of the Aston. Or she was being paid by someone to find out something about him. If that was the case what? He wasn't straight and narrow but he had no secrets worth the effort of a professional plant. Professional women, honey traps didn't come cheap, at least the good ones didn't and he should know. And from what he'd seen of Bree, if she had been hired, she must be costing someone a small fortune.

What to wear? If he was to take precautions he had little choice. It was a made to measure jacket and trousers, he'd purchased from a specialist tailor in Milan. The trousers were especially sewn so they could hold a gun and silencer without being too obvious. It didn't make them particularly comfortable to wear, but better safe than sorry. With the faint hope that Bree really was after his body or his money, he'd be delighted if she was, he wore his shirt as is the modern style, outside his trousers. His belly still tested the material but it was a vast improvement from tucking his shirt in. Pot belly designers could only be responsible for the fashion that was the loose hanging shirt and John wanted to thank them all personally. Dressed, he checked his gun. He ejected the cartridges until there were just four left. If he needed more than that he'd be starting a war. Tucking the gun into the specially sewn holder, he once again self-critiqued his image in the mirror. He would do he thought, he would do. I'm on my way to meet her now, he sent Roger a text. A text immediately came back, it simply read, 'photo, take care and enjoy.'

Five minutes later he was approaching Covent Garden Tube. He immediately spotted Bree. WOW, was his immediate reaction.

Mont D'hubert – France

Antanois watched in horror as the surgeons prepared Armani for, for what? He wasn't sure. What looked like a tv monitor was being wheeled in front of the patient. One of the surgeons stood with his head beside Armani's. He gave the thumbs up. What happened next was a complete shock and Antanois almost vomited. One of the surgeons, with a scalpel simply cut off Armani's eyelids. Armani's face muscles contorted horribly as he attempted to scream.

"What are they doing?" It was Seth who asked. This was not normal procedure.

The Egyptian obviously delighting in the spectacle turned to face both of them. "The whole operation will be filmed and this way the patient will be forced to watch. He can't now close his eyes, no matter how much he'll want to. Oh and he will want to." The Egyptian laughed, a sordid, grotesque laugh, one that was almost inhuman. A fourth man entered the room carrying a digital video camera. After a little fiddling an image of Armani's abdomen appeared on the television monitor. One of the surgeons, Antanois assumed an anaesthetist, prepared a drip, inserting a cannula into a vein in Armani's left arm.

Both Seth and Antanois could tell the Egyptian was smiling under his mask. "We're going to start harvesting, he laughed. The one difference is, this patient won't be dead, he'll be very much alive and forced to watch every step of the procedure on the monitor. Today we're going to remove his kidneys and liver. The intravenous drip won't knock him out, the anaesthetist will administer just enough to stop his body going into shock and granting him an early exit. The human body can sometimes survive up to three days without these organs. This will allow our patient plenty of time to reflect on his stupidity before he eventually meets his God. Stupidity that has caused the organisation a great deal of trouble, and trouble that could have gotten a lot worse. This will be a lesson to others. We are broadcasting this live to your unpaid workers, it will help them to think carefully before doing something that may cause us a problem."

One of the surgeons turned to the window and gave the thumbs up. The Egyptian as though he were a Roman emperor lifted both thumbs. The signalling surgeon nodded and turned back to the patient. 'Patient,' that was a laugh thought Antanois, the poor guy was a victim. This wasn't what he'd signed up for. He knew Armani's days were numbered but he didn't deserve an end such as this. After speaking to his two colleagues the surgeon signalled to the cameraman. Another thumbs up. Apparently all were ready. After wiping where the first cut was to be with a swab the scalpel started to cut through Armani's outer layer. His face contorted with the pain made all the worse by being forced to watch what was causing it. With his head strapped down and his eyelids removed Armani had no choice. He wanted to die and die quickly. Why wasn't he dying? How could his God allow such inhumanity. His tortured mind still strong, Armani started to pray. The camera zoomed in as the retractor was positioned to hold back human tissue. Clearly visible one of Armani's kidneys. As one of the surgeons carefully started to cut away, Antanois was violently sick between his legs, he couldn't hold it any longer.

The Egyptian patted him on the back. "Don't worry Antanois. It affects nearly everybody like that the first time they watch. Doesn't it Seth. Seth nodded, she had seen hundreds of kidney harvests but never one quite like this. Although what was happening horrified her she wasn't affected in the way that she felt physically sick. Mentally though it would scar her for life. "You see," the Egyptian laughed, with a bit of luck this will be over in a couple of hours then we can make a start on the liver." Antanois retched again throwing his vomit all over the base of the window. One of the security, standing behind stepped forward to wipe it off. It wouldn't do to spoil the view. The Egyptian turned to Seth. "A coffee will help settle his stomach, with the liver we're likely to be here a while. Can you organise some coffee, a pot to share would be good and perhaps some cake as well." Antanois retched again and more vomit started to circle his shoes. The Egyptian laughed, louder and louder. He was enjoying himself.

Hotel De La Plage – Calais Plage, France

Fatima had been told to expect the capitaine around midday. Today she would try and make verbal contact, allow him to enjoy her mind as well as her physique. Orange Blossom wasn't needed this morning, she only ever needed the song before the first contact or before she was going in for the kill. Today, everything was down to her and her alone.

Instead of a dress, she chose a mulberry coloured blouse and a skirt that ended just above the knee. Standing up the skirt would look matronly, sitting down, if she wished she could expose a great deal of thigh and it would look anything but. The blouse buttoned up, like the skirt when standing, looked positively professional. Loosen just one button and it became a little suggestive, loosen two and a window was opened onto what could be. As was the Persian way Fatima made up her face to accentuate her already strong features. For her head she chose a mauve hijab with a touch of sparkle and after spraying her neck and back of hands with the blue lotus perfume, her final touch was to take an oil, infused with the same blue lotus scent and rub it gently into the folds of her skirt. After slipping on a pair of strong high heeled shoes and examining herself in the mirror, she hung a jacket loosely over her shoulders and strode boldly up the corridor towards the bar and restaurant.

It was ten minutes before midday and there were only three tables taken. One by a single male. Police, Fatima immediately recognised. You could tell even when they weren't wearing a uniform. A second by two couples sat facing each other. Plastic carrier bags, though plain, sitting on the floor between them almost certainly denoted they were English and the last table with his back to her a smartly dressed man with tussled curled hair. Pierre, she recognised him instantly. Pierre didn't know how to dress down. Casual for him was not to wear cufflinks. As she passed Fatima gently rubbed his right shoulder.

"You look a million dollars, even from behind Pierre," she complimented sitting down.

"I have to, it's my job."

"Rubbish Pierre, you wouldn't know to look anything less."

"Maybe not," Pierre shrugged his shoulders smiling. "You all set Fatima? I've just had word your target has just left the gendarmerie, he should be here in ten minutes. He's meeting the man sat behind us, with his back to us."

"You mean the policeman," Fatima ordered a Ricard from the hovering waiter.

"He's a bit more than a policeman Fatima, he's from the BRB." Fatima didn't look impressed.

"He's still a policeman." Pierre shrugged his shoulders.

"If you like."

Her Ricard arrived and after pouring water into her glass, Fatima gave the clouding liquid a swirl before taking a sip. Resting her wrists on the table she leant forward so she was within inches of Pierre's face. "What is it you want me to find out Pierre?"

If Pierre felt intimidated he didn't show it. He took a sip of his coffee first. "There's a gendarme operation, investigation, call it what you may, that could distract even ruin our operation here. I'm sure you have heard the discovery of several severed heads." Fatima lifted her head, not taking her eyes off of his. She meant yes. "Well they were found very close to where we have a hidden operation, quite a major operation in fact. The gendarme and the media interest has forced us to temporarily suspend our activities here. We need to know where they are going with their investigation and when it's safe for us to start up again. Every day we are closed down is costing the organisation a small fortune."

"And the operation is?"

"You know I can't tell you that Fatima, not yet anyway. If your cover was blown anything you know could endanger us, you know how it is." Fatima nodded and sat back.

"I know," she admitted verbally. It would just help if I knew something. These heads, are they our doing?" Pierre was about to answer but Fatima stopped him. She could read his eyes and their expression, no matter how hard he tried to hide it, told her yes. As a Femme Fatale you very quickly learnt to read eyes. Eyes can't keep a secret. "I see. Then I think I can guess pretty much what the organisation's operation here is." Pierre ignored her last remark.

"London are discussing, if it gets worse implementing a diversionary tactic but it wouldn't be without risks."

"Let me see what I can find out first."

"He won't be an easy nut to crack Fatima. He married his childhood sweetheart. They've been together for nearly thirty years and have a daughter and recently a granddaughter who he dotes over. As far as we know he's never strayed and never been tempted to stray. He lives and plays by the rulebook. There probably isn't a more upstanding citizen in Calais."

"He hasn't met me yet," Fatima gave a hint of a smile.

"No he hasn't," Pierre agreed, he almost found himself feeling sorry for the capitaine. Fatima had her head raised.

"Here he is now." Pierre turned to look and waved.

"Hello capitaine, what brings you here?" Fatima though surprised by Pierre's greeting was professional enough not to show it. Capitaine Maubert strolled across, signalling to the man from the BRB he'd be right over. He hoped his drumming heartbeat couldn't be heard around the restaurant. Pierre was actually in conversation with the woman he was hoping to see again.

"The two men shook hands. "Capitaine, this is Fatima. We used to work together, she's come to. Why are you here Fatima?" Fatima held out her hand and held the Capitaine's a little longer than was necessary, she had one finger on his wrist and smiled inwardly as she felt his raging pulse. She had him, just to be sure, she made certain her eyes were a magnet and they were. He was hopelessly floating in the dark pools either side of her nose.

"I wanted to see what La Nord was like. I've watched the film, Bienvenue Chez Les Ch'tis, four times. Every time it made me laugh. I bought the book and am here to see where everything was filmed and to see if I have the same experience as the poor postmaster. Pathetic, perhaps even childish but I'm intrigued capitaine. If you're not too busy perhaps you could show me some of the sites, if you know them of course. Pierre do I have to call him capitaine, it's so formal. Don't you know the man's name?"

"It's Thierry," Thierry offered, "but everybody calls me capitaine. To be honest I prefer it.

"Well if we're going to become acquainted Thierry, I'm not going to keep calling you capitaine. It sort of makes you my master and I'm not going to let you be that." Everybody laughed and subtly Fatima had got a sexual suggestive across. From the expression in the capitaine's eyes she knew it had hit home even if he dare not believe it. After all, she was presenting herself, very obviously, as a Muslim woman.

"Anyway, I'm sorry, someone's waiting to see me." The Capitaine signalled to Baptiste. "Nice to see you Pierre, nice to meet you Fatima, Bienvenue, (welcome)."

"Les Ch'tis," Fatima added the title of the film. "And I thought you were here to see me." Fatima gave him a saddish look. The Capitaine, caught out, blushed. Annoyed at his uncontrolled reaction he went over to Baptiste, apologising profusely.

Pierre looked at the lady opposite him, she was brilliant, he had to give it to her. He'd been struggling, searching for an excuse for her being here. Fatima had told him to leave it to her, the film was a brilliant reason. "Have you ever seen the film Fatima?"

"No," Fatima admitted, smiling. "So Pierre, how's our Lady in London doing?"

Pierre looked at his watch. "I think she's meeting her target as we speak."

Covent Garden Tube Station – London, England

Maureen alias Bree, smiled broadly as she saw her target approaching. He looked nothing without the Aston she thought sadly, but a mission was a mission.

John couldn't believe his eyes. The plant if she was that, was wearing a faux fur coat which ended more than a little way above the knees. There was no sign of a skirt and the black shine of her hosiery shouted stockings not tights. Her coat was open enough to promise a pronounced cleavage and Bree was wearing her shortish hair in such such a way to made her look masterful. In charge of everything around her.

After dodging numerous tourists John was standing beside her, feeling old, fat and extremely under dressed. In short unworthy. If Bree was disappointed she didn't show it.

"Hello, you," she beamed kissing John on one cheek, leaving a mark which she immediately proceeded to wipe off with spittle and fingers. "There, good as new." Bree stood back to admire her handiwork.

"What would you like to do Bree?" It was all John could think to say. He was pathetic.

Bree clapped her hands. "Let's stick to Covent Garden, something to drink, something to eat and then see how we feel. It's too cold to be trudging around the streets. Let's be tourists in Covent Garden today." This suited John, he was not one for trudging but food and drink he was good at.

"Hang on Bree, I want a memento, let me grab a photo." Bree needed no encouragement, she posed in exaggerated fashion allowing for all the shots John needed and when he'd finished grabbed him, then his phone to take a selfie.

"Smile John," she laughed, holding his phone out in front. Hugging him close Bree took several pictures. John didn't want her to stop, her faux fur was delicious and her scent even more so. For a few seconds he was in heaven. Bree pushed him away laughing. "Come on, let's be typical tourists, what's that pub with an outdoor balcony?"

"The Punch and Judy."

"Yes. Let's start there," and linking her arm in his she started marching John, expertly dodging tourists, towards the pub.

Two hours were spent in the Punch and Judy. Bree attacked pornstar martinis as though it were her last day on earth and John feeling bloated after a couple of pints turned to white wine. 'Wine after beer and you're in the clear, or beer before wine and you'll feel fine,' conventional wisdom dictated. He hoped after centuries of experimentation that the results were fool proof. After the pub John treated Bree to a meal in a swanky restaurant in King Street. Here his companion had to remove her faux fur, revealing a rather daring mini dress that tended to ride up her legs every time she moved or in Bree's case wriggled. John after more wine was past caring if she was a plant or not. He couldn't care less if he died that night, just as long as his burning arousal was satisfied first. Anyway when in the Punch and Judy he'd WhatsApped Roger the photos. He should have the results back pretty quickly.

The results came back conveniently as Bree left to relieve herself. John read, not really caring what his old colleague in the NCA had found, he was having too much of a good time.

"Hi mate. You can relax. Her name is Maureen Fowlis. Widow now living in Wissant France but can't guarantee if that last bit is still the case. Can't see anything against her, not even a speeding offence. I think you're safe mate. Enjoy yourself."

John didn't know whether to feel relieved or dissapointed, the thought she may be a professional honey trap had actually excited him. And Maureen! Really? Maureen as he now knew her was once again sitting opposite him, grinning, her ample breasts threatening to escape their low cut support.

John decided to take the bull by its horns "Bree, that's an unusual name, where does it come from?"

Maureen leaned forward giggling. "It's not my real name," she whispered loudly. "My real name is Maureen." She laughed.

"Why Bree then?" John found himself laughing too, he didn't know why.

"Well," Maureen thought about her answer. "I love sex and Bree sounds like a name of someone who'd enjoy sex, Maureen on the other hand sounds as though I enjoy doing the washing up and I don't!" They both laughed and during their laughter their hands connected and remained connected.

Chapter 14

Minutes later they were in Maureen's room at the Fielding. As John exited the bathroom Maureen slow and provocatively removed her faux coat. Throwing it on the floor she placed one foot on the bed, revealing a stockinged leg and suspenders. "Come here Mr Aston," Maureen made a finger gesture whilst pouting her lips. John trying to look cool and failing, slid off his jacket as he approached. When in arms reach Maureen pulled him close sliding one hand under his shirt, brushing his left nipple. They were so close now they could feel each other's breath. Maureen felt his hardness against her body.

"Now John, is that a gun in your pocket or are you just pleased to see me?"

She felt John fumbling. "A gun," he said pulling out a pistol, with something attached.

Hotel De La Plage – Calais Plage, France

There wasn't much of an update to give Baptiste and the Capitaine was a little mystified as to why he'd needed to see him at all. What he told him across a table could have just as easily been said over the phone and backed up electronically. Baptiste tended to go with the theory, that the missing officer, looking at the initial evidence had probably wanted to disappear and there was no law against that. He also emphasised that unless somehow they could prove people were being murdered for their body parts, the BRB had bigger fish to fry. The Capitaine updated him on the latest stages of the operation and that house enquiries had started this morning, on people who had in the last five years, moved into the area. Baptiste wished him luck on that but suspected it wouldn't really come to anything. He hoped he was wrong of course. The Capitaine quietly agreed but they had to do something.

All the time they were talking, the Capitaine couldn't take his eyes of Fatima. Although sat at a table that was in a line adjacent, she was almost sat opposite. Not once though did she even look across at where he was sitting, she was too engrossed in conversation with Pierre to even notice he was still there. But just like yesterday he had the feeling her body somehow seemed to be talking directly to him. Wanting him to notice it. And her leg, yesterday was just a glimpse, today her leg was on show. Not intentionally he was sure but the way her leg sat across her knee the skirt had virtually dropped half way down her thigh. Without warning and in one move Fatima looked across and at the same moment dropped her leg and pulled down her skirt. She must have felt him staring at her. Fatima was once again engrossed in conversation with Pierre. Hopefully she hadn't seen his reddening cheeks.

By 2pm Baptiste announced he was ready to leave. Standing the Capitaine shook his hand with more promises that he'd keep the man from the BRB updated. As protocol dictated he escorted him to reception where final farewells and bonne chance, (good luck), were exchanged. As the capitaine turned to return to the restaurant and finish his coffee he almost collided with Pierre who was also leaving.

"Nice to see you capitaine, we must catch up some time."

The capitaine agreed and apologised for having to ask him a question. "Pierre, have you any idea why one of my officers was calling in your licence number?" Pierre didn't have to act surprised, he genuinely was.

"Isn't that sort of thing logged?"

The capitaine scratched the back of his head. "Normally yes, but he was off duty and now he's disappeared." The capitaine withdrew his hand and shook his head. "I'm sorry for asking Pierre, I thought you may have had an idea."

"Sorry, no. Perhaps he simply liked my car and was checking the number to ensure it wasn't stolen."

"Possibly," but the capitaine didn't sound sure. "Anyway don't let me hold you up."

"You're not," and Pierre left the reception, heading for his Merc, the car that all the fuss was about. Capitaine Maubert watched him exit the car park. Something wasn't right, he had that illogical sense that the British called, "gut feeling." Pushing Pierre from his mind he returned to finish his coffee. Where Baptiste had been just a few minutes before, sat Fatima. She was gazing out of the window whilst playing with a chain, silver probably, hanging around her neck. As she played the top button on her blouse slipped loose from its hold causing the two sides to part a little. It was unintentional of course but the Capitaine couldn't wait to take a closer look and went to sit down. Perhaps the unintentional may be repeated. He hoped so.

Mont D'hubert – France

It was early afternoon when the horror that was the harvesting of Armani's liver and kidneys finally came to an end. After the surgeons had cleaned up, Armani was left alone to literally slowly watch himself die, courtesy of a TV monitor. Without eyelids he wouldn't be able to sleep. He would have to witness every dying second of his wretched life slowly wither away. The expression fate worse than death didn't apply to Armani for, for him the two were cruelly combined.

Antanois felt mentally and physically exhausted by what he had witnessed. Seth being from a medical background simply felt disgusted at the inhumanity she had just witnessed and the Egyptian, well the Egyptian reacted as though he'd just watched a really good horror movie.

"Well that was great," he expressed at the end. "Excellent, excellent. Seth can you give me and Antanois," he slapped Antanois on the back, "a little tour before we leave. We both may never be privileged enough to see this place again." Seth hoped not.

"This way." Seth gestured for them to follow her. After only a few paces they passed an identical operating theatre. A red lit figure 4 indicated this one was also being used. Three surgeons, just like in theatre 3 were operating on a body. Unlike the previous operation the body was covered, open only where the surgeons were working. There was no cameraman and no tv monitor. The eyes on the exposed head were closed. Antanois recognised the face immediately. It was his chief engineer, the Scotsman.

Antanois felt another pat on his back. "Don't worry Antanois, we were kind to your man here. He didn't even know he was dying. We put him to sleep if you like. With the rupture in the wall, he knew too much. We couldn't risk him talking. His body will be put to good use I promise."

Antanois simply nodded, he was too exhausted, too tired and too shocked to give any sort of answer. For support he was leaning on an identical set of viewing chairs to the ones facing theatre three. The Egyptian rested his right hand on the nearest chair. "Do you know these are the original chairs installed during the second world war. They were to allow the German high brass to witness medical experimentation. Ingenious." The Egyptian shook his head in apparent wonderment. Whilst Seth and Antanois were taking this in, two medics passed pushing a covered body on a gurney. Seth looked on in astonishment.

"Is that a new patient? You're taking a bloody risk if it is. The gendarmes and the police might still be watching this place, not to mention the media."

The Egyptian nodded. "Yes it is and I know, I know. It's a huge risk but we had no choice. It wasn't my doing. Something unexpected took place and it had to be dealt with. Anyway, I think you'll find he's a fine specimen. He should be fit, for he was a gendarme."

Seth and Antanois stared open mouthed. A gendarme! The body was wheeled into the next theatre, theatre five. The figure 5 turned from green to red. Another harvesting was about to start.

The Egyptian either didn't see Seth's and Antanois' shocked faces or chose to ignore them. Whichever it was he insisted on Seth continuing with their tour. Theatre six was the last theatre after which they passed a shining wall of what looked like highly polished stainless steel. A huge sign on the wall announced. "Strictly authorised staff only."

"What's behind here?" The Egyptian didn't appear to know. Seth's expression turned from shock to one of pride.

"This," she said proudly, "is where we store our harvest, especially organs. In fact behind these doors is probably the most advanced organ storage facility anywhere in the world. Until a few years ago a harvested organ would have immediately been put on ice to prevent cells from being damaged, making the organ unusable. The shelf life of the organ using this process would normally be no more than twelve hours, often a lot less. As a result many patients needing a transplant often died even though an organ had become available. What we have on the other side of this wall, is something called, Nature Biotechnology. We have literally recreated the conditions of the human body using mechanics. The pressure and temperature in the machines inside are identical to a perfect body. The harvested organs carry on working as though they're still in a body, except they're not, they're in a machine. We believe for example we can keep a liver healthy, ready for transplant for up to a year in here, maybe longer."

"Brilliant, think of all the lives we can save." The Egyptian seemed to forget how cruelly he was ending one. The Nature Biotechnology room was the end of the tour. Back at the reception area, the Egyptian shook hands with Seth and Antanois as though they'd just finished a pleasant business meeting. "I hope you both won't be offended if I say, I hope we won't ever meet again." Both smiled their understanding, they both hoped so too. With that the Egyptian and his entourage left in two waiting cars. Antanois and Seth after he'd gone, hadn't really anything to say to each other. Mumbling goodbye Antanois started the long walk back up the tunnel to his life on the surface. Seth being the overseer of all things connected to the harvesting and transportation of body parts, returned quickly to the medical facility to see what was happening with her two new patients.

On the summit of Mont d'Hubert the Tunisian restaurant had five new male customers. Three had chosen Couscous and three Poulet Meshi. All were washing it down with mint tea.

If the walk down the tunnel had seemed to take an age the walk back felt a lot longer. Antanois still believed in the organisation but what he had just witnessed had severely shaken him and his faith. It had also made him realise what a tightrope he was walking. Surely the master of everything hadn't intended such cruelty. Discipline yes, loyalty yes. In such a large outfit you had to have these, but to control with such cruelty really wasn't necessary. Perhaps the master simply wasn't aware, Antanois theorises, suddenly stopped. A red light was flashing above the false wall to the garage. A red light meant there was movement at the farmhouse. Antanois switched on a television monitor set into the wall. Stood at the door to his farmhouse were two gendarmes, their car parked in the drive. He watched as they rung and then knocked on his front door. They waited for just over a minute and presumably accepting no one was in returned to their car and drove off. They made no attempt to search outside the property which was a good thing. If they were onto something, at least a quick look around would have been inevitable. Antanois waited a good ten minutes before opening the false wall. Fifteen minutes later he was back in his farmhouse. Nothing looked to have been moved. He needed a drink, Antanois moved to pick up his decanter, it was empty from the night before. MERDE. He was out of beer too. MERDE. He couldn't wait, after all that had just happened he needed a drink. He'd have to go to Wissant to make a purchase. Grabbing his coat he opened the front door. A man stood in his way, a tall man dressed in expensive clothes and a head covered with a mass of tussled curls.

"Pierre!"

"Hello Antanois, may I come in. We need to talk." Without waiting for an answer Pierre pushed Antanois aside and stepped through the threshold.

Antanois closed the front door and followed his unexpected guest into the lounge. MERDE.

Private Hospital – South Kensington, London, England

The American was receiving dialysis when the doctor knocked and entered. He was bored with dialysis, he was bored with these four walls and he was bored of watching television. He'd paid over a million fucking bucks for this shit and every day he stayed here the hospital were charging him more. It was daylight fucking robbery. He hated them but they had him by the short and curlys. It was either them or goodbye to this life. And they fucking knew it. He fucking hated them.

"What?"

The man in a white coat remained unphased. "Good news," he said waving a paper. "We've found you a liver."

"It's not from someone with a funny colour, I don't want no Negro shit inside me"

The doctor held back from repeating what he really thought. He had to remain professional but bloody hell it was hard with customers such as this. "No, they're from people like you and me."

"People?"

"Yes you actually have a choice, French or Scottish, which would you prefer?"

"Scottish, we speak the same language."

"Great, Scottish it is then. We'll operate tomorrow. I'll get my assistant to come and explain the procedure." The Doctor quickly closed the door.

Hotel De La Plage – Calais Plage, France

"I hope you don't mind," Fatima smiled engagingly as the Capitaine sat down. "Only it seemed rude to remain over there now we've been introduced.

"Not at all." Mind? He was delighted. He went to finish his coffee only to find it cold. He called for another.

"And I'll have a Kir, merci." Fatima smiled again. "I hope you don't mind."

"Not at all," the capitaine repeated. "So how do you know Pierre?"

"Oh, he helped me a long, long time ago, when I was just a girl." Fatima looked out of the window. The Capitaine sensed it was a subject she didn't want to expand on so left it at that.

"So you're a film buff?" Fatima's hand was still fingering her necklace though now she was playing with the jewellery the necklace was supporting, a kind of ornate cross. The capitaine couldn't help being mesmerised by the playful movement of her hands, it was verging on the hypnotic. And her scent, it was vaguely familiar. For some peculiar reason it made him dream of the sea, a warm blue sea with flowers floating between the waves. As he watched her hand play teasingly with her jewellery another button came loose revealing an ever greater hint of what lay underneath. He was sat in plain view, in a restaurant and yet strangely the capitaine felt he was in another world and losing control in that other world. He had to do something, say something to bring him back to the here and now, to this world. "That's a beautiful cross," he could barely get his words out.

"Thank you," Fatima held the cross just above her recently revealed cleavage. "It's called La Croix d'Agadez. These," Fatima with one finger touched, one by one, four points of the cross. " These represent the four cardinal points of direction." So you asked if I was a film buff Thierry, sorry I absolutely, refuse to call you capitaine. The answer is no, not really, I just love this particular film and wish to see where it was made."

Fatima had snapped, unknowingly for him, the capitaine out of it. She had him under her complete control, exactly where she'd wanted him. Despite Pierre's reservation, it had been easy, too easy. His fidelity and innocence made him all the more vulnerable, he was like Adam before he bit into the apple. The capitaine was already hers. Tomorrow she'd take it a step further and after that, for the capitaine, there'd be no going back.

New Dawn Hotel – Bayswater, London, England

Habib found a man waiting for him when he returned to his hotel. He was sat at a table on the small terrace out front. The receptionist told Habib the man had asked after him.

"Pitgam," the man whispered loudly as Habib approached, "walk with me." Habib did so, almost as though he were following orders. Together, they walked up Inverness Terrace towards Kensington Gardens. "Well done Habib you have passed your practical exam with flying colours." He handed Habib a brown A4 envelope. "Tomorrow you start your work with us. After breakfast, book out of your hotel and call a taxi to take you to this address. The stranger handed him a card. "This is your home whilst you work for us. I can assure you it's very comfortable. A car will pick you up from there at two pm sharp and take you to your promised place of work. Tomorrow will be something of an introductory, after that we'll keep you busy. I promise. This is the last time we'll meet Habib." The stranger held out his hand. "Good luck Habib, I wish you every success in your new life." The stranger broke from the shake. "You can go back to your hotel now." The stranger walked briskly away, at the end of the Terrace turning left along Bayswater Road.

Habib, almost trancelike walked back to his hotel. By the time he entered reception he could remember, in detail, everything he'd been told but nothing about the stranger who had instructed him. He had simply disappeared from his mind.

The Fielding Hotel – Covent Garden, London, England

John had no idea what reaction he'd get by producing a gun but roars of laughter wasn't one of them.

"I hope you're not thinking of using that on me," Maureen laughed. "There's no way I can take that." John found himself laughing with her, the whole scenario was beyond the ridiculous. Still laughing they collapsed on the bed together, both anxious to unclothe the other. In the process the gun dropped to the floor, it was forgotten.

Maureen recognised from the way John manoeuvred he was a man of some experience and had to use all of hers to make sure she remained firmly in control. Using her mouth, arms, legs and at times weight, she sometimes battered her target into submission, making him do what she commanded, not what he thought he wanted.

John had never experienced a woman like her, he was helpless and made to worship her body the way she wanted. At no time did she fully let go of him. If she needed her arms for something else, her legs clamped him firmly and vice versa. If she needed both her arms and legs freed she'd use her body weight along with her strength to keep him under her control. The result for him was a continued excitement that never quite spilled over into orgasm. And thank God, because if not their passionate embrace may have been over in a couple of minutes.

Twice Maureen felt John try to enter her. How dare he, all men should learn you should satisfy your woman first before you even attempt such a move. His attempts made her even more demanding. She would make him pay. After around ninety minutes Maureen swung herself over so she was sitting astride his face. She clamped his arms between each leg and leaned forward, supported by the headboard. She stared into his eyes as she began to grind herself on his mouth. He was helpless, the combination of her weight along with the way her legs held his arms meant he was there for the taking and she took him. After minutes of grinding she leant back and pushed herself forward so his tongue had nowhere to go but deep inside her. Maureen groaned with pleasure and wanting more, leaned back pushing harder, all the more forward. John felt as though his neck might break but didn't want her to stop. Never had he'd been so aroused. After a series of minor orgasms, Maureen decided it was time to finish him off and reward herself at the same time, by cuming hard. Loosening her left leg she freed John's right arm and helped his hand find his straining phallus. Mission accomplished she pushed down on John's forehead with both hands and started to grind herself over his mouth with much more force than before. She could see his eyes bulge as he struggled with her weight. Sitting back slightly, Maureen cupped her hands under his head and pulled his head up burying his tongue deep into her vagina. He could feel him struggling to breathe but that simply turned her on. If he worked magic with his tongue she would release her hold a little allowing him seconds to take a breath. If his tongue failed to please her he was in danger of dying. One thing Maureen quickly discovered, John knew how to use his tongue, at times it felt as though her clitoris was being tickled by a thousand feathers. She'd read once that the clitoris had no other use than to give pleasure. If there was a God, she must be a woman for man had been given no such gift. As John fought hard for survival, Maureen felt his body tense and his right arm speed up. She knew he was close to orgasm and wanted her pleasure before it was too late. Grabbing his ears she positioned John's mouth exactly where he wanted it. Keeping it there she started pushing and pulling hard, in short sharp thrusts. She could feel the orgasm rising inside her. She felt John jerk underneath her as he came. Seconds later Maureen exploded, her full weight thrusting down with immense force on John's face. Several more orgasms followed, each one battering her target's face. Slowly Maureen's orgasms faded and she began to hear muffled cries coming from the man beneath her. Slowly she rolled off, collapsing onto her back beside him. John, gasped then gulped, his mouth opening and closing like a fish.

After he'd managed to catch his breath, John turned. "Jesus Bree, you almost killed me."

"Bree not Maureen then." Maureen laughed. "Now after that, do I deserve a ride in your lovely car?"

John still struggling for breath, laughed. "The car's not mine, I was just getting it back for someone. For the rightful owner."

Maureen slid out of bed and into her heels. She knew too well how to hold a man's interest. Walking across the room, naked except for her heels, she picked up John's card from the dresser. She flicked it. "I knew that car was too nice for a mere baker."

John laughed again, coughing because laughter required air he didn't have. "I'm not just a baker," he spluttered.

"What are you then?" Maureen reached down and picked up his pistol. Stood naked in her heels holding his gun in both hands was an image John would never forget. "And this, is it real?"

"Yes it's real, put it down Maureen." Maureen to his relief did as he requested.

Maureen stood, legs astride with hands on hips. "What were you intending to do John, shoot me?" Maureen could not believe how cool she was in the face of a real gun. She should be a quivering wreck but she was quite the opposite. She felt confident, powerful even.

John started to laugh again. "No it was for protection, I though you might be a femme fatale."

"A what?"

"A honey trap, paid to get information from me, and you're not, you're just Maureen." John started to cough again as he struggled to laugh.

"So what do you do John, when not baking cakes."

"I'm a debt collector."

"Debt collector?"

"Not the car clamping kind because you haven't paid your parking fine, I specialise in big debts, people who owe hundreds of thousands, sometimes millions. Or precious items like the Aston." John knew he was saying too much, but without the Aston he had to impress the magnificent woman standing in front of him. He already wanted to experience what they had just done again.

"Does that pay well?" Maureen sounded doubtful.

John forgot all his training. He was desperate to keep this woman. "Over quarter of a million from my last job."

Maureen's eyes widened. "What the car?"

"No it wasn't just the car, the same guy owed a lot of money."

"Must have been a lot if you got paid a cool quarter of a million."

John laughed again, the alcohol and lack of air were taking their toll, he wasn't thinking properly. "It was the person who owed the money, who paid me the quarter of a million, not the person who was owed.

Maureen was confused. "Why on earth did he do that?"

"Because I got him off the hook."

265

"How? I mean to pay you quarter of a million, you must have worked some sort of magic. What did you do."

John tapped his nose. "That's for you to find out."

"I will," Maureen challenged him, "just you wait and see."

An hour later John was walking home. Maureen had told him she was meeting a friend. The cold was helping him sober up. He'd had an incredible afternoon. It had been so good it was almost too good to be true. And that bothered him. It had been too perfect. Thinking back to their time in bed he pushed any doubt from his mind. So what, he didn't really care. Anything was worth risking for what he'd just experienced.

Maureen gave it half an hour after John had left, before she left the hotel herself. She was now dressed for protection from the cold, rather than dressed to impress. Even so she still managed to turn several heads as she marched with purpose down Shaftesbury Avenue. She quickly found the half-price ticket booth at the entrance to Leicester Square. It was just as Mahon had described and as depicted in the flyer he had given her.

Maureen suddenly felt nervous about approaching the ticket booth, and worse, silly almost, asking for a show called Pitgam. Back in France, how Mahon had explained it, it had all felt very exciting, now here in London it simply felt stupid. A minute later she found herself in front of a gum chewing woman sat behind a Perspex screen. "Have you tickets for a show called Pitgam?"

"Yes Madame but we don't sell them here, I'll call someone who can show you where to buy them. Please wait over there." The woman signalled for her to wait to one side.

"This way please Madame." A man in his forties, Maureen guessed. Wearing wildly contrasting jacket and trousers and a dogs dinner shirt ushered her to another booth several doors down. "Tickets for which show Madame?"

"Pitgam, p-i-t-g-a-m."

"Ah yes, a fringe show. Please wait in here, we'll have to phone the theatre." The man opened a door at the back of a small waiting area. Maureen stepped through into a dimly lit corridor. At the end a flight of stairs doubled back over her. A stronger light flowed from an open door to her right and it was through here she was directed. Inside, stacked high were cases of soft drinks and crisps. In the middle of the room were two cheap plastic chairs. One was occupied by a woman, her skin wrinkled from years of smoking than from age. The other chair was empty and the woman motioned for Maureen to sit down.

"Mahon told us to expect you, but not so soon. You caught us on the hop." The woman's voice too had been affected by her smoking habit. It was gravelly and didn't suit a female Maureen thought. How this woman knew Mahon, heaven only knows. Style wise she was as far away from Mahon as Pluto is from the sun. "So you've made contact."

"Yes," Maureen nodded.

"And?"

Maureen hesitated, she still wasn't sure what she was supposed to find out. "Well, he's not just a baker, he's also a debt collector. He's just returned a car, an Aston Martin, I think." The woman looked pleased and nodded for Maureen to continue. "He told me he'd been paid quarter of a million for the job."

"What?"

"Yes but not by the people who had sent him. By the person he was sent to get the money from. Oh and today he was carrying a gun, I think it had a silencer."

Surprisingly the woman didn't seem to find the gun important. "Did he tell you why he was paid quarter of a million?"

"He said," Maureen searched for the words John had used. "He said it was because he helped get him off the hook, yes that's it, off the hook were the words he used."

The woman looked thoughtful and it was several seconds before she spoke. "Look Maureen, we already knew he was a debt collector and what you have told me raises some questions. You've done really well so far. When are you meeting the target again?"

"Tomorrow, around lunchtime. I'm going to call him in the morning."

"Where do you have breakfast? Your hotel doesn't offer it."

Maureen shrugged, "this morning I just got a take away, coffee too, I brought it back to my room."

"Well tomorrow, take breakfast here," she handed Maureen a card. It's a café in the market, It's easy to find, and it's more your style than here." The woman grinned displaying a set of yellow stained fragmented teeth. "Before you arrive buy a Times newspaper, leave it open at the page with the crosswords and start filling one in with this." The woman handed Maureen a pen. It's green ink," the woman explained. "It doesn't matter which letters you put, you're not answering a clue, just leaving a sign. One of the waiters there will recognise the sign and know who you are. They will organise a contact. If ever you need to contact us in future do this and always use the Times printed on the day, never an old one. From now on never use our code unless you're asked for it. We will though use it if we need to contact you. Be there nine o'clock sharp tomorrow. That's when the café opens. I need to speak to someone to check where you go from here. Oh and well done Maureen."

Maureen blushing, made to leave. She felt the woman touch her arm. "Madame your tickets." The woman handed her a stiff, sealed vanilla envelope, still grinning. Maureen took it, puzzled.

"Thank you," she said and left. Outside the sky was darkening and London was preparing for another lively night. Normally Maureen would have revelled in the atmosphere but now suddenly she felt exhausted. Buttoning her coat against the cold she decided on an early night. So much had happened in one day. In under twelve hours she had been propelled into an alien world. A world until today she thought only existed in films. Fifteen minutes later she was soaking in her bath. In another fifteen minutes she was dry, scented and in bed. Fifteen seconds after her head snuggled the pillow, Maureen was asleep.

Ardres – France

Dinner was waiting for Thierry when he arrived home. He immediately felt a deep sense of guilt that was too quickly quashed when his mind wandered back to Fatima and their time together. The two had lunched together before Thierry, the capitaine had had to return to his gendarmerie. He had loved, no adored every moment he had spent with Fatima, who he now knew to be Persian. Never had he met anyone with such a sense of mystery, everything about her was mysterious. Almost as though she was from another world. Yes that's how he thought of her, as someone from another world. He couldn't wait to try and unravel the many secrets that he knew she carried with her. And her scent, he could still smell it, it toyed with his senses, releasing feelings that he dare not think about. He had only just met the woman and already he was 'meurs d'amour.'(Love-sick). That was dangerous, very dangerous and Thierry knew it, but he simply didn't care.

As was routine his wife kissed him lightly on the forehead before turning in for the night. Thierry as was the norm, retired to his office for his nightly fix of hard rock. That night he decided on Yungblud again, he'd liked what he had heard before. Tonight he didn't feel like sitting. As the first notes of, 'The Funeral', started to play, Thierry started to dance, dancing like a man possessed. On reaching the chorus he started to sing and sing loudly. Forces in the room listening to the words, forces we can never explain became worried that Thierry, the capitaine by singing the song was perilously tempting fate.

Farmhouse – Escalles, France

Pierre strode across the lounge, coming to rest in front of the window looking out on Mont d'Hubert. Hands in pockets he stared wistfully at the steeply rising slope. Without turning round he spoke.

"We have a problem Antanois, well several problems in fact. The Egyptian has dealt with a couple today. I can't say I like his methods but you can't argue that he's not efficient and he always gets results." Pierre, fell silent. Antanois thought it best not to reply. Pierre was once more taking in the view of Mont d'Hubert. Again without turning he spoke. "Everything I have worked for is under that hill Antanois, I will not let it fail just as we're about to go into full production." There came another, what seemed like to Antanois, eternal silence. Finally Pierre turned to face him. "Do you know why the gendarmes were visiting you?"

Antanois shook his head. "I've no idea."

"You know if you slip up Antanois, the Egyptian can always come back."

Antanois' face drained of all colour, the memory of Armani was all too fresh. To imagine it could be him strapped to that table was too much to bear.

Pierre suddenly smiled. "I'm sure that won't be necessary Antanois but I can't, the organisation can't, afford any more slip ups. You do understand that don't you?"

Antanois nodded, he tried to speak but all that came out was an unintelligible rasping sound.

Pierre took the sound as confirmation Antanois more than understood. "Good, then you'll understand why I can't have you staying in this farmhouse anymore?" Antanois didn't reply, he was on the verge of freezing with fright. "After I've gone, I want you to pack your bags and move into the bunker. Quarters have been arranged for you, you will be living in residence four. You're lucky, it was designed and equipped to accommodate an officer. Oh and as a measure of my gratitude, take your decanter for I have arranged for your favourite tipple to be regularly stocked. As for the outside world, you will be flying back to Lebanon, though of course it wont be you. Your car will be sold. In two days' time you will no longer exist in France, except of course you will. It's just that no-one will know. Any questions Antanois?"

Antanois hung his head. He just managed to whisper 'no.' He was a condemned man. Nobody as far as he knew got out of the bunker, not once you were living there. Everybody spoke about the day they'd retire or get out and how they would spend their earnings, saved whilst in the bunker, but nobody actually left. Those that did were carefully watched before silently disappearing, usually within hours of leaving. As far as those still inside were concerned, those who had left were out living the highlife with the incredible money they'd earnt whilst living and working below ground.

"You know the organisation always rewards loyalty Antanois, don't look so glum." Antanois managed a faint smile. "Good, I'll be informed when you're nice and cosy. Your role in the bunker won't change. Good evening Antanois." Pierre made to leave. "Oh and Antanois," he waited checking to see he had the condemned man's full attention. "Don't do anything stupid will you, I have a fondness for you Antanois. I don't want to see you come to harm." Antanois' lips moved but no sound projected from them. "Good," Pierre smiled. "Have a good evening Antanois, sleep well." The silence left after Pierre was gone hung heavy in the air. For a second Antanois considered running, in the next second he dismissed the idea. Running was futile and he'd probably end up like Armani. No he would simply have to take his chances in the bunker. Maybe one day the master will recognise his loyalty and reward him. Maybe being the operative word. MAYBE. Three hours later Antanois was installed in residence four. His residence consisted of a lounge a bedroom and a bathroom. All fitted to a high standard. There were no cooking facilities but in the lounge there was a small fridge. On opening it he'd found it to be full of Lebanese beer. So the organisation had known all along. He actually managed a smile.

Today hadn't gone well. Pierre hoped Bree and Fatima were faring better. Tomorrow they were starting operations again though be it on a very small scale. He couldn't afford for anything else to go wrong. It worried him that a gendarme had been following him, had called in his number. The one positive, it looked as though he'd been acting alone. His gendarmerie knew nothing about his quest. Hopefully Fatima would find out more.

He was genuinely sad about Antanois. He honestly liked the man. Antanois wasn't aware but he'd had to fight tooth and nail to prevent the Egyptian having his fun with him. Yes he'd stuck his neck out to save him and as a compromise had had to have him condemned to the bunker. Antanois would never thank him, just blame him. If only he knew.

Now there was the problem of the farmhouse. He couldn't risk a stranger renting it. As a solution the organisation were using their members to rent it as a normal holiday let, two weeks or one week at a time. It had been a real pain to organise and expensive. The sooner the bunker was running at full capacity the better. All the trouble and extra expense would hopefully then, quickly be forgotten. Sliding into his cockpit he swung his car onto the coast road heading for Boulogne. He'd booked a table for one only at Le Matelote. After the day he'd had, Pierre felt he deserved it.

Bayswater – London, England

Behind an instantly forgettable door off Westbourne Grove, up an instantly forgettable flight of stairs and on the first floor in a very dull office with frayed carpet covering the floor and decades old wallpaper covering some of the walls, sat three men. All three were in deep conversation and all three were speaking in hushed tones. They were worried about the way things were going in France. The purpose of their meeting, could they do anything to alleviate the situation. To take the heat off. A diversionary tactic was, all agreed, the best option but it would come with huge risks. Were the risks worth taking, this was the multimillion dollar question.

In the end all felt it was. They would put their plan into action tomorrow night. The reasoning that swung their decision, if by their actions they came under heat, they could go for the government's jugular. The organisation had done it before and it had worked before. Politicians were always easy targets. They had too much to lose.

CHAPTER
—15—

Calais – France

Dawn was breaking and migrants from every part of Calais were slowly making their way to one of the charitable food stations that had set up to serve a hot drink and breakfast. Breakfast being normally, either buttered baguette and confiture or buttered croissant. Some migrants arrived carrying with them everything they owned, sometimes this would be nothing more than a blanket. Others had left what little they still possessed where they'd slept for the night, trusting others to keep guard. The mood considering their plight was often surprisingly joyful.

That morning a face, a female face nearly all recognised was asking more questions than normal. She'd been doing the same at supper yesterday. Both charity workers and the migrants had noticed the change, her increased interest. And it wasn't at just one station, she'd been touring all the established stations and asking about new food stations too. One worker who was so anti- establishment she was close to being an anarchist, suspected a rat. She would keep a close eye on Marie. She was determined to find out what she was up to.

Covent Garden – London, England

It was a good job she had left early Bree pondered, for she soon found that buying a newspaper in Covent Garden these days was no easy matter. It had taken an amazing amount of time and a lot of leg work before she could declare success. Dead on nine o'clock though she was sat in the named café with a large cappuccino and two buttered croissants, one with salami and cheese, the other with butter and marmalade. Actually situated in the Piazza, the menu declared that the café had French origins, starting as a bakery in Reims. It was beautifully furnished and had that delightful early morning smell that somehow always faded as the day matured. As instructed she lay the paper, open at the crossword page face up on the table. With the green ink pen she had filled in some of the squares to the cryptic crossword. Rather than just put the odd letter she had created words or phrases, such as, no idea, or headache. By nine thirty she was on her second cappuccino and wondered if whoever it was, was actually going to show up. Just as fate does, as Bree was about to give up and leave, a tall elegantly dressed gentleman pulled out a chair and sat down. Pulling off a pair of gloves he held out a hand.

"Sorry I'm late, delays on the Central line. No change there I suppose," and laughed at his own humour. "Morning, my name's Charles by the way. A real pleasure to meet you Bree, that is your name isn't it, most unusual."

"Actually it's Maureen," Maureen knew the organisation or whatever it was knew her real name, she had no idea why this man was using Bree.

"Yes, yes, of course it is, just my little test. Bree sounds so much more exciting though doesn't it. Maureen sounds as though you should be at home doing the dishes, don't you think?" He laughed at his own joke again. Very funny Maureen thought, had he been listening at their table yesterday. Charles, if that was his real name clicked his fingers and ordered a double espresso. Maureen watched with interest. He was rather like an English version of Mahon in France, around the same age too. Except where Mahon was all smoothness and charm this man was clumsily polite. And another major difference, she desired Mahon whenever she set eyes on him, she could never imagine herself desiring this man in that way. Charles' espresso arrived and immediately he took a short sip, after which he smacked his lips in satisfaction.

Pleasantries finished, Charles, to Maureen's surprise, got straight to the point. "So Bree tell me about what you have found out about our chap so far. I've gathered for your first assignment you've done really well."

Bree wallowing in pride recounted what she had told the woman yesterday. Charles listened carefully.

"Hmmm," he expressed after she'd finished. "You're not a stupid woman are you. I think you can see where we're going with this. We need to find out why a man who owes money, pays someone who has come to collect a debt, a great deal of money to. As you say he told you it was 'to get him off the hook.' You see Bree we have a theory and we need to find out if our theory is right. A few years ago someone who worked for us got himself into a lot of debt. Hundreds of thousands of pounds. Silly boy. Anyway, your John got him 'off the hook' too. He paid just £50,000, not quarter of a million. I suppose where debt is concerned it's all relative. Anyway he told us that John had somehow made him disappear. What that means, we have an idea, but need to find out for sure and how he does it. Make people disappear I mean. There Bree, that's your mission. Exciting isn't it?"

Exciting wondered Bree, maybe but how the hell was she going to find all that out. The next moment the man was standing to leave. "There it is, sorry must dash, when you've found out something come back here. Same routine, I won't be more than an hour," and with that he was gone. Gone and leaving her to pick up the tab for his espresso. Maureen looked in her bag for her purse, had what happened really happened?

She shook her head, her mission was starting to turn out to be something like Alice Through the Looking Glass. She'd been catapulted into a quite mad world with even madder people. Tucked beside her purse lay the envelope given to her last night, she still hadn't opened it. She'd do so now. Inside she found a ticket for tomorrow night's performance of Tina the musical, and £500 in £20 notes. Quickly closing her bag she wondered, if she pinched herself whether she'd wake up from a dream. This world she had fallen into was beyond madness. As she replaced her purse her phone rang. It was John, he was keen, good.

"Bree," he was so kind. "Are we still on for today?" Maureen confirmed laughing, of course she was, especially after yesterday.

"Good, will you let me show you some of my Covent Garden?"

"That sounds ominous," Maureen half joked.

"No, I'm serious, just one pub then I'll cook for you, my flat's just up the road. I think I might surprise you, I'm a good cook." Maureen hesitated, she was remembering the gun. In her hotel she'd been safe, in his flat she would be at his mercy. John could hear her doubt in the silence. "Oh and don't worry, I promise I won't shoot you." She heard him laugh.

"You'd better not," Maureen managed to laugh too. "Where's this pub, is that where we're meeting? And what time."

"Lunchtime," John came back quickly, "say just after midday. It's called The Cross Keys and it's at 31 Endell Street, you can't miss it. It's five minutes' walk from your hotel. Your hotel, if they're worth their salt will tell you how to find it."

"Don't worry, I'll find it."

"Great, I'll wait outside for you." John waited for Bree to say something else but she didn't so he rang off.

I've got to think, Maureen considered and the place she normally solved all her problems was in the bath. And that's just what she'd do next, have a bath.

John held onto the receiver for several seconds after he had rung off. Was he being stupid. What had this woman done to him. He felt like a kid with a new toy. The trouble was he loved his new toy, he loved the feeling and he didn't want it to stop.

Back at her hotel, Maureen was enjoying her soak in the bath at the bottom of her bed. She was loving the new world Mahon had introduced her to but at times it could be a little overwhelming. She wasn't sure who were the good guys and who were the bad guys but Mahon she was convinced was on the good side and that was all that mattered. Even though some of his colleagues were a bit weird. She reached down for her handbag and pulled out her ticket for Tina the musical. Was this another strange rendezvous and if so who with. Was someone going to sit in the seat beside her and pass her something. She'd seen that happen in films. Well she'd find out tomorrow evening wouldn't she. She let the ticket fall on the floor, coming to rest on an untidy pattern of £20 notes. She lay back so that her vision easily took in the TV. It was on but she wasn't really watching it. She thought of John, his mysterious debt collecting world and his even more mysterious methods. How could she get to the bottom of it without making him suspicious. Closing her eyes she let her mind relax. Within a few minutes an idea had started to form, a few minutes later she saw that the idea definitely had potential. Could she pull it off though and could she be convincing enough to attempt it that afternoon. In under half an hour she had a plan and better still, she was ready to put it into action. Her brain, exhausted, took some much needed time out. Her senses having lain dormant, whilst her brain worked overtime, returned. They made her feel sleepy. Bloody hell her bath water was cold. Maureen pulled the plug and stepped out in a hurry dripping bathwater over her Tina Turner ticket and a good number of £20 notes. You idiot Bree, Maureen scolded herself, Maureen would never have done that.

National Crime Agency – Vauxhall, London, England

The meeting was almost over. A plan had been put into place. The investigation in Havant revealed that around the time the deceased had moved to Langstone he had been in contact with a bakery in Putney. A similar investigation in Spain revealed the same. Not long after there were phone records to a mobile but in both cases it was to an anonymous pay as you go phone. The two numbers were different. The owner of the bakery was one John Mitchell, Ex MI5, ex special forces. Was this one of their own turned bad? Was he responsible for both murders and if so why? And why so brutal?

Roger had done his best to dampen down such views but he was walking a tightrope. He didn't want any investigation, doing a U-turn and focusing on him. The plan was to be a sting operation, not to arrest but to find out how his debt collecting operation worked. They already knew it must be a cash operation or something very cleverly run for there were no suspicious payments into his bank accounts and his side-line hadn't been registered with HMRC. His debt collecting operation was completely off the radar.

To start the ball rolling an undercover officer was to contact the bakery number. They were to play the part of a creditor, claiming to be owed a hell of a lot of money and requiring a specialist to get his money back. No questions asked. The last address he'd have for the guy was empty, his debtor had obviously done a runner. All he had was a mobile number and that had gone dead. The NCA would do the necessary, in case their target checked, to set up an empty house and false records of the last known resident. The debt it was decided, needed to be big. You only caught the big fish with a bait attractive enough to reel them in. The figure decided on was £250, 000,000. Quarter of a billion. Roger prayed he'd never need the crime agency to come up with it, or his career would be history.

After everyone had left his office, Roger pondered about warning his ex-colleague. In the end he decided he simply couldn't risk it. John was on his own on this one. The NCA already knew their past connection and that he'd interviewed him at his Covent Garden flat. For all he knew, they may even be watching him, though he doubted that. No, John was definitely on his own with this one. Anyway John wasn't stupid, he'd almost certainly smell a rat. Whatever happened, he prayed that they would never discover his connection in all of this.

South Kensington – London, England

Habib was busy exploring his new home. As instructed, he had booked out of his hotel that morning and taken a taxi to the address that was to be his home whilst working for the hospital. His housekeeper had let him in. HOUSEKEEPER! His new home was a basement flat housed in an ornate brick Victorian house in a very smart South Kensington Street. It had one large bedroom, a large lounge diner, fully fitted kitchen and a bathroom with a bath and a walk in shower. The flat was fully decorated and some of the pictures on the wall were of scenes from his country, Tunisia. There was even an old photo of his home town. His new employers, had it seemed thought of everything. He couldn't wait to start working for them, to pay them back for their attentive kindness. His family back home would be so proud. At 2pm sharp, a taxi arrived to transport him to the hospital where he was to be a surgeon. A surgeon specialising in transplants. He would, he'd been told either be saving lives or at the very least improving peoples lives. He couldn't wait to get started.

Bergues – France

After a morning at his office Capitaine Maubert was, at least he thought, taking a much deserved afternoon off. The house visits were well under way but so far nothing remotely suspicious had turned up. He was beginning to wonder if Ismail had been hallucinating and the heads had been washed in from the sea after all. Drug use, he'd been told was almost epidemic amongst some of the migrants. Anyway just to check he'd arranged to meet Marie at her friends' house in Les Attaques later that afternoon, even though it would be in his own time.

He'd picked Fatima up at her hotel at midday and now they were enjoying traditional Flemish cuisine in Le Bruegel, Bergue's most famous Estaminet. Housed in a 16th century building, the owners had recreated a traditional ale and food house. It had been popular from the day it had opened but after featuring in the film Bienvenue Chez Les Ch'tis, you nearly always had to book.

Fatima appeared to love it and dressed in colourful and stylish Muslim attire, covered almost from head to toe, she became almost as much an attraction as the estaminet itself. After their meal Capitaine Maubert gave her a tour of the medieval town, pointing out many of the places featured in the film. Back in his car Fatima thanked him profusely exclaiming he had given her the best day of her life. To thank him she clasped his head with her hands and gave him a kiss on the cheek. It was a moment the capitaine would remember as long as he lived.

Before driving her back to her hotel, the capitaine asked if she'd mind if he stopped on the way. He had some official business to attend to. Her answer as he'd expected was, not at all.

It was nearing five in the afternoon when they pulled up outside the rather nondescript house belonging to Marie's friends and where Ismail had been sheltering the last few days. Marie showed him in. The capitaine found Ismail sitting at a largish kitchen table covered with a plastic cover decorated with colourful images of fruit. He looked a lot better since the last time he'd set eyes on him and he also looked genuinely pleased to see him, not scared. That was good, it would make their conversation easier. Marie was about to shut the door when she saw there was a passenger in the capitaine's car. At first she'd exploded. What was he thinking of risking Ismail's cover by bringing a stranger to the house. Her friends' house too at that, or had he forgotten. Marie calmed down when the capitaine explained who she was, why she was with him and that she hadn't a clue as to why or what he was doing there. It was Ismail himself who prevented any further argument. Coming to the door to see what all the fuss was about he couldn't help but spot Fatima and to both their surprise and shock he ran out of the door to greet her. Ismail was fed up with strangers, living a strange culture. Here was someone who was from his world, who understood his way of life. Here was a true friend.

A few minutes later all were sat around the kitchen table and a strange gathering they looked, Capitaine Maubert couldn't help thinking. Not one of them were remotely similar, circumstances, tragic circumstances had brought them all together. Fatima as it turned out although it wasn't her natural tongue, nor the Arabic she was used to, did understand most of Ismail's Arabic and was therefore able to translate. Often the two would, rather annoyingly disappear into conversation as if the other three weren't there. It became Marie's job to keep bringing them back, at which both Fatima and Ismail would laugh, and both apologise profusely. What had initially been intended as a follow up interview ended up turning into something of a social event. Perhaps it was better that way, far from being guarded Ismail was all smiles and chatter. The result was the same though. He was adamant what he had recorded on the capitaine's Dictaphone was what had happened. And even more frustrating, he could remember nothing else, he had told them everything he could remember. He was sorry but there it was.

Just as they got up to leave, the capitaine's phone rang. He excused himself, it was his wife, he'd take it outside. His wife he realised by her tone was severely stressed. Her first question, "where are you," caught him by surprise. Without thinking he answered truthfully, Les Attaques.

"Thank God Theirry, you're only minutes away. My mother's had a fall, quite a bad one. Can you pick me up and drive me over there. Our daughter's borrowed my car as hers is off the road. Remember? How long will you be Thierry?"

Before he knew it he had told her, ten minutes. His wife had immediately put the phone down. Fuck, it was too late now, he'd promised her. He looked back at the house, both Marie and Fatima were stood in the doorway. Fuck, what a bloody mess. What was he going to do.

Covent Garden – London, England

John had been right, the Cross Keys was no more than a five minute walk from The Fielding. And he was right on two counts, you couldn't miss it. A myriad of plants adorned the pavement outside. John she noticed looked a lot more casual than yesterday and thus more relaxed. Instead of a shirt and jacket he was wearing a half zip fleece, and not a cheap one, she could tell. He smiled broadly on seeing her approach. His eyes, she was very aware, almost devoured her. That was good. It was what she wanted as well as intended. Once again Bree was dressed to kill.

John ushered her inside, "This place gets busy early, we need to get in quick if we want a table."

To Maureen, inside, the pub to her resembled something like an Aladdin's cave. Every possible spare space was taken up by sometimes extravagant antiques, pop memorabilia, huge mirrors and anything remotely eccentric. It was a virtual palace. They found a table and

The Cross Keys, Endell St, Covent Garden

Maureen sat down whilst John went to the bar to order. A large gin and tonic for Bree and a real ale for himself.

"This place never changes," was the first thing John said as he sat down. "I've been coming here since the eighties and it's still the same. The only thing I don't think they do any more, when I was a lad, on a Sunday there were roast spuds on the bar."

"I love it," Maureen admitted looking round and she did. The atmosphere compared to yesterday was much less frantic between them. Though both had the same goal in mind their build up today was much gentler. John especially in, 'his' pub was much more at ease. He loved Covent Garden and purred over its past glories. The café Diana's Diner, famous for its English cooking and customers who were household names. The Rock Garden, a music venue, where bands such as U2, The Police, Iron Maiden and The Smiths once played. The African Centre where genuine bands from that continent played in the basement. Long Acre with its weird and wonderful shops and Stanford's, a shop that sold just about every map you could find in the world. When travel was an adventure and had to be earned. All now sadly distant memories. Covent Garden had lost its soul he bemoaned. Thankfully Café Pacifico remained, London's first Mexican restaurant and Pineapple the world famous dance studio. The pubs, the theatres and of course the Opera House were all still there, but not the places that had once made Covent Garden the centre of the universe.

Maureen loved listening to John talk, his enthusiasm for this place was sincere and she found herself getting completely caught up in the Covent Garden he painted. When John got around to asking her if she was hungry, Maureen, probably more Bree, had far too easily downed three large pink gin and tonics and walking in a straight line would now take all of her concentration. The two of them laughed together as they bumped their way back to John's front door. And Bree kept collapsing in fits of laughter as she mounted the steep narrow stairs to his flat on all fours.

"Water please," Bree cried out as she slumped into his sofa. John obliged.

" Don't sober up too much, I prefer making love to women when they're drunk."

"Why," shouted Bree between peels of laughter, falling backwards and exposing nearly all of her bare legs.

"They don't seem to care then about this," John patted his stomach, Bree roared, spilling most of her water. John disappeared into his kitchen only to reappear wearing a red and white checked apron. "Salmon or pate for starter?" Bree almost choked as she curled up with fits of giggles.

"I dare you to cook, wearing just that and only that." John said nothing but disappeared once more into his kitchen. When he reappeared he was completely naked except for his apron. Bree collapsed once more, this time rolling onto the floor. Shrieks of laughter echoed around the room as she tried and failed to get up.

"Let me help you," John stood over her, intending to help pull her up.

"Hello Scottie, " Brie bawled laughing even more loudly looking up at his collection of dangles. She held out her hands, John took hold and pulled but Bree was stronger. Within seconds he had toppled beside her. Bree attacked him, devouring him. John was right about drunk women and sex, he was about to experience what a drunk woman could really do. Would he survive that was the question.

Private Hospital – South Kensington, London, England

Habib was having his tour. The hospital was the best equipped he'd ever seen, it was like a medical palace. It had everything both a doctor and a patient could wish for. The atmosphere was calm, almost like that of a hotel and the company's slogan, 'we care,' was plastered everywhere. He was shown to his theatre, it was incredible, far better than anything he trained or worked in before. He was going to enjoy life in London, of that he had no doubt.

After the theatre, whilst being escorted along a corridor he passed another doctor. It was the same person who he'd recognised at the GMC building where he'd taken his practical exam. A flicker of recognition passed between them, it was a split second only and then it was gone. Why were they forbidden to communicate, Habib simply couldn't understand. And if we were honest, the instruction, made him a little uneasy.

Anis recognised his fellow doctor immediately. He had trained in the same medical centre as him though they'd never actually spoken. He'd also attended the same practical examination at the GMC centre on Euston Road. Anis had recognised him there too but as instructed by the organisation, had made no attempt to communicate. As far as everyone else was concerned they were complete strangers. He'd been shown his accommodation that morning, it was nice, very nice. It was a shame where it was, that's all. In the centre of this decadent civilisation with little or no morals. He was born in Tozeur, South West Tunisia. His parents had been farmers and had owned a considerable date plantation. In the eighties Western money had been invested in the town. A row of enormous hotels had been built, to accommodate mainly tourists from Europe. The water they used meant some of the oasis dried up destroying many farmer's livelihoods, including his parents. It had been a horrible time. To add insult to injury a stupid brightly painted train would carry uneducated tourists around the oasis, gawking and taking photos of the people who lived and worked there as though they were nothing more than animals in a zoo. Many of the women wore the shortest of shorts and the briefest of tops corrupting the thoughts of good Muslim men. The whole thing was disgusting, he hated the West. He'd gone into the medical profession to help his own people. The organisation, he had no idea what the actual name of the company was, when they first approached him, promised to fast track his qualification. They had certainly done that. Now they wanted him to work in London. If you want revenge on the West they had told him, London was the place to do it. Just be patient. He was being patient, he was prepared to wait.

Les Attaques – France

Marie watched them go. Seeing Fatima climb in the passenger seat, she'd felt a little jealous. Why was that? The Capitaine gave her a wave as he drove off. She loved his smile, so un-gendarme like. Quite the opposite, it was so human. She'd promised to come back with her findings regarding the food stations tomorrow. The trouble was she hadn't found anything untoward and some of the migrants, because of her constant questioning were starting to be wary of her. She couldn't have that. Rather than call the capitaine she would go to his office. It was easier. She looked forward to it, she just needed something of interest to tell him.

Within seconds of driving off, the capitaine was struggling to find what to say, how to explain to his female passenger. He had no choice but to introduce Fatima to his wife. His mind was in a turmoil, yet he'd done nothing wrong. At least he tried to convinced himself of that.

"What's wrong Thierry?" Trust a woman to see through him. The Capitaine, grabbing her offer of an open door, spat out his problem. It came garbled and rambling but just about coherent. The hardest part was explaining to Fatima that his wife had no idea about him taking the afternoon off to show her around. His admission left him exposed that he might, with his actions, have had an ulterior motive. Exposed his true feelings and worse intentions. He physically cringed as he explained the difficult situation he now found himself in.

To his surprise, Fatima laughed. "Don't worry Thierry, I'm flattered," she patted his hand. "Tell your wife I'm helping with your investigation, after all I am Persian, I speak Arabic. The people you are studying, many of them speak both, am I not right? It's natural you should seek my assistance."

The capitaine breathed a huge sigh of relief. She had got him off the hook and she hadn't been offended. There was something else. "Thank you Fatima, I'm glad you understand. But there's one more thing."

"What's that Capitaine Maubert? That I call you capitaine, not Thierry, am I right?" Thierry nodded wearily, Fatima was one step ahead of him. "Oh and capitaine." Thierry looked her, she really was quite stunning and Fatima was looking at him in in a special way. "You know capitaine, you honestly are a very good looking man, and I really am very flattered."

"Thank you," the capitaine managed a smile and put his foot down. He knew his wife would be outside the house waiting. And she was, and with an overnight bag at her feet. His wife hugged him tight as he got out of the car.

"Thierry thank God, thank you for doing this for me, I know how hard it is for you to leave work."

"It's nothing." Fatima got out of the front seat to sit in the back. "This is F.."

"Hello," his wife smiled sliding into the front seat. "Thierry can we hurry please. My mother cannot be left alone, not for one minute more."

"Of course, sorry. " Thierry to his wife, capitaine to his passenger on the back seat, climbed into the driver's seat and within seconds they were on the D231 heading towards Guines where his mother-in-law lived. He looked at the bag sitting on his wife's lap. "What's that for?"

His wife looked guilty. "I thought I'd stay over Thierry, you don't mind do you? You can go to the friterie for your dinner can't you?"

The Capitaine caught Fatima's eyes looking at him in the rear mirror. "No of course not, of course I don't mind."

Fatima smiled. So her God was watching over her. A gift had just landed on her lap. There would be no better opportunity than tonight. She also knew by the expression in the capitaine's eyes, that he knew it too.

Somewhere In East Sussex, England

A Boring white van parked beside a wooden quay, at the end of which was moored an ageing motor cruiser. A couple of men were loading bags on deck. In minutes they were finished and the van left, heading home to South Kensington. Two more men covered the bags with a heavy tarpaulin and roped it over, checking when they'd finished to ensure their cargo was secure. Satisfied, the cruiser loosened her moorings and motored silently into the English Channel. A little further down the coast a smaller, faster craft started to follow.

Covent Garden – London, England

After nearly two hours of intense body contact Bree and John lay breathless on his carpet.

"Salmon or pate?" John repeated and both laughed.

Whilst Bree showered, John cooked dinner, chicken breast baked with Quark cheese and wrapped in Bayonne ham. The starter in the end was salmon and instead of dessert he had put together a cheese platter. John to her surprise really was a good cook, today she had seen a completely new side to him. A side that she both liked and had enjoyed. After their love making she had sobered up but after sharing a very decent bottle of Merlot with their meal she knew she was on the slide again. She had to complete her mission, to put her plan into action.

"John may I tell you something personal, I need your advice."

"Depends what it is," John chuckled to himself, he was feeling, very, very relaxed.

"Well you're a debt collector as well as a baker?" John nodded.

"Uh huh."

Maureen stared into her glass, " I'm embarrassed to tell you."

"Tell me what, it can't be that bad."

"It is," Bree wiped a tear from her eye, "you see I'm in debt John, a lot of debt. You see when my husband died he left me a lot of money. I've been enjoying it ever since. But recently I've discovered he owed a lot of people a lot of money, a great deal of money. Millions in fact and apparently now he's dead his debt passes to me. I've been threatened John and I don't know what to do."

"I see,"

"I'm not looking for you to give me the money, well I was initially but you're too nice John. Now I'd just value your advice."

John looked reflective, he felt a sense of calm he hadn't experienced in years. "Who was that man you were with at the restaurant, the day you asked for a lift in my car."

"Just a friend." Maureen had to think on her feet. "It was him who suggested I'd try to make your acquaintance. With a car like that he told me you must be loaded. I didn't do badly did I?" Bree giggled.

"No you didn't," John smiled, "and now here we are, you me and my gun."

"You wouldn't." Bree laughed again.

"No I wouldn't," John admitted and the trouble is for me, you know I wouldn't Bree. Bree smiled, shrugging her shoulders.

"Give me a thousand pounds Bree and I'll make your problem go away. You'll have to move though. Get a new identity but I can help you with that too."

This was so sudden, Maureen wasn't expecting it. Well she didn't know what she'd expected, certainly not this. "Just exactly how will you make me disappear John, I need to know before I give you a thousand pounds."

John laughed and poured himself another glass of wine. "Ok I'll tell you, I have a friend who works for the GRO."

"The GRO?"

"General Register Office, it's where all the births deaths and marriages in the UK are registered. My friend, for a thousand pounds will give me a death certificate and register it correctly in the records office so no one will know any different. The man in Spain, paid me quarter of a million to do this. Not a bad profit eh?" John laughed.

Maureen suddenly felt sober, she had accomplished her mission. She couldn't believe it. In the end it had been so easy. She needed to report back.

"Can I think it over?"

"Of course, I'll tell you what Bree I'll even do it for nothing, that is if you promise not to disappear."

"I won't, I promise," Bree reached across and took his hand. "It was a lovely meal John and I've really enjoyed today. But I do honestly have to go now. I'm meeting another friend. Trouble is they work during the day. Do you want to meet again tomorrow?"

"Certainly," John held up his glass. "Till tomorrow." Maureen tightening her coat blew him a kiss. I'll see you tomorrow then, ring me in the morning."

"I will." John watched her close the door. In just a few seconds he had given away his closest guarded secret. Would he really see her again tomorrow. Somehow he doubted it.

Bakery – Putney, London

The Caller had said he was chasing £250,000,000, quarter of a billion pounds and he didn't care how he got it, just as long as he did. He hadn't realised he was calling a bakery, he'd simply been given this number by a friend. No he wasn't prepared to say who. Had he a name? No, not at this moment anyway. Perhaps later.

" Ok, let me put you in touch with someone who may be able to help, is this the best number to contact you on?" The caller confirmed that it was and asked when he might be contacted. "Tonight probably," and the receiver rang off.

Two minutes later, the receiver, the man at the bakery who had taken the call was talking to, his boss, John Mitchell. Who he thought, sounded very relaxed. Too relaxed almost.

"That's a hell of a lot of money," John commented. "Do you think he's for real?"

" He'd sounded very pissed off, so yes probably." John wanted to know how the man had got their number. "From a friend and no, he wasn't willing to say who." His boss had accepted this, it was the norm, non-disclosure was an unwritten law in the murky world of money. Ok, John agreed to call him in the morning.

The man who had taken the call replaced the receiver. This was not at all like his boss. Normally with an opportunity such as this he'd be jumping at it. Not phoning till the next morning, was most unlike him. He hoped everything was alright.

Mont D'hubert – France

Armani had no idea how long he had been awake watching himself slowly die. At first every second had felt like a year, now his brain may as well be dead for time was no longer an entity, it simply didn't exist. The

TV monitor was his life, his only life and the fixed camera didn't move. The live image of his mutilated body had almost become acceptable.

Now, after God knows how long there was a new colour on the screen, it was green. A beautiful fresh green and he could smell flowers, the beautiful perfume of flowers. There was birdsong too, happy, joyful birdsong, he wanted more. Armani was walking through a garden, a beautiful, beautiful garden. Realisation dawned on him, he was at last dying, this was death. A single tear rolled down his left cheek. It was the last physical action his living body managed.

Half an hour later, three surgeons entered the theatre. They started to work on Armani's corpse, it was important they harvested as much as they could whilst the body was still fresh.

R.I.P. Armani

Hotel De La Plage – Calais Plage, France

The drive to Fatima's hotel was made in almost total silence. Neither hardly said a word but the sexual tension spoke louder than anything joined together with letters.

"Shouldn't you be staying with your mother in law," Fatima had asked. The capitaine's response had been negative, that he'd only be in the way. Fatima knew he was lying. This was going to be too easy but she had to make it count. She had to make him crave her, to risk everything for her. To die for her if she asked him.

The capitaine had made an awkward and stumbling offer of dinner. Fatima had accepted but on condition that it was at her hotel restaurant. She wasn't used to the cold and she didn't feel like going out again. The capitaine had hurriedly agreed, too hurriedly. He'd made it very obvious he was keen and at the same time not used to what was happening to him. He wasn't a natural adulterer. Quite the opposite, he was a loyal and devoted husband and she was about to destroy all of that. Fatima almost felt sorry for him. Before they had dinner, she needed to freshen up and had asked the capitaine to give her a couple of hours. The capitaine thus dropped her off and returned to his gendarmerie to catch up on what had been happening. They'd agreed to meet in the bar at eight, in just over two hours' time. Within minutes of being dropped off Pierre had appeared for an update. Fatima told him about their visit to the house in Les Attaques, about Ismail and his account of being drugged and kidnapped in a van. Pierre had visibly stiffened as he'd learned of this. He'd requested the exact address and Fatima had given it to him. She had noted it. Thanking her he left, wishing her good luck with the capitaine.

"I don't need luck," she'd called as she'd waved him off. Then again it had been luck, cruel luck for his wife and mother-in-law that had thrown her and the capitaine together tonight. Perhaps she should stop being so dismissive of the world no one can explain. Maybe she should embrace it, encourage it even. Accept that sometimes luck could be on your side, to try and keep it that way, only worry when it was not. With that thought, Fatima went to her room to prepare.

Covent Garden – London, England

Why did she feel guilty? Maureen couldn't understand the feeling. She had accomplished what Mahon had wanted her to find out. She should feel elated, but she didn't. She felt flat and very guilty. Today she had thoroughly enjoyed her afternoon with John and now she was left with a strong sense of betrayal.

Pushing it aside, she was just being stupid, Maureen purchased a Times newspaper and headed for the café. The café was busy and she had to wait for a table to become free. Whilst standing she hung the

Times loose from her hand with the crossword page open, and just three squares filled in using green ink. She hoped that whoever was the contact had spotted her. She didn't fancy spending all night here. She was past being knackered. She was ready for bed.

Ten minutes later she was called to a table. Black Americano, she ordered as she sat down, and a double espresso please a familiar voice sounded, following.

"That was quick work, what have you got for me." Her English equivalent of Mahon, she was discovering quickly, didn't like to waste time.

"Hello," Maureen replied pointedly.

"Sorry, how rude of me," Charles apologised. "good afternoon?" Bree smiled widely and a little salaciously.

"Yes very good, thank you."

"And you've something for me?"

"Yes," Maureen was back and she repeated what she had found out, what John had told her.

Charles sucked air in through his teeth. "Well, well, well, we suspected something like this but a thousand pounds only, that's a bargain." He laughed. Maureen watched him, she didn't feel like laughing. The man looked pensive for a moment. "Look, Bree, you've done extremely well, incredibly well. Can you wait here a few moments, I need to take advice on this but I think we need to strike whilst the iron's hot. Do you mind? Just a few minutes."

"If it's only that, I'm knackered."

"Of course you are. I'll be right back." And off he went.

It was a good forty minutes before Charles returned and Maureen was becoming coffeed out. He immediately apologised.

"Sorry it took longer than I thought." Maureen glared at him. "Look have you made arrangements to meet this man tomorrow?"

"Only loosely."

"Good, good. Look do you think you can persuade him to meet you at Khans restaurant in Bayswater, it's on Westbourne Grove. It's quite famous you know."

"What time?" Both Maureen and Bree liked a good Indian so, no Maureen didn't mind.

"Let's say one ish, shall we. If you can get there a bit earlier we'll tell you our plan of action."

Bree liked the sound of this. It all sounded exciting. So quickly gone, her feelings of guilt. Maureen had been brushed aside. Bree was back on the case. She was also paying for the man's coffee again.

La Manche – The English Channel

It had been dark for well over an hour and the cruiser was almost mid channel. The lights outlining the French coast were becoming ever closer. Navigation lights moved through the water, warning that a vessel was ploughing the water. But not with the cruiser and the boat shadowing, they had no desire to be seen.

Two dull pops sounded accompanied by two dull thuds as bodies fell to the floor. The smaller, faster boat that had been shadowing accelerated, and within minutes pulled alongside. A third man who had been on the cruiser leapt onto the deck of the smaller boat, which immediately turned, accelerating towards the English coast.

The cruiser, with no one left alive on board continued on a slow path, heading for the French coast. It was a good twenty minutes later when a small sea cargo vessel noticed something was wrong and radioed ashore. A nearby French fishing vessel hearing the call diverted to take a look. From what the crew could see the cruiser was travelling blind, without anyone steering her. Le Cross and the Gendarmerie Maritime based at Cap Gris Nez were immediately informed. Two vessels were quickly launched, one piloted by the Gendarmerie and one a lifeboat by the French SNSM.

At around the same time the Gendarmerie Nationale at Calais received a call from an English mobile. In bad French a man told them there was a boat stranded near the French coastline that the gendarmerie would most certainly be interested in. The caller had rung off before he could be questioned. A call was quickly made to Le Cross who confirmed that indeed a pilotless cruiser was drifting in French waters and that a Gendarmerie Maritime vessel was on its way along with the SNSM. Keep us informed, asked the operator in Calais. Of course came the expected reply.

The operator thought for a second and dialled Capitaine Maubert's mobile. Their boss would want to know what was unfolding. With everything that was going on this could be significant. To his surprise the capitaine's mobile went straight to answer phone. He tried again, the same result. The capitaine's personal mobile was also listed as an emergency contact. He tried that one, but that too went to answer phone. He quickly checked with the operator to see if his phones were out of range. No both were switched off. How odd, the capitaine was always contactable.

Hotel De La Plage – Calais Plage, France

Fatima, drying herself after her shower, then proceeded to oil all of her body. Oiling by using sensual circular movements, taking her time, not rushing and not with brisk short strokes. Preparing her body, respecting its feelings and where necessary arousing them, was as important as preparing her mind. Satisfied she sprayed herself with the scent made from the blue lotus flower. In particular round her neck, on and under her bosom, over her abdomen and lower down. Satisfied she put on her heels and stood in front of the mirror. Except for the Croix d'Agadez hanging from a silver chain around her neck and a golden chain around her waist from which hung an arrangement of delicate Persian jewellery, she was naked. She liked what she saw. She was a woman not a girl and in the prime of her life. She could make any man fall to his knees and worship her.

Before getting dressed she went to the curtains and started rubbing the oil infused with a concentrated essence from the blue lotus into its folds. Next she reached for the hijab she'd be wearing that night and draped it into position. Once more she went to the mirror and this time using her phone started to play Orange Blossom's version of Ya Sidi through her Bluetooth speaker. Watching herself in the mirror she began to writhe to the music. Her hands above her head she started to intwine her arms to the music her fingers stretching reaching for something that she hadn't yet found. LOVE.

Quarter of an hour later she was dressed and ready. One final touch, she oiled the lower sheet. If Thierry wasn't intoxicated by her he would by the magic of the blue lotus flower. Before leaving her room she took one more look at herself in the mirror. She was dressed smartly but sexually in western styled clothes. Her blouse she wore open enough to reveal a deep and plunging cleavage and her skirt ended quite a way above her knees. Covering her head she wore a pale orange hijab. Tonight Fatima had deliberately created a look that shouted contrast. A clash of two very different cultures.

The Capitaine couldn't stop a gasp as Fatima paraded up the corridor. She looked beyond magnificent, never had he seen such a perfect representation of the female form. Waiting in reception, he'd begun to feel guilty. He should be with his wife caring for her elderly mother. He had phoned her and offered to come over but his wife had refused, as he knew she would. Her husband had enough going on without the added burden of her and her mother. Too readily, he had replied, well if you're sure. Now settling his eyes on Fatima all feelings of guilt were extinguished, replaced only by desire. A raging, uninterruptable desire, a desire that had, just had to be satisfied.

What happened the rest of the evening and most of the night, frustratingly for the capitaine remained, afterwards something of a haze. Nothing was quite clear. He vaguely remembered laughing a lot whilst sat in the restaurant. Being intoxicated by Fatima's beauty and her scent. Her scent. Her scent was like a snake that wrapped itself around you and pulled you in to be devoured by whoever was wearing it.

His body felt as though he had been sprinting for 24 hours without a break and yet all he could remember about his time in Fatima's room was of a heavy but heavenly, intoxicating aroma and a vague recollection of her nakedness. Naked except for her jewellery and hijab. This memory alone ignited a fire somewhere deep inside him. Tomorrow he would see Fatima again, that was for sure. The Devil himself wouldn't be able to stop him.

As he drove, the capitaine remembered his phones. He'd turned them off. Perhaps his wife may have needed him. He at once felt very guilty though still not remorseful. There were no messages on his personal phone but his gendarme phone pinged continuously. There were stacks of messages. Before he could check them or call in to see what was happening his phone rang, shattering all thoughts of Fatima.

"Maubert."

"Capitaine? We've been trying to get you all night."

"Sorry I've been out of range, what is it?"

"I know it's the early hours, but I think you need to come down sir, somethings cropped up."

"Cropped up? To do with what?"

"I think it's to do with our big investigation, the organ trafficking, we have fourteen more bodies, twelve of them are children."

The capitaine's blood ran cold, fourteen bodies! Twelve children. YOU'VE GOT TO BE KIDDING!.

"Capitaine?"

"I'm five minutes away, I'll be right there."

"Yes sir." The officer stared into space. Why had the capitaine lied, he hadn't been out of range. He'd had both his phones switched off. It was probably nothing but he'd enter it in his report. Just in case.

CHAPTER
—16—

Gendarmerie Nationale – Calais, France

The gendarmerie was buzzing when the capitaine pulled in. Something definitely very big was taking place.

"Can somebody come to my office to brief me," he instructed the night officer manning reception. "Oh and ask them to bring me a coffee."

"Yes sir."

The night reception officer and a couple more hovering in reception stared at their capitaine as he left through the swing doors. To all of them he looked dishevelled, almost as though he'd been in a fight for he looked exhausted too. And he smelt of something none of them could recognise, something vaguely exotic. All glanced at one another, asking, 'what the fuck.' Never had they seen their capitaine with one hair out of place, and from what they had just witnessed he had everything out of place.

In his office the capitaine went straight to his private bathroom. My God, he looked a mess and Fatima's intoxicating scent hung over him like a dense fog. Quickly he splashed his face, combed his hair and adjusted his clothing. It wasn't great but it would have to do. After all it was nearly four in the morning.

There was a sharp tap at his office door. Before he could answer his officer in charge of the night shift stepped in followed by his second in command. "Sir," both said in unison as the capitaine gestured for them to take a seat. "Good night sir?" His officer in charge couldn't resist a smirk.

The capitaine managed a smile. "You could say that. Now tell me what's going on. Fourteen bodies, twelve of them children, is that right?"

Both nodded. The officer in charge spoke. "Yes sir," and launched into a detailed account of events during the night. He told him of the call received from an English mobile. They'd already tried to trace the call but their English counterparts had come back to say it was a pay as you go phone and therefore untraceable. What they could confirm was the call was made from somewhere in Bayswater but nothing more accurate than that. They had a recording of the phone call, if the capitaine wanted to listen, which he did but later, not now. His officer thought the accent sounded North African and therefore almost certainly Egyptian, otherwise his French would have been more accurate.

The boat the caller was warning about, turned out to be a leisure cruiser. It was spotted in French waters off Cap Blanc Nez, without navigation lights and apparently with nobody piloting her. The Gendarme Maritime and the SNSM attended. Crew from the SNSM boarded first, to bring the cruiser under control and to activate the navigation lights. She was stranded in a major shipping lane and could have caused a major incident. What they found when they boarded were two men lying dead, apparently each killed by a single shot through their heads. This has yet to be verified, the officer hastened to add. The gendarmes then took over and started to search the boat, mainly to see if anybody else was on board.

On deck, they'd found a heavy tarpaulin strapped to the deck, covering some sort of cargo. When the tarpaulin was released, underneath they'd found a heap of what appeared to be a number of large sports bags. When they started to unzip these what they found inside horrified them. In two bags, inside black dustbin liners they found a total of twelve heads, all children's and all with their eyes removed. Just like the heads that were picked up after the storm, the officer added. In the other bags were torsos only. Presumably belonging to the severed heads. At first glance it looked as though the bodies had been butchered. Another bag contained legs and arms and an early examination estimated that if there were twelve torsos around half the legs and arms were missing. Oh and none of the arms had a hand attached, they'd been severed. So far there's no evidence of severed hands on board so God only knows where they are."

"Jesus," the capitaine whistled through clenched teeth. "Where's the boat now?"

"It's been towed into port sir, well away from everything else. We've closed off all access roads leading to the area." It was the second in command who offered this information.

The Capitaine nodded. "Good, have the media got hold of any of this?"

"No sir, not yet anyway." The commanding officer for the night confirmed.

"Then make damn sure they don't, make sure everybody investigating this keeps shtum. Under no circumstances must this get out. Do you understand? The capitaine looked sternly at both his men.

"Yes sir," both replied in unison.

"Right, I need to take a look at this boat."

"We're just going sir, want to travel with us?"

"Yes, good idea, let me just change into my uniform, I'll meet you in reception."

The two officers glanced at each other, "yes sir."

Ten minutes later all three officers were travelling to the port. When they arrived, they found two ambulances were present, along with four cars belonging to the gendarmerie as well as a single van. A forensics vehicle was also present and two unmarked cars. Six officers stood guard with several more on the boat. Even more officers were guarding access roads. Calais would just have to look after herself for the rest of the night. On deck a photographer was busy recording the grisly scene.

A man in coveralls approached the Capitaine. "Morning Capitaine, what a bloody mess."

Capitaine Maubert pulled a face which acknowledged that yes, it bloody was.

"Provided the holdalls are handled with gloves I see little point in keeping them on board. Poor sods deserve a bit of dignity. I assume they're to go to the morgue in Boulogne."

The capitaine nodded, "yes ok good, get it done, has anyone contacted the morgue to warn them?"

"Yes sir, I have." The commanding night officer responded. "Apparently no examination can take place until we've contacted the British authorities. The bodies were found on a British boat and the call we received was from England."

"I'll do that," the capitaine told him. Interpol need to know as well. This is a major incident."

"Sir."

The man in coveralls cut in. "Capitaine, if your men have finished, I'd like to start our examination, I have a team waiting. I'd like to start below deck, if that's ok with you."

"Yes of course, have we finished?" The capitaine turned to the commanding night officer.

I'll check," the officer moved off to find out.

"First impressions?" The capitaine turned to the man in coveralls in charge of forensics.

"I'm not a pathologist sir but at a guess I'd say those bodies are at least days old. What they were doing on that boat, well that's your job."

"Thanks."

"You're welcome." There came a shout.

"All clear sir"

"Ok, do your best."

"We will and we'll let you know straight away if we find anything."

"Please do that," the Capitaine watched as the man joining two of his team boarded the boat. At the same time his officer re-joined him. "Anything?"

"Nothing sir. Not as far as we can see. We searched everywhere, careful not to disturb any possible evidence of course, but nothing. No drugs, no weapons, just an ordinary boat."

"What do you think?"

The officer paused to think. "Well the obvious answer is they were planning to dump their bloody cargo at sea, the bags, were weighted. It's possibly even the same boat where the other stuff came from, washed up after the storm. It all fits."

"And the men who were shot?"

The officer shrugged, "who knows, typical criminal gang squabble and these two came off worse."

"And where's the shooter? Is he an Olympic swimmer?" The capitaine was doubtful, something wasn't right. It was all too convenient, too neat.

"Or she," the officer responded. The capitaine shrugged, touché, one must never assume. "I don't know, I did wonder about that. The boat didn't get where it was found without someone piloting it. Someone or something must have taken he or she off."

Exactly the Capitaine thought, this has all been carefully planned. But why? For what purpose? It was almost as though the whole incident had been staged for their benefit.

National Crime Agency – Lambeth, London, England

It was exactly eight am when Roger took the call. It was the head of the Gendarmerie Nationale in Calais. He knew what was coming, he had already been given early reports. This was massive, twelve children and two adults dead, almost certainly murdered. If this turned out to be true and he could see no reason why it wouldn't, this would be recorded as the largest mass murder in decades. And children, bloody hell. The authorities in Calais wanted to know if they could go ahead with a post mortem at their morgue in Boulogne. Roger agreed, the sooner a post mortem was carried out the better, pointless bringing the remains back here. Not yet anyway. What he did need, and fast were the DNA results, the two adults may have been naughty boys and as a result their DNA recorded on their database. You never know.

Roger also took the number of the mobile phone used by the caller, he'd get it checked again and details of the boat. It should be registered.

Ten minutes later, Interpol called, offering their services and promising to send the NCA any information they considered may help with the UK's investigation. If there was no objection they'd send the same information to the French. There was no objection.

Fucking hell, Roger slammed his desk. How the hell did this happen, why weren't the people who'd done this on their radar. The events overnight had caught him and his organisation, completely by surprise. His boss would want to know, the Home Secretary would want to know. And if this got out, which invariably it will, he had no doubt, the whole bloody nation would want to know. How could something as big as this have escaped their attention. And where the hell had the children come from. Twelve, that's not something if they were missing, that would go unreported. Parents would be kicking off. It just didn't make sense. He needed the autopsy report and the DNA results like yesterday. Their bloody pathologist better not take the traditional two hour lunch break they enjoyed across the water.

Roger thought some more. He picked up the phone, the direct and secure line to MI5. If those bastards were hiding something from him he'd bury them all under a tarpaulin and put them on a slow boat to China.

The Fielding Hotel – Covent Garden, London

Bree was enjoying luxuriating in her bath. GMTV played on the TV screen, she enjoyed the banter and the magazine style of the programme. Her husband had called it Grandma TV which to her was a joke. Looking back now, after the life she'd discovered since his death, he'd already become a Grandpa by nature, the day she'd married him. What right to an opinion did he have.

She felt better this morning. She was on a mission and mustn't let sentimentality get in the way. She'd been a soppy cow yesterday. This morning she was Bree, Bree the special agent. On a high she felt the floor for her phone. Finding it she dialled John's number.

John had just stepped out of his shower when his phone rang. Drying his hands he picked it up, it was Bree, well he hadn't expected this. He really must stop worrying. She was just Bree a dippy woman who needed his help, as well as his body. He smiled, the thought made him feel good though the same couldn't be said for his body. His body felt as though it had been through a mangle.

"Hello Bree, you're keen." He heard Bree chuckle. He loved her constant happiness.

"Don't you start getting big headed Johnny boy, how do you fancy a rematch?"

"What? When?"

"NOW. I'm outside your door, naked under my coat," Bree lied. John felt himself stumbling, not now, not yet. He needed time to recover. He was more of a CV2 not a Ferrari. He heard Bree roar with laughter.

"Ha, John, had you worried didn't I." more roars of laughter. "Don't worry Johnny, I'm in my bath getting ready for later"

"Later?" John wished he didn't sound so nervous.

"Yes how do you fancy buying me an Indian, you can't get a good Indian in France." More laughter. "My guide book recommends Khans in Bayswater, apparently it's one of London's original Indian restaurants."

"I know it." John did, it was rather no nonsense and didn't sell alcohol but the food was authentic. He'd always had a positive experience there.

"Great, then you'll be able to find it. I'm seeing a friend first so I'll meet you there, say one ish. Then you can surprise me afterwards. Am I scaring you Johnny Boy?"

"Ok," before he had even begun his sentence Bree had rung off. He wasn't sure if he could cope with another physical session with that woman. It was beginning to look as if he had little choice. What had he got himself into.

Private Hospital – South Kensington, London, England

A patient, an American was being wheeled to an operating theatre. Today he was due for his liver transplant. "About bloody time," he told everybody who cared to listen.

His doctor the night before had gone over the procedure in some detail and at the end he'd signed a consent form. "I've got little bloody choice," he'd muttered, finishing his signature with a flourish.

Although loud, it was mostly bravado. He was nervous, no ,scared. He knew the risks, they'd been explained to him in some detail. If he didn't have the transplant he'd die anyway. He had several grand-children, he wanted to see them grow up. He had the money so he'd paid New Dawn Health Services for the operation. They'd insisted it being done in London. And now paid, New here he was. Dawn or dusk? Dawn he hoped. Several surgeons were waiting in the operating theatre, one who was the anaesthetist started to explain how he'd be putting him under and measuring constantly so that, one, he was never at risk and two, he wouldn't feel a thing.

His regular doctor, the man he'd abused on a regular basis appeared, carrying two bits of paper. This is your donor, the doctor held up a picture of a man with red hair. He's, or rather he was Scottish. And this is his death certificate. The doctor held up a second piece of paper. The death certificate was a forgery but he wouldn't know that. "You see, he's as white as you and me."

"Thank you doctor and sorry for being a grumpy old man."

"Forget it," the doctor patted him on the shoulder. "These men will start to get you ready, your main surgeon will be along in a jiffy."

With that the doctor left. As he walked up the corridor he passed the man's surgeon coming the other way. Born in Ghana, he was an ethnic Ghanaian. He'd been brought to England by his parents when he was eight. He'd always wanted to be a surgeon and had passed his medical exams with flying colours. New Dawn Health Services had offered him a career he could up until then, only dream of. He earned good money and a flat came with the job. As they passed the two shook hands. After which the doctor carried on along the corridor, laughing out loud as he went. The surgeon shook his head. What had got into him. Seconds later he pushed open the doors to the theatre.

"Morning, Mr Lewis. My name's Kofi, I will be in charge of your operation today. All you have to do is relax."

Gendarmerie Nationale – Calais, France

Capitaine Maubert was fading fast. He'd had no sleep for over twenty four hours and the biggest crime operation in Calais' recorded history had just landed in his lap. In just a few days, twenty dead bodies or parts of bodies had been discovered all close to, or on shore, one of his officers had disappeared and an immigrant had claimed that he'd been part of a drugging and attempted kidnap. And he was not even one step from solving any of it.

After forensics had started their investigation he'd interviewed both the men from SNSM and the Gendarmerie Maritime. All were in shock and all couldn't really throw any light as to what had happened. The one thing that stood out, after they boarded, was, they discovered, everything on the boat, they discovered that everything was operational including the navigation lights. The cruiser also had a working Automatic Identification System and this too had been disabled. Whoever was responsible was very aware of what they were doing, and how to do it. This was in no way an amateur operation.

The pathologist had arrived just before five. He quickly examined the two men who'd been shot and agreed that there wasn't much else he could do. What was needed was a post mortem and that could only be done back at the morgue. The ambulance crews then had the grisly job of carrying the corpses off of the boat and transporting them back to the morgue at Boulogne.

At nine the Capitaine remembered to phone his wife. She was fine she'd told him and so was her mother. Her mother was shaken and had a nasty gash on her forehead but she would live. She would probably stay over tonight as well. If she did, the capitaine had promised her he'd pop by.

"Thank you Thierry, I love you."

"You too," he'd just about managed to mumble.

Shortly after phoning his wife, Baptiste from the BRB in Paris had phoned.

"I hear you have something even more major going on." The Capitaine wondered how he'd gotten to know so quickly, Interpol maybe. The BRB, he knew had ears everywhere.

He told Baptise what they had found, without going into too much detail.

"It looks as though this may be an offshore operation after all, Thierry, doesn't it. Perhaps you need to be looking for a hospital ship operating in French waters. The Gendarmerie Maritime and Le Cross can help you there. If you need my help let me know."

"Possibly," the Capitaine still wasn't so sure. He was still suspicious, and he was a little surprised that Baptiste had jumped to such a conclusion so quickly. The way this was building he fully expected the BRI or the BRB to come flooding into Calais and taking over operations. So far that hadn't happened and he prayed that it wouldn't.

Baptiste told him the latest in Paris and rather vaguely the leads the BRB and BRI were chasing but it really wasn't much more than he already knew. He was sure Baptiste was holding something back, but what? If he had something that would help with the investigation, why not reveal it? Why hold it back? Unless it had something to do with national security. It was the only reason he could think of.

As if he hadn't enough on his plate, late morning Marie phoned. She was in floods of tears. After he had managed to calm her down, she sobbed out her story. That morning she'd continued her mission, trying to find out if anything untoward, anything suspicious was happening around the food stations. She'd thought she'd been discreet but obviously not, for, whilst walking between stations, she'd been accosted by four masked migrants and threatened with a knife. They wanted to know why all the questions and what was she up to. She'd convinced them that she was doing it for their own good and they had let her go, but not after they'd warned her that a good many others, like them, were becoming very suspicious. And to take great care as, unlike them, some of the others who were becoming suspicious of her, may not listen and take matters into their own hands. If she didn't heed their warning, harm may come to her or even worse. " It's because of what they've been through Thierry, they trust no one." And now she was scared, really scared. Worse still, she could no longer work with her extended family. They didn't trust her any more. "They were my life Thierry, my life. My raison d'etre." She once more burst into floods of tears. Once again the capitaine found himself to calm her.

"Look Marie, I've got a lot on this morning but I'll pop by and see you some time this evening. We can talk it over." Marie thanked him profusely, she'd wait for his call. Oh and even with all her questioning, she discovered nothing, nothing at all.

Covent Garden – London, England

John made a few work calls before getting dressed. There was a nip outside so he chose to wear a jumper over a shirt and then a jacket on top. Finally a navy Barbour Rokig jacket. Standing in front of the mirror, John was pleased, he looked quite stylish. What woman could resist him? He stopped holding his breath and reality hit home. MOST! If not ALL! But he didn't care, Bree appeared to adore him and though he still had underlying doubts they were fading all the time.

Pulling out a box from a bedroom drawer he selected a pay as you go mobile from the many inside. He charged them all regularly, ready to use. He never used a phone for more than one call. After that one call they were destroyed. In America, using phones in this manner, has given rise to the expression 'burner phones.' He thought the term ridiculous, for if you did try to burn your phone it would certainly attract unwanted attention. He liked to simply snap the sim in two and crush the phone underfoot or under a wheel of a vehicle.

Placing the phone in his pocket he left his apartment to meet Bree at Bayswater. It was a short walk to Covent Garden Station, where he took the tube to Holborn, changing there to take the Central line, travelling west and getting off at Queensway. From Queensway station he deviated a little, taking in Kensington Gardens Square. Here it was a lot quieter and here John stopped to make a call. Taking out his pay as you go mobile he dialled the number given to him yesterday. After just two rings a male voice answered.

"Yes."

"Hello, I understand from a colleague that you need help recovering some money." There came a long pause before the man again answered.

"Yes."

"Can I enquire, how much?"

"Two hundred and fifty million," he confirmed.

"You know my fees are 20% of everything I recover and a non-re-fundable down payment of ten thousand pounds, if I succeed in recovering your money or not."

"Jesus," came the reply.

"Yes, or no."

"Yes, ok," the man said quietly, it was obvious the man wasn't happy with the arrangement but he had little choice. And John knew it, he was the best in the business and had contacts that were second to none. Including a guy in the upper echelons of the NCA.

"Do you have a name? I need a name, and your real name. I have to check you out you understand."

"Paul, Paul Taylor."

"Thank you Paul, and is this the best number to contact you on?"

"Yes, I bought this phone especially for our use." This confirmed to John that the money was almost certainly dodgy. And that HMRC knew nothing about it. "Is this the best number to contact you on?"

"I will do the contacting Paul and I will never use the same number. This is for your security as well as mine. You understand that don't you?"

"Yes, yes I do."

"So Paul, tell me how you came to lose quarter of a billion pounds." Paul launched into a tale of honour amongst thieves which ended in betrayal. The man who had taken it, had meant to be looking after it for him, helping him launder it. Not once did the man, Paul Taylor, explain where the money had come from in the first place, just that this bastard had absconded with it.

"Have you a name for me?" John asked. The man had, one Greg Warnford and he even had an address, an apartment on Chelsea Embankment. They didn't come cheap.

"I've been there though," the man added and I've had the apartment watched. He's not there. Bastard."

"Ok, that's enough to go on for now, how do you want to pay me? I won't start until I've received your down payment. I have to know you're serious. If you only bank in this country or Europe it will have to be cash, if you have a bank outside…."

"South America." So it's drug money, John wasn't surprised. He gave the man details of an account in Panama to pay the money into. Once I've received it I'll make a start, John promised.

"You'll have it in an hour," the man promised. "One thing."

"Yes."

"How do I know, you won't run off with my money."

"I was recommended to you Paul."

"Fair enough," and the line went dead. Twenty minutes later the money arrived in John's Panamanian account. John looked at his watch, he had fifteen minutes before meeting Bree. Using his own phone he called his bakery. Once he'd got hold of the right person he asked for a check on the address given to him by Paul Taylor. He needed confirmation on who owns the property and for how long and that it's not rented. If it is, who by. Easy peasy had come the reply. Before he did anything else, John took out the sim, snapped it in half and tossed it in the Gardens. Next he put the mobile in a small plastic bag and crushed it under foot. He would dispose of it in the next bin.

Using his own phone John phoned Roger, his old colleague at the NCA. Roger didn't always pick up, not during working hours but on this occasion he did.

"Denton."

"Roger, it's me."

"What the fuck do you want now?"

"Good morning to you too. Can you do a trace on a couple of names for me, not just a normal check dig a little deeper. Pleeeeease."

"Why the fuck should I John?"

"Quarter of a billion, Roger. I think it's drug money. If I find anything, I could accidently drop some info into your lap."

Roger sighed, "Ok, shoot, give me some names." John gave him Paul Taylor and Greg Warnford and the address he'd been given for Mr Warnford. "I'll do my best John, but no promises." He rang off.

Ten minutes later there was a knock on Rogers door. One of his senior officers stepped in. "He's taken the bait sir, we've had to transfer £10,000 but it's recoverable. Do you want to have him tailed?"

"Not yet, It's too risky. Remember he's trained to spot a tail. Lets see what he does next, try and set up a meeting. We've got a line set up, haven't we?"

"Yes sir, this is the number." The officer slipped a post it note across the desk with a number neatly added.

"Ok, let me know your progress, and tread carefully. If he smells a rat all of this will have been for nothing."

"Of course sir." The officer left. Roger swallowed. He couldn't tell his officer that he already knew his old colleague had taken the bait. He was walking a tightrope, he hoped, no prayed he wouldn't fall off.

Bree had taken the tube from Covent Garden just half an hour before her beau had done the same. She'd just passed Tesco on Queensway when she heard 'Pitgam' whispered in her ear. A man of Mediterranean appearance joined, walking in step beside her.

"Walk with me Bree but say nothing." Bree did as she was told, they were simply two strangers walking in the same direction, held together because of the crowds. Within five minutes they were standing outside Khans on Westbourne Grove. "Follow me in Bree, I'll show you where to sit. Once there you wait for your companion. Act normally, enjoy your meal. Don't look for me. Understood? Bree nodded. How exciting.

The man led her past up-lit pillars made to look like palm trees. Through a false Mehrab style arch to an arrangement of tables set into an alcove beside the door to the toilets. The stranger signalled for her to sit down and disappeared through the door marked Toilets. Of all the places to sit Bree thought, this was the least romantic. She wasn't sure what her first impressions were. The restaurant was certainly decorative but at the same time functional. She'd hardly call it romantic though. All the same she loved it. It was like nowhere she'd eaten before. A waiter brought her a menu, she asked for a second as she was expecting someone. The waiter obliged.

Ten minutes later John arrived, Bree thought he actually looked quite stylish. He waved cheerfully on seeing her. "Why on earth are you sitting here?" were his first words.

Bree, shrugged her shoulders, she'd thought exactly the same thing, she had to think on her feet. "Oh it's cosy, we're rather hidden here, no one can really see us." She grinned and squeezed John's thigh.

"Fair enough." John slid in opposite her. Bree handed him the menu. She had already examined it and chosen the non-vegetarian thali. The way it was described it looked a virtual feast. John said he'd have the same. His stomach could handle it after all, they both laughed. And that was how their meal continued, casual chat, lots of laughter, all very relaxed. Except Bree couldn't help constantly wondering where the man had gone and was he ever going to reappear.

Hotel De La Plage – Calais Plage, France

Capitaine Maubert had no idea if Fatima would be there or not. After having not eaten all morning he needed a good lunch. Before meeting Fatima he'd often grab lunch at the hotel's restaurant anyway. It wasn't that unusual. Although not fine dining the food was always good and the parking easy. Before he'd left, he'd phoned Jean-Paul at the morgue in Boulogne. He'd sounded under pressure and had made it clear the fewer interruptions the quicker he could get on with his work. And yes he knew Thierry was under pressure but so was he and ok he could come over if he must. They'd agreed around three that afternoon.

"And Thierry, what in God's name is going on?" They were the pathologist's last words before he rang off.

"Fatima to his delight was sitting, having lunch herself when he entered. She was dressed modestly but at the same time making the most of colour. As always she was wearing a hijab. The hijab she'd explained the night before, for her was an emblem of pride. It was who she was, even though she didn't always live by the same rules. She smiled as he sat down. "A man in uniform Thierry, are you testing me?"

"No, no, after leaving you last night I had to go straight to work."

"Really? Fatima raised her eyebrows. "Well I think you look very smart, tired," she grinned, "but very smart all the same." As she said this she leant across and smoothed his collar. The capitaine immediately began to relax, what magic did this woman possess that she could have such an instantaneous effect on him. His stress was leaving him in droves. He could feel it even. A waitress appeared with a menu. The capitaine didn't even look at it, he ordered the Salade du Ch'tis accompanied by a small bierre pression. Fatima he noticed was drinking a Kir Royale. She declined the capitaine's offer of another drink.

"So tell me Thierry, why did you have to go straight to work, why do you look so stressed.? Tell me everything, Let me take your pain away." She rather sensuously kissed her fingers and brushed them across his lips. The capitaine conscious he was in uniform looked around nervously. "Don't worry Thierry, no one is looking, I checked first. It's just us."

The capitaine felt all resistance drain from his body to be replaced by total calm. He felt at one with this woman, he felt almost vulnerable when he was with her and yet not once did he consider she may be his nemesis. He trusted her completely. Proof that Fatima was the ultimate professional. The definition of a Femme Fatale.

"So tell me Thierry, tell me all your troubles, tell me everything, absolutely everything and I can help blow your troubles away." And he did, he did tell her. Everything, absolutely everything and it was all being recorded, by a microphone hidden under her hijab.

Bayswater – London, England

Bree and John had finished their meal and now both were enjoying a coffee before they left. Both of them had thoroughly enjoyed their food and the time had passed incredibly quickly. At one point Bree had seen an employee wearing an apron and had burst into fits of laughter that lasted on and off for a good ten minutes. Her laughter was infectious and John felt his ribs hurting as he tried to block the image of him wearing something similar only yesterday. After he'd paid the bill John excused himself. He needed the toilet. "Old mans trouble," he told her as he pushed open the door marked Toilet.

Whilst standing relieving himself a man of Mediterranean appearance entered the toilet to use an urinal adjacent. Both men gave a single nod. Finished, John washed his hands and made to re-join Bree. Seconds later the other man stepped in behind. John, miles away, still laughing a little failed to notice. Re entering the restaurant he found to his surprise two men sitting beside Bree and Bree was no longer smiling. She had guilt written all over her face. Too late he realised he'd walked into a trap. Before he could even think about escaping the man who'd shared the toilet, kneed and pushed him expertly onto a chair. John recognised instantly the work of a professional. He'd been trained to do the very same so as not to attract attention. The largest of the three men smiled reassuringly.

"Don't worry, John, we have no desire to harm you, we just want you to do a job for us. However we can't discuss it here. Please come with us." All three men stood up. He knew there was no point in trying to resist. He could cause quite a commotion but it would put both him and more importantly Bree at risk. He still cared even if she had betrayed him. The perfect honey trap. He smiled inwardly, she'd had him fooled all the time. She was bloody good. No, he would simply have to see what these men wanted from him, how he could work with them. At that moment he hadn't a clue what they wanted. He'd soon find out.

"Wait until we're gone Bree, don't leave before we're out of the door." The man who had, met her in Queensway told her this.

Bree would never forget the look on John's face as he was led away. It wasn't one of anger, just one of immense disappointment. His lips were even turned up at the edges. His expression cut through her, like knife through butter. Still trying to regain her composure, Bree stood, a little shakily, ready to leave. It was all the more painful because she'd really enjoyed John's company over lunch. Before she'd taken a single step a young fresh faced male, Indian she thought, handed her an envelope. "For your services Ma'am." Bree knew what was inside.

"You can damn well keep it," she hissed and knocked the envelope so hard it flew out of the man's hands and flying across the floor. Looking shocked the young Indian skuttled across to pick it up. The waiters, all looking a little concerned, bid her goodbye as she strode across the floor to the exit and hoped that they'd see her again soon. Outside she virtually marched up Queensway, what had she just done? What was she responsible for, they'd better not hurt him. God, how she regretted getting involved. You stupid, stupid bitch. Not far behind, taking care not to be seen another man followed her. The woman was unstable, she was a loose cannon. They'd have to keep a careful eye on her from now on. The organisation wouldn't accept taking a risk with someone like her.

The Morgue – Le Centre Hospitalier, Boulogne-Sur-Mer, France

It was nearer four when the Capitaine pulled into the parking area, reserved for visitors to the morgue. He'd spent longer with Fatima than he'd intended, very easily done, she was such tantalising company. He'd received, whilst with her, several calls from his gendarmerie. One, related to the cruiser they had tied up in the port of Calais. The English authorities had failed to trace the owners of the vessel. The new owners hadn't registered the cruiser and had given the seller a false name and address. The seller insisted that the buyer had provided proof of ID, as he'd paid cash, but 'rather stupidly,' hadn't taken copies. The English authorities had told his team that they had no reason to disbelieve the man. Great.

The rest of their time together had simply been harmless banter. She'd made no attempt to seduce him and their sexual liaison the night before was only briefly referred to and even then with humour only. The capitaine, casually mentioned that knowing his wife, she would probably spend another night with her mother. Well if she does Thierry, Fatima had said, you know where I am. Now as he entered the morgue the capitaine's nerves were tingling with anticipation. He couldn't wait. It was wrong, all of his concentration was needed elsewhere.

Jean–Paul met him personally in reception. "I've never had to deal with anything like this Thierry, never" The pathologist looked shaken. All his life he'd looked for clues in dead bodies, and this was the first time the capitaine had seen him show any kind of emotion. After donning coveralls, a mask and gloves, the capitaine followed Jean-Paul into the theatre. The smell was even more sickening than normal. The pathologist first showed him to two tables where his assistants were busy carrying out a detailed examination. "These are the two adult males found on deck. Cause of death, bullet wounds to the head. When they died, I can't give an exact time until further analysis, but a professional guess. I'd say not more than hour before you found them, perhaps considerably less for, from what I can see the bodies show no signs of deterioration and I understand that when the boat was boarded the bodies were still warm and their blood wet." The capitaine nodded, that was correct.

The pathologist then guided the capitaine to another table. He was used to seeing dead bodies, attending post mortems but what he was presented with here shook him to the bone, his belief in any sort of God. Laid out in pieces, were a torso, two legs, two arms, missing hands and what was unmistakably a girl's head, minus her eyes and with a missing scalp. It was hard to believe this had once been a living person.

"I have the parts, or some of the parts of eleven other children in refrigeration storage. So far this is the only child I've managed to match the body parts to completion. Like the torso we found after the storm all the organs have been removed and in the arms, her bones, poor child." The pathologist's voice cracked. "Whoever did this Thierry has no respect, no respect and no sense of decency. I'm finding it hard, Thierry, really, really hard. Never did I think for one minute that I would experience such inhumanity."

"We'll get the bastards," answered the capitaine, his voice lacking any sense of conviction.

"You'd better Thierry, you'd bloody better. I hope I get them on my bloody table." The pathologist took a deep breath, composing himself. "It is obvious, all of the children have been butchered for their body parts. The rest by the way are all boys, this is the only girl. All have been scalped for their hair. Skin has been taken from some as well and as with the previous torso, at one point their bodies were drained of blood." The capitaine listened intently, the pathologist paused. "You know Thierry after what you told me, I've been looking into this red market theory. From what I can tell with what I've got here and from what I've read, these poor children, dead, to the traffickers, if that's what this is, are worth tens of millions of Euros. Transplant tourism is how the English describe it but that innocent sounding phrase hides a disgusting industry."

"I know and we're looking at London, can you tell me anything else?"

The pathologist looked thoughtful, "It's early stages Thierry but I think I can safely say that all of the children have at some point been stored in cold storage. Not frozen but refrigerated. And it's only a guess and you know I don't like guessing, but I think I can safely say from physical appearances alone, that all of the children come from a similar area"

That was interesting, the British authorities had told them they had no reports of numerous children going missing, only the usual teenage hormonal desire to rebel. Nothing with children this age, under ten, twelve at the oldest. Where had these children come from then. Who was missing them. Somebody must be.

"You know the English have requested their DNA."

"Samples have been taken and sent for processing, first thing I did," the pathologist replied rather defensively. "They'll have them first thing tomorrow morning. Best I can do and believe me, DNA results that fast are almost a miracle."

The capitaine smiled, "I know Jean-Paul, I know, we do appreciate your efforts you know." With that the capitaine left. It couldn't be soon enough. Once in his car he took several minutes to think things over. All the findings so far had been at sea or sea related. Perhaps they should be looking at a hospital ship, if you could call it that. But what about Ismail's account of attempted kidnap, how did one explain that? Unless he was being paid to create a diversion, a distraction. To put the authorities off the scent. After all, his officers and Marie had found no evidence to back up his story. It all made sense. Why hadn't he thought of it before. Bloody, bloody hell. Putting his car into gear, he pulled out of the car park heading for the A16 and Calais. He called Marie. Her phone didn't even ring once before she answered. She was waiting for his call, poor girl.

"Thierry?"

"Yes I'm on my way, where are we meeting?"

"Café du Centre, like the first time, how long will you be?"

"Twenty minutes," the capitaine put his foot down.

Bayswater – London, England

John was led across Westbourne Grove, through a small inconspicuous unmarked door the other side, and up a flight of stairs to a small first floor office. The office had definitely seen better days. A frayed carpet covered the floor and what looked like decades old wallpaper covered some of the walls. The only furniture was an unused bookcase, a table covered in cigarette burns and four basic wooden chairs, probably from the forties. One of the men pulled a chair in front of the door and sat down, the other two sat behind the desk indicating to John he make himself comfortable on the remaining seat.

"We're not here to harm you John," it was the large man talking again. It was quite obvious he was in charge. And John knew they weren't, from their stance, intending to hurt him. The way these three men handled themselves it was obvious to his trained eye, that all three were professionals. They were all very capable of doing him a great deal of harm without actually killing him. No they needed him, that much was clear.

"Then what do you want from me?" John got straight to the point. The sooner this was sorted, the sooner he'd be out of there.

"Ok, I'll get straight to the point." The large man lit a cigarette, took a puff and lay it on the desk. We want you to provide us with death certificates, we'll pay the going rate, of course." So that was what Bree had been after, how he got the death certificates and he'd handed it to her on a plate. How could he have been so bloody stupid.

"What do you call the going rate?"

The large man grinned, we'll double what you pay. £2,000." So Bree had even given them that. They had him by the short and curlies and they knew it.

"How many?"

"Twelve." John spluttered.

"TWELVE!"

"Twelve, every week." John choked.

"Impossible, one at the most and to be safe, every two weeks. Twelve a week is simply impossible."

"Then make it possible," there was a pause, "Johnny Boy." The man laughed. We won't take no for an answer.

'Johnny Boy', they were bugging Bree's phone. "I'll do my best, that's all I can promise."

"Twelve John, we'll pick them up from your flat a week from now. Oh and a friendly warning. I think you know better than to cross us." The man stood up and held out his hand, "then we are partners, good. We will pay you cash of course." John took it and shook. He had little choice. The other two men then came over and shook too, smiling as if they were best of friends. As he left he heard the leader call out "Hhazz sa'a -id." So they were Arabs. He hadn't been sure.

"Thank you," he called back.

Outside, John took a deep breath. The only way out of this was death or to disappear and disappearing sounded much more appealing. He knew, even if he could provide twelve death certificates every week, his usefulness would one day come to an end and then he'd become a liability. And there was only one way in the criminal world to deal with a liability. He had to act now, and fast. To disappear success-fully, required a great deal of money, especially if you wanted to live out your final days in comfort. He already had a great deal of money but not enough. Maybe the Gods had been smiling on him when Paul Taylor and his quarter of a billion landed on his lap. He'd check out the address on Chelsea Embankment. Now was a good time. Walking quickly he took the backroads to the Bayswater Road. He was pretty sure nobody was following but to be sure, almost opposite the Russian Embassy, he hailed a cab seconds before it had passed and jumped in. "Chelsea Embankment." The cabbie started the meter and they were on their way. If there was anyone following him now it could only be a government agency.

There was a hint of sun when John was dropped off and the Thames almost looked inviting. He hadn't wanted to be dropped directly outside, just in case. The apartment was a good fifty metres and he started to walk. He made a call to his bakery. After being passed to the relevant individual he asked if he'd had time to check the land registry and more. Yes had been the response, told you easy peasy and the apartment did belong to one Greg Warnford, and he had purchased it seven years ago using a twenty five year mortgage. As far as he could tell there was no one renting, but you could never be one hundred percent sure. John realised that and thanked him.

Ten minutes later he was standing in front of a red brick, elegantly finished building four storeys high. Mr Warnford's apartment was on the third floor. He looked up, the windows looked dull, almost certainly there was no one at home. Going to the front door, after looking around John slipped the lock. Within seconds he was in an intricately tiled hallway full of lush green plants. Everything shouted Victorian. A wide staircase with a sweeping banister climbed to an arched window. John started to climb wishing for the umpteenth time that he'd taken better care of his body. A fairly modern door was a giveaway that Mr Warnford's apartment was a relatively recent conversion. Seconds later, John was inside. Easy peasy. As he'd expected there was no one home. The flat was tastefully furnished and everything although old, appeared to match, to be carefully put together. A clue that somewhere along the line an interior designer had been at work. There were clothes in the bedroom and all perfectly put away. There was food in the kitchen cupboards but nothing in the fridge. On the surface the flat didn't look lived in but there were two contradictions. Everything was spotless which meant a cleaner, and two, there was no post. Somebody must be collecting it. He could ask the neighbours but he didn't want to bring attention to himself, no he'd have the apartment watched. Satisfied, he left, and outside hailed a cab for his flat in Covent Garden.

Rather than going all the way to his door he asked to be dropped off near the Savoy in The Strand. He needed a drink and where better than the Coal Hole, a pub rumoured to have once been the coal cellar for the famous hotel. The pub still retained many of its original features from when Queen Victoria reigned and John loved the overall feeling they evoked. After ordering a pint, he found a seat in a convenient corner. He looked at his watch. His contact at the GRO will have finished work. He gave him a call.

He got the reaction he'd expected. No way, he'd be found out. He was taking a huge risk already. No bloody way, it was impossible. John hinted he might be in trouble, serious trouble if he couldn't help him but his response had been predictable. Well that's your bloody problem, you shouldn't promise what you can't deliver. John had to agree but his colleague wasn't aware under what circumstances he had made his promise, and there was no way he was going to tell him. One last favour then, and that would be it. He would pay him five thousand as it was to be the last time. His contact in the GRO agreed to this. He refrained from telling him the last death certificate he needed was for himself. Thank you. John heaved a sigh of relief. This Paul Taylor thing better come off. Next he rang Roger. He wasn't expecting him to reply but he did.

"It's your lucky day John, Mr Warnford is known to us. In fact a while ago he was actually a police informer, one of our more reliable contacts." John's heart missed a beat. "For some reason he dropped out," Roger continued. "But we still have a number for him and we've checked. And guess what, it's still active. You owe me big time John."

"I accept that Roger. On this occasion only. I'll see you right, you know I will." There was laughter on the other end of the phone before the line went dead. John thumped the air with his fist. Yeees, yes, yes, yes. After all the shit earlier, things were actually beginning to look up.

Café Du Centre – Marck, France

The capitaine loved Marck. There was always street parking to be had. He pulled up only a couple of car spaces from the front door of the café. There was quite a noise coming from inside. The café was busy with people stopping by for a drink on their way home from work. As he stepped through the door, nearly all conversation stopped. Of course he was in uniform.

"Bonjour, messieurs--dames," the capitaine smiled his greeting. It was accepted and everyone went back to their conversation. He spotted Marie sat by herself in a corner. She had almost finished what looked like her second glass of wine. She looked horrified on seeing him.

"Thierry you're in uniform" she mouthed, "I'll meet you outside." She signalled this with her hands as well as mouthing it. Together they made her request more than clear. Embarrassed he made a quick exit and went back to his car. He saw Marie exit, looking for him. He flashed his headlights. Seconds later she was sat in his car.

"Are you mad Thierry, if any of my family see me with you, I'm finished, if I'm not already." The capitaine could smell alcohol on her breath and her words came a little slurred. He guessed she'd probably been drinking most of the afternoon. By family he knew she was referring to the migrants she cared or tried to care for.

"I'm sorry Marie, I've had a bit of a day, I wasn't thinking."

"Have you? She reached across and touched his cheek with the back of her hand. It was over in a second but it had felt good. "So have I, Thierry I thought they were going to kill me." Marie started to sob. The Capitaine was struggling to accept this was the hardnosed, cantankerous Marie who had once given him and his gendarmerie so much trouble. He wasn't sure what to do now she was in his car. "Do you mind taking me home Thierry," she managed between sobs, "I'll direct you."

"Calais?". Marie nodded and to his discomfort rested her head on his shoulder. As they drove Marie started to fall asleep. Waking her briefly, the capitaine asked for her address. She just about managed to mumble it before falling into a much deeper sleep, bringing her right arm across and resting it on his chest. The capitaine punched it into his GPS, he knew roughly where it was anyway. It was in one of the older parts of Calais, well known for its rows of Flemish brick houses. Just over fifteen minutes later he was in her street looking for a parking space. After driving up and down a couple of times a neighbour obligingly pulled out and the capitaine quickly took advantage. Another neighbour couldn't believe what she was seeing. Marie in a car with, not just in a car with, but snuggled against the shoulder of their arch enemy. Worse still the man in charge of their arch enemy, Capitaine Maubert of the gendarmerie. She'd known Marie had changed her spots, the way she'd been asking questions at the food stations. 'Quelle connasse.' She'd been right to get some of the migrants to threaten her. They'd come back telling her Marie was all good. Really, well now she had evidence she'd been right after all. Stepping back into her doorway she pulled out her smartphone and selected camera.

"Marie, Marie, you're home," Capitaine Maubert shook Marie gently, attempting to wake her up. Marie shook her head and looked up to the capitaine's face. Instead of preparing to get out she started to talk. Half crying, and very passionately she related her attempts to find out if anything untoward, if someone meaning her family harm, had infiltrated the food stations. How one of her original colleagues had turned a little hostile towards her and how a group from her family, yes her family had threatened her with a knife. Capitaine Maubert was listening but he was also enjoying the smell of her perfume and the feel of her body against his. He had recently tasted the other side and like a Class A drug, the other side was very addictive. Marie finishing her story opened her eyes, staring into Thierry's, instinctively the capitaine leant down placing his lips on hers. To his surprise she responded and for seconds they were caught in an embrace. Almost at the same moment both pulled back, shocked by what they had just done.

Marie started to laugh, "are you a wolf in sheep's clothing Capitaine Maubert?" The capitaine was struggling to find a way to apologise. Marie touched his arm. "Don't Thierry please. It proves you're human, not just a robotic gendarme. You have feelings. I didn't think anyone who joined the gendarmerie did."

"Well now you know."

"Yes now I know," smiled Marie. "I'll say bonne nuit Mr Wolf."

"Will you be ok Marie?"

"I'll be fine, thanks for listening." Marie cracked the door.

"Marie," the capitaine remembered, for him, the main reason he'd wanted to see her. The capitaine told her about his theory that Ismail had been paid to make up his story to throw the gendarmerie off the scent. To his surprise Marie didn't dismiss the story but added something else. Since this morning she hadn't managed to reach her friends housing Ismail, nor Ismail himself. Her friends had given Ismail a mobile but none of their phones were responding. She'd phoned a neighbour and she, at her request had gone round but no one had answered. No one had been home, she was sure.

"Wait here, I have a key to their house. I'll give it to you, perhaps you would check on them for me." Capitaine Maubert promised he would. Two minutes later Marie came back holding an old fashioned brass key. Winding down the car window the capitaine took it from her. "Let me know they're ok." Once again the capitaine promised he would. "Merci," Marie leant inside the car giving him a peck on his lips. It was innocent but framed in a photo suggested much more. Her neighbour was delighted, the whole of Calais will soon learn of their affair.

Covent Garden – London, England

John spent only a few minutes in his apartment. Just long enough to pick up another pay as you go phone. Feeling quite a lot better now that he had something positive to aim for and perhaps a solution to his recent problem, he strode with a spring in his step to Covent Garden tube. It was only three stops to Kings Cross/ St Pancras, where he alighted, after which it was just a short walk to the St Pancras Renaissance Hotel. There he ordered a cocktail in the Booking Office 1869 bar. John loved the bar, it was once the Victorian booking hall for St Pancras Station and my God did those Victorians have a penchant for extravagance and eccentricity.

Finding his usual quiet corner and after taking a long sip of his cocktail he opened the pay as you go phone. Locating the number Roger had given him, he dialled. Whoever or if there was anybody at all, took a long time to answer and just as John thought his call was going to be directed to answer phone, a man's voice answered.

"Yes?" the voice sounded nervous.

"Mr Warnford, Mr Greg Warnford?"

"Who's calling?"

"Greg, my name's John, we have a mutual friend, a Mr Taylor, oh and Greg, if you know what's good for you, speak to me. I'm here to find a solution, not to kill you." There was no reply but whoever it was he was talking to didn't ring off. That was a good sign. "Maybe I can help you Greg, it's wise that you talk to me."

"Why should I trust you, I've got the money to be able to disappear."

"Nobody disappears Greg, my speciality is finding people who try to disappear and I need to warn you, I have a one hundred percent success rate. I've already found your phone number, haven't I" There came a pause, whilst Mr Warnford, if it was Mr Warnford thought about this.

"Ok, I'm listening."

"Good Greg, that's a good start. Listen it's in my interest that you don't come to any harm. What we have is a problem and we need to find a solution that makes everybody happy. Now Mr Taylor has employed me to recover a quarter of a billion pounds you have of his money." John deliberately refrained from using the word stolen.

"It's not as simple as that, anyway I no longer have quarter of a billion."

"It's never as simple as that, there's always two sides to a story. I'm not here to judge Greg, as I said before I'm here to find a solution that suits everybody. I'm sure Mr Taylor is a very reasonable man." There came a splutter on the other end of the phone which John took to mean Paul Taylor was far from being so. "Listen Greg, you say you don't have all of the money anymore, that's why we need to find a solution and I'm sure I can help you with this."

"How?"

"I'm not going to discuss that over the phone Greg, you'll have to meet me."

"I'm not sure…." The man was obviously scared.

"Listen Greg I know the thought of meeting me can be scary, and if the truth be told when people see me I tend to scare them but that's simply because I'm an ugly bastard. Listen think about it and I'll call you back sometime tomorrow to see where we're at."

"OK, what time will you ring?"

"Before midday."

"Ok. I'll think about it." You have little choice thought John.

"Yes, ok but a friendly warning. Don't turn your phone off, don't try and disappear. If you do I promise I will find you and you won't like it when I do. Work with me Greg and you'll soon discover I may become an asset."

"I promise."

"Good, have a good night Greg." John rang off. He was pleased, that had gone well, he could see his life pension before him and he knew how to disappear.

One last call. He dialled Roger's mobile. "Another favour? I've already done it."

"Done what?"

"Put a trace on the phone, he's somewhere, close to Hyde Park Corner. Can't tell you more than that I'm afraid."

"Thanks Roger, that'll do."

"It will bloody have to," and Roger rang off.

Work over, John's thought's turned to Bree and a touch of sadness started to creep over him. He couldn't believe she'd created her persona especially to snare him. It had been too real, too raw, he was certain or liked to think it hadn't all been an act. John ordered another cocktail and after a couple more began to willingly wallow in self-pity. What the bloody hell was wrong with him.

Maureen had discarded Bree, she no longer liked anything she stood for. Back at her hotel room she opened a bottle of champagne, a bottle she'd bought at duty free. Pouring the soft bubbly liquid into a bathroom tumbler, she drank. It tasted lovely. In seconds she'd finished her first glass and hurriedly poured a second. She wanted out and it was just beginning to dawn on her that, that may not be so easy. How could she have been so stupid. Her imitation Victorian bath looked inviting, she always thought better in the bath, it's where all of her best ideas came from. She opened the taps and dropped in a bath bomb she'd bought from reception. Finishing her second glass she undressed before pouring a third. Climbing in she took the bottle of champagne with her. She hadn't been soaking for five minutes when she'd finished her fourth glass. There remained a tiny amount and rather than waste energy pouring, she finished what was left by drinking straight from the bottle. Laying her head back on the rim of the bath Maureen closed her eyes. Her head was spinning. Sleep came to her quickly, her hand loosened and both her glass and the bottle dropped to the floor. Before consciousness left her she made one decision. She had to see John again. She had to explain.

Calais Plage – France

Fatima hated the cold but enjoyed the sea wherever it was, even La Manche. La Manche was very different to La Mediterraneenne, from her short experience it sometimes looked wild and unforgiving. Perhaps from all the bloodletting over the centuries.

Pierre walked beside her, taking in the fresh sea air as they took advantage of the town's long promenade. The beach was lined with colourful beach huts and even with a stiff cold breeze some were being used. Kite flying was popular all along the coast and several were being flown expertly as they walked.

Their conversation was deep, intense. Fatima was concerned about the bodies of the children found on the cruiser. She wanted to know if the organisation was responsible for this. She was a woman after all and although she hadn't ever had children, not by choice but because of the torture she'd endured when she was young, she still had a mother's instincts. Pierre assured her he simply didn't know and didn't believe that they were. We both joined the organisation to bring good into the world, to stamp down on the evil and corruption that is everywhere he told her. And from what he could tell the organisation's sphere of influence was steadily growing, even within the higher echelons of Western Governments. Soon they would be in a position to start taking action. Fatima trusted Pierre and was satisfied, for the moment at least.

Their conversation next turned to Capitaine Maubert. Fatima was pretty sure they'd be meeting that evening but she wasn't sure if he had anything more that was useful to them.

"Do your best Fatima, if he has I'll know you'll get it out of him." His next line surprised her. "Anyway it looks like your work is finished here, you're needed in London. Young Bree sadly has proved to be too emotional." Fatima could tell Pierre was a little emotional himself over her failure. She knew he felt very protective over his recent protégé. It was so unlike him.

"I need to remind you Pierre that I have refugee status in France, I am not allowed to travel." Pierre didn't appear to be fazed by this.

"We'll sort your travel documents, don't worry, bank cards the lot. And you'll still be Fatima, don't worry." Fatima having pointed her status out knew, Pierre would sort it. Her mind was already elsewhere, she was deep in thought, pondering over a question she'd been wanting to ask for months.

"Pierre, who or what exactly is the organisation. What's it called. I have given who or whatever it is a good service, I have always got results. No questions asked and yet I still don't know who or what I am working for. I don't even know who's at the helm. What his name is, where he's from."

"It's a question I ask too Fatima, and I can't help you. I don't know either. All I'm told when I ask the same question, is that the organisation's anonymity is one reason it's so successful. Nobody really knows if it exists even. What I do know, is, the creator is shortly travelling to London. But I've no idea where he's staying or for how long. I shouldn't even know he's going to be in London. The Egyptian let slip. Most unlike him."

So the powerful Pierre knew little more than her, how interesting. Well she was determined to find out. She wasn't prepared to work for a ghost any longer.

Ardres – France

After dropping Marie, the capitaine drove to her friend's house in Les Attaques. He found the door locked and no lights burning. After knocking it was obvious no one was home. He wondered about using the key Marie had given him but decided it were better if he came back the next day, during daylight. Turning the lights on may attract the wrong type of attention. And he wasn't overly concerned, her friends may simply be visiting friends and hadn't wanted to leave Ismail alone in the house for that period of time. It was perfectly understandable.

Afterwards he went to visit his wife and mother-in-law in Guines. His wife he found was fine and his mother-in-law even though she had taken a tumble had made him four baba au rhums for which Thierry had given her an almighty hug.

At home he demolished two, the other two he'd have for breakfast. He then, just in case he spent the whole night at the hotel went about making it look as if he'd spent the night at home. A precaution, in case his wife, tomorrow, came home before him. Unlikely, but best to be sure. This meant untidying the bed, leaving a cd out in his office, a glass of wine still with sediment in the lounge and an unwashed coffee cup in the kitchen. After a much needed shower, he shaved, dried and dressed in a smart but casual two piece suit and a crisp white shirt. After spraying himself liberally with Vintage Lacoste, the capitaine considered himself to be ready. Hopefully Fatima would be waiting for him.

Covent Garden – London, England

Maureen woke to find herself sitting in bath of cold water and with a muzzy head. Groaning she stepped out. Through her window she could see a night sky. What time was it? There was a clock in the room, nearly half past eight. Shit, she needed to see John. She had to. After taking a couple of headache tablets she finished off her ablutions by taking a cold shower. The combination worked. She was beginning to feel, once again, a bit like Bree. Maybe she needed Bree tonight. A double agent, the thought appealed to her.

It was well past nine before she felt ready to put into practice her own mission. Dressed to kill and wearing her favourite faux fur Maureen or was it Bree marched to John's apartment. She was pleased to see his lights were on. He'd gotten home safely, she was beginning to wonder if he would. She rang the doorbell longer than was necessary. After a few seconds she heard steps descending the stairs. The door opened and John stood there wearing nothing but a bathrobe. He gave her a look of bad taste.

"What do you want Bree, come to gloat?" Bree changed quickly to Maureen. From the way he spoke she could tell he'd been drinking.

"Not at all John, I've come to apologise, I had no idea that was going to happen." John stared back at her, she could tell he was trying hard to focus.

"Is this another one of your tricks Bree or should I say Maureen, did you know they'd bugged your mobile?" He noticed, even in his inebriated state that he had genuinely shocked her. No matter, he was finished with her and that came next. "Anyway Bree, I don't want to ever see your face again, a new job has fallen into my lap, one that I can retire on. In a few days I'll be well away from here. Have a good life Bree." He shut the door, the last image he'd ever have of Bree were tears rolling down both her cheeks. John sat on his second step, dropped his head in his hands and started sobbing.

Hotel De La Plage – Calais Plage, France

The capitaine was pleased to see Fatima sitting in the restaurant and just like yesterday she'd almost finished her meal. Unlike yesterday she was dressed in a long robe that matched her hijab and her make up done in the Persian style, she looked both exotic and gorgeous. She smiled a smile that had 'welcome' and 'pleasured' written all over it. The capitaine was finding it difficult to believe that he'd actually had sex with her yesterday. Sex that he'd never imagined possible, it had been beyond euphoric.

"You're late Thierry, trying to resist me?" The capitaine shook his head.

"No I've had one hell of an afternoon." Fatima leant forward and brushed his cheek with the back of her hand, just as Marie had done only hours earlier.

"It can't have been worse than your morning." The capitaine considered this.

"Almost." Their conversation followed up on what he had told her lunchtime. He was oblivious to the fact that he was telling an almost complete stranger the ins and outs of a heavily guarded gendarmerie investigation. Not once did he even tell her that their conversation should go no further than their table. After watching him down a couple of brandies Fatima led the capitaine, like a lamb to the slaughter, to her room.

Like yesterday she had prepped everything. The capitaine was immediately hit by the heady scent. It enveloped him, made him feel weak at the knees and above all incredibly sensual. Every sexual nerve burned his body.

"Undress Thierry and lie down." The capitaine did as he was told. Fatima started to play a song on a speaker he hadn't seen. As the song played Fatima started to dance, turning and turning and as she danced she slowly disrobed. The capitaine had never heard music like it. It was beautiful, soulful and mysterious all at the same time. Like her perfume it played with his senses. As the music finished Fatima stood with her back against the door, legs apart. All she wore were her headdress, the cross thing around her neck, her abdomen jewellery and her heels. "Come to me Thierry, kneel."

Once again the capitaine did as he was told. Fatima grabbed his hair and guided him forcefully towards her crutch. Holding his head just where she wanted it she felt his tongue start to explore her clitoris. She didn't experience sexual pleasure but she loved the power. Here was one of the most powerful men in Calais kneeling naked between her legs, doing her bidding. Her bidding, a woman from Persia who when she was young had been nothing but a commodity for men's pleasure. How the tide had changed.

She kept him there for a good half hour, at times pulling his hair so hard that she could feel him wince with pain. Even so, not once did he stop trying to pleasure her. On the bed she controlled every move, he was at her mercy. For Fatima, her ultimate power was being on top. Using her strength along with her weight to crush her target into submission. As part of this she crouched over the capitaine facing away from his head. As she played with his erection she slowly sat over his face. Slowly she brought herself up. She had a strong back and she knew men liked to look up at her as she smothered them. Slowly she brought herself down so that her full bodyweight rested on the capitaine's face. To breathe he would have to open his mouth and place his tongue deep inside her. She could feel him struggling for breath under her weight but his stiffening erection told her he didn't want her to stop. Sitting straight she felt his tongue slip into the orifice that was her anus. Fatima started to shake, she had never experienced this feeling before. She pressed down and let out a groan as the capitaines tongue pushed deep into her back passage. More, she wanted more and started to writhe and push, searching for the most pleasure she could from the capitaine's tongue. Slowly she felt a pressure begin to build inside her, deep, deep inside her. It needed to be released, it needed to explode and it did. Fatima cried out as she felt a rush of liquid flow down her back passage. She wanted more and as the capitaine spluttered she pushed down hard and the second explosion came. Exhausted she collapsed and rolled off the struggling capitaine. She was shocked by what had just happened. Shocked and scared. She turned to the capitaine who was coughing violently.

"Thierry I'm sorry but you have to leave and leave now."

Covent Garden – London, England

Maureen walked back to central Covent Garden. Never had she felt so upset. She couldn't go back to her hotel, not yet. She didn't want to be alone with her thoughts in her room. Not yet. As so many people do when in a crisis she'd seek solace in alcohol. Holding back tears she walked to the Punch and Judy. A couple, one with a guitar and the other singing were churning out popular hits outside the cellar bar. The music was just what she needed. Ordering a large pink gin and tonic, Maureen drank heavily taking in the music. Her tears never quite left her and after her third large gin she was luxuriating in her emotions. A young good looking chap started talking to her. He was nice, sensitive, charming. Above all he was understanding and wanted to know what was wrong. He bought her a fourth gin and as the music slowed he invited her to dance. They kissed and both knew the next step was her hotel. She'd told him where she was staying.

At three am Maureen woke. Her head thumped and the room smelt of something familiar, sex. Sitting up she realised someone was in bed beside her. Shaking his body in anger, she hissed.

"You have to get out and get out now."

Chapter 16

Outside the young man walked to Longacre. The tube had finished for the night. He was exhausted and his head hurt. He couldn't bear the thought of waiting for a night bus and looked around for a taxi. Conveniently a car slowed beside him. The driver wound down the window and leant across.

"Taxi Sir?" The lad knew it wasn't an official taxi but he didn't care. He was used to taking illegal taxis and they were often a lot cheaper.

"How much to Chesham?" The driver thought before quoting a price.

"Payment in advance. Cash only" The young lad handed over a wad of notes and climbed into the back seat. He was surprised to find a glass wall separating him from the driver. You couldn't be too careful these days he supposed. As they drove he sensed something he couldn't explain. A funny sort of smell. He began to feel sleepy, no it was more than sleepy, he started to feel faint and the next minute he was gone, gone forever.

A lone figure stood not far from The Fielding. They would have to deal with the woman too.

Chapter
—17—

The National Crime Agency – Lambeth, England

There was a loud knock at Roger's door. He knew what it was about. They'd received the DNA results in impressive time from France and there'd been a hit on all twelve children. Not so the two males. His officer had said on the phone that what they revealed was shocking and didn't feel comfortable relaying it over the phone. What was so shocking? He was about to find out.

The officer entered on bidding and sat down. In his hands were several files which Roger assumed contained details of what was so shocking. "Go on then shock me." And his officer did.

Holding on to the files and scanning them after his officer had left Roger phoned his boss, the Director General of operations. "Sir I think the Director General should see this and with some urgency." On hearing what Roger had to say he agreed. A meeting was arranged to convene in half an hour. A record his boss told him. In half an hour exactly they were sat in the Director's office. The Director read through the files and asked a few questions. Picking up the receiver of a bright red phone she pressed a single digit and waited. A female voice answered.

Their Director didn't have time for pleasantries. "Pamela, it's Jane, NCA, I need to speak to the Home Secretary."

"He's busy I'm afraid."

"Sorry Pamela, this can't wait." Silence and then a male voice spoke, a voice everyone recognised as belonging to the Home Secretary.

"What can't wait Jane, I'm really busy."

"I need to come and see you and straight away Sir."

"I need some idea of what this about Jane." The Director gave him a brief resume. The Home Secretary didn't hesitate. "Ok, you'd better come over."

The Director, Jane stood up. Come on you two we've got a meeting at the Home Office.

A House In Tottenham – London, England

There came a knock at the door, nervous Zahra asked her daughter to answer it. Staying in the UK illegally she found it sometimes difficult to breathe let alone answer the door to a stranger. The knock as it turned out, had been a delivery man. A largish parcel had been left on their doorstep. The driver took a photograph for proof of delivery and left.

Zahra's daughter, her tenth birthday yesterday carried it in and placed it on a very worn coffee table. "Perhaps it's from Daddy, perhaps it's my present" she said excitedly, jumping up and down. Possibly, for very few people knew where they were staying. Daddy's name was Ismail, for months now he'd been stuck in Calais trying to cross the water that separated France and England. They'd been in daily touch and every day he told her tomorrow will be the day. But for the last two days, there'd been only silence. Zahra wasn't too worried. Circumstances meant there were often prolonged silences. She was used to them.

Unable to contain her excitement the little girl started to tear back the masking tape. Once freed she lifted up the flaps and peered inside. Clasping her hands to her mouth she started to shake, tears rolling down her cheeks.

"What is it love?" Her mother held her daughter to her waist and peered inside, puzzled as to what there could be that had so upset her. Some sort of joke probably, her father was always playing tricks, sometimes he loved to play scare his daughter. After peering inside her mother's reaction was far more extreme, she screamed throwing her arms in the air and running out of the house. A car's brakes squealed as a driver made an emergency stop to avoid hitting her. Seconds after a little girl followed shrieking. Several passers by rushed to help. Two men nervously entered the house, half expecting to find a dead body. What they found was a lot worse. In a box in the lounge, sat a severed head. The eyes had been gouged out and in the mouth, which had been stretched open to its fullest were stuffed the man's genitals. One of the men was instantly sick, the other ran out gasping for air.

"Somebody call an ambulance," he just about managed to gasp, "and the police." Several bystanders went to their phones.

The woman clasping her daughter lay in the road screaming, repeating over and over. "It's my husband, it's my husband, Ismail. Isssssmaiiil, Isssssmaiiiil, she wailed over and over and over again."

Covent Garden – London, England

It was ten in the morning before Maureen woke a second time. She groaned loudly as she gingerly left her bed. Her head was thumping, when would she ever learn? The room smelt heavily of sex, her body felt of sex and inside, her body was telling her she'd had sex but she could hardly remember a thing. She vaguely remembered throwing……, she couldn't even or didn't even know his name. Had she even asked? Going to her bag she, with tepid water, swallowed four headache tablets. Next a shower, as cold as possible.

An hour later Maureen was ready for the world. Yes she was fragile but she'd been here before and knew how to deal with it. She needed to see John, she couldn't leave it like this. Five minutes later she was ringing his bell. No reply, no heavy steps sounding on the staircase. She rang again for longer. Still nothing. She put her ear to the door. Not a sound, he wasn't in, she made herself a promise to come back again later that day.

It was now gone midday and as always the case with drinking too much alcohol, when you stopped feeling ill, the stomach immediately sends a message to the brain demanding food. The message was coming through loud and clear. She suddenly realised she was starving.

"You look awful."

Maureen spun round to see her contact, the clumsy but posh sounding Englishman who always came after messaging whoever with green inked crossword puzzles. He was smiling warmly and had a concerned look on his face. Maureen was caught off guard, she felt she should be putting up defences but his harmless manner allowed him an open drawbridge.

"I don't feel great, " Maureen admitted, "too much to drink last night."

"Are you hungry?" Maureen smiled yes, how did he know. "Come on, a bit of spice is the answer to the demonic drink. I know a good restaurant." He held out his arm and Maureen took it.

The restaurant turned out to be Café Pacifico, she remembered John talking about it. John, where was John? She could see why John had purred so positively about the place. Though quiet when they entered it had an ambience that comes only with years of rowdy clientele. An ambience even the cleverest interior designers find impossible to recreate. The Englishman, Charles turned out to be good and charming company. He was just what she needed. He played down her experience in Bayswater, explaining it was the only way they'd get him to talk to them. He hasn't come to any harm he assured her and with the reassurance, asked if she'd seen him since.

Bree returned as easily as she'd left. She was, with immense enthusiasm tucking into a plate of slow cooked pulled pork chilli tacos and this after a starter of nachos. Charles was right, the spice was definitely helping as was the fresh passion fruit and spice mojito, her second.

"I saw John last night," Bree told him, "he wasn't happy with me though." She tossed her head back and laughed. Taking another mouthful she added noisily, "anyway I don't think he's too bothered. He told me, let me think," Bree perched her fork in the air as she went through the process. "Got it, he said another job had fallen into his lap, one so big he'd be able to retire."

Changing the subject Charles asked if she'd enjoyed Tina, the musical. "I forgot all about it" admitted Bree. "Oh was I meant to meet someone there?" With her recent experience she realised that the ticket may have been a cover for a clandestine meeting. Passing notes across chairs. Charles laughed, no he told her. I just thought you'd enjoy it.

They finished by downing a couple of tequilas. As soon as they left, the contrasting cold air hit Bree like an arrow between the eyes. She felt very dizzy, faint and almost helpless. A black cab was waiting outside. Charles stepped forward and opened the rear door.

"To show my gratitude, I've organised a little tour for you, you'll love it." Bree needed to sit down and gratefully slumped into the rear seat.

"Aren't you coming?" she mumbled as Charles went to close the door. He smiled.

"Sorry no, work calls. Just enjoy the tour, I've already paid for it. You'll see the best of London." Closing the door he waved her off. The taxi pulled forward and he was gone. She felt strange, dizzy and for some reason she felt unable to move, none of her limbs were working. She saw landmarks she recognised as the driver expertly manoeuvred through the streets of London. She wanted to sit up, to fully appreciate them but something inside her was stopping her. She felt the taxi suddenly descend, they were somewhere underground. Bree was intrigued, what surprise was this. Parked outside there were a row of ambulances. Bree's eyes started to close, never realising the ambulances would be her very last vision. Maureen would be so disappointed.

Gendarmerie Nationale – Calais, France

The usual officers were gathered in the incident room for that morning's briefing. Capitaine Maubert on entering sensed a mood change amongst his officers. Perhaps it was the pressure and frustration enveloping the case. Before he'd arrived for work he'd popped back to check on Marie's friend's house. He still hadn't found anyone at home. He'd tried the key Marie had given him but it hadn't worked. She must have given him the wrong key. Before he left he checked the windows. Everything inside looked neat and tidy. No signs of a struggle. They must surely be away. Strange though that they hadn't told Marie. He tried her phone to see if she had any news but she wasn't picking up. As he left he failed to spot two men sitting in a parked car, watching his every move.

At the briefing, in the light of recent events, he threw open the theory that perhaps after all they should be searching for a so called 'hospital ship' and that Ismail had been paid to deliberately mislead them. The theory received some positive feedback but if this was the case why put the dead bodies on a motor cruiser. Why not just dump them overboard? Because that wasn't foolproof one officer pointed out. Look what happened during the storm. There was more general discussion before the meeting broke up and officers left to endure more knocking on doors.

Chapter 17

Back in his office the capitaine reflected on Fatima and her strange behaviour last night. He simply couldn't work it out. Had he done something wrong? He didn't think so, he racked his mind trying to find something but no, he could think of nothing. He had to let it go. He was becoming obsessed. Anyway he'd pop to the hotel at lunch, just to check. As his mind was elsewhere other than police business a knock on the door brought him back to the here and now.

"Maubert." Colette entered, she looked nervous, troubled.

"Are you ok Colette?"

"I don't know, are you Mr Maubert?" The capitaine frowned, what was she talking about. Colette stepped forward handing him a piece of paper. "London want you to call them, it's about those small children, poor devils. Sounds urgent, and if you ask me something big is going on over there."

"Thank you, I'll call them after you've gone, anything else?" Colette hesitated, she looked even more nervous.

"Yes Mr Maubert," she wouldn't look at him. "Are you seeing someone, a woman?" The capitaine's blood froze. This hit him like a terrorist's bomb, completely by surprise. Had Fatima been secretly filming him. It didn't bear thinking about.

"Why do you ask Colette?" the capitaine tried to look cool and failed miserably. He knew he had 'guilty' written all over his face. Taking out her smartphone, Colette came round the desk so she was standing beside her boss.

"These are all over Facebook," Colette held her phone so her boss could see. The capitaine hated social media and so didn't belong to that world. He had no idea what Colette was about to show him. Colette started sliding her fingers across the screen, one after another, photos of him with Marie yesterday appeared on the screen. Several showed the two of them kissing.

"What!" The capitaine was shocked. "But that's not what it seems, not at all." Colette stared at him, disappointment etched all over her face.

"It doesn't matter what I think Mr Maubert or what it was, but I think you need to talk to your wife before she sees these, if she hasn't already." The capitaine started to physically shake, his wife was hardly ever on social media but his daughter was very different. Social media was like an extension of her brain. "It's lunch Mr Maubert, I suggest you go home."

"Thank you Colette," the capitaine virtually flew out of the door, "thank you" he said again.

As the capitaine drove it was as though his mind and his car were in a race with each other. He couldn't get home quick enough, that is if his wife was there at all, perhaps she was still with her mother. And his mind was racing, trying to understand it all. Who had taken the photos, who had been watching them? Who could be so vindictive. As he approached the family home, his heart sank. He knew he was too late. Outside was parked his daughter's car and on the doorstep a holdall and a small suitcase.

The walk to his front door, felt like the march of death. He truly understood for the first time the expression, 'heart in mouth.' His was in his mouth and waiting to be vomited out. As he got close the front door opened and his daughter came out screaming.

"Dad, how could you do this to mum, to me you, batard, batard, batard. Conard. You utter conard." She reached down, picked up his holdall and briefcase and threw them at him. Through the windows he could see his mother-in-law holding her daughter, his wife in her arms. His wife was obviously in tears. If only he could turn back the clock, how many people over the centuries had wished that. He'd never for a day thought he'd be one of them. Picking up his bags he turned and walked back to his car. Everything was too emotionally charged right now. He'd come back when it was less so. Then he could explain everything. He tried Marie's phone again but this time it was off. God what must she be going through?

Before he went back to the gendarmerie he stopped at The Café de Paris in Rue Royale. He needed a beer and ended up having two. On returning to the gendarmerie he was both frustrated as well as annoyed to find a car in his reserved space. Reversing, he swung into a space reserved for visitors. Walking into reception, Colette came running over.

"Mr Maubert, Mr Maubert there's some men waiting to see you in your office."

"Thank you Colette." The capitaine mounted the stairs two by two. Who could it be that they presumed to have the right to barge into his office. Baptiste, the BRB, possibly. As soon as he opened the door, he knew he was in trouble.

The Home Office – London, England

You could cut the atmosphere with a knife, it was that tense. The Home Secretary was sitting behind his desk flanked by, as the late Diana would describe them, 'men in grey suits.' Roger, the Director and his direct boss the Director of operations were sitting in a semi-circle, facing.

The Home Secretary was holding the files that had started all the fuss. "There's no way someone could have made a mistake?" All three from the NCA shook their heads.

"Sadly no." Jane the director spoke for all of them. The Home Secretary threw the files on his desk.

"Shit, what a bloody mess." Silence followed his outburst. "Who was meant to be protecting these children and how come we've got their DNA?"

It was Roger who spoke up. "It's the responsibility of the local authority to ensure their safety, but of course they're overstretched." The Minister threw his hands in the air. "As for the DNA, its been our policy, not secretly but we haven't shouted about it, that we take DNA samples of every illegal migrant, for fairly obvious reasons."

"It was on the orders of your predecessor," the Director cut in.

"Including children?"

"Including children yes." The Home Secretary scanned the files again.

"And these children found on the boat, they're all from Albania?"

"Yes." The director gave a single nod. "Yes, they were all housed in a hotel in Eastbourne, they went missing just over three months ago."

"And nothing was done to try and find them?" The Home Secretary was incredulous.

"The local authority and the local police did their best but it's all down to resources."

"It's always down to bloody resources," the Home Secretary slammed the desk. If I chucked everybody a couple of billion more I'd still continue being told with every mistake it's down to resources. How many more Albanian children are missing?"

It was Roger's turn. "Another ten from this hotel sir, two hundred and seven in total."

"Fuck and they could all end up like these poor devils if they haven't already." The Home Secretary stared at the three from the NCA. "Do you three realise the shit we're in if this gets out, the biggest pile of shit since shitting records began that's what. JESUS, I don't believe it." The Home Secretary took a deep breath. "So that brings us to the next question, what do we do now?"

"The local police are stepping up patrols and mak......" Roger was stopped.

"Yes, yes, I'm sure they are, I mean how do we stop this from getting out. Where are the bodies now?"

"With the French authorities, at a morgue in Boulogne." Roger told him.

"Well we can't trust the bloody French to keep a secret can we, we need to get the bodies back."

One of the men in a grey suit spoke for the first time. "The French won't want to keep them Sir, not for longer than is necessary. The real problem is, what do we do with the bodies when they're back on British soil?"

"What do you mean?"

"Well we can hardly admit to the Albanians what has happened, it's best if they believe the children are simply missing."

"Well can't we, at least, give them a decent burial?" The three from the NCA watched as the conversation went back and forth.

"Hardly Sir, it would risk bringing too much attention to the case and burials normally have to be recorded, what would we put?"

"Then what do you suggest?"

"Short term, we freeze them until we can think of a solution or the timing is easier."

"Jesus, is there no other way?"

"Can you think of one?"

"Who would be responsible?"

The man in grey looked at Jane. She responded quickly.

"Oh no, don't get my department involved in this."

"Leave it to me Sir," the man smiled. The Home Secretary changed tack.

"And this, organ trafficking, the so called 'red market.' Are we taking it seriously?"

The Director struggled to give an honest response. How could she explain to him that his predecessor had intimated to her, to turn a blind eye. That in many ways the organ traffickers were doing an over stretched NHS a valuable service.

"Well that went well," the Director commented as they left the building. "Don't you think?"

Hyde Park – London, England

John was sat on a bench in Hyde Park looking back to the Hilton Tower and Hyde Park Corner. The sun was shining and the weather was pleasantly balmy for Autumn. He punched Greg Warnford's number and waited. The phone rang twice before the voice he recognised from last night answered.

"Morning Greg, have you thought over our conversation from yesterday. I'm being honest when I say I think I can help you and it will cost you a lot less than quarter of a billion."

"I don't see that I've got any choice."

"There's always a choice Greg. It's just choosing the right one and I'm the right one. I promise. As I said yesterday, I don't want you to come to any harm."

"Then I suppose we need to meet." Greg Warnford sounded resigned to his fate.

"Tell me where you want me to meet you Greg and when."

"In public," Greg replied quickly, I'm not risking a private meeting, you understand."

"Perfectly Greg, where?"

"At Windows, the Hilton, Park Lane, do you know it?"

"Of course." So that's where he's staying. "How will I know you?" There came a pause as Greg quite obviously thought about this.

"I went to the theatre last night, Tina Turner. I bought a program, I shall have it with me."

"You can't meet today?" John was impatient to close the deal.

"Sorry no, promise I'll be there tomorrow, two in the afternoon."

"Deal, don't do anything silly Greg."

"I wont and I'll be there." He rang off. The NCA officer punched the air, they had him. Now to put the sting operation into place.

John disposed of the pay as you go mobile in the usual way and started walking back towards Covent Garden. He didn't feel like taking any form of transport, he needed the walk to freshen his mind. He wondered about Bree, she had looked genuinely upset yesterday. Perhaps he'd been too hard on her. He wondered about going to her hotel but decided it was a bad idea. If he pulled this off maybe he'd ask her to escape with him. Yes he'd do that. Feeling much better his pace quickened.

Gendarmerie Nationale – Calais, France

Sat behind his desk was a man he recognised as the Commandant des Regions, Hauts des France. With him were two officers he didn't recognise. The Commandant, unnecessarily pulled out his ID. Take a seat Capitaine Maubert. The capitaine did as he was told, it felt strange sitting on the other side of his desk.

The commandant looked at the clock on his wall. It read three pm. "You're an hour late capitaine and by the smell of alcohol on your breath I assume it wasn't work." The capitaine hung his head, for the commandant to be here he knew he was in some kind of trouble, now he really was in the shit. What had gotten into him. Why had he behaved so stupidly?

"Capitaine, we received a call from the British authorities this morning, they've been trying to reach you." Merde, the capitaine remembered Colette telling him. He'd forgotten to ring them.

"Apparently you're hiding an informer, a migrant called Ismail, is that correct capitaine?"

"Yes sir."

"And recently he went missing?"

"He's just not..." The commandant held up his hand.

"Well the British have found him." The capitaine looked up, surprised. "Well I should say found part of him. I'll spare you the gory details but his severed head was delivered to his wife yesterday, by courier." The capitaine was visibly shocked and he could see what was coming.

The commandant slid a number of photos, face up on the desk. They were of course prints of the photos placed on Facebook. "By the look of these you've been having an affair with this woman, Mademoiselle Marie Chevalier". The capitaine started to proffer an explanation but again the commandant held up his hand. "You will have your chance to defend yourself at the appropriate time. For now I just want to lay out what we know and what action will be taken." The capitaine stared silently at the floor. He knew his time in the gendarmerie, his whole life, everything he'd ever worked for was finished. And now if he knew what was coming he'd be lucky to escape prison. "We interviewed young Marie," the commandant tapped one of the photographs, "this morning." She told us, despite the obvious dangers you brought a complete stranger to the house, is that correct capitaine?"

"Yes."

"I didn't hear you, capitaine."

"Yes, sir, stupid of me I know, but yes."

"Very stupid capitaine, a woman?"

"Yes."

"Her name?"

"Fatima."

"Her whole name."

"I don't know sir." Christ what had he done?

"How long had you known her capitaine?"

"Two or three days." He was dead meat.

"So let me get this right capitaine. You brought virtually a complete stranger, not even knowing their surname, without having had them checked out, to a house where someone you suspected at being at risk was hiding."

Yes sir." The capitaine wished the ground would swallow him up.

"Bloody hell capitaine, how could you have been so stupid, what were you thinking of. Where were your brains? In your trousers apparently, is this her?" The commandant slid another photo on the table. It had obviously been taken from a security video at the Hotel de la Plage. "Is that her?"

"Yes sir."

"And you say she's called Fatima." The capitaine nodded.

"Well I can tell you capitaine she may be using that name but she booked into the hotel using false ID and a bank account falsely obtained. It was not an amateurish job capitaine. Your one saving grace, if you can call it that, is you were duped by a femme fatale, a professional and she was obviously sent to target you. Did you tell her anything else?" The capitaine still had honour if nothing else. He told them the truth. That he had told her everything. A heavy silence fell on the room. The commandant shook his head, "Jesus capitaine, you do realise that you are almost certainly responsible for this migrant, Ismail's death and whoever she's working for. Well they'll be streets ahead of us now. We might as well all pack up and go home. And before you ask capitaine, your so called Fatima booked out first thing this morning. She's disappeared though all of Europe is looking for her. I assume you two were having sexual relations, don't bother, the receptionist told us you went back to her room. More than once, you weren't playing tiddly winks were you." The capitaine lowered his head, at that moment he wanted to die.

The commandant slid another photo onto his desk. To the capitaine's surprise it was a photo of Baptiste, though when he was a little younger.

"Who's this?" The capitaine's face showed his surprise, he shrugged his shoulders.

"It's Baptiste, he's from the BRB."

"Wrong capitaine, yes he's Baptiste but he resigned or rather he was forced to resign from the BRB over a year ago. What's he doing here? With You, in your gendarmerie."

The next two hours were spent with the capitaine answering some very difficult questions, especially regarding Baptiste. Apparently he too, like Fatima had disappeared. He'd often thought it strange that he was always alone, the BRB normally travelled in pairs and he'd always had to ring a mobile, never a landline. Or had he, he couldn't remember. At the end he was asked to give up his Carte Professionel, (warrant card), and escorted from the building. He was warned not to leave the local area. The commandant with some grace told him that he believed the capitaine had behaved stupidly and not corruptly and therefore was prepared to trust him, before formal disciplinary action could be taken. Which it would, undoubtedly.

The Hilton – Park Lane

Fatima stared at the view through her window. She was on God knows whatever floor of the iconic Hilton hotel on Park Lane in London. The view from her window was beyond magnificent, before her stretched Hyde Park and the lights that were London seemed to her to stretch to infinity and beyond.

She had travelled to London with Pierre. He had business in Hatton Garden, after all, officially he was a diamond dealer. Although the organisation had always paid her well they had never placed her in a hotel such as this and she was wondering what was different this time around. No point in worrying, she'd find out in time. All she knew for now was that she may be needed to take over from Bree. Where Bree was she had no idea.

Her mind wandered back to Calais and Thierry. How he had made her feel had shocked her, scared her even. When she was still a girl men abused her, taking what they wanted for their own gratification, not caring about her. Men who called themselves Muslims but were anything but. As she grew older she became a bride for sex. It had been her only way to survive. A corrupt Iman accepted payment from men so they could marry, have sex and then divorce her at the end of the day. For her services she would receive a cut. In total she had been married and divorced eleven times. Eventually the Iman had fallen foul of the mainly decent local population and been drummed out of town. It left her free from abuse but without a means to support herself. Enter Pierre, he'd been working for a French charity and seeing her plight managed to rescue her to France. Not believing he would do this for nothing she had offered him her body. He was and still is the only man who had refused her. He was simply helping her because it had been the right thing to do, nothing else.

It was perhaps because of her past she liked to dominate men, to hold power over them and why she never let them indulge in full sex. No man had ever gone where Thierry had, last night. The fact that she'd enjoyed it had shaken her, to experience what she now realised was her first ever orgasm. The result was she hadn't been in control. And that scared her, control was her profession, it's why she got paid. If men could do this to her, her power over them was coming to an end. It would be the other way around. The thought scared her to hell yet she wanted to experience that feeling again.

For the first time she realised she wanted out. She wanted out. She wanted if possible to meet a decent Muslim man, someone who would love, respect and cherish her. Look after her, enjoy life together, grow old together. She wanted to find the faith she'd been given at birth. A tear rolled down one cheek, wanting and achieving were two very different things. She had no idea how to get out and even harder how she'd go about finding a man who would accept her for what she was. Tomorrow Pierre had told her, she may be needed to take over Bree's target. Maybe. Whatever happened she was determined it would be her last job for the organisation.

Hotel De La Plage – Calais Plage, France

Thierry, for he was no longer capitaine had left the gendarmerie in a daze. He was struggling to take everything in. In just a few days he'd managed to bring his whole world crashing down. He had no idea where he was going, wanting a sense of recent familiarity he chose the Hotel de la Plage. He wanted to try and experience Fatima one last time, the surroundings in which they met would help him achieve that.

The bar and restaurant he found to be fairly busy when he arrived. Looking at the reception desk he decided he'd book in. He couldn't go home and though the woman he'd met here had destroyed him, he somehow still wanted a piece of her. Thierry wished now he'd asked her what the name of the song was she'd played when dancing for him. It had been magical, mysterious, almost painful at times as though it were a cry for help. At reception he asked if the room they'd used was free. The girl behind the desk, looking a little nervous, apologised. It was still being cleaned. However the room next door was free. He took it.

Chapter 17

Thierry wasn't hungry but he needed a drink. Sipping his bierre pression, he mulled over the brief reunion he'd had with Fatima. It had felt so real, he was struggling to understand how on her half it had all been an act. He remembered seeing a documentary once about America's failed invasion of Cuba. The Cubans knew everything about the American's plans because of a paid femme fatale. He was beginning to realise why some governments paid them so much money. They were an incredibly powerful weapon.

Theirry downed his third bierre. He still wasn't finished but he had a sudden compulsion to see where it had all began. He could enjoy more of the golden stuff when he returned. Going to his car he grabbed his two bags and placed them in his room. Memories lingered even if it wasn't the actual room. Shaking his head he walked briskly back to his car. Gunning the engine he exited the hotel car park at speed. Putting his foot down he stared up at his intended destination. Cap Blanc Nez

Covent Garden – London, England

A man who had no business being there, slipped past reception at The Fielding. He knew Bree's room and where to find it. Within seconds he was inside. The room had been serviced, everything looked very neat. Quickly he gathered Bree's belongings. It took him just ten minutes. Waiting to ensure the coast was clear he left. Bree no longer existed. Not in London anyway.

John lazed in his bed with a scotch and a take away curry. None of this would be possible if he lived with Bree, with any woman. He smiled to himself, curry in bed was one of the advantages of being a bachelor, having the leftovers for breakfast was another. Tomorrow was all set, one last job and he'd be able to retire.

National Crime Agency – Lambeth, London

They were going over the final plans for the sting in Roger's office. The officer pretending to be Greg Warnford and who'd already made contact with their target would wait outside in a car. Whilst five officers, three men and two woman would take their places in the bar, mainly to assess the situation. When their target was in place and there were no obvious suspicious circumstances they would give the all clear for the made up Greg Warnford to come up. They couldn't risk the officer playing Greg Warnford being miked, as their target was trained to spot such things. But he would be wearing sewn into his trousers a transmitter, so if need be they could track him. One of the officers in the bar, a woman, would be sat close enough, hopefully to overhear their conversation. No arrest would be made in the bar, it would be too messy but the officer playing Greg Warnford would try and entice their target to a hotel room, which would be bugged. If after the information they'd captured, it was felt that it would be more advantageous to let him go in the hope of catching maybe larger fry, that decision would be made on the day. For his own safety the officer impersonating Greg Warnford, would be the only one responsible for making the decision. Any arrest it was decided, if there was to be one, would be made outside the hotel where several unmarked cars would be waiting. All the officers involved in the operation would be fully armed as they knew their target may be carrying a weapon. The only exception would be the officer playing the part of Greg Warnford.

Minutes after everyone had left, Roger's phone rang. John, perfect timing.

"Yes John."

"Evening, be a little more civil, do you know if my target's still there."

"Yes actually, I'm monitoring him and he's still there. I'm assuming he must be staying in one of the hotels. Perhaps the Hilton."

"Thanks Roger."

"Yeah sure." Roger leaned back, his hands behind his head. He couldn't let his men arrest his old colleague, he had too much to lose if John spilled the beans. Somehow tomorrow he would have to create a circumstance under which John would be shot and killed.

Cap Blanc Nez – France

Apart from his own, there was one other car in the car park at the summit of Cap Blanc Nez. The windows were slightly misted and a song he recognised, Tahitialamaison by Keen'V was playing loud enough to be heard outside of the car. It was a song his daughter was always playing.

Thierry walked to the very edge of the cliff. He looked down at the sea below, its mood was restless, verging on anger encouraged by a stiff breeze. Waves, continuous in their torment crashed one after the other against the rugged chalk cliff. The waves were mesmerising, this is where it had all begun, in the waters far below. This is where his very own torment, a torment that had ruined his life had begun. Down there, in the sea the English liked to call their own, here in France simply known as La Manche. 'The Sleeve'. Thierry braced himself against the stiffening breeze. There, down below, may have been the beginning but he had no intention of it claiming his end. His fate would not be the same as the photographer's, who'd lost his life to the storm. His wife and daughter might have no wish to see him but they might still need him and he was determined to always be there for them. What happened to him in the near future was beyond his control. May God smile kindly on him.

He scanned the sea before him. Ships as well as boats, their navigation lights illuminating the inkiness that was the sea, moved slowly to and forth. Should they be looking for a so called hospital ship, plying its bloody trade in international waters? Thierry still thought the answer must lay closer to home, somewhere in Calais. He still believed Ismail's recollection. God rest his soul. How could he have been so gullible, so bloody stupid. Anger started to rise, he clenched his fists. The lights of Dover shone bright. Could the answer lie over there, across the water in Britain, Thierry turned his head, left then right, to the lights of Wissant and then Calais. No he was sure, very sure that the answer lay somewhere close by. What had he, they missed? He started to rack his brains.

He sensed rather than heard someone behind him. He spun round, a man dressed all in black and wearing a face covering had somehow crept up on him. His first instinct told him it was Baptiste, but no, the man's build was wrong. Under the mask Thierry sensed whoever it was, was smiling. In a natural response Thierry started to smile back. The car with the steamed windows was still there. Tahitialamaison was still playing, the music sounded a little louder.

"Goodbye Capitaine."

Thierry thought he felt something, a push maybe and suddenly the ground beneath him was no longer there. The sea, only moments ago that had so mesmerised him was approaching at speed, closer and closer at greater and greater speed. There came a sickening sound, a crunch as bone shattered, repeated seconds later by another. Thierry was walking through a garden, a beautiful garden, a garden full of bird song. He was confused, where had the sea disappeared to? His last memory before the garden took him was of Fatima and the kiss on his cheek she had given him when they were in Bergues. Seconds later Thierry's body hit the water, the waves picked it up and slammed it again and again against the base of the cliff. The Devil could do all he wanted, it didn't matter. The most important ingredient, the soul, had already left.

Shortly after Thierry had left this world a van pulled into the carpark on the other side of the road, the carpark that serviced the restaurant at the summit of Mont d'Hubert. Slowly it approached the restaurant's service area. A wide door opened and the van edged inside, the door quickly closed behind. Inside another door opened and two men slid open a door to a huge freezer. The van once more carefully edged its way in. A woman wearing a white coat, picked up a fire extinguisher, pulled out the safety pin and squeezed the handle. No powder came out but the rear wall of the freezer slowly slid open. On the other side a road descended deep underground. The van driver slowly edged the van forward. Fully onto the road the freezer wall closed behind him. A little while ago the mechanism that operated the wall had been broken. They'd had to unload the van on the surface and transport the cargo in small batches below. It had been a real pain. Thank God, it had been repaired and he could now drive his cargo into the bunker, as had always been intended. Waiting for him in the service area were Seth and Antanois. He lifted the rear door to reveal a collection of human bodies slumped over one another. Antanois climbed in and started to count, moving a lifeless form here and there where needed. When finished, he jumped out. Eighteen he said to Seth. Excellent came the reply, we'll get started straight away. Men and women, all wearing white coats started to lift the bodies onto gurneys and wheel them away. A sense of relief swept away the tension that had hovered the last few days. Everything was back to normal. Excellent.

CHAPTER
—18—

The GMC Building – Euston Road, London, England

Ammon waited nervously, he was part of a group all waiting to take their practical exam so they could legally practice in the UK. There was a face amongst the group he recognised. A second's glance had passed between them, and Ammon knew the familiar stranger had recognised him too. The organisation, that's the only name he knew it by had drummed into him that he must never show a hint of recognition and he was determined not to.

Minutes later several men and women, all dressed smartly in black welcomed them to the General Medical Council. One who was obviously in charge explained how the practical exam worked. Firstly all personal belongings had to be handed over, especially mobile phones and there was to be no conferring. Each of them would be chaperoned, even when they went to the toilet. Ammon took a deep breath, the next few hours would determine his future. He was determined to pass, both for his family and for the organisation which had so successfully fast tracked him.

The Hilton Hotel – Park Lane, London, England

The guests enjoying the uniqueness of the Windows Bar on top of the Hilton were oblivious to the tension between the plain clothes NCA officers. Everything was in place, what could go wrong? Anything and everything was the short answer, which was why everybody was so tense. Their target was being followed from his flat in Covent Garden. He'd left a good half an hour ago, his ETA? Any minute now.

Fatima had woken to find a photograph of her target slid under her door. First impressions weren't good. He was overweight and his face wore signs that he'd indulged in too much of everything. Days ago she wouldn't have flinched. It was her job but now the idea of sleeping with someone like him disgusted her. Hopefully she wouldn't be needed. Her instruction today was just to observe, nothing else. As she prepared she played Orange Blossom's rendition of Ya Sidi. This morning she didn't need the song as a stimulus, quite the opposite the passionate tones today were helping to relax her.

Arriving in good time, Fatima found an unoccupied seat by a corner window overlooking Hyde Park. It was approaching midday and the bar was starting to fill up. Several of the customers, quite obviously their first time, went straight to the telescope, facing East. It was twelve fifteen when she saw her target enter. He actually looked better in the flesh and she could tell that once upon a time, he'd worn a toned, as well as muscular physique. After ordering a beer from a waiter, he chose a seat in the centre of the bar. Not long after, a woman sat closely beside him. They were quite obviously strangers and Fatima found it odd that the woman had chosen to sit quite so close when there were still so many empty places with far more arm room. Perhaps the woman was a prostitute. Fatima noted her, just in case.

John found the bar to be two thirds empty when he arrived but it was beginning to fill up. After ordering a beer from a waiter, he chose a seat somewhere in the centre of the bar. Not long after a woman sat almost next to him. It was an annoyance but nothing more. The bar would be full soon anyway, something that would probably make him feel safe. He'd made his mind up to ask for fifty million to obtain for his client a registered death certificate and a new identity. In other words to help the man, Greg Warnford, disappear. With the other two hundred million Mr Warnford could live out a very nice and carefree life. He looked around the bar, in a corner beside a window sat a woman. She was dressed very modestly and obviously a Muslim for she was wearing a hijab. For some reason he found her captivating. Although very different she also somehow reminded him of Bree. He shook his head, 'stop it John, you needed to concentrate.' Moments later he saw his client enter the bar. He could tell it was him for in his hand he was holding a programme for Tina, the Musical.

The officers waiting in the Windows Bar, discreetly watching their target received a signal. Their colleague playing the part of the made up Greg Warnford, was in the lobby and about to take the lift. He would be there in a matter of minutes. Everyone of them tensed. The sting they'd been so carefully planning was about to be put into action.

The officer impersonating Greg Warnford, felt strangely relaxed. He'd played a role similar to this, many times before. He was usually chosen because he had such an unassuming character, to others he always appeared harmless. A very valuable tool. Windows was on the 28th floor and world famous for its views over London. On the seventeenth floor two men joined him in the lift. Whilst passing the eighteenth floor he felt his neck click strangely, and before the lift reached the nineteenth floor he found himself walking through a beautiful garden, a garden filled with sweet smelling flowers and alive with birds singing . On the nineteenth floor the two men got out and deftly marched their fellow passenger into a carefully pre reserved room. Another man took the Tina program and entered the lift. Minutes later he entered the bar,

John seeing the program stood up and signalled. The man waved and joined John in a beer. John shook his hand warmly, he wanted Greg Warnford to feel relaxed.

Puzzlement buzzed the officers surveying the sting. Who was the man talking to their target. He'd done everything right but no one recognised him. Perhaps he was a last minute replacement. Strange they hadn't been told. In the operations vehicle below there was equal puzzlement, their agent's tracker placed him on the nineteenth floor. Why had he got out? He was meant to go straight to the Windows Bar, seconds later the tracking signal was cut. Shit! something had gone wrong. They had to play it cool, any sudden moves could ruin everything. Their officers were still watching their target, five of them, they could worry about the officer on the nineteenth later. Maybe he'd simply visited the bathroom. Signals were often lost in such places. They'd all be shitting themselves if they were in his shoes.

John found Greg Warnford surprisingly personable, he even liked the man. Over a couple more beers John slowly hinted at how he maybe able to get his client out of a hole. It was a little too noisy in the bar to concentrate and John suggested it may be wise to find somewhere a little quieter to finish their discussion. Well I'm staying here Greg pointed out, we could always go to my room. John knew it, he had suspected as much all along and he'd been proved right. Finishing their beers the two men left. Mr Warnford's room was on the thirteenth floor. John programmed in the floor and seconds later they were descending. One of the five NCA officers, discreetly followed behind. He watched the indicator on the wall as the lift made its way down. The room they'd booked was on the 16th floor but the lift hadn't stopped, it had passed by. It was now stopping on the twelfth, what was going on?

John followed Greg Warnford out of the lift. A few paces along the corridor Mr Warnford did an about turn.

"Shit I'm always doing this, we're on the wrong floor, mine's on the thirteenth."

"Easily done." Both men laughed. Taking an adjacent lift the two were soon on the thirteenth.

"Ah, this is my room." Greg held open the door "After you please." John thanking him stepped into the room.

As soon as he had done so John realised he'd been an idiot. He'd been snared in a trap. Waiting for him were three men. Three men he recognised immediately. They'd originally met in Khans Restaurant on Westbourne Grove and had been escorted by them to their grubby office. Then they had been all handshakes and smiles. This time their demeanour was completely different, they looked menacing. John knew by their stance that he wasn't leaving that hotel room alive. So this was to be his end. He'd read somewhere that people who had had near death experiences had found themselves walking in a beautiful garden, full of bird song. He hoped this was true and he'd be walking through that garden quickly. The man impersonating Greg Warnford kicked him hard on his calves. John collapsed to the floor. It was a full two hours later before John found himself walking through the garden, he had read about.

Fatima watched her target follow another man out of the bar. She was relieved, she simply couldn't manage another coffee. She was about to get up when a woman in bright Arab robes and wearing a hijab, seemingly coming from nowhere sat opposite her. She addressed her by her name which was an immediate surprise.

"Fatima," the woman held out her hand, Fatima reciprocated and their hands touched briefly, there was no shake. "Fatima, my name's Nefret, I'm here to escort you to the head, your boss, my boss too."

"Boss, what of the organisation?" Fatima started to shake. The woman nodded, yes.

"Please, follow me." The woman stood. Fatima followed, her legs feeling at anyy moment as if they were going to give way. She was going to meet the man who all this time had been a ghost, an almost imaginary figure. She tried to imagine what he'd look like, she'd always thought of him to be a long bearded follower of Islam. Perhaps she'd been wrong all along, perhaps he was a westerner, maybe he was neither. The truth was she simply didn't know. They took the lift to the twenty sixth floor, her boss was staying in one of the hotel's suites. The woman held open the door. "Please Fatima our boss wants to speak with you alone."

Fatima almost exploding with nerves entered the room. The suite was gorgeous but there was no one there. The room was empty. Or so she first thought. Silently a woman, Arab in appearance and wearing the traditional black Abaya with a black hijab and laced black niqab so only her eyes were visible, seemingly glided to a place where she stood facing her. Fatima held her breath, she dared not breathe. She stood transfixed, held by the eyes of the woman before her. Round her neck Fatima saw for the first time, hung a fine silver necklace with an intricately worked silver Croix d'Agadez. Unknowingly she began to finger her own Croix.

"Axsti." The woman's voice was soft, luxurious and at the same time contained a current of underlying strength.

"Axsti, Fatima just about managed to whisper.

The woman held out both her hands, "It's a pleasure to meet you Ariana, my name is Orme and I am the leader of what you know as the organisation."

As she spoke a dull thud sounded and the windows shook. In the distance a cloud of smoke could be seen rising slowly above the streets of London.

Ariana, alias Fatima stood transfixed, she didn't notice, her vision was held by the woman's eyes. She hadn't heard anyone call her by that name since she was a child. It brought flooding back many, many happy memories. Ariana's gaze, not for one second deviated from the woman's stare. The moment their eyes had met knew she'd do anything for the woman standing before her. Even lay down her life if necessary.

Wissant – France

Two days later.

The air in the apartment hung heavy with mourning. If inanimate objects could cry, everything, every piece of furniture would be shedding a tear. Their mistress over the past few months had brought an energy to the air inside that positively shimmered with 'joie de vivre'. Laughter, music, excitement all had exuberated with the zest for life their mistress had chased so enthusiastically after. For far too long, the apartment had been dull and boring. The four walls and every object inside had welcomed, the new Maureen. She had brought a breath of fresh air to, what had previously been a sterile environment, carefree adventure that one and all had luxuriated in. Now there was a terrible feeling that their mistress was never coming home. Her body, they weren't aware would live on, scattered all over the world, living in the bodies of others but the most important ingredient, her soul had left and left them. The vibrance that had brought them, however briefly, so much joy had moved on to another world. The air inside hung heavy in mourning. Humans would never understand that bricks and mortar, wood, metal could be touched by a human soul. They would never believe or accept they could experience sadness. Unquenching sadness.

A door opened. A man who had no business being there stepped over the threshold. A man in his thirties, who was tall, wearing expensive clothes, and on his head a mass of tussled curls. In his hands he held a single rose. Walking to what had been their mistress' bedroom he placed the rose on the bed. After wiping a tear he left as silently as he had entered. Days turned into weeks, weeks into months. The rose slowly turned black and as the months passed it became no more than a stain on the bed cover. Months turned to years, Every week, every month, every year bills were paid automatically from an account set up long ago by a devoted husband. A husband who in case of his death, wanted his wife to live on without the worries that he'd always had to deal with. The name Maureen lived on in Wissant for a little while. The playful English woman, was how residents of Wissant fondly remembered her. Everyone assumed she was back in her home country, and everyone expected her to one day return.

As the years passed, sand blown in by the wind slowly gathered on the balcony that Maureen had once so enjoyed. The glass doors to the balcony, the eyes of the apartment, every passing day stared out to sea, hoping always for a sign their mistress was on her way home. The hope of course was in vain. Thus another chapter ends.